Praise for The Master of Samar

Lambda Literary award winner Scott (*Shadow Man*) sets a solid mystery plot within an aristocratic, Victorian-esque commonwealth held together by magical curses. // Scott hits all the expected beats, and her dark magic system keeps the stakes high. Fans of Victorian fantasy will want to check this out.

— *Publishers Weekly*

Intricate and elaborate scheming both civil and magical, in a wonderfully-realized city. I am in awe!

— Ellen Kushner, author of the fabled *Riverside* mannerpunk novels, host of the influential WGBH/PRI series *Sound & Spirit*, winner of the World Fantasy and Locus awards

Intrigue and bricolage. Complicated characters. Action and unpredictable mystery. This is exactly what I want in a fantasy, and *The Master of Samar* delivers.

— Sherwood Smith, creator of the immersive Sartorias-deles and Wren universes, Nebula award finalist

In 1985, I picked up a new novel with the intriguing title *Five-Twelfths of Heaven*, a second novel by a writer new to me. I haven't stopped reading her since, because Melissa Scott is that good. *The Master of Samar* is one of her best.

— Cynthia Ward, co-creator (with Nisi Shawl) of the acclaimed fiction writers workshop, *Writing the Other: Bridging Cultural Differences for Successful Fiction*

//...a rousing and exciting story, and Melissa Scott is a master of the genre at her best. My heart was in my throat more than once. The magical system is intricate and fascinating, and the last several chapters are unstoppable—you are compelled to keep reading straight through to the satisfying conclusion. *The Master of Samar* is a gorgeous fantasy novel. Longtime readers of Melissa Scott will be reminded of her popular *Points* series. I hope there's a sequel—I would love to visit this world again!

— Jo Graham, author of the acclaimed *Numinous World* historical fantasies and *The Calpurnian Wars* space operas

Melissa Scott's *The Master of Samar* is a character-driven fantasy whose strong use of contract magic, old secrets and the lies we tell each other and ourselves shapes the past, present and future of the characters and the city-state that they are bound to. It is an immersive and enthralling read.

— Paul Weimer, SFF book reviewer and Hugo finalist

THE MASTER OF SAMAR

MELISSA SCOTT

Candlemark & Gleam

For information, address
Candlemark & Gleam LLC,
38 Rice Street #2, Cambridge, MA 02140
eloi@candlemarkandgleam.com

Library of Congress Cataloging-in-Publication Data
In Progress

ISBN: 978-1-952456-16-9 (paperback), 978-1-952456-17-6 (ebook)

Cover art by Heeseon Won
Book design and composition by Athena Andreadis

Editor: Athena Andreadis
Proofreader: Patti Exster

www.candlemarkandgleam.com

List of Characters

Gilmyssin Irichels di Samar, cursebreaker, only surviving heir of the Samar family

Envar Cassi, chirurgeon and feral mage; Irichels's lover

Arak min'Aroi, swordswoman of the min'Aroi clan, Irichels's bodyguard

Martholin, former housekeeper of the Samar family

Karan, house servant and boatman, Martholin's lover

Romello, house servant

Antel, house servant and boatman

Tepan, a street boy

Bartol Samar, deceased, Irichels's uncle and former Master of Samar

Galeran Samar, deceased, Irichels's uncle and former Master of Samar

Illiana, deceased, Galeran's wife

Bretigil, Jacen, Hafen, Jilla, and Debes, all deceased, Galeran and Illiana's children

Hamel Samar, deceased, Irichels's uncle and former Master of Samar

Maritsa Samar, deceased, Irichels's aunt and former Master of Samar

Gellis Ambros, Master of Ambros

Halyssin Ambros, eldest son of Ambros, Irichels's friend and former lover

Valens Ambros, younger son and heir of Ambros

Innes Manimere, Master of Manimere
 Felisan Manimere, her cousin
 Kasia Manimere, her daughter
 Nerin Manimere, her son
 Canamun, her factor
 Deion Argerin, sea captain, in Manimere's employ

Nallin Cambryse, Master of Cambryse
 Seresinha Temenon, his second wife
 Alaissou, his daughter

Radulph Temenon, Master of Temenon
Fane Temenon, his brother
Oredana Temenon, Oratorian, Fane's daughter
Margos Temenon, Fane's son
Per Gethen, Master of Gethen
 Merete Temenon, his wife

Conart Jeroen, High Constable of Bejanth
Tyrn Arlechin, lawyer and acting head of Arlechin
Zaffara, contract mage and cursebreaker
Leonor, an Oratorian searcher

CHAPTER ONE

It had been years since Gil Irichels had poled a boat through the canals of Bejanth, but some skills were worn so deep into the bone that they could not be forgotten. His bodyguard Arak min'Aroi crouched in the center of the boat with the piled baggage, her hunched shoulders the only sign of her unease. By contrast, Envar Cassi knelt barefoot in the bows, already holding the mooring rope. He, too, had been born in Bejanth, and had not forgotten how to navigate its waters.

The house loomed ahead, three stories with an alley to one side and a narrow cut-through canal on the other, shutters closed and the black wreaths still on the upper windows. The canal channeled the wind, and the dyed feathers were looking bedraggled: time and past to have them down, Irichels thought, adjusting his stroke to bring the boat alongside the narrow platform.

Envar leaped the narrowing gap, mooring rope in hand, and Irichels shifted his pole to stop the boat from colliding with the crumbling stone. Envar walked backward along the dock, pulling them forward until he could loop the rope over the bollard and draw it tight. Irichels racked the pole against the outside gunwale and stepped ashore to fasten the stern tie. Arak looked up at him, one hand still clutching the nearest cleat. "This is your house?"

For my sins. That was a dangerous comment, here where the house could hear him, and Irichels merely nodded.

"Most impressive," Envar said. He came back down the

dock, and Irichels saw the moment he thought of offering Arak his hand. Arak's glare dissuaded him, and he came on down the dock, looking up at the house. "You'll need to take the wreaths down, of course. Unless they're for your arrival?"

That was closer to the bone than Envar could have known. "The advocate said no one has been living here since my aunt died."

"Not even staff? How unfriendly of them." Envar continued staring up at the house, pale eyes noting every crack in the plaster, the peeling paint, the time-blurred carvings on the shutters and the downspouts. Even the once-brilliant peacock blue door had faded. Behind him, Arak wobbled to her feet and stepped awkwardly onto the dock, straightening with a scowl that dared anyone to comment.

"Now what?"

Irichels took a deep breath. "Let's get the baggage up, and then we'll go in."

Envar stepped back into the boat to toss their bags to Arak. Not nearly enough of them, Irichels thought, not for his new status—master of Samar with the family vote in the Lower Assembly—though they had seemed more than sufficient for a traveling cursebreaker. Three sets of saddlebags, a larger, shapeless bag still stained by the straps that had held it to the mule, the cases that held their weapons, and an incongruous woven basket that Envar had acquired that morning: it was lucky the house should still contain some furniture. Irichels could feel the weight of the key in his purse; and because he wouldn't give the house that satisfaction, he drew it out and stepped briskly to the door.

The lock resisted for a moment, or perhaps that was only his imagination. He pressed harder, and the tumblers caught, drawing back the heavy bolt. He pushed the door open all the way, and saw for an instant the inner courtyard ablaze with light and color. The vision vanished, replaced by reality: the dark hall, the filtered sunlight in the inner court, the utter silence where there had once been the music of birds and water. He hoped someone had released the birds when his aunt Maritsa died, if they were not going to maintain the house.

He crossed the threshold and felt the subtle shift that meant the house was aware of him. There was the familiar smell of cold ashes, sour and oddly comforting, and the sense of weight receded, vanishing into the shadows. Behind him he heard Envar's quick intake of breath, glanced back to see the chirugeon's considering expression. "You didn't mention *that*," he said.

Arak dropped the first load of saddlebags on the tiled floor, set her cased crossbow more gently beside them. "There is something here."

"It's a very old house," Irichels said, and heard his voice defensive.

"And your family's lived here for centuries," Envar agreed. "But *that* doesn't always happen."

"No." Irichels' mouth tightened in spite of himself.

"A spirit," Arak said. "Yes? A daemon of the house?"

Irichels knew the highland term that Arak really meant, and hoped the house didn't. "In a sense."

"It's more that the house has been a center of the family's attention for long enough to become a daemon," Envar said. "Every one of you, family and household, must have acknowledged it for generations, and that's fed it." He gave Irichels a sidelong glance. "You don't much like it, my heart."

That didn't need to be said out loud. Irichels swallowed the words, said instead, "It never much liked me." He heard Arak mutter something, curse or propitiation or both, and straightened his shoulders. "Let's get everything inside, and see what they've left us."

All in all, it was better than he had expected. The newer, smaller pieces of furniture had vanished, of course, and the family plate was—he hoped—locked in the vault of the Moravai Bank, but the massive old-fashioned pieces that he remembered from his childhood were not only still present, but tucked neatly under linen dust covers. The mattresses that belonged on the heavy four-posters had been rolled up and stored away, but there were linens in the press, sweetened with herbs, and the curtains had been knotted up against the dust. When he turned the tap in the first bathing room, there was a rumble and then a rush of cool, sweet water from the rooftop cistern.

He carried his bags to one of the bedrooms at the front of the house, where the windows looked out onto the canal rather than the houses across Weaver Street, and wrestled with inner and outer shutters until he could retrieve one of the tattered wreaths and let in the afternoon light and a breath of warmer air. He turned back, wreath in hand, to find Envar waiting in the doorway. "Not the master's bedroom?"

"I want a fresh mattress first." It was the best excuse he could think of, and from the look on Envar's face, he didn't believe it either.

"Where do you want us to sleep?"

Irichels set the wreath beside the cylindrical stove. "Wherever you like. There's no shortage of rooms."

"Well. I'd like to sleep with you, of course—"

"And you know you're welcome," Irichels interjected, hoping to deflect the conversation, but Envar went on implacably.

"But you must know that's not a good idea. You're the master here, you have to act it. It wants a master."

"It doesn't want me," Irichels said.

"You're what it's got," Envar said. He came forward to rest one hand on Irichels's cheek. "You have to assign us rooms, my heart, or it'll give us no peace."

That was probably true. Irichels closed his eyes for a moment, letting himself lean just a little into the touch, then straightened with a sigh. "All right. Let's take a look." Envar stepped aside, letting him return to the hall, and he leaned over the balcony to call down into the courtyard. "Arak! Come up, will you?"

There was a moment of silence, and then Arak came into view, scowling and wiping dirty hands on a rag. "Right now? I was trying to get the boiler started."

"It can wait," Irichels said, and a moment later Arak appeared on the stairs.

"Are there beds, even?"

"You can try the mattresses if you want," Irichels said, "or use your bedroll. I'll have someone bring fresh stuffing tomorrow or the next day." He looked along the hall. "These front bedrooms have box beds, so they'll be more comfortable until we can get settled properly. I'm taking this one. Arak, Cass, you can have the next ones along—Arak, you take the one next door." He saw Envar give a faint, approving smile, and thought he felt some of the distant pressure ease.

"All right," Arak said, and pushed the door open. "I'll get the fires going, and then bring the bags up. There's about two days' worth of fuel in the coalroom, if we're careful, but you'll want to order more."

Irichels nodded, not trusting himself to speak. He had never wanted this, never wanted the house or its insatiable needs; and now that he had them, his first instinct was to flee the city. The house would need staff—a cook and housekeeper at minimum, a few maids to be the housekeeper's hands and feet, someone to do the rough work, and maybe a boatman for the errands—and he felt the weight descending, cold and airless as misery.

Arak was already heading down the stairs, apparently oblivious. Envar touched Irichels's shoulder. "There must have been servants when your aunt died. Is there anyone you could get back? Someone that you'd want back?"

The advocate had given him a list, among the sheaf of papers he'd turned over. Probably there was no one he remembered—it had been years since he'd been back in Bejanth—but it was a start. "I can see."

"Good." Envar nodded. "Then let's take another look round before the light goes. You'll feel better once you've gotten more settled."

To Irichels's surprise, he found that was true. There was no point in opening up the formal parlor or the grand dining room, but he found the controls of the fountain and set it going again, the water a welcome break in the silence. The bird cages were all empty, for a mercy: empty and swept bare before the servants left, and he hoped the birds had found good homes somewhere. Arak had taken over the low-ceilinged kitchen with its door opening to the water alley, and there were fires in the stove and the boiler. The massive worktable had been built in place and could never be moved, but there were sturdy chairs and stools, and Envar's basket proved to contain a ham and bread and half a cheese as well as bottles of wine and brandy.

"What we're shortest of is oil and candles," Arak said, as night fell and they retreated to sit around one end of the table in the fluttering light of an eight-branched candelabra. Irichels remembered that it had once graced his grandfather's workroom, a heavy piece of bronze with cups shaped like tulips. "After that, charcoal. The weather's warm still, but we'll want it for cooking and the boiler."

Irichels nodded, and tossed off a glass of the brandy. There had probably been better in the wine pantry, but those shelves had been emptied along with the rest of the portable goods.

Envar carved himself another sliver of cheese. "Did you find anyone you'd want to bring back?"

"I haven't looked." Irichels poured himself another generous glass, then added a second reckless measure. Neither of the others said anything, and Irichels sighed. "Hand me the folio, then."

Arak stretched to reach the leather folder, and Irichels sorted through the documents, squinting in the dim light. He found it quickly enough, was surprised to see a familiar name at the head of the list. Martholin had been the cook when he was a boy, but apparently she'd risen to housekeeper over the years. That was unexpected, and unexpectedly pleasant: she had always been kind to him, had always been willing to let him sit in a corner out of sight, always had a smile and a taste of whatever was on the stove. The list gave an address, on the edges of the Palinade: she might be glad of a job, if she was living there. "I'll write her in the morning," he said, and tied the folio shut again.

Envar tidied the food away while Irichels finished his glass, and Arak leaned back on her stool, head cocked to hear the sound of the fountain. "This must have been a fine house once."

Irichels was aware of Envar's swift look, and answered carefully. "Busier, anyway."

"You were raised here?"

Irichels couldn't blame the hillwoman for the note of surprise. He looked nothing like the sort of man who would come from a house with a seat in the Assembly: too broad in the shoulder, too dark, too hairy, with coarse blunt hands and feet as big as barges. Envar looked more like an aristocrat, thin and sharp-boned, for all that he had been born in the Limmerwil, the slums on the seaward edge of the Orangery. "I was born in Bellem," he said, abruptly unwilling to deny the father he could only just remember. "My father was Ystelas min'Yver, the tarmynor of Cal'Innis—"

"I knew that," Arak said, her posture shifting slightly in response to the hillfolk title, not a clan chief but leader of a collateral branch of the family. *Otherwise I wouldn't have taken service with you*, her tone implied. The min'Aroi had lost lands and power when the high king Venarak ascended the Sede, and the warriors of their service caste had been reduced to common free-swords, but they had lost none of their pride. "Why weren't you raised there?"

"My mother Irichel was a preceptress in the tarmynor's household," Irichels said. "She renounced her vows to marry him as one of his third-rank wives. He died when I was five, and Mother had no allies in the household, so we came back here to live with my grandfather." Much good that had done them: his grandfather had never acknowledged the marriage, which was why Irichels carried her name instead of the family's, but there was no point in saying so. "When I was fifteen, Mother rejoined the Oratory, and I went to the University in Tarehan. I proved good at curses, and—well, the rest you know."

Envar's eyebrows flicked up at that, but he said nothing. Arak said, "And you never came back?"

Irichels shrugged one shoulder. "There was never any need." His mother had had three brothers and another sister, though Maritsa had also chosen the Oratory. At least two of the brothers were married, each with at least one child, but somehow in the twenty-five years he'd been away, the family had died off; not just the direct line but all the cousins, until there was only himself left to claim the mastery of Samar. He frowned then. On the road from Tarehan, he had been too nervous to think clearly, too preoccupied with the responsibilities he had never wanted, had always avoided. But now—

"I wondered when you'd get there," Envar said.

Arak looked at him sharply. "You think something's wrong? Besides the daemon?"

"I think it's odd that the entire family is dead," Envar said.

"It's been twenty-five years," Irichels said, but there was no force behind the protest. "People die."

"I'd look twice if it was business," Arak said, and Irichels couldn't help nodding.

"And that's another thing I suppose I'll have to do. Look into it, I mean. But not tonight." He set down his empty glass and pushed himself away from the table. "Come on, let's lock up and then to bed."

It took nearly half an hour to make the rounds of the ground floor, making sure all the doors were locked and the windows were barred from the inside. Irichels climbed the stairs in the light of a single candle, Envar at his heels, and paused in the door of the room he'd chosen for himself. "I would like it if you'd sleep here."

Envar smiled. "Always."

The floor of the box bed was sound, and easily big enough for two. There was no pitcher to match the heavy stone basin in its cabinet, but there was a lighter basin in the bath that would serve, and Irichels washed quickly, not bothering to heat the water, while Envar laid out his own blankets. He left the water in the basin, blew out the candle, and climbed over Envar to put his back against the wall. Envar settled against him, and Irichels touched his cheek to feel his smile.

They lay comfortably entangled, both sets of blankets drawn over them for now. Irichels closed his eyes, drifting toward sleep, and jerked upright at a thud from the adjoining room. "Arak?"

"I'm coming to you." Arak's voice was grim.

Envar propped himself up on one elbow. "What's wrong?"

"Your daemon." The connecting door clicked open, closed again, and Arak came toward the bed, the dagger in her hand glowing softly. "Tell it to leave me alone."

"To me," Irichels said, and reached for the familiar warding spells as Arak fetched up against the box bed's wall. Behind her, the shadows seemed deeper than before, and Irichels could feel a presence behind them, old and heavy.

"Wait." Envar caught his hand before he could form the first sign.

"What?"

"Don't." Envar tightened his hold. "Arak, put the knife down."

"No."

Envar went on as though the hillwoman hadn't spoken, pressing close to Irichels's ear. "This is your house, your home, your family—your daemon. You can't shut it out, that's what upsets it."

It hates me. It's always hated me. Irichels swallowed the words, knowing better than to say them aloud, and flattened his hand against the wall of the bed. But Envar was right, he did belong here—no matter how much he wished he didn't—and he tried to put that conviction behind his words. "Leave Arak alone. Leave my friends alone."

The darkness thickened, flowed closer. Arak bared her teeth at it, but lowered the dagger to her side. Irichels held himself very still as it rose like a wave. In his inner sight, he could see flashes of its power, colors that weren't there tracing shapes in the dark. It had always been present, part of the house. It had slipped into his room when he was a boy, trailing nightmares, and lurked in the corners when he was older, jealously herding him away from the things that weren't his. He wanted nothing more than to draw the charm, set his wards flashing into place, but he trusted Envar. *One more step*, he thought. *I'll give it one more step, two more, I can wait, there's time—*

And then it was gone, between one heartbeat and the next. The darkness was as absolute, but lacked color and weight, and once again Irichels could make out the faint blue gleam of Arak's knife. "It's gone."

"Gone where?" Arak demanded.

"One of the back storerooms, under the master's rooms," Irichels said. He had been there once, on a dare, him and three cousins huddling and poking at each other until they all crossed the threshold in a rush, to see sagging shelves piled with boxes and bundles, and beyond them a white stone set into the foundation wall. They had all felt it turn to them, and then the candles had gone out, and they had fled back to the courtyard and the sunshine and the songs of birds. He worked his shoulders, and felt Envar sit up beside him.

"You belong here," the chirurgeon said again. "So you can't shut it out."

"I don't want it," Irichels said softly. "I don't want any of this."

"And you can settle it and go away again," Envar said. "But you have to settle it. It's...been grieving, here all alone."

Irichels tipped his head back against the wall, feeling unexpected pity welling up in him. Samar had fed the thing for years—centuries—and then in a few short decades the family had dwindled and died and left it alone in the empty house, alone and bewildered and, yes, grieving, insomuch as such a thing could grieve. "I'm...sorry for it," he said, and knew that in the morning he would pour the dregs of the night's wine at the base of its pillar.

"I'm still sleeping in here," Arak said.

Irichels woke late and dragged himself downstairs in the unforgiving sunlight to find tea and toast already made, and Arak and Envar arguing about how much charcoal to use to keep the boiler going. "We'll order more tomorrow," Irichels said, and Arak scowled in his direction.

"Can you afford that? Fuel can't be cheap here."

"There is money in the bank," Irichels said. "Enough to keep us for a while." *While I decide what to do.* Envar's eyebrows twitched at that, but he kept the toasting fork steady above the fire.

"They'll let you draw on it?" Arak sounded even more skeptical than usual, and Irichels sighed.

"I really am the heir. Everything here is mine." *My responsibility as well.* That was less comforting, and he scowled at the tea. If he was going to return to Bejanth, he was going to take up its more expensive habits. "We need to order kaf, too."

"Now that would be a treat," Envar said, and withdrew the fork from the fire. He plucked the bread off the tines and tossed it in Irichels's direction. Irichels caught it, juggling it for a moment until he could rest it on the chipped saucer one of the others had found.

"I will not drink that disgusting stuff," Arak said.

"You can have all the tea you want," Irichels said. He took a bite of the bread and reached for the folio he had gotten from the lawyers, his heart sinking as he glanced through the first few sheets of paper. There was, if this could be trusted, plenty of money and a decent amount still coming in from investments, but they couldn't be left to run themselves, at least not in their current state. And if he was going to live here, he needed supplies, charcoal and food and wine at the very least, and staff to manage the daily work. He would need to write Martholin straightaway, see if she would come—and of course he had neither paper nor pen to hand. He swore under his breath and crammed the last of the toast into his mouth, pushing back his stool. He had ink and pens in his saddlebags, and almost certainly a few scraps of paper; if any was left in the house, it would be in the workroom tucked into the corner behind the stairs. He should check there first, and see what had been done with the books.

"Gil?" Envar asked, and Irichels waved a hand.

"I need to get to work. I'll be in the workroom if you need me."

"And where would that be?" Arak muttered, but softly enough that Irichels could ignore her.

The courtyard was drowned in sun, the water chiming gently in the fountain. The colored flagstones outlined spaces for planters and birdcages and delicately wrought metal benches, but all but a few of the largest planters were gone. The trees—oranges that had been there and fruiting since he could remember—looked wilted; restoring the fountain should have also restored the hidden irrigation system, and Irichels hoped it wasn't too late to save them.

The entrance to the library was in the shadows under the stairs. He pushed open the heavy door, expecting in spite of knowing better to be chastised for interrupting, but there was only darkness and the dim shapes of looming furniture. He shook himself and felt his way past the heavy chairs and the enormous worktable to unlock the shutters. The light from the street was blinding, great squares of sun crossed by the bars that protected the narrow windows, and he blinked hard as he opened the next set of shutters.

The windows gave onto Weaver Street, and were set high enough that passersby couldn't see in; by their light, he could see that the shelves along the outer wall had been plundered, only a handful of forlorn-looking volumes remaining. The locked presses on the other wall seemed to have fared better, the unmatched bindings still familiar after all these years, and he wondered if Maritsa had had to sell the lesser part of the collection. Surely not, if the lawyers' accounts were accurate—unless she had chosen to live beyond her means, which was possible. He sighed, and fumbled with the chatelaine's keys until he found the one that fit the cupboard where his grandfather had kept his supplies.

It had not been touched, it seemed, and he stared for a moment at the familiar contents: the stacks of squared paper, the brass pots for ink powders, the heavy glass flasks for oils and water, the brushes and rubbing stone and ink sticks for formal correspondence. The sticks of wax had melted, were fused into a single multicolored lump, and he was aware again of the house seal resting in his purse along with the keys. He would need it now, if he was going to persuade Martholin to return.

He set the folio on the worktable and mixed himself a bowl of plain iron ink, then took it and pen and paper back to the worktable. It felt strange to sit in the chair that had been his grandfather's, and he felt the daemon stir at the presumption. *Grandfather is dead*: the reminder was as much for himself as for the daemon, and he trimmed the reed pen carefully before he began to write.

The letter to Martholin was easy enough, a simple request for her help in re-establishing the household, with an offer of generous pay for even a temporary visit. The note to the bank was just as easy, a request to reopen the family accounts, as was the letter to the lawyers asking for another appointment to review some of the papers. Even the official letter to the Assembly stating his claim to Samar was easy enough: there was a copy of the Formulary in the cupboard, along with the brushes and night-blue ink sticks and the polished paper. He found the correct model and read through it three times while he rubbed ink into the stone, then copied the stately phrases in his best calligraphy. The Formulary advised him of the proper fold, and informed him that he could use the Samar house seal as long as it was formally defaced.

Instead, it was the orders for fuel and food that defeated him—how much, who to patronize—and finally he bundled the papers back into the folio and locked everything back in his grandfather's cupboard, then headed for the kitchen. No one was there, of course, and he stepped back into the portico that ran along the courtyard's south side. "Cass? Arak?"

For a moment, there was no answer, and then Arak leaned over the railing from the second floor. "Yes?"

"I need—" Irichels stopped, sighing. What he needed was staff, not friends who were strangers to the city. "I need someone to find a post-boy to take some letters."

"And exactly how do I do that?" Arak came down the stairs, frowning.

"I can show you." That was Envar, emerging from the direction of the empty ballroom. "Or I could go myself if you'd rather."

"If you'd show Arak, I'd appreciate it," Irichels said, and sighed again as Arak bridled.

"I am your bodyguard, not a page. I should stay with you."

"I need you to get to know this neighborhood," Irichels said. "I'm going to need people I can trust." Arak's frown eased at that, and she accepted the bundle of letters.

"We should also fetch in more supplies," Envar said. "And—listen to the gossip while we're about it?"

"That couldn't hurt," Irichels said.

"Is there anything in particular we should ask about?" Envar asked.

"I wish I knew," Irichels answered, and reached into his purse for a handful of coins.

When they were gone, and the street door locked again behind them, Irichels stood unhappily at the foot of the stairs. He knew what he should do, of course, and knew equally well how much he didn't want to do it. Maybe it would be better to wait until they returned—he might need their support, after all—

He shoved the thought away, and went back into the kitchen, rummaging through their scant supplies until he found an unbroken cup and the nearly-empty bottle of wine. He poured the cup half full and left the kitchen by the side door.

This part of the house was a maze of small, badly-lit halls and storage rooms, but he remembered the way well enough. Down the hall behind the portico, then past the workroom and into the middle room where various bits of equipment had been kept. It was as emptied as the rest of the house, and when he snapped his fingers to light the single lamp, the wick sputtered and died: no oil left in the reservoir. He swore under his breath, and conjured up a marsh-wisp instead, the pale twist of flame floating in the air above his head. By its light, he found the door to the next room, and the key, and turned the lock. For a moment, it resisted; then the door sagged back, the hinges groaning softly.

The room was much as he'd remembered it, filled with racks and shelves to store valuables that were only used in certain seasons—festival ornaments, the enormous wine bowls for the family's public feast day, chests that probably held linens and formal wear. It was less picked over than the rest of the house: either the lock or the daemon's presence had protected it. Irichels snapped his fingers at the hanging lamp and it grudgingly caught, casting more shadows than light.

It didn't matter. He could see the white stone, vivid in the gloom, set into the southeast corner of the foundation where land and sea came together. He could feel the daemon, too, sullen and massive, an almost tangible presence in the cluttered space. He took a step forward, threading his way between the racks, and overhead the lamp winked out. Out of oil, he thought, and scowled at his own reaction. He knew better than to dismiss a sign like that, and sure enough he felt the daemon rouse and surge toward him, rising like a black wave that dimmed the stone. Every instinct screamed at him to ward himself, but he held himself still. Envar had been right the night before, it was Arak's warded blades that had set it off. In the past, he'd tried to block it out, as though it and he were strangers. He was Master of Samar now, and the daemon was bound by that blood inheritance, no matter how much it hated the bond.

He took a step forward, into the looming dark, and it parted for him. He could feel how much it grudged that concession, could feel its anger and frustration and, yes, a strange wild grief, a hollowed thing that echoed the empty house. However much it hated him, it hated what had happened more.

He paused at the base of the stone, plain white marble that had once been carved with symbols. In the wavering light of the marsh-wisp, there was no making out what they had once said; he doubted he could read them without bringing in paper and charcoal to trace the shapes, and there was no need to provoke the daemon that far. Instead, he poured the wine in a thin stream onto the depression at the base of the pillar. In spite of his care, a few drops splashed, spattering the stone like blood.

"I am sorry for the losses to the house," he said aloud. "I honor your mourning." The daemon swirled, swelled, cold air rushing out of nowhere to pluck at his sleeves and hair.

You never wanted—

"I'm Master of Samar now," Irichels said.

Chapter Two

By the time Envar and Arak returned, Irichels had brewed another pot of tea and had spent enough time by the kitchen fire to get warm again. Envar gave him a sharp look but unloaded his basket without comment, setting bread and cheese and various pots and jars on the shelves while Arak examined the range and the boiler.

"Where does the water come from? Not the canals, surely."

"Idra forbid," Envar said. It might have been involuntary, except that Envar never spoke without intent.

"We—this house has cisterns on the roof," Irichels said. "We catch rainwater in the winter and there are spells and filters to keep it from spoiling." He sighed. "Which is another thing I should look into, I've no idea of the last time anything was renewed."

"The water's sweet enough," Envar said.

"What of the folk who don't have a house like this?" Arak asked. "We saw…"

"We walked by the Palinade," Envar said.

That was unkind. Irichels swallowed the words, knowing that neither of them would appreciate the comment. The Palinade was one of Mercies's poorer districts, a maze of silted cut-throughs and stinking water-alleys and tumble-down houses perched between the Shore Road and the Dawan Canal. There were worse in Bejanth and in most southern cities, but the people of the hills had nothing like it. "There are neighborhood catch-tanks," he said. "And in the dry season, the high constable will send barges from the mainland to provide a basic ration."

"Some people will try filtering the canal water," Envar said, "but that's best avoided unless you have no other options."

Arak grimaced. "I hope the wine is cheap."

"And tastes it," Envar said.

Martholin responded to the note even more quickly than Irichels had expected, a grubby post-boy knocking at the street door with a much folded scrap of paper that proclaimed Martholin's interest in the job and her intention to arrive that afternoon, with baggage. She was as good as her word, her boatman ringing the bell at the door beside the coal-room a little past mid-afternoon. Irichels slid back the inner door and unlocked the metal gate to find a broad-bodied, flat-bottomed haug snugged up to the wall, and Martholin smiling up at him from amid a pile of luggage. The striped awning had been lowered to make more room for the bags, and the hoops that supported it rattled against their sockets as the boatmen held the haug against the wall. "Little Gil! I never expected to see you again."

"Nor I, at least not under these circumstances." Irichels offered his hands, and she stepped neatly from the haug to the hall, wide trousers swaying over cut-leather slippers. Her calf-length gown was plain but well made, and not much mended. He hoped that meant she had been managing well enough. "Cass, would you and Arak—?"

A boatman was already handing bags into the hall. Envar sighed and nodded, and Irichels waved toward the courtyard. "Let's go in the kitchen, Marthie—Keeper, I should say."

"Marthie's fine for now," she answered. "Takes me back. Though I should call you Master now."

"It's a strange thought, I know," Irichels answered, and held the kitchen door for her. "I hope you'll excuse us, we've made free of the place."

She gave the room a sharp glance, and seemed to relax a little. "No harm done, and I hope you have more with you than those two."

"They're my friends and colleagues, Marthie. Arak min'Aroi and Envar Cassi."

She snorted. "I don't mind the hill folk, they've manners even if they're not our manners. But that Envar's a slum rat if ever I've seen one, and they're not to be trusted."

"Cass is a chirurgeon," Irichels began.

"And feral, too, I'm bound." She gave him a challenging look. "Tell me that's not so."

"And my very dear friend."

"Oh, is that the way of it?" She shook her head. "Very well then, I'll say no more. Just—have a care of him, that's all."

For a moment, Irichels felt twelve again, perched on a stool in the corner while the work of the kitchen bustled on around him and Martholin passed him a taste of the day's baking between tending the pots on the range. And that would never do. He deliberately chose a place at the long table, where he had never been allowed to sit as a child, and gestured for Martholin to take a seat as well. "You're right that I can't manage with just the three of us, and it's not their place, anyway. I need at least a housekeeper and a minimum staff, and I'm hoping you'll step in for me."

"Of course," she answered. "Though you talk as though you're not staying very long."

"I haven't decided yet," Irichels said. "There are a number of things that have to be settled, so I'll have to be here at least a month. Maybe two."

"That's not very long."

Irichels shrugged. "As I said, I haven't decided. What would you need to keep house for me for two months?"

"Well, if you're to be gone again, there's no point hiring a cook." Martholin counted off the posts on her fingers. "A kitchen maid, scullery boy, maid of all work—two of them, if you're going to open up all the bedrooms—a couple of men for the heavy work and to handle the boat, and probably a page?" Irichels nodded. "So that makes seven, and myself. If you stay longer, we'll want a second cook." She gave him a sharp look. "I can find you good people, but they'll want top pay."

Because of the daemon. Irichels nodded again. "Just be sure they're suitable." He paused. "Even after my aunt died, it doesn't seem the house was short of money. Why didn't the lawyers keep you on?"

Martholin hesitated. "I'm sure I couldn't say."

"Marthie."

"When Master Maritsa died, she was the last," Martholin said. "They'd forgot about you, I suppose. And the whole house felt it. The windows cracked, the shutters wouldn't hold, the iron grates on the alley-side rusted overnight and had to be replaced. The respectable ones wouldn't stay, not with all that going on, lights and shadows and wanderings about the house after dark, and I wouldn't trust the ones who said they were willing, they were just after what they could take. The lawyers called in a curse-reader, but she didn't find anything."

"A curse-reader?" Irichels said, in spite of himself.

"Did they not tell you, those lawyers? I thought that might be why you didn't want to stay."

"I break curses for my living," Irichels said with a wry smile. "They don't frighten me."

"And it's not like that one would harm you." She tipped her head toward the locked storage room.

Irichels wasn't entirely sure of that, but he managed a smile. "Why did they call a curse-reader? Surely some… demonstrations…were to be expected after Aunt Maritsa died."

"Well, but it wasn't just her," Martholin said. "It started with your grandfather, Idra guard his soul."

"He'd had the marsh-fever since I was a boy," Irichels said, startled. "Unless—?"

"It wasn't the normal marsh-fever, that's for sure," Martholin said. "It came on at the slack of the year, waxed and waned with the tides. He had the physickers to him, of course, seemed like it was all the physickers in the Scholastica, and half the priests of the Oratory, too. But every time it came back just that little bit worse, and lasted longer, until he was trapped in his bed and dying by inches. All they could do was try to make him comfortable, and they didn't manage much of that. A bad way to go, Master."

Irichels nodded. He had never really known his grandfather, who had disapproved of his mother's hill-country marriage and made it very clear that Irichels himself should never have been born. Irichels had stayed out of his way as much as possible, and been glad to escape to the University. "Idra grant him rest."

Martholin seemed pleased by the conventional phrase. "Then after that, there never seemed to be any luck. Master Bartol moved in, with that actor of his, and you know how they drank. No surprise their boat overturned one dark night when they were trying to sneak home after curfew."

Irichels had always liked Bartol, who hadn't cared about his sister's marriage or lack thereof, who wrote plays and never made any pretense of honoring the family or managing a house. Grandfather had kept him on a vanishingly small allowance all the time Irichels had known him. If anything, his actor—Tevas Antelorian, leading jewel of the Calder Theater—had been the one to pay most of their bills. Irichels had been in the hills above Antrim when he heard the news of their deaths, and had been sorry for it.

"It was your Uncle Galeran who came next," Martholin said, "and that was nice for a while. Illiana was lovely, a perfect lady, and—well, you knew the children."

"I knew Bretigil and Jacen," Irichels said. "Hafen and Jilla not so much." He and Bretigil had been of an age, with Jacen five years younger; they had played together when the cousins visited—it had been Bretigil who'd dared them to visit the daemon—but they had never had the chance to become close.

"Debes was born after you left," Martholin said. "The only one of them born in this house, while Galeran was Master. And I'm sorry to say it, I could wish it had never been, for all they doted on the child. But Illiana was never right after the birth, and the boy, well." She shook her head. "I won't say it was his *fault* that Jilla fell on the stairs, but he knew better than to play there. Poor thing, she hit her head and never did come right. We nursed her half a year, but she wasted away. Mistress Illiana didn't last much longer, a fever took her that winter. And then Hafen died of a winter flux. The whole city was taken bad with it, Idra rest him."

"Jacen was killed at Migon Ford," Irichels said. It had been a particularly pointless border skirmish, fought and lost under an expansionist Senate and Assembly; he had been in the south at the time, and wouldn't have noticed if someone hadn't bothered to send the news of his cousin's death. He hoped he had thought to send some formal acknowledgment.

Martholin nodded. "And Bretigil was drowned in the Slackwater. He'd been on the Plana, he was trying to beat the storm back so his wife wouldn't worry. Poor girl, she didn't even have a child to remember him by. She went home to her own people after that."

"And the youngest one?" Irichels asked. He was ashamed to realize how little those deaths had touched him. He'd been up and down the coast, building his practice, earning patrons and winning Envar, and it hadn't seemed to have much to do with him.

"Ah." For the first time, Martholin wouldn't meet his gaze. "What did they tell you about him, then?"

"Nothing. I don't think I even knew his name until you said it."

"More grace to you, then. Debes, he was called, after Illiana's grandfather, and he was never…never quite what he should have been. We couldn't keep birds once he got older, he'd break their wings—to keep them from escaping, he said, but I always thought he just enjoyed it. And then there was Jilla's fall. Even Master Galeran had to notice in the end, but he couldn't break him of it. Debes took to sneaking around the house to play tricks on people—and he'd learned a few cantrips then that were just cruel. I had a scullery maid who, well, Idra was looking the other way when they came to hand out sense, but she was cheerful as a bird herself. Not graceful, she was a dumpy little thing, but he had a cantrip would make her dance until she cried, and one day he kept her at it until her feet bled.

"I told Master Galeran then that something had to be done, and he sent the boy to the Oratory. And he never forgave me for it, either, for Debes was found hanging in the bell ropes. They said it was an accident, but no one could quite say how." She paused. "I left the house then, Master Gil, for I wasn't wanted, and I stayed away until Master Galeran died. It was Master Hamel who asked me back, and then Master Maritsa had me stay after he went."

"Uncle Hamel had a family, I thought," Irichels said. "What happened to them?"

"His first wife divorced him," Martholin said. "She couldn't keep a child with him, lost two as babies and I don't know how many she miscarried. His second wife ran off with a musician, left him with a sickly daughter and not even a wet-nurse to care for her. I thought we'd pull her through, but no. There was a boy, I never saw his mother, but he drowned in the canal when he was five. And then that dancer he had in keeping drank poison when she was with child... After that, it was just him and Master Maritsa. And then just her."

It was a litany of disaster enough to make Irichels blink. Marsh-fever was endemic in Bejanth, and a certain number of people drowned every year in the canals, but such an unrelenting parade of mishap and illness was enough to catch his attention. The worst of it seemed to have been focused on Galeran and his family, possibly through the last-born boy— but Debes was dead, and surely someone had had the sense to make sure any ghost stayed laid.

Before he could ask, the kitchen door rattled open. "There's a cage full of birds," Arak said. "What do you want done with them?"

"I told her to put them in the courtyard cages," Envar called, "but she would ask you first."

Irichels looked at Martholin, and saw that she was blushing. "I hope you don't mind, Master Gil. I took some of them home with me when the house was shut up, but it's no life for them in a little house. I brought them back—I thought it might make the place nice again."

"It was a kind thought," Irichels said. "Would you help get them settled? They know you better than us."

Her blush deepened at that but she bustled out after Arak, and a few minutes later Irichels heard the first bright notes of birdsong from the courtyard.

Martholin took up her duties with a vengeance, and by nightfall had hired in a man about her own age to help with the boat. His name was Karan, and if Irichels suspected he and Martholin shared a bed, it was none of his business. Karan brought a vague-looking scullery boy with him, all legs and shaggy dun hair, who answered to Romello and reminded Irichels strongly of a pack horse he'd once owned. The three of them set to work, driving Irichels and Arak back to the library and Envar out to wander the streets. Martholin had called it correctly when she'd named him feral, and Irichels knew the chirurgeon was reestablishing old ties. Cats and mages run free in Bejanth, the saying had it, and for the same reason: to keep down the vermin.

Licit magic came from the Oratory and the University, filtered through contracts and structures centuries old that attenuated the risk of dealing with the powers that ruled outside the material world. Illicit magic—feral magic— was won through bargains made directly with those powers, contracts every bit as binding as legal ones, if far more dangerous. Irichels's own magics came from the University, from a bond established at its foundation, but he had a healthy respect for feral magic. Badly made, it could be deadly—and indeed at least half his business as a cursebreaker had been to undo feral contracts. But a well-chosen web of contracts could give a person far more power than the legal bonds, and Envar's contracts were more cleverly woven than most. Exactly what had caused him to leave Bejanth, Irichels didn't know, but he knew Envar had kept up correspondence with a number of colleagues here.

Dinner was served in the dining room, with the three of them clustered at the head of the enormous table with a twelve-branched candelabra between them and all the sconces lit. The plates and the food were from a nearby taverna, but Karan served them with stiff-backed formality. It had been years since Irichels had eaten in state but the rhythms came back to him with alarming ease, and he made a note to make different arrangements for later. He might be Master of Samar, but surely he could find a more pleasant place to dine in his own house.

He had managed to hold firm about the bedrooms, however, despite Martholin's protests, though once she'd had time to hire maids and arrange for the mattresses to be freshened he knew he would have to move. Still, she had lit a fire in the front room's stove, driving back the night's damp, and there was new oil in the hanging lantern. It was already lit, and he was unsurprised to find Envar perched on the edge of the bed, the curtain bunched behind him. He wore only a thin, much mended shirt, pale as a spirit against the shadows. "Arak says she's going to try to sleep in her own bed tonight. She said if 'that thing' comes back, she'll ask you to banish it."

"I can't do that."

"No?"

Irichels sighed, stripping out of hip-length gown and narrow trousers. Barefoot and in his shirt, he moved to the cabinet, unsurprised to see that Martholin had found a pitcher somewhere. "I suppose, yes, technically I could—though it might take more than me to manage it—but I want to figure out what's going on first."

"So you've decided that something's not right." Envar sounded faintly amused.

"I spent some time talking to Marthie about what happened," Irichels said. He poured water, traced a glyph to take the chill off, and washed his hands and face. "And then I made some lists. I'm surprised no one took action before it got so bad."

"Someone doesn't like your family, my heart," Envar suggested.

"Always possible, of course, but—most people liked my uncle Galeran. He's the one who was hit hardest." Irichels dried his hands on the waiting towel and turned to the bed. Envar sketched a sign in the air, then blew through it toward the lamp. The flames winked out, and Irichels called a twist of marsh-light to hover beneath the bed's ceiling. In its light, Envar's eyes seemed to shine for an instant, reflective as a cat's, before he blinked and looked away. "He was in the house the longest after Grandfather, he and his children, and the one born here was either cursed or a changeling, to hear Marthie tell it."

"Is she likely to be right?" Envar settled against him, the weight comfortable and comforting.

"When I knew her, she was the cook," Irichels said, "and there wasn't anybody in the house or in the markets who could get the better of her in a bargain. She's as shrewd as she's loyal."

"So, yes, then."

"Yes."

"Was it bad?"

Irichels sighed. "Bad enough. He tormented the birds and at least one of the maids, and he may have caused his sister to fall on the stairs. She died of that, eventually. Galeran sent him to the Oratory."

"And?" Envar asked, as the silence stretched between them.

"Marthie says he was found hanging in the bell ropes," Irichels answered.

He felt Envar sigh in turn. "That could be anything. The bells could have taken him—they're spelled to do that—or he could have done it himself if the Oratory had persuaded him to remorse, or it could even have been an accident. But a cursling child—that's no small thing."

"I know." Irichels shook his head. "The house must have been cleansed once he left. Marthie couldn't say, she'd left on account of the servant girl, but I can't imagine it wouldn't have been. There must be records, even if it's just the account books. I'm going to go through them tomorrow."

"Was the boy a mage?" Envar asked.

"He knew at least one cantrip," Irichels said. "That's according to Marthie. But he was young when he died, there's no telling whether he'd have kept up his studies."

"Could it be your daemon causing all this?"

"I don't know," Irichels said. "I suppose it could be, but I can't see why it would turn on us after all these years. Unless someone didn't give it its due? I suppose I'll have to check that out as well, though I'm not sure how." He shook his head. "It didn't look unfed."

"So you went to see it?"

"Yes."

"You could profitably have taken one of us with you." Envar's voice was sharp.

"There wasn't any need. As you said yourself, taking protective measures was more likely to annoy it." Irichels felt the other man's body relax slightly, and followed up his advantage. "I don't suppose you heard anything useful?"

"Not yet." Envar was sounding sleepy now and they shifted, settling more comfortably among the pillows. "There are some folk I could see tomorrow."

Irichels nodded. "I'll have a word with the lawyers. There are a handful of cousins in the Plana, I want to know why they didn't take the house."

"I can't imagine," Envar said with a sleepy chuckle, and Irichels closed his eyes.

CHAPTER THREE

Breakfast was served again in the grand dining room, the three of them clustered around one end and the morning light streaming in through the canal side windows. Martholin had clearly kept back a few dishes from the previous night's dinner, and that was still smarting when she cornered him in the library for the ritual review of the day's work.

"Being that there's nothing fit to cook with, never mind to serve a meal on, bar a few pots I brought with me, it would be a help if you could at least have the plate brought back from the bank. And I've sent to the Exchange to see what sort of people they have on their books."

"I trust you with the hiring," Irichels said. "In fact, I leave it entirely up to you. You've done well so far." In the library's subdued light, it was hard to tell if she blushed. She looked again at her slates, the squared slabs neatly bound in leather with the inner faces smoothed to take the chalk, and Irichels went on quickly, "As for the plate, I'd rather wait a bit. I don't like having that much silver in the house with only five us of here. The house must have accounts—order what you need for cooking and for a decent table service, for us and for you in the kitchen. And, speaking of that, have Karan and the boy move a table into the family parlor. We'll dine there from now on, except when we've guests."

For a moment, he thought she'd protest, but she swallowed any objection she might have had. "Yes, Master. I'll need a note under your seal for the shops."

"I'll write you one." Irichels went to the cabinet, took out more squared paper and the ink he'd made up the day before.

"Very good." She looked at her slates again. "I've nothing in the way of stores. It'll cost a pretty penny to put things to right. And I don't know how many to buy for, or how long."

"Let's plan on having the night meal from the taverna for the next couple of nights," Irichels said. He could almost hear his grandmother's voice, giving the daily orders, and was mildly appalled at how easy it was to fall into the familiar routines. He had been out from under this roof for nearly thirty years, but the old habits remained. "That will give you time to get everyone settled. I'll be home for the noon meal today, but that's likely to be an exception. If you'd keep bread and cheese for us, that would be appreciated. Arak drinks tea; please keep a pot handy for her. Cass and I will drink kaf; you'll need to get that in, and all the fixings."

Martholin scratched something on her slates. "Very good, Master. Once I get the bedrooms sorted out, we can move you into your proper room. Will Dot're Cassi have the mistress's room?"

Irichels hoped he wasn't blushing. He was used to a traveling life, where any disapproval was temporary and generally wiped out by the cold silver of the rent, and where anyone might sleep two or even three to a bed to save a penny or two. Setting Envar up as an acknowledged lover felt very strange, particularly when sodomy was at least technically against the city's laws. But then, so were most curses, and that never stopped anyone. "Yes, for now. Put Arak in the room Grandfather's valet used." That would keep the three of them together, with only two doors between them.

"Very good," she said again. "So I'll just need that note for the shops, Master."

Irichels found the correct page in the Formulary and copied the request. He scrawled his full name under it, the one he never used—*Gilmyssin Irichels di Samar*—and added the family seal. Martholin dropped a curtsey as she took it, and for an instant, he could feel his grandfather standing behind him. "I'll want the boat this afternoon, assuming you can spare Karan."

"Of course. What time?"

"I'll let you know when I have the appointment," Irichels answered, and she curtseyed again and backed away.

The Arlechini lawyers—a branch of House Gethen, who were connected to Samar by marriage and commerce—professed themselves delighted to arrange a meeting for that afternoon at the eleventh hour. It was later than Irichels would have liked, only an hour before sunset, but there didn't seem to be any reason to try to change it. Instead, he put on his best gown, neat knee-length dark wool trimmed with a narrow edge of fox fur, and did his best to look like a man who could take his seat in the Lower Assembly. He didn't own the robes for that, of course, the ankle-length draperies of pure white wool, and the old-fashioned broad hat and the blank black mask that went with it. He'd have to acquire them if he stayed—but only if he stayed. He put that thought aside for now, a decision for later, and came out into the courtyard.

Martholin's birds seemed to be settling into the largest of the three cages. At the moment, they were clustered in the carved tree, murmuring to themselves, and the floor of the cage was scattered with birdseed. That and the sound of the fountain hit him like a cantrip, and for an instant it was as though he had never left, as though any moment his grandmother might step from the workroom, or his grandfather appear to complain about his presence, or some of his cousins come dashing down the stairs.

"It's bad luck to have birds in the house," Arak said. She had dressed for the occasion as well, looked every inch a hill-country free-sword in her embossed leather jerkin and full breeches, the steel points glinting in the late afternoon light. She carried both sword and dagger, and had Irichels's belt and dagger over one arm. She held them out and Irichels took them, fastening them into place.

"That's not the custom here."

"So I told her," Envar said, emerging from the shadows of

THE MASTER OF SAMAR

the portico. He was wearing his usual ragged black academic's gown, a worn satchel slung over one shoulder, and Irichels couldn't help raising an eyebrow. "Karan is bringing the boat to the front door. I thought I might ask you to drop me at the Orangery on the way."

"All right," Irichels said, and heard Arak sniff.

"Best not be seen with him, looking like that."

"Nor will you," Envar answered, and Irichels started for the door.

As promised, Karan had the boat waiting, and Irichels stepped down into the hull to settle himself on the padded bench. At his gesture, Arak seated herself beside him while Envar crouched in the bow, looking like a cormorant in his rusty black.

"Had you something particular in mind?" Irichels asked, and Envar's eyes flicked briefly to Karan, leaning on the oar, before he answered.

"Just some people I wanted to see. It's been a long time since I've been in the city."

Irichels nodded, trying to relax and let himself be ferried. When he was younger he'd been taken to school by boat, along with any cousins who either lived with them or were on the way; as soon as he was old enough to handle an oar, he'd claimed the use of one of the spare boats, freedom from the house and his duties and the thing that lurked in the shadows, ready to punish him for his missteps.... But he was grown now, and Master of Samar; the daemon would answer to him.

Karan took them down the canal with long, easy strokes, and edged them into the wider channel of the Eastern Water, keeping close to the bank and out of the deeper water where sailing barges and haugs and the occasional eight- or twelve-oared gallemin competed for space. Lawgivers' Isle loomed ahead, the gilded tower-top of Idra Mistress of the World catching the setting sun and reflecting it like flame. The Senate and Assembly House rose before it, the dome reaching halfway up the spire, the pale stone reddened by the sunset.

Irichels could see the robed figures, senators in black with white masks, assemblors in white with black masks, tiny as dolls. Here and there an Oratorian added a flare of scarlet or purple, their faces hidden behind gilded masks of Idra's face. They gathered in clusters on the raised plaza, servants hovering at a discreet distance, one or two holding a fringed parasol to mark a senior member. Neither body was in session but there was always work to be done, or so his grandfather had always said. He could remember him leaving the house in his full white robes, mask already in place even though it technically wasn't required until he reached the Isle. And that was another responsibility he didn't want. Irichels looked away, pretending to examine the houses on the opposite bank, and knew Envar was watching him.

Karan brought them under the Processional Bridge and then across the Serenna to glide along the shore of the Boot. He brought the boat close inshore at the foot of the Soliman Bridge long enough for Envar to leap ashore, then turned toward the entrance of the Langtan Canal. Irichels looked over his shoulder long enough to see Envar crossing the bridge to the Orangery, but then they had entered the canal and the buildings cut off his view. The houses were newer here, and the canal was crowded with boats carrying men and women along its agate-brown waters.

Arlechin House was built facing the Langtan, an imposing structure with a wide dock and an alcove to shelter a man to tend to any arrivals. Karan brought the boat alongside the steps with something of a flourish, and the tender came to catch the bow line. "Help you, Messires?"

"I have an appointment with Tyrn Arlechin," Irichels said. He rose to his feet and stepped quickly onto the dock, taking three steps inland to draw the tender's attention. "Irichels di Samar."

"Of course, Messire. I was told to expect you." The tender bowed.

Out of the corner of his eye, Irichels saw Arak stumble ashore and straighten instantly. "Then announce us, please. The boat will wait."

"Yes, Messire," the tender said, and knocked briskly on the main door. A peep-door opened; the tender said something too quietly for Irichels to hear, and then the main door swung back and a footman in red-and-gold striped livery bowed them in.

Tyrn Arlechin was waiting for them in the courtyard, where a fountain played and birdsong mingled with the sounds of a lute from an overhanging balcony. He was soberly dressed, but the cloth of his unbelted gown was black-on-black brocade, and the brooch that clasped his collar was the fine-worked gold of the hills. He was the eldest son, Irichels remembered, but the old man was bed-ridden, and had been for some time.

"Irichels."

"Arlechin." They joined hands and exchanged the kiss of kinship, even though by Irichels's reckoning they couldn't be more than some sort of cousin. "May I present my bodyguard, Arak min'Aroi?"

"Messida." Tyrn gave a polite nod, and Arak bowed more deeply. "I hope you don't feel the need of protection in my house, Irichels."

"Old habits," Irichels said vaguely. "And of course Samar hasn't prospered of late."

"Nothing that a bodyguard could have done about that," Tyrn said. "But I understand you'd want to make inquiries. This way." He waved toward the middle of the three doors that led out of the courtyard, but before he could herd them toward it, a girl's voice called from the stairs.

"Father! One quick moment, please?" Irichels turned to see a young woman hurrying down the stairs from the balcony, rose-red trousers cut daringly short to show jeweled slippers and a glimpse of ankle. "You've not yet said if you'll be here for dinner."

"My daughter Nemissa," Tyrn said, in a tone between embarrassment and pride. "And I will join your mother for dinner—perhaps you'd care to join us, Irichels?"

"I'd be delighted, but I'm otherwise engaged." Irichels bowed. The girl was lovely, honey-skinned, black eyed, a great mass of black hair caught up with a scatter of pins that must have taken an hour to arrange to that effect. The lighter red overgown was cleverly cut to show her figure to perfection, and he wondered abruptly how long she'd been waiting to make that entrance. Samar retained enough wealth to make even him a reasonable catch.

"Master," the girl said with a fleeting smile. "Perhaps— another time?"

"I'd be honored," he said with another bow, and resolved to stay busy for the foreseeable future. Though whether he stayed or not he would have to do something about an heir....

The girl headed back up the stairs, though she managed one swift, backward glance and another quick smile. Irichels averted his eyes and followed Tyrn into the lawyer's cabinet. It was a pleasant room with a pair of barred windows that overlooked a cut-through canal, book-presses on both side walls, and a worktable and secretary's slanted desk arranged to catch the best of the light. There were lamps as well, and the air smelled faintly of flowers. There was no sign of the secretary, and Tyrn cleared his throat, waving toward a padded chair that stood opposite the worktable.

"I sent Frederlin away, I thought you'd want to be private."

"I certainly need to speak freely," Irichels answered, and seated himself. Arak leaned against the back of his chair and did her best to become invisible.

"Yes. I thought so, when I got your note." Tyrn rummaged in a stack of papers and slid two sheets across the table. "You asked about your relatives in the Plana. The short answer is, there are none left living."

Irichels's eyebrows rose. He pulled the pages to him, scanning the list of names. Most were unfamiliar, though here and there he saw a cousin he remembered. "That seems... unlikely."

"Unlucky, certainly," Tyrn said. "Though not necessarily for you."

"How so?" Irichels kept his voice steady, though he felt Arak stiffen behind him.

"There's no one who can contest your claim," Tyrn said, as though he could have meant nothing else. "Given that your grandfather never acknowledged your mother's marriage, that's just as well."

"The marriage was legal under canon and civil law," Irichels said, and managed to sound bored. "As Grandfather very well knew. But that's not at issue."

"No, indeed," Tyrn said, in a tone that hinted it might well be.

"Our former housekeeper says that a curse-reader was called in when Aunt Maritsa died." Irichels was watching Tyrn's face, but it was his hand that betrayed him, a quick, convulsive clenching that might have wanted to form a warding glyph.

"That's so." Tyrn's voice was calm enough. "It seemed wise under the circumstances."

"I'd have insisted on it myself," Irichels said. "And?"

Tyrn turned his hands, palms up and empty. "She found nothing. The house spirit, of course, but—other than that, nothing. She said, perhaps…Samar is an old house, and there was not much new blood. Some families simply die out."

Not in a single generation, Irichels thought. He said, "Maybe so. Who did you have in?"

"Ah." Tyrn sorted through a second stack of papers. "Her name was Zaffara. She was experienced, and very well recommended. I have her address here."

"Thank you." Irichels took that paper as well, glancing quickly at the directions in neat secretarial hand. Envar would probably know her.

"I've been informed that you've reopened the family's accounts," Tyrn went on. "Does that mean you've come to some decision about staying?"

"Not yet," Irichels answered. "But it's clearly going to take some time to settle things. I see no reason not to be comfortable."

"No, of course not," Tyrn said. "It's just—neither the house nor the neighborhood is what it was."

"Do you say? I'd not been here long enough to see." Irichels cocked his head.

"Mercies has seen better days," Tyrn said. "The Falloni abandoned it for Quintava, and there hasn't been a family of stature there since. It was better when Galeran was alive, but—neither Hamel nor Maritsa, Idra defend them, were particularly *active* personalities. They didn't really do much for their people. And of course the Palinade has just expanded since the drought two years ago."

Hamel was a scholar and Maritsa a preceptress like his mother; Irichels doubted either one of them had wanted to inherit the house any more than he did. "I did have one more question. Galeran's youngest son, Debes. What do you know of him?"

"Very little, I'm afraid. There was a tragic accident while he was at school, or so I heard."

And that is the first flat lie you've told. But I don't know why. "If there were any papers," Irichels said, "any settlement with the school—he was at the Scholastica, I think?"

"I believe so. I can find out which congregation he was assigned to, if you'd like."

"Thank you."

"I'll send word." Outside, a tower clock was striking, the cascade of tones that marked the evening service. "Ah. It's esperin. I won't keep you—"

"Nor I you," Irichels answered, and folded the papers to tuck them in his purse. Tyrn walked them to the waiting boat—a mark, Irichels thought, of unanticipated favor—and saw them off into the thickening twilight.

"He shouldn't speak that way about your honorable mother," Arak said abruptly.

"No. But it's something to hold against me." Irichels braced one foot against a cross-rib. The tide had turned, and the water was choppy. "It doesn't mean anything."

"In Bellem, his words would be actionable." Arak's voice was perfectly calm, and Irichels frowned.

"I don't want any action taken."

"Not yet, certainly. But it might be a useful thing later."
Irichels sighed. "You're not wrong. I'll bear it in mind."

They dined that night in the family parlor, where the furniture
had been hastily rearranged to accommodate a table. There was
a fire in the fireplace, enough to take the chill off and to make
the colors dance on the carved and painted salamander above
the mantel. Martholin had bought candles by the hundred,
and the great wheel-candelabra was fully lit, casting a mellow
light. The meal itself came mostly from the taverna, as did the
plates, but the dessert was of Martholin's own making, balls
of sweet dough studded with currants and dusted with spice,
then soaked in a butter-and-brandy syrup. The three of them
cleaned the platter, and Irichels was still licking his fingers
when Martholin made her ritual appearance. Irichels offered
heartfelt praise, and she dipped a curtsey.

"I'm glad you're pleased, Master Gil, and things will
be even better tomorrow. In the meantime, I wanted you to
know I've moved your things into the master's rooms—and
the dot're's and Messida Arak's, as you requested. I had the
luck to find a girl who could start today helping with the
rough work, and I've moved her and all of us upstairs. I'm
interviewing some more help tomorrow."

"Very good," Irichels said. "You're working miracles,
Marthie."

"Idra forfend, Master," she answered, but sounded pleased
in spite of herself.

The curfew bell was sounding as Irichels made the rounds
of the first floor doors and windows, Arak at his heels with
her sword still at her waist and a branch of candles in her
hand. All the windows were barred on the outside, and the
inner shutters were inch-thick wood and iron-bound, with
an iron bar across. Most of them hadn't yet been opened
since they'd arrived, but Irichels walked through each room
anyway, making sure nothing had changed. He checked the

doors as well: the canal door, the street door, and the three service doors on the water alley. All were locked, and he drew the bars across, setting them in the heavy brackets.

"Will you do this every night?" Arak asked.

"Someone had better."

"I meant, shouldn't it be a steward's job?" They had reached the courtyard, and the moonlight spilled over the patterned stones, silvering the water in the fountain.

"Eventually." Irichels looked at the stairs leading up to the second floor, aware that he was avoiding the moment when he'd have to take over his grandfather's bedroom. *Maritsa's bedroom,* he told himself. *And Hamel's, and Galeran's— Grandfather's been dead since I was seventeen.* "But right now, I feel better seeing to it myself."

"I can't say I blame you," Arak said. "Will you stay? Messire Tyrn seemed to think you should."

"I don't know." It felt as though he had been saying that entirely too often in the last two days, and Irichels forced a smile. "What do you think, should I turn myself into the Master of Samar?"

"I think this city could use a good cursebreaker," Arak said, and started up the stairs.

That was a possibility Irichels had not considered, keep the house and title and still practice his profession. There were precedents—the Arlechini were lawyers, the Moravi and the Tenebri were bankers—so perhaps it could be a viable solution. He put the idea aside for later, and followed Arak up the stairs.

The master's bedroom was at the top of the right-hand stair, the door thrown open and candlelight spilling out into the hall. Irichels made himself step briskly in, to find Envar prodding at the fire beneath the carved mantel. It displayed another salamander, collared and chained in its bed of flames, though the wood here was unpainted. Envar straightened, setting the poker back in its place. "I gather I'm across the hall?"

"Officially," Irichels said. Martholin had lit the wheel-candelabra here as well, and the space was brighter than he had ever seen it, unexpectedly so. The enormous bed with its wooden canopy carved like a giant crown stood on a raised platform against the far wall; the velvet bedcurtains fell in heavy folds, so dark they looked black in the candlelight. There was more dark velvet on the bed, and a somewhat lighter fur, and he could just see the spotless linen beneath the formal pillows. "As you can see, there's more than enough room."

"You could sleep five in that and never notice," Arak said.

There were a pair of high-backed carved chairs on either side of the fire, and a couch and a set of padded stools had been arranged to form a sitting area. There was a carved console that Irichels thought had been in the grand parlor, complete with flecked mirror and a matching pair of candelabras, and in the corner by the head of the bed someone—Maritsa, presumably—had set a prayer desk, the kneeler embroidered with stiff scarlet flowers. Irichels looked away, and found the doors the led to the bath and the dressing room.

"And I'm across the hall," Envar said again. He looked at Arak. "Want to see?"

They all trooped across to find the smaller room just as meticulously prepared, a fire in the painted stove and the bed made up just as lavishly, though the wheel-candelabra was unlit. There were lamps instead, and a faint scent of roses. The sitting area was smaller and more comfortable, with a long couch and padded chairs that didn't quite match, with a bright rug between the chairs, and Irichels gave Envar an apologetic glance. "Marthie's doing her best."

"She means well," Envar said. "Though I'm surprised the connecting door is to Arak's room."

"That was Grandmother's dressing room," Irichels said. "And then Grandfather's valet's room, after she died. Is it all right?" He looked at Arak, who nodded.

"It's comfortable enough—a good box bed and all. Though it's two doors between us, unless you sleep with Envar."

"And that, I think, would be unwise," Envar interjected. "There's no need to upset your daemon."

"You'll get no argument on that," Arak murmured.

"There's another door," Irichels said. "A direct passage." He moved toward the screen that hid the close-stool, trailing his fingers across the painted panels until he found the ear of wheat that shifted at his touch. "Here." The others pressed close, and he tilted the carved grain sideways. There was a soft click and the panel sagged outward, turning on concealed hinges to reveal a narrow passage. Irichels snapped his fingers for a marsh-light and sent it floating ahead of them to hover at the blank end. "There's another door that opens into the master's room."

"Show me," Arak said, and they squeezed together down the passage. The door was easy to see from this side; Irichels ran his hand down the edge until he found the iron ring, then lifted the latch. The door was low, and they ducked through it, emerging in the corner of the master's room under one of the sconces.

"Very clever, my heart," Envar said, "but why would there be a secret passage from the wife's room?"

"There are times when it's better not to count the last time she and the master slept together," Irichels answered, and Arak shook her head.

"Are there any other passages like this?"

"Not that I know of," Irichels said.

"Does that mean there might be?" Arak eyed the open door with some suspicion, then pushed it closed. It disappeared into the paneling.

"No—" Irichels stopped, considering. "Well. It was one of my cousins who told me about this one. I suppose it's possible there are others, but I can't imagine where."

"A back way out?" Envar said, and Arak nodded.

"I'd expect as much, myself. I'll take a good look in the morning. And in the meantime—with your permission, Gil, I'll sleep in here tonight."

"That's hardly necessary," Irichels began, and stopped, shrugging. It wasn't as though they didn't already know each other's secrets. "If you think you must."

"It'll keep her safe from your daemon, at least," Envar said, "and spares me playing the blushing bride."

"That was never required," Irichels said, and Envar gave him a slanting smile.

"But it would disappoint your household, Master di Samar."

CHAPTER FOUR

A rak fetched blankets and a pillow from her room and made up a bed on the couch by the fire, while Irichels stripped and slid between the heavy sheets. He hadn't felt anything like them since boyhood, cold and heavy, the edges worked with a band of fretwork, and as he extinguished the candles with a gesture he saw Envar running a finger over the threads.

"Fine work, my heart. And suitable for a bride."

"I'm sure there is a wedding set," Irichels answered. "Probably dyed scarlet and embroidered in saffron."

"Not white to show the blood?"

"Not every bride's a virgin," Irichels said.

"Wise of your house to notice that," Arak said from the couch, and they settled to sleep.

Irichels woke in darkness, already listening, though he couldn't have said for what. He held his breath as though that might help, but heard only the soft sound of Envar's breath beside him, and the rustle of blankets as Arak shifted on the couch. Irichels propped himself up on one elbow, straining to hear. Was that something moving, somewhere beyond this room—the courtyard, maybe? Was that the scuff of foot on stone or just his imagining, fear weaving sound out of silence? He thought he heard it again—on the stair?—but then there was nothing. The daemon hadn't roused: surely that meant there was nothing wrong. The air was warm, heavy with dreams; he closed his eyes—and shot bolt upright at a woman's scream.

Not Martholin, he thought, scrambling out from under the sheets. He snapped his fingers for a marsh-light, and saw Arak on her feet in shirt and breeches, sword and dagger glowing blue in her hands. "Where—?"

"Upstairs," Irichels answered, groping for his own sword, and felt the daemon rouse at last. He felt it rush upward, through and past their room, and saw Envar stagger as though he'd been struck. "Come on."

Arak was ahead of him on the stairs, blades ready, but at the top she faltered and Irichels swallowed an oath. There was light ahead of them, the wavering light of a single lamp, and either Karan or Romello braced in the doorway holding a smoking candle; but between him and the stairs the shadows were unnaturally dark, and if you looked at them sidelong, they seemed to roil and swirl like water over rocks.

"Marthie!" Irichels put his shoulder against Arak's. "What's happening?"

"We're not hurt, Master Gil—" Martholin's voice was high and strained, and a part of the shadow lunged toward it. Karan blindly thrust the candle at it, and it recoiled. Irichels sketched a charm, calling on a contract of defense and dispersal. It blazed up, not quite light, and Irichels caught a glimpse of a shape more or less like a man's before it batted away the charm with a sound like glass breaking. It lunged toward them, a purple spark snapping like a whip, and Arak caught it on her glowing dagger. Then the daemon surged up from the courtyard, a vast soundless weight like a roaring sea, and the shape pushed past them to flee back down the stairs. The daemon flowed over the edge of the balcony and vanished into the dark below. There was a thump and a cry, instantly cut off, and a brief sense of satisfaction.

"Is it gone?" Karan leaned against the doorframe, the candle shaking in his hand. "Master—"

"It's gone," Irichels said, choosing the simpler answer for now. "Are you all right?"

"No one's hurt," Martholin repeated, but behind her rose a hiccupping wail that resolved to "—want to go home!"

Irichels snapped his fingers for another marsh-light. "Someone tell me what happened."

"I'll do that, Master." Karan blew out the candle and set it carefully on the floor. "Best let Marthie deal with her."

Irichels nodded. "Well?"

"We were all abed," Karan said. "Marthie has us in adjoining rooms this side of the courtyard for now, and we'd put out the candles long since. I heard the midnight-bell from Idra-of-Mercies, and then I thought I heard a foot on the stair. I grabbed a lamp, not knowing who it was and not wanting to offend, but then I heard the lock break and I knew that wouldn't be anyone here. So I went in by the connecting door, and Marthie had the watch-candle lit, and I grabbed it and got between it and the others. And then you came. And *it*."

"Did it cross the threshold?" Envar asked. He was naked except for patched braies and his nose was bleeding. He dabbed at that one-handed, his iron-shod quarterstaff still ready in the other.

Karan looked at him, and then back at Irichels. "No, Master."

If the sending hadn't crossed the threshold, then the others should be safe enough inside while they searched the rest of the house. "Go back in your room," Irichels said, "light the watch-candle and keep it lit. We'll deal with this."

"Yes, Master." Karan picked up the candle and ducked back into the room, closing the door behind him.

"It's gone now," Arak said. The blue light was fading from her weapons.

"Yes, but what was it?" Envar was shivering visibly. "Let me get some clothes on, and we'll find out where it came from."

Irichels dressed hastily himself, keeping his own sword within reach and his ears cocked for any more trouble. The daemon had withdrawn to its regular spot, if anything quieter than usual. That was not particularly reassuring and he was glad to see Envar return, dressed and carrying an open censer. His nose was still bleeding, and Irichels frowned. "What happened there?"

"The sending struck me." Envar used the hearth tongs to pluck embers from the hearth and set them in the censer, then produced a small brass vial. He sprinkled a few grains of its contents onto the coals and waited for the smoke to rise. "I wasn't expecting it, or I would have dodged faster."

"I would have said it was a fetch," Arak said, "but I didn't see its face. And what would a fetch be doing here?"

"That's uncommon outside the hill country," Irichels said. A fetch was usually intended to take someone's place, and that didn't seem to make sense.

Envar lifted the censer, now trailing thin tendrils of smoke. "Let's see if we can find it."

Irichels followed him out into the corridor, the resin almond-sweet in his nostrils. This was one of Envar's own blends and sure enough, as they approached the stairs, the smoke waked a fugitive sparkle from the polished stone. There were two tracks, one regularly spaced, the other leaping from stair to stair: one coming in, Irichels thought, and the other fleeing. "Let's see where it came in."

They followed the regular tracks back down the main stair and across the courtyard. It circled the fountain, then entered the ballroom, the flecks of light brighter in the dark. They ran the length of the room, and then went back out the other door to the courtyard.

"That's odd," Arak said. "I'd have expected it to come through these windows."

Envar took the censer closer, moving carefully in the dark, swung it so that the smoke washed up and over the first of the locked and barred doors that led to the portico that opened onto the alley. That was how guests had arrived for the balls, Irichels remembered abruptly, not through the main door on the canal but down the alley, hung with lanterns and banners, hurrying in and out the ballroom doors that spilled light and laughter and music into the street. He had always been too young to attend, but for a while his room had been above the ballroom, and the narrow balcony had given him a cramped view of the arriving guests.

There was no response from the first door, not even the faintest flash of light; Envar checked the other three and turned back, shaking his head. "It didn't get in this way."

"How, then?" Irichels called a marsh-light to examine the locks himself, but there was no sign of tampering.

Envar shrugged. "All I can say is not this way."

"The tracks lead back to the courtyard," Arak said. "Maybe we missed something."

They followed the tracks back to the fountain, where they were crossed by the line of tracks fleeing under the portico. Arak shook her head in frustration. "They don't go anywhere near any of the doors. Could it have come through the courtyard?"

Irichels looked up at the glass-and-lattice network that kept out the rain. "That should be warded—was warded, I thought, though I'll admit I didn't check it closely." Another thing to do in the morning, he thought, and Envar gave a wry smile, as though he'd guessed the thought.

"There's one other possibility. Suppose it came in the way it ran out?"

Irichels turned to look where Envar was pointing. A broader trail of sparks spread across the stones, wiping out the leaping footprints. Both led under the portico, and then down the hall toward the storage room where the daemon laired. But that hall ended in a service door, opening to the water-alley, and Irichels braced himself. "Let's take a look."

The hall seemed darker than was natural, and the smudged marks seemed all the brighter by contrast. The broader trail had covered most of the footprints, ended abruptly outside the storage room's locked door. Envar swung the censer again, and a great patch of twinkling light bloomed on the door itself, as though someone had thrown a ripe fruit to spatter against the wall. "I think your daemon ate whatever it was, my heart."

Irichels tugged at his beard, unable to disagree. "No bad thing, all considered."

"No, indeed." Envar's voice was for once entirely respectful.

There were no marks on the floor beyond the storage room door, not even when Envar sketched a glyph that sent the smoke billowing out of the censer, nor did they find any others anywhere else. The doors on the first floor were locked and barred, unchanged from when he had checked them before bed, and he shook his head. "I'll tell Marthie all's well, and then let's to bed."

It was a late morning and a meager breakfast, served by Martholin herself with sleeves rolled up and her working apron still in place. "Vette's left me this morning, wouldn't even stay for the pennies she'd earned, said to send them after her along with her box. So it's toasted cheese and bacon and you'll have to wait for the kaf till I can strain it."

She hurried out without waiting for an answer, and Envar said, "One can hardly blame the girl."

"No, indeed." Arak sniffed warily at her tea, which was blacker than usual, then took a cautious sip. "Do you think she was the target? If it was a fetch, I mean."

"I didn't get a good look at it," Irichels answered. "Unless you did, Cass?"

Envar shook his head. "And I'm not that sure it was a fetch. To what end?"

"Replacing the maid puts an agent in the house," Arak said.

"But this is Bejanth, not the High Hills," Envar said. "Servants are often strangers. It would be just as easy to bribe an ordinary girl as to call up a fetch to take her place."

"Unless there was cursing to be done," Arak said.

"Maybe." Envar didn't sound convinced.

"I want to know how it got in," Irichels said. "We'll need to check the wards, tedious as that is. I'd hoped to track down the curse-reader they consulted after Aunt Maritsa died."

"Did this reader have a name?" Envar asked.

"Zaffara." Irichels leaned back as Martholin reappeared with the tray for the kaf and all its fixings, and saw her eyes flick up at the name. "Were you here when she came, Marthie?"

She set the tray on the table, poured the narrow cups half full, drawing the pot up to get a layer of froth on top. "I was."

"And?"

She set the first cup in front of him, and slid the tray closer so that he could choose from the little dishes of coarse sugar and spices and candied orange peel. "She stank up the entire house with her smokes and potions, and we weren't any the wiser after she'd left. She *said* there was nothing to find, but the trouble continued just the same."

"What sort of trouble?" Envar asked. Irichels finished dosing his own kaf and slid the tray toward him.

Martholin gave him a swift glance, but answered as though it had been Irichels who asked. "Noises in the night, things moved that shouldn't be, cold drafts from nowhere—and of course itself was troubled. But she swore there was nothing to find."

"That does seem odd," Irichels said. "Thank you, Marthie." She dipped a curtsey and returned to the kitchen, and Irichels took a soothing sip of his kaf.

"I know her," Envar said, frowning. "Or I did. She's certainly competent."

"Would she meet with me?" Irichels asked.

"I would think so," Envar answered. "But it would be better not done here. I can send a note, if you'd like."

"That would help."

"There's a thought occurs to me," Arak said. "After you showed us that passage last night—suppose there were more? As I said, I'd expect some back bolt hole in a house like this."

"We're not in the High Hills," Envar said again, and Arak ignored him, her eyes on Irichels.

"I don't know of any," Irichels said. "But there's a good chance I wouldn't have been told. That's another thing we should look at—after we check the wards."

That took well into the afternoon, crawling from the hidden compartments on the first floor to the roof with its cisterns and the lattice over the courtyard, but everything seemed to be functioning properly. At least there was a breeze on the roof and Irichels lingered there, turning his sweating face into the moving air. From here he could look down the length of the Hadolon Canal and across the rooftops of Mercies to the dome of the Senate and Assembly on Lawgivers' to the south, or if he craned his neck he could look west to the taller houses crowding the Boot.

It was a pretty sight, the city brighter and cleaner from this height, and he stood for a moment, watching the seabirds turn against the pale sky. But he was hot and filthy, his knuckles bruised from wrestling with recalcitrant doors and covers, and he wanted nothing better than to sink into a hot bath. Instead, he and Envar took turns standing in the tub under the cold tap, rinsing off the worst of the dirt, and then Irichels returned to the library to see if he could find any of the house papers that might show a plan.

"Do you really think your architect would include the secret passages?" Envar asked, hauling another double folio out of the shelves and letting it fall onto the worktable. Like the last two, this one's cover was embossed with the Samar chained salamander and seemed to contain deeds of purchase. Why someone had decided to have them bound into a single volume, Irichels couldn't begin to guess, but it was the best he had to work with right now.

"Invisible ink, maybe," he said aloud. "Just in case someone died off without sharing the secret. Or—more likely—it was a later alteration and I might find the bill that paid for it."

"I just don't know." Envar perched on the edge of the table. "Where would an escape passage come out? On the street seems entirely too obvious—if you were attacked, that's where the mob would be coming from, not to mention it would be overlooked by all the neighbors. The same goes for the alley. And the canal."

"There's the water alley," Irichels said.

"Which is water," Envar said. "You'd need a boat, and

surely that would be a bit obvious. How many boats sit there for hours? Not so many, I'd bet."

Irichels nodded. "But the wards are intact, so how did the sending get in last night?"

"How would you do it?" That was Arak, coming in the door in her shirtsleeves. She'd obviously bathed, her cropped brown hair still plastered to her scalp, and the light fabric emphasized the breadth of her shoulders. Even barefoot, she was barely two fingers shorter than Irichels: a typical hillwoman, and shaped by her profession.

"No luck?" Irichels asked.

"Nothing." Arak gave a crooked smile. "Which is why I was wondering how you'd do it."

"I'd break the wards," Envar said.

"But if for some reason you couldn't," Irichels said, his voice trailing off as he considered the problem. Depending on how the wards had been set, it was sometimes possible to find a weak spot and wear away the ward at that point only. But it was much harder to keep the wards from unraveling once they were damaged, and harder still to mend the fabric of someone else's magic. There had been no sign of such interference, and the house wards had been designed to minimize the possibility.

"I'd try to have someone bring it in unwittingly," Envar said. "Send it in the wax of a seal, or among the supplies, maybe? But for that you'd need to bribe the housekeeper not to find it, and I can't see your Marthie agreeing to that."

"No," Irichels agreed. "And the only letter I've received was from the Arlechini, and I'd have noticed if there was anything in it. That's something else we'd better watch for, though."

"What's beneath the house?" Arak asked, after a moment.

Envar gave her a look. "Water. Pilings and water."

"These canal-front houses were built on platforms that sit at the tide-mark," Irichels said. "There are dozens of pilings sunk into the rock and held together by crossbeams and copper fastenings, and then the platform and the stone on top of it."

"There are places in the slums where there are grates that open to the water," Envar said thoughtfully.

"In some of the oldest houses, too." Irichels frowned. "I think? There was one in Casteven House, I recall, with an iron cover and a lock."

"I'd lock it, too," Envar said. "And of course you hear tales of thieves sneaking through the pilings at dead low tide and cutting into warehouses and such, but I've never heard of them breaking into a well-built house."

Arak shrugged. "Well, it was a thought."

"I've a thought myself," Envar said. "We should leave here."

"I can't," Irichels began, and Envar raised a hand.

"I don't mean leave the city, I mean move out of this house. Rent rooms somewhere pleasant and far away while we figure out what's going on, and you decide what you're going to do."

If I leave now, I'll never come back. Irichels swallowed that shameful certainty and said, "It's not a bad thought, but if I do, it'll look as though I'm not certain of my claim."

"But there's no one else, is there?" Envar tipped his head to one side.

"The Senate and Assembly have to acknowledge me," Irichels said. "And the holdings of the house go to the high constable if they don't. Or they can appoint someone in my place, if they can find a collateral relative." He managed what he hoped was a careless shrug. "Besides, I've just hired Marthie back."

"Are you sure she wants to stay?" Arak asked with a grin.

"I'm sure she wants employment," Irichels answered. "Besides—we can handle this."

CHAPTER FIVE

The next day dawned cloudy, with an edge to the air and a chop to the water even in the canals. For Arak's sake, Irichels decided they'd walk to Zaffara's house on the Quadrata. The Quadrata lay against Mercies's southeast edge, linked by a pair of bridges; and as they crossed Irichels looked east to see the tower guarding the mouth of the canal, the red-gold-and-white stripes bright against the lowering sky. There was a similar tower at every point where the canals opened to the sea, bespelled by the Oratory as part of the city's defenses against the sea demons who lived in the depths of the Narrow Sea. They were kin to the land demons, and like them a source of feral magic, though fewer ferals bargained with them than with the more accessible demons who haunted the Plana and the hills beyond. Theory suggested that creatures like the house daemon were a lesser form of the same substance, and could eventually become true demons, but if Samar's had not, Irichels thought, he doubted any would.

"Rain before sunset," Envar muttered, but not loudly enough that Irichels had to take notice. They were all dressed soberly, to draw no unwanted attention in the shabby district behind the Eastern Harbor; and among the sailors from a dozen nations, not even Arak stood out as particularly foreign. The houses here were old and much divided, with shops crowding the ground floors. There were public cisterns in the narrow squares, each with its brass taps and the donor's bust picked out in plaster; they all seemed to be working, though Irichels could remember dry summers when even Grandfather had to send men to queue at the dock for a ration. With luck, he'd be gone before the next summer set in.

Zaffara lived on the second floor of what had once been a modest townhouse, with her own stair and a balcony that overlooked the courtyard and its fountain. A maid led them into the study, where the curtains had been pulled back to let in as much light as possible, and the walls were lined with shelves and locked book presses. Zaffara rose from the worktable, dismissing the secretary who had been working at the slanted desk, and gestured toward a set of chairs that waited in front of the cold fireplace.

"Master di Samar. I was glad to get your note. I thought you might consult me, so I've been reviewing the matter."

Irichels bowed politely. "Thank you, Dot're. Let me introduce my colleagues, Dot're Cassi and Messida Arak."

"Honored." Zaffara took the high-backed master's chair, and Irichels and Envar seated themselves opposite, Arak leaning lightly on the back of Irichels' chair. "Am I correct in assuming you want to know what I found after your aunt died?"

"Very much so," Irichels answered.

"I wish there were more to tell. I understand you're of the community yourself?"

"I've worked as a cursebreaker these twenty years and more."

Zaffara nodded. "That makes this a little easier, perhaps. In a word, I found—nothing. Your house spirit was active, perhaps more so than usual, and I could read its presence all over the house, but there was no real sign of anything else."

"No real sign?" Envar said.

"There might have been something," Zaffara said. "I could never quite put a finger on it—it was like at night, when you see better if you look sideways, but the thing vanishes when you look head on. I think there was something else in the house at some point, but I couldn't tell you what it was. It might even have been something your aunt or uncle had done, that hadn't completely unraveled with their deaths."

She paused. "Are you experiencing the same things?"

"A bit more than that," Irichels said. "We had what seemed to be a sending, possibly a fetch, but the daemon destroyed it before we could be sure."

"Your spirit is very loyal," Zaffara said.

Irichels swallowed his instinctive response, and Envar said, "I assume you also checked the wards."

"Of course." Zaffara spread her hands. "And again, nothing. Everything was in order. They'd been renewed only two or three years before, and it was skillfully done. There was no sign they'd been breached."

"And yet," Irichels said after a moment, "you wouldn't swear there was nothing."

"As I told you, I thought—there might have been? It worried me, though I couldn't put a finger on it. You'll know the feeling."

Irichels nodded. He knew exactly what she meant, that niggling uncertainty, as though there was something just out of sight that might mean something important, or might be nothing at all. At the University, there had been innumerable attempts to classify those traces, to develop some taxonomy, but all anyone could say for certain was that sometimes magic overspilled its bounds, like a flood tide washing up over the top step, and a trained practitioner could see the stains it left behind. "You were also asked about the deaths. Maritsa's and Hamel's—Galeran's, too?"

"Yes. That was a different question—wasn't it?" Zaffara gave him a startled look, and Irichels shrugged.

"Tyrn Arlechin thought so, anyway. Did you read on them?"

"I did." Zaffara rose from her chair and went to the worktable, pulling a large square of paper from among the litter of sheets and tablets. "I have the record here."

Irichels joined her, turning the paper so that they could all see. It was a nine-card spread, laid out in the familiar tree, with the Hanged Man at the crown and the lightning-struck Tower at the root, each card noted with quick brush-strokes. This was a practitioner's copy, not the elaborate painted version that could be handed to a client, with each card depicted in detail; this was just the names of the cards, and the time and date noted in one corner, with the relative positions of sun and moon and tide.

"Do you read the cards?" Zaffara asked.

"I know the meanings," Irichels answered. "I've no talent for their use."

"Well, then." She touched the crown. "That must have been you—suspension, irresolution, waiting for something, in this case someone. And you can probably tell me what lies at the root." She touched the rectangle marked 'Tower'. "I would guess that's something in your family's past, but all I can say is that it was some kind of catastrophe."

"Possibly? I don't know," Irichels said. "I wasn't brought up to think of myself as a di Samar, and no one shared the family stories with me."

"Ah." Zaffara touched the two cards above the Tower. "Nine of Coins and Nine of Staves. Whatever it was, it didn't quite come to fruition. The house is built, but must be defended. And that leads to—" She touched the cards to their left and right. "The Four of Coins and the Seven of Swords. Parsimony and avarice on the one hand, theft and treachery on the other. And then, in the main line, Death. Whatever came before was overthrown, and that leads to the Ace of Cups and Six of Staves. That overthrow led to prosperity, to victory, but that was temporary. I drew clarifying cards here, to see if I could find what ended the good times." She pointed to the side of the drawing, where smaller rectangles were labeled 'Five of Cups' and 'Page of Staves'. "Five of Cups for disillusion, dissatisfaction. Whatever the Ace brought, it wasn't enough. And the Page..." She touched the sheet again, her expression thoughtful. "Again, you'd know better than I. A child, or perhaps children, hot-at-hand, angry."

"That I do know," Irichels said. "My Uncle Galeran's youngest son...." He stopped, not wanting to say more, but Zaffara merely nodded.

"And that brings us back to the Hanged Man, waiting for resolution." She cocked her head, studying the drawing again. "I can only tell you what I told Messire Tyrn, the roots of this are deep in the past."

"Are those roots being acted on in the present?" Envar asked.

Zaffara shrugged. "That's not in the scope of this reading. All I can say is that I found no immediate supernatural cause for these deaths, and so I certified to Messire Tyrn."

And that was as far as they were going to get, Irichels thought. She'd done her duty and been paid for it, and it was clear from her stance that she had no desire to become any more deeply involved. "Could I get a copy of the reading? I'll pay, of course."

"A client's copy?" Zaffara sounded doubtful, and Irichels shook his head.

"A copy of your working copy. You've made me curious about the family history."

"Twenty zekki," she said. "If you'd care to wait, I can have my secretary copy it for you now."

A maid escorted them into a side parlor, where a fretted screen overlooked the courtyard, and brought a tray with barley-water and candied fruit. Other servants came and went, all in easy earshot, but Irichels had nothing to say anyway, still pondering what Zaffara had said. He wondered how much she knew about Samar's history—certainly she had seemed to know about Debes, though his death would have been enough of a scandal that he should probably assume all Bejanth knew about it. He could hear the soft whir of a spinning wheel from some inner room, and once a woman's laughter, but nothing more.

At last the secretary appeared with the rolled copy. Irichels handed over the coins, and the secretary bowed them down the stairs. There was a taverna on the far side of the square, and they made their way into the main room to see if the noon meal was still available. It was, and plenty of open tables as most of the patrons headed back to work, and Irichels ordered wine to take the taste of barley-water from his teeth.

"That was interesting," Envar said, after they'd claimed plates of the day's meal. "Possibly useful."

"Do you think?" Arak gave him a doubtful look.

"Well, we know she didn't find anything more than we have," Envar answered. "And the reading is interesting. Do you know what's at the root, Gil?"

Irichels shook his head. "I told you, I didn't get much in the way of family stories." Mostly he had spent his time trying to stay out of people's way, because his mother had never much exerted herself to protect him. She had been worn out with grief and with the loss of her vocation, something Grandfather had never allowed her to forget or to mend. He had only softened in the last year of her life, and had allowed her to return to the Oratory as a lay sister. At least she had died within the walls of Idra-of-Mercies, in the shadow of its sanctuary and the embrace of its bells.

It had begun to rain by the time they left the taverna, a thin drizzle that promised worse to come. It was still light enough to risk a shorter cut through the edge of the harbor slums, and they hurried over a smaller canal, the bridge depositing them in an unswept square. This one was ringed on three sides by an open portico, and instead of a cistern there was a fountain, Idra's loyal servant Benaion spilling water from a sieve. Children were playing some sort of complicated skipping game on the cracked pavings, their feet blurring the chalked marks more than the rain, and a crowd had gathered at the far end of the square, just outside the shelter of the portico. A rasping cry like a gull's came from that direction, and Envar lifted his chin.

"What is it?" Arak asked, one hand already on her sword.

"Nothing, I hope," Irichels said, and Envar gave him a searing glance.

"Prophecy." He stalked off toward the sound without waiting for an answer.

Irichels loosened his own sword in its scabbard. "Stay close," he said to Arak and followed, Envar's ragged gown billowing like a sail ahead of him.

By the time they reached the crowd, Envar was already shouldering his way into it. Irichels put himself at the chirurgeon's right, Arak automatically taking the left, and under that force the listeners gave way, letting them through to the front row. A filthy boy sat on the flagstones dressed only a tattered shirt, his brown hair hanging in greasy elflocks. At the moment, he was picking at the sole of his foot, heedless of his exposed crotch. A woman stood behind him, poorly dressed but clean, and another boy waited with a basket on a long stick. The woman's expression brightened, seeing their arrival. "Come to have your fortune told, Messire? Hurry, now, this chance won't last long." The boy with the basket waved it hopefully in their direction.

"He's possessed," Envar said.

"He has the falling sickness," the woman answered, "and when the fit's on him, he sees things that may yet be."

Irichels's mouth tightened. That was an old belief; sometimes it was an enterprising parent seeking to wring some good from a child's affliction, but just as often the fits were faked. Or someone called a demon to make the pretense more plausible. What it did to the child was beside the point.

"He's possessed," Envar said again. "And if you don't care about the child—well, I hope you read your contract carefully."

The crowd shifted uneasily, about half taking heed of Envar's words, the rest annoyed that he was spoiling their fun. Irichels said, "He's right. You should—"

He had meant to suggest that they take their answers and let the boy go, but the boy's head shot up as though jerked by a string. He shrieked again, the sound high and inhuman, and a much deeper voice spoke through him.

Lightning-struck! Turned your back on the water, did you, and did it do you any good? Have you found your answers yet? Shame will take you still—

"Enough!" Envar gestured, shaping a glyph that blazed bright with his anger. The boy jerked backward, his eyes closing, and the woman skipped back a step, caught between fear and fury. Something like smoke oozed from the boy's nostrils, rising and solidifying, and Irichels formed a second sign, flicking it at and through the smoke. This was the moment when a demon was most vulnerable, and this one hadn't been very strong after all. It keened and vanished, the smoke shredding to nothing, and Irichels turned on the woman before she could speak.

"Be grateful you're free of it."

Envar went to his knees beside the boy, sketched a sign over his forehead and then another over his chest. "He's clear."

"And no good to me." The woman found her voice with a gasp. "What am I to do without him?"

"Without your demon?" Irichels could feel the crowd at his back, unsure who to turn against. "Be glad you're done with him so easily." He heard a murmur of agreement: everyone had seen the boy freed and the demon destroyed. He reached into his purse, found a gold sequin, and placed it firmly in the palm of her hand. He saw her eyes widen—gold, far more than the boy would ever be worth—and said, "Make a better bargain next time." Out of the corner of his eye he saw Envar heave himself to his feet, the boy hanging unconscious in his arms. "Let's go."

The crowd parted for them and he marched toward the closest exit, the hair prickling at the nape of his neck. Arak was behind them, walking with the exaggerated swagger of a hill-country fighter, but Irichels didn't relax until they'd turned a second corner.

"Is he all right?"

"I don't know." Envar was out of breath, but shook his head when Irichels would have stopped. "Let's keep going."

"Is he hurt?" Arak asked. "I can take him, if you'd like."

"Later." Envar looked around. "Which way?"

"Toward the Eastern Water," Irichels said, and turned in that direction. "Is he hurt, do you think?"

"I said, I don't know." Envar shook his hair out of his eyes. "He doesn't have any obvious injuries, but you just don't know with demons."

By the time they'd reached the edge of the channel, the boy was stirring. Envar set him down on one of the low walls that separated the street from the steps that led down to the water, and Irichels supported him with one hand while Envar crouched at his feet. "It's gone," he said quietly. "It's gone and you're free."

The boy gave him a doubtful glance, then shrugged first one shoulder and then the other as though testing his limbs. He flexed fingers and toes and then his ankles, a frown deepening on his dirty face. "Who—" He choked on the word, coughing as though it pained him, and Envar winced.

"Don't try to talk. I've a syrup at home that will help you." The boy managed a nod, and Envar looked up at Irichels. "Can we find a boat, do you think?"

Arak moved to support the boy's shoulders, and Irichels dropped down onto the steps, scanning the water for a boat for hire. There were small craft in plenty, but they either carried house livery or they were fully occupied. "I'll look—"

"Gil?"

Irichels turned to see a stranger about his own age coming down the steps. He had obviously been heading for the gallemin pulled in close to the bank; its flaunting blue-and-silver livery matched the badge on the man's hat. Then the years dropped away and he recognized the man after all. Halyssin Ambros was the eldest son of one of the three families who controlled the Senate and competed for the office of high constable; they had been at school together in Bejanth, and briefly in Tarehan, and had been friends then.

"Hal?"

"It is you." Halyssin held out both hands. Irichels took them, and Halyssin drew him in for the cheek-to-cheek kiss of equals. "I'd heard you'd come home at last."

"I hadn't much choice," Irichels said. That was the most honest and least offensive thing he could say at this point.

"I was sorry to hear about your aunt," Halyssin offered. "And your uncles."

"We weren't close."

"No." Halyssin gave his wry smile, more familiar and welcoming than Irichels had expected. "That I also remember. Look, we can't talk here. Will you come home with me? I've my own suite of rooms now, you won't have to put up with any of the rest of the family. Idra's Bane, it's good to see you again!"

For an instant, Irichels was tempted, but a glance behind him recalled him to his business. "I'm sorry, I can't. We have to get the boy home."

"What's wrong with him?" Halyssin's expression was sharper than his lazy tone.

"Someone called a demon into him to issue prophecies," Irichels said. "Cass and I dealt with it. But the boy needs tending."

"Of course." Halyssin nodded. "Can I take you—no, this thing will never make it up the Hadolon. Though I have a punt I could put at your disposal?"

"That would be greatly appreciated," Irichels said, and Halyssin put jeweled fingers to his mouth to whistle for his boatman. He gave the orders with brisk efficiency, and didn't blink as Envar steered the boy down the steps.

"Poor little brat," he said, in a voice calculated to reach the boatman. "You'll let me know how he gets on."

"Yes." Irichels turned toward the boat himself, and Halyssin caught his sleeve.

"Look, my father's hosting a party two nights from now. Let me send you an invitation—it'll improve things immeasurably."

"I haven't been acknowledged yet," Irichels said.

"All the more reason to be seen at our house," Halyssin answered. "And who knows, Father might even approve. The high constable will be there, too. I'll send a note." He turned away without waiting for an answer. Irichels shook his head, and joined the others in the punt.

"Who was that?" Envar asked. He was holding the boy almost in his lap, the filthy head cradled against his shoulder.

"Halyssin Ambros," Irichels answered. "He and I were at school together."

"It was good of him to loan us the boat," Arak said.

By the time they returned to Samar House, the boy was fully awake again, though still not able to speak. Envar settled him by the kitchen fire and vanished upstairs to fetch herbs and potions, while Irichels explained the circumstances to Martholin. She had hired another pair of kitchen girls, who listened slack-jawed until she set them to heating milk and water. By the time Envar returned, the milk was ready. He poured a spoonful of thick syrup into it, and gave another to the boy directly. He had also brought smallclothes and a pair of trousers, and the boy scrambled into them eagerly. And all the while Envar talked to him, calm and soothing and as ordinary as though this sort of thing happened every day.

"I expect you'll want a bath, but I warn you: it'll put you right to sleep, and I want you to get this bottle down you before you go to bed. It'll ease your throat, and tomorrow you may be able to talk again. Can you write?" The boy shook his head, and sipped obediently at his milk. "No matter." Envar's voice stayed even but Irichels could see the tension in his hands, could feel the anger building like a wave. "There, Marthie has some ganji for you. It's not too hot, and you need something in your stomach. Try a taste, now."

The boy turned his head away, but Envar coaxed him to take a bite, and then a second, and after that he fed himself, wincing a little as even the soft porridge caught in his throat.

"I'll keep him in my room tonight, Dot're," Martholin said, and Envar nodded. "Chelle can make up a bed for him, and draw a bath—you're right, he wants one, and you're right that he'll sleep after, too."

"Yes." Envar poured out a final spoonful of the syrup.

"Here, finish that, and you'll have more in the morning." He looked over his shoulder. "I'll stay with him until Marthie comes up."

"I'll send a tray, then," Martholin said.

"I'm not hungry."

"You'll want it later," Martholin said.

Dinner was plain and hastily served, Martholin's attention obviously on caring for the boy. Irichels ate without really tasting it, then made the rounds of the ground floor, making everything secure. Arak trailed after him with the candles.

"Is Cass all right?"

"He's upset," Irichels said.

"It was upsetting," Arak agreed. "Maybe you shouldn't have paid off that woman."

"I couldn't just kill her," Irichels said. "Not in Bejanth. And with the demon banished, there was no case to be made. I thought, better to be rid of her and help the boy."

"If he can be helped."

"It was just the demon in him," Irichels said, and hoped it was true. "Most of them don't understand people, how our bodies work. That's why possession can be so harmful."

Arak made a noncommittal noise and they turned into the ballroom. "Halyssin Ambros, you said that was? Who loaned us the boat?"

"Yes." Irichels checked the lock, and dropped the first bar into place. Beyond the barred glass of the door the portico was in shadow, but the alley showed torchlight toward the far end.

"That's a Senatorial house, yes?"

"Yes." Irichels set the next bar in its brackets. "More than that, it's one of the three great houses that dominate the Senate. The only reason a Jeroen is high constable this year is that the Three couldn't agree on which of them would win." It had been a long time since he'd paid much attention to Bejanth's politics; it was disconcerting to find it all coming back so easily.

"You were friends at school," Arak said, giving the word the twist that meant 'lovers'.

Irichels sighed. "What of it? That was twenty years ago—more. And why are you minding Cass's business for him?"

"Because it's been a difficult day for all of us," Arak answered.

Irichels swore under his breath and dropped the last bar into place. "Hal was my friend at school, nothing more."

When he got upstairs, Envar was standing by the fire, one hand on the mantel, kicking moodily at a log that had split and rolled. Irichels could see the tension still stiffening his shoulders, and when he looked up his face was pale and set.

"How's the boy?"

"Asleep." Envar kicked the log again, swearing as it crumbled into a shower of embers. "He should be better in the morning."

"And you?"

"I'm fine."

"Did you eat?" Irichels moved cautiously closer, and was relieved when Envar didn't turn away.

"I told you, I'm not hungry."

Someone, probably Martholin, had brought the tray in anyway, and it sat on the sideboard beside the brandy bottle. Irichels nodded, knowing better than to press the issue, and laid a cautious hand on Envar's shoulder.

"I hate them so much," Envar said quietly. "Anyone who'd do that...to their own child is worst, but to any child—I hope she dies slow and hard. Something wasting, and painful. And that her kin abandon her to it."

"I know." Irichels waited, not daring to move, to offer everything he wanted to give; and after a moment Envar turned into his arms, resting his face against Irichels's shoulder. Irichels tightened his hold, and felt Envar sigh.

"I told you, didn't I? That was me?"

Irichels nodded. "You did. And if I could kill him again—"

Envar managed a smothered chuckle. "Too late, my heart, I already did that."

"You said." Irichels rested his cheek against Envar's hair. "I only wish I could have helped."

"You wouldn't have liked it," Envar said. "You wouldn't have liked me." Irichels made a soothing sound, though he suspected it was might have been true. He didn't have Envar's stomach for revenge. He stroked Envar's back instead, and felt some of the tension ease. "When did I tell you?" Envar asked. "I don't remember."

"We were drunk," Irichels said. "In Abesscie." He remembered it all too clearly himself, huddled in the back room of an inn overlooking the rocky harbor, the windows thrown open to bring in what breeze there was at the height of the southern summer. It had been a hard job, and a messy one, and they'd been bruised and battered enough to take to their bed with a bottle of the local gin, passing it back and forth to dull the nagging sense that somehow they could have done better.

Sometime in those hours, Envar had blurted out the tale, how his mother had sold him to a fortune-teller, who'd called a demon into him. Envar had fought it, he couldn't imagine Envar doing anything less, but to no avail—*like beating your fists against a stone wall ten feet thick, and all the while it puppets you, and no one cares if you're hurt or what it makes you do. And it likes it, every stupid filthy thing it makes you do.*

"I was lucky," Envar said. "I figured out how to ward myself, how to keep it from getting in, and when my master couldn't beat me into submission, he sold me to another feral—thirty zekki and a cask of brandy. But she was a decent sort, and taught me well. I inherited her contracts when she died."

"Yes."

Envar pulled back, and Irichels let him go. This was an old ache and one he couldn't soothe, no matter how much he wished he could make it go away. Envar rubbed his face, thrust both hands into his hair, and shook himself hard. "Well. At least the boy should be all right. I don't think there's anything permanently wrong with him, it was just the demon."

"That's good news." Irichels crossed to the sideboard, poured himself a glass of brandy. "Want some?"

Envar shook his head. Irichels settled himself in one of the tall chairs by the fire, stretching his feet to the flames, and after a moment, Envar came to perch on the arm of the chair. Irichels leaned against him. "What did you make of Zaffara?"

"I'd trust her reputation," Envar answered. "And that reading is certainly intriguing. It's a pity you don't know the story behind it, my heart."

"And even more of a pity there's no one left to ask." Irichels took a sip of the brandy, and Envar intercepted the glass before Irichels could set it aside.

"There was one thing—whatever answer that demon was bound to provide, I think that message was definitely meant for you."

Irichels recovered his glass and took a deeper drink. "I'd rather not think that."

"No more would I, but I think it was." Envar accepted the glass again. "'Lightning-struck' it called you—of course I think of the Tower. 'Turned your back on the water.' You left Bejanth? And then it threatened you with shame." He handed the glass back. "I hope that doesn't mean me."

"I'm not ashamed of you."

"This isn't the mainland," Envar said. "And we're not wandering scholars."

"I don't care," Irichels said. "I won't give you up. If any pressure is brought to bear—I never wanted this. I can leave, and there's nothing anyone can do to make me come back. In fact, I wonder if I shouldn't do that anyway." He felt the daemon stir, as though it had heard the words, and Envar grimaced.

"Best not say that too loudly, my heart." He paused. "You can't think of anything it might have meant?"

Irichels swallowed the last drops of the brandy. "Unfortunately, no. Though Hal is something of a scholar, he might be able to help."

"It did help, him loaning his boat," Envar said.

"He's a good man."

"And a good friend, I gather."

"That was a long time ago," Irichels said firmly. "Over long before I met you." He felt Envar relax again, and pushed himself to his feet. "Let's to bed."

Chapter Six

As promised, the boy was better the next morning, able to whisper his name—Tepan—and to confide that he was eleven years old and could neither read nor write. He did prove capable of understanding the basics of kitchen work and seemed eager to cling to Martholin's skirts, so Irichels left him to it and retreated to his study to go through what were left of the family books. Envar reported the boy essentially unharmed, but probably not particularly talented: if he could be taught more than the basics, he would surely want to learn how to protect himself. Instead, he shrank from the offer and from Envar, who shrugged it off, but Irichels thought he was hurt by the rejection.

The invitation arrived as promised, a brightly-inked square sealed by Gellis Ambros himself. A second seal had been used to attach a hand-written note from Hal inviting him to a light supper before the main event, and Irichels sent back notes accepting both. There was no time to have new clothes made, but Irichels found a tailor and ordered new gowns for himself and Envar, and formal livery for Arak. There would be more parties like this, and he wanted them to be able to attend.

Martholin had finished hiring essential staff, and he ordered the family silver brought from the bank and returned it to the house's strongroom. He dug through the chests and found a livery badge for Arak—not the heavy shoulder chain and badge, but smaller, elegant, with a jeweled salamander lying on a bed of golden flames. It was the badge of a trusted retainer, for someone of gentle birth, and Arak hesitated when it was offered across the remains of their meal.

"That's—too good for me."

There was a note in her voice that hinted she was thinking of her banished clan, and Irichels hoped he hadn't inadvertently hurt her. "It's how I see you."

"I'm a hire-sword you won in a card game," Arak said.

"You haven't been that for seven years." For an instant, Irichels could see the tavern in Jondamer, dark and smoky even with all the oil lamps lit, and Arak's lifted eyebrow when the caravan-master staked her contract against the pot. Irichels had displayed his hand, and she had picked up her sword and crossbow with exactly the same expression.

There was a moment of silence, and then Arak gave one of her rare smiles. "True." She fastened the badge carefully at the base of her collar, the stones flashing in the candlelight. "What about Envar?"

Envar laughed. "This isn't Bellem. There's no word for 'favorite' here."

"Ah." Arak blushed. "One forgets."

"Anything more on the boy?" Irichels asked, and Envar shrugged, accepting the change of subject.

"He's improving daily. Marthie seems pleased."

That lasted them through the sweet, but after the table was cleared and Irichels gathered his keys for the nightly round, he saw Arak catch Envar's sleeve. "You know I didn't mean—"

"I know." Envar touched her hand. "There are times I miss the Hills myself."

"Indeed."

They made the rounds of the doors in silence, and parted at the end of the hall that led to the main bedrooms. Envar was sitting by the fire, long legs stretched out to the hearth, and looked up as the door opened. Irichels came to sit on the arm of the chair, looking down at him. "How much do you mind not coming to this party?"

"Not as much as I'd mind if I had to go," Envar answered lightly.

"I'm serious."

"So am I."

No, you're not, Irichels thought, but knew better than to push. "I meant it. If I stay—and as long as we stay—I won't hide you."

"Get the Senate and Assembly to confirm you first." Envar straightened. "That's what matters."

"I know. That's why I'm doing this party. If Gellis Ambros acknowledges me, that's one of the Three on my side."

"Will he?"

"I think so. For Hal's sake."

"Tell me about him."

For a moment, Irichels wished he'd had more sense than to mention the name. "We were in school together here in the city—some of the Senatorial families clubbed together to set up an academy outside the Oratories, and somehow my mother persuaded Grandfather to pay the fees. We had a regrettable passion for the same tutor, who had eyes only for Delsie Temenon—this was one of the schools that admitted girls as well as boys—and then at University we were lovers for a bit. He's a scholar, and a good one. No particular talent for magic in practice, but he knows a great deal of theory, and even more of the history of the art. He's the eldest son, so he must be married now. I didn't think to ask."

"He sounds useful to know."

"He was a good friend," Irichels answered, and hoped it was still true.

The evening of the party was cloudy and chill; there would be no moon, and Irichels was grateful for the new boatman Martholin had found for them. Antel was young and built like a small ox, and admitted to knowing how to use both crossbow and short sword. "Are we expecting trouble, Master?" he asked, and Irichels shook his head.

"No more than usual."

They arrived at Ambros House at the end of twilight, and were greeted by Halyssin himself, waiting in the shadow of the long portico that fronted the canal. He told the boatman where to wait, and then led Irichels and Arak down the portico and past the half open doors, where they could see last-minute preparations still in progress, and through a door that gave onto a spiral stair. Irichels followed him, to emerge into a pleasant sitting room, with a table set for three and windows that looked out onto the canal and the narrow alley that ran alongside the house.

"I'm glad you were able to join me," Halyssin said, waving them toward the table. A woman in Ambros blue and silver livery came out of an inner room with a pitcher of wine and filled the waiting glasses as he spoke. "But I was expecting to meet your friend."

Irichels said, "Arak min'Aroi is my companion and bodyguard. It seemed...ill-advised...to bring a lover before I knew what I was getting into."

"You're wiser than I am, then," Halyssin said. "You'll still join us, of course, Messida Arak."

Arak slanted a glance toward Irichels and Irichels tipped his head in agreement. "Yes, thank you, Master Halyssin."

"Messire only," Halyssin corrected, and grinned. "But you missed all of that, Gil."

"Evidently." Irichels took his place, and accepted a plate of tiny clams. "What exactly did you do?"

"Renounced my inheritance," Halyssin said. "Father agreed, and we all know Valens will do a better job than I would."

"May one ask why?" Irichels thought he could guess, but it was better to get things out in the open.

"I'd give you three guesses, but they'd be wrong," Halyssin answered, and for the first time there was the hint of something bitter underneath the cheerful words. "I fell in love, my dear. And, to everyone's shock, with an entirely suitable girl. Only she had promised herself to the Oratory, and wanted none of me. And so I said I was done with it."

"And your father agreed?" Irichels kept his tone light with an effort. If Gellis Ambros was still angry with his son, it might not be such a good idea to pursue the friendship.

"He was glad of it, I think," Halyssin said. "Valens is a better choice, and I'm happy to act as advisor when called upon. We drew up a proper settlement, I've a nice income that doesn't drain the house, my own rooms, and peace." He speared a pastry from the next platter, and added, "And that's been almost a decade ago now, so you needn't worry. Father will be glad to see you, I think."

"I could use his support," Irichels said. "Not that there seems to be anyone left to question my claim, but still."

"Yes. Samar's had a terrible run of luck," Halyssin said. "I thought it would get better after the boy died—did you hear about that? I know you were gone by then."

"Debes, you mean? Galeran's youngest?"

Halyssin nodded. "Your uncle sent him to the Oratory, and there was talk he was a cursling. He hanged himself in the bellropes, or so they say."

"That's what I'd heard," Irichels answered. "He mistreated the servants, certainly."

"It happens," Halyssin said. "But usually that ends the bad luck."

"Not necessarily," Irichels said. "A great deal depends on whether the cursling was a natural event—a demon slipping in between conception and ensoulment, say—or inflicted from outside. If it's the latter, the curse has to be lifted." He paused. "But you know this as well as I do."

"I wondered which you thought it was."

Irichels paused again. "Inflicted, I think. We've had some...problems...since I came home, which was another reason I wanted to talk to you."

"However I can help," Halyssin said.

"After Aunt Maritsa died, they—the lawyers, we use the Arlechini—had a curse-reader in. And she did a card reading that said the root of the matter was in Samar's past." Irichels spread his hands. "You know Grandfather didn't share any of that with me. I wondered if you might know where I should start looking."

Halyssin blinked. "I can certainly make the obvious guess. Do you mean you never heard of it?"

"Heard of what?"

"The Shame of Four Houses." Halyssin gestured for the servant to leave the pitcher, and poured for all of them. "It's not talked about, but I would have thought someone would have told you."

"You know how much my grandfather loved me."

"True." Halyssin gave a wry smile. "Dreadful old man. But anyway. The story is that, long ago, there were twelve families in the Senate, not ten, but they fought for power just the same as they do now. And two of those families conspired with two families of the Assembly to contract with the sea demons to protect the first part of the city that was built out into the shallows. They wrote a clever contract, one that bound all sides absolutely—and then they provoked a war with Dalmate, that's Dalmas now, in the Plana.

"As the families had known, Dalmate had its own contract with the land demons, and they broke our army and devastated old Bejanth, but couldn't touch the new city without running up against the sea demons, which they weren't prepared to do. The Senate and the high constable figured out what had happened, but by then the city was rebuilt in the shallows, and they couldn't punish the houses without breaking the contract and opening up the rebuilt city to attack. So they demoted the two Senatorial houses to the Assembly, confiscated every bit of moveable property, and dared the survivors to challenge the decision. Samar was one of the Senatorial houses."

"I did not know that story," Irichels said. Certainly it was something Grandfather would never have shared, except grudgingly and only with his acknowledged heir. Nor would he had given anything but the most necessary details, and would have tried to bluster through without admitting any act of treachery. Treachery it certainly was, to destroy half the city to profit from ruling the other half—even if in the long run it had been better for Bejanth to be built on water. But that would certainly be disaster enough to have been symbolized by the Tower.

"What of the other houses?" Arak said. "Your pardon, Messire, if I spoke out of turn."

"No, it's a fair question." Halyssin topped up their glasses again. "Manimere was the other Senatorial house. Cambryse and Morellin were the Assembly houses."

Irichels nodded slowly. Samar had always had ties with Cambryse and Morellin; Manimere had dwindled over the years, becoming little more than a merchant house, with a few ships to its name and a crumbling house on the far side of Mercies. Grandfather had always spoken of them with loathing, but if they were the other demoted Senatorial house, that would explain it. "I wonder how they're doing these days."

"Manimere is as it has been," Halyssin said, "though Innes—she's Master now—seems to have a better hand on things than her father ever did. I haven't heard anything about Cambryse and Morellin—there's been nothing like what's happened to Samar."

"That clarifies things," Irichels said. "Thanks, Hal."

"Oh, certainly," Halyssin said. "May all your difficulties be as easily resolved." He pushed back his chair. "And now we really should go down."

The ballroom was lit by four great wheel-candelabras, and the sconces along the walls held pillar-candles as thick as a man's arm. The air smelled of beeswax and perfume and the lavender that had preserved the embroidered linens that covered the long table at the end of the hall. There were already several dozen guests present, talking loudly over the sound of the consort tuning in the middle gallery, and when Irichels looked up, he could see several small heads peeping through the carved stone railings of the upper gallery. Halyssin saw where he was looking, and grinned.

"Valens's brats. If they're good, I'll send some treats up later."

Irichels remembered, sharp and sudden, crouching at the edge of the middle gallery of Samar House to stare down at the guests crossing the courtyard, or paused by the fountain to gossip, the lights and music spilling from the ballroom just out of sight. It would never have occurred to anyone to send a treat to the children of the house. "Who did he marry?"

"Gemina Celest," Halyssin answered. "Not precisely a love match, Valens is too dutiful for that, but they seem well-suited. She's given him three sons and a daughter, so something's working."

"Evidently." Irichels let himself be steered down the length of the ballroom, toward a knot of blue and silver that resolved into Gellis Ambros and his second son, both in ankle-length silver-on-blue brocade, and a sharp-faced man with steel-gray hair all in black, who wore the chain of the high constable across his shoulders.

"Father," Halyssin said. "You remember Gil Irichels, I think? The Master of Samar?"

"I can't claim that yet," Irichels protested, and Ambros held out both hands.

"I do indeed. Welcome home, Samar—Irichels, then, for now."

Irichels let himself be drawn into the kinsman's kiss, conscious only of an overwhelming wave of gratitude. He had not expected to be welcomed, much less have his claim acknowledged so publicly. And then the gratitude vanished, replaced by caution: what price would be exacted for that support? "Ambros." He nodded to the younger man, dark-haired and a little flushed in the ballroom's warmth. Valens looked happier than Irichels had ever seen him; seemingly the exchange suited everyone.

"And of course Conart Jeroen, High Constable for this term." Ambros gestured casually, and Irichels made a formal bow.

"High Constable."

The high constable nodded, a movement carefully calculated to convey polite social recognition and nothing more. It was a difficult office, responsible for the city's safety and bound to it by contracts that prevented him from leaving it for any length of time: of course he'd give nothing away. "Irichels. I don't believe we met before you left the city."

"No, High Constable. I went to University when I was quite young." They exchanged a few more pleasantries, and then the high constable turned away, the others bowing politely to his retreating back.

"It is a pleasure to have you home again," Ambros said. "I hope we can count on you to dine here someday soon."

And there was the request for payment, though the touch was the finest velvet. Irichels gave a half bow. "I'd be delighted."

He let himself be eased away, joining Halyssin against the outer wall as the first figure formed for the dance. "That was generous of your father."

"He's always liked you," Halyssin said. "More to the point, he disliked your grandfather."

"Do you know what he wants in exchange for his support?"

Halyssin gave him a startled look. "Your support in the Assembly, I would think. Generally speaking, I mean, I don't know of anything in particular that he has in mind."

Irichels nodded. That was reasonable enough, and Ambros had always been on good terms with Samar. A movement at the door caught his eye, a group of three women—no, two women and a girl barely old enough to fill out the bodice of her expensively embroidered gown. She was very pale and very thin, her copper hair cut chin-length and barely confined by a jeweled net. "Who's that?"

"Cambryse's second wife and her sister," Halyssin said, and rested his shoulders against the nearest pillar with the air of a man settling in for a good gossip. "The girl is called Alaissou, she's the daughter of the first wife, but there are two bounding baby boys behind her."

"She doesn't look well." Her skin had the unhealthy color of whey, not improved by the vivid pink gown and the bright embroidered flowers, and the short hair suggested recent fever.

"She's never been healthy," Halyssin said. "Or so I hear. Word is, her stepmother wants to marry her off and get the advantage of it before they lose her."

"I'd have thought they'd be glad to save the dowry." Irichels watched as the older woman spoke to a young man, winning a bow and a lackluster curtsey from the girl. "Those dresses must have cost a small fortune."

"Ah, but Cambryse has several large fortunes, thanks to this new marriage," Halyssin said. "To put her out of her father's sight might put her out of mind as well, and they'd all grieve less when she goes."

A different young man seemed to be asking Alaissou to dance but she shrank back, shaking her head. The stepmother said something, and Alaissou took the boy's hand. She had not yet smiled, Irichels thought, and felt vaguely sorry for her. He felt Halyssin stiffen then, and followed his gaze to see a pair of Oratorians enter the ballroom, their rose-red robes seeming very plain against the play of colors. They were a man and woman, both bare-headed, but Halyssin's eyes were fixed on the woman. "Is that—?" Irichels began, and Halyssin nodded.

"Oredana Temenon." She was making her way through the ending dance, and he broke off, smiling, as she came up to them. "Sister! Renounce your vows and run away with me! I've almost finished my book, and I've all of ten ducats a year in income."

"Don't be ridiculous," Oredana answered, but she sounded more amused than annoyed.

"Then dance?"

"You know I don't dance."

"Then permit Gil to fetch us wine and little tarts."

"I'll permit you to fetch them," Oredana said. "And make sure you get the ones with olive paste. Your cook has a way with them."

"If you'd marry me, you could have the cook and the tarts," Halyssin said.

"It would be cheaper and easier to hire the cook," she answered. "And far less trouble. Be off with you, now, I want to talk to Samar."

Halyssin flourished an extravagant bow and backed away. Oredana gave him a thoughtful look. She was not particularly beautiful, with the Temenon beak of a nose, and there were threads of gray at her temples, but Irichels could recognize the spirit that had appealed to Halyssin. "You are Samar? You have the look of your cousin Jacen. I knew him at University."

"I'm not yet acknowledged," Irichels said. He was going to get tired of saying that soon. "But, yes, I'm Irichel's son, and the last heir."

"I doubt there will be much opposition in the Assembly. Or the Senate, for that matter." She paused significantly, and Irichels smiled.

"And the Oratory?"

"The Oratory will have no objection as long as you do your duty. Marry and get children. Samar cannot be allowed to die out." She returned his smile. "That is a message from the Concourse, by the way."

"I'm touched by their concern."

Oredana shrugged. "You have a reputation—an excellent one—as a cursebreaker, you and your companions. But other rumors have reached them as well."

"Envar Cassi and I have been lovers ten years and more," Irichels said deliberately. "And I don't intend to give him up."

"I told them you wouldn't say otherwise," Oredana said. "Nor, in fact, is that required. But you must marry."

"I would have thought it was to the Oratory's advantage to take their share of the house property," Irichels said. "Samar is still rich enough to be worth plundering."

"There are more important things than money," Oredana answered. "Especially in the city of curses."

Irichels lifted his eyebrows at that, but she was already turning to greet another woman with outstretched hands and a kinswoman's kiss. Halyssin reappeared as well, trailed by a servant with a tray of dishes, and the conversation became general. Irichels finished another cup of wine and a handful of what really were excellent pastries, and let a matron in cloth-of-silver persuade him to a round-dance. He partnered her cousin for another, and friends of hers for three more, then pleaded the need for air. He slipped out onto the streetside portico, Arak at his heels, and leaned against the nearest pillar.

The light from the ballroom and the enormous flambeaux and braziers out on the street threw the portico into even deeper shadow, and it took a moment to realize that there were a few couples standing close together in the darkest spots. It took him a moment more to recognize Oredana and a man—Halyssin, surely—standing so close that they could have kissed. That was the last thing he'd expected—he'd been sure that she meant her refusals—but before he could be sure, the door behind him banged open. He whirled to find himself in the path of a tall man in red and white, who scowled at him.

"Out of my way, you. Oredana!"

Arak moved smoothly up beside him, head tilted in question, and Irichels nodded. Arak kicked sideways, knocking the man's foot backward just as she caught his shoulder with an outstretched palm. The man stumbled, swearing, and Irichels caught him, pinning his arms in the process.

"Messire. Are you all right?"

"You tripped me!"

Irichels mimed wide-eyed innocence. "I? No, Messire, the stones are uneven—"

Oredana emerged from the shadows, the other Oratorian at her shoulder. "Margos? You were looking for me?"

"You should not be on the portico alone," the stranger said. "It's a disgrace to your robes."

"But I'm not alone," Oredana said. "And it's not your business what I do."

"You're still my sister," he answered. "And I won't have you disgracing our house." He shrugged his shoulders, seemingly startled to find himself still held. "And you, let go of me."

"Of course." Irichels stepped back, lifting his empty hands, well aware that Arak was poised to defend him. "I'm glad you're unhurt, Messire."

The man glared at him, then switch the glare to Oredana. "I warn you—"

"You have nothing to warn me about," Oredana said firmly. "Come inside, if you wish to talk." She took his arm and drew him away, the other Oratorian closing the door softly behind them.

"Charming," Arak said.

"Quite." Irichels shook himself. "And not, thank Idra, our problem."

"So you say," Arak muttered.

Irichels made a propitiating gesture, and saw Arak grin. "It should be safe to go back in."

The music was louder than ever, and there was no sign of the stranger or Oredana. A country dance was forming, taking up most of the hall, and Irichels found himself pressed back against the doors again. Before he could decide if he wanted to slip away, Halyssin appeared, carrying three glasses of wine.

"I owe you for that, my dears. Drink up."

"He tripped," Arak said straight-faced.

Irichels said, "Who was that?"

"That," Halyssin said with loathing, "was Margos Temenon. Second son of the second son, and Oredana's brother. A swordsman of some skill, and doesn't he swagger with it."

"He seemed…" Irichels considered. "Officious."

"Oh, there was a scandal with one of the other Temenon daughters—ran off with a flute-girl from the hill country *and* her low-caste husband. It doesn't help that she's the toast of Bellem, or maybe they all are. He'd like to be high constable next year, so he's touchy about the family."

"He won't win any elections that way," Irichels said, and saw Arak nod.

They left well after curfew, a lantern dangling from the boat's bow to light their way, and a pass signed by Gellis Ambros in Irichels's purse. There had been a great bowl of them waiting by the door, ready for anyone to take, and Irichels had been happy to take advantage. Probably he could have written one for himself, as Master of Samar, but it seemed unwise to take a chance. He leaned back against the cushions, letting exhaustion wash over him. He was a long way from drunk, but he was tired, and the sound of the oar was soothing. There were no other boats on the water; there were dozens tied up along the canal side or tucked into narrow docking spaces against the housefronts, but that was all. The tide was on the turn, beginning its long retreat, but the water was still high enough that they had to dodge the lanterns hung beneath the smaller bridges.

"I think I heard that tale," Arak said sleepily.

"Which tale?"

"The girl who ran off with the flute-player. They made it to the court in Dahlamar, and the king there granted them his protection and the freedom of the court."

"I don't know what he's complaining about, then," Irichels said, and Arak made a noise of agreement.

Another bridge loomed ahead, a lantern hanging from the keystone of its arch. Irichels yawned, wishing they were home, and something moved behind the parapet. He frowned, and beside him Arak sat upright.

"Crossbow."

In the same instant, they heard the snap of the release and the bolt whistled past. Antel cried out, but there was no time to see if he was hurt. Irichels could hear the ratchet working and hunched his shoulders, pressing his palms together. Beside him, Arak went to one knee, a throwing knife in her hand, but Irichels ignored her, reciting the protective cantrip, his lips against the tips of his fingers. He felt the spell seize and lock, the energy flowing out of him to congeal in the air like an invisible shield between them and the bowman.

The release snapped again. The bolt struck the shield with

a sound like a hammer on an anvil, and glanced off, landing harmlessly in the water. Irichels absorbed the blow, wincing, and braced himself for another shot, but the bowman had had enough, and ran clattering down the stairs. Arak flung the knife after him but it fell short, bouncing off the end of the railing and splashing back into the canal. She sank back into the boat, swearing, and clutched at the sides for balance.

Irichels released the shield and turned to look at the boatman. "Are you all right?"

"No. I mean, yes, it missed me—"

"He's gone," Irichels said, and tried to sound as though he were confident of that. "Home now, quick as we can."

Karan had waited up to tend the door, and took Antel into the kitchen while Irichels checked the rest of the locks. Karan emerged long enough to report the other man unhurt; Irichels prescribed a glass of brandy for both of them, and climbed the stairs to his room.

Envar was awake as well, sitting by the fire wrapped in an old dressing gown and a fur rug, a branch of candles pulled close to let him read. He set his book aside as the door opened, his lazy smile turning to concern. "What's happened?"

"Someone took a shot at us as we were coming home." Irichels pulled off his gown and dropped it on an empty chair. "No one was hurt, but I had to shield us."

"Let me see."

Irichels held out his hands and Envar drew him into the candlelight, turning his palms upward. Sure enough, a bruise was blooming at the heel of his left hand, and he winced when Envar pressed it. "Ow."

"Mm." Envar released his hands, tugged at his shirt strings, and bared his chest to run a hand down the length of his sternum. Irichels grimaced as Envar found the matching bruise, the energy of the crossbow bolt reflected through the shield, and Envar nodded. "Anything else?"

"No."

"Arnica, then." His fingers lingered. "That was close range."

"We're lucky it was a moonless night."

"Evidently." Envar released him and went to the cabinet where he'd stored his kit, came back with a familiar wide-mouthed jar. Irichels shivered at the cool touch, but felt some of the soreness ease. "Was it robbers?"

"I assumed so," Irichels said. There were bandits in plenty in Bejanth; you knew the risks if you stayed out after curfew.

"But?"

"There was only one of them. He shot at us from a bridge."

"Hard to collect the spoils that way," Envar said.

"I know. I have to think it might have been personal."

"It would be wise to consider it." Envar anointed his hand as well, then began snuffing the candles as Irichels stripped out of the rest of his party clothes. He called a marsh-light to take them to bed, and once they were settled among the pillows let it drift upward to float beneath the canopy.

"I'm almost afraid to ask," Envar said, "but was there anything else of interest?"

"In fact, yes." Irichels settled himself more comfortably, drawing up the heavy coverlet. "I think I've found the Tower in Zaffara's reading." He laid out the story as Hal had told it, Envar listening intently, and when he had done, Envar nodded.

"That would fit. It's certainly a disaster and far enough back to fit, and the Nine of Coins and the Nine of Wands make sense following on from it. Though I'll want to look at it harder in the morning."

"Of course," Irichels said. "There should be people I could ask about it myself, if I can just think who."

"It's a start," Envar said. "Anything else?"

Irichels hesitated, tempted to put off the matter of marriage until the morning, but knew it would be no easier then. "A Sister of the Oratory had a word with me, unofficially official. The Oratory will support me, so long as I marry and produce an heir."

If they had not been lying so close together, he would not have felt the faint shiver that ran through Envar. "Well. You had to have expected that, my heart."

"I suppose. Just not so soon, or such a blatant trade."

"You are the last of the Samar," Envar said, and sounded plausibly content.

Chapter Seven

The next few days passed quietly enough. The lawyers brought over the draft of the formal claim to be presented to the Assembly and the Senate, and Irichels affixed his signature and seal. It would be several weeks before the Senate would meet, and Tyrn Arlechin sent notes encouraging Irichels to build up alliances ahead of time.

"I'm not sure exactly what I have to offer them," Irichels said. They were sitting in Tyrn's courtyard, sunlight pouring in through the colored glass. "I can only promise so much without having a better handle on Samar's business ventures."

"If you want my advice," Tyrn began, and Irichels nodded.

"Please."

"Your grandfather and your Uncle Galeran generally voted with Gethen—the eastern faction, it's called, since most of the houses are on the eastern islets. So that's Gethen, Alteplana, Neis, and Anstellin. And their dependents, of course. I don't think you will disadvantage Samar if you support them."

Arlechin was a dependent of Gethen. Irichels said, "That's helpful. I'll bear that in mind."

"Also..." Tyrn gave him a measuring look. "There is you. Your marriage." Irichels did his best to keep his face expressionless, but something must have shown, for Tyrn spread his hands. "You must have known you would have to marry. There are no other heirs."

"Yes."

"It needn't be a hardship," Tyrn said. "Dot're Cassi seems a sensible soul. Pick an older girl who understands the situation—someone who's been to University, perhaps—and it can all be arranged quite happily. There are several women who'd be interested in such an arrangement."

That was almost certainly true, Irichels admitted. Marriage brought any number of freedoms for women, and any marriage he made would come with contracts that guaranteed income and spelled out the duties and privileges on both sides. It need not be unfair or even unpleasant, but it was hard to make himself like the idea. "Do you have any particular thoughts on the matter?" The suggestions would come from Gethen, of course, but it was as good a place as any to begin.

"There are any number of suitable matches," Tyrn said. "Anstellin's second daughter is of appropriate age, educated—a nice girl, a friend of my daughter's. And of course I have two daughters who might be considered, though I leave that entirely to you. Gellis Ambros has a niece he might like to see married well. I know you're friendly with the family, and any child of that line won't be surprised by the dot're." He frowned, visibly moving down a mental list. "Pars, Casteven, Radechan: all of them have daughters more or less in the right range. If you're feeling particularly political, I believe there's a Jeroen cousin who was widowed young."

"Gethen approves of the current high constable, then?"

"Conart is a sensible man, and has Bejanth's interests at heart," Tyrn said.

Irichels nodded, remembering his conversation with Halyssin. "What about Innes Manimere? I heard she was managing the house. Is she married?"

"Oh, no," Tyrn said. "Anyone but her!" Irichels blinked, startled, and Tyrn forced a smile. "Well, perhaps I put that too strongly. But she's steering Manimere into the arms of the merchantry. You don't want to be allied with that. Also, I doubt she's one to accept her husband's lover."

"If you say so." Irichels made a note to find out more about Manimere's current alliances: if Gethen disapproved this strongly, it would be worth finding out why. "A second question, then. If I die before I'm acknowledged, what happens?"

"Idra forfend!" Tyrn sketched a ward, flicked it away.

"But if?"

"Normally when the main line of a house becomes extinct, there are collateral lines. Or sometimes a deathbed adoption brings in a relative by marriage. We try very hard not to see our old families disappear." Tyrn gave a wry smile. "But in this case…if there are no heirs at all, the movable property is sold up, and the proceeds are shared out among the families of the Assembly. The house is destroyed, down to the pilings, and no one may rebuild there for thirty years."

"I had no idea." Irichels shook his head. The house gone, nothing left but slack water and rotting pilings…. To his surprise, he found he hated the idea. "It's hard on the neighbors."

"As I said, we go to considerable lengths to avoid such a thing," Tyrn said.

"Someone took a shot at me coming home from a party," Irichels said. "A crossbowman on a bridge. So I wondered."

Tyrn's eyebrows rose. "No one was hurt, I hope?"

Irichels shook his head again. "But the bowman got away."

"Footpads. They're getting worse every year."

Except that a footpad wouldn't have attacked men in a boat. Irichels swallowed the words and took his leave. Coming down the curve of the Hadolon Canal, he saw Samar House rising from its platform, the pale stone bright in the sun. Martholin had pulled down the rest of the tattered wreaths and had the brilliant turquoise door repainted, and one of the maids was sweeping the dock as the boat pulled alongside. It all looked ordinary again, bright and busy as it had been when he was a boy, and he realized he wanted it to live. He felt the daemon stir at the thought as the maid opened the door to let him in.

Envar was in the workroom, the upper shutters open to the sun and the table covered with papers and stacks of books. There was a tray on the sideboard, the plates half emptied; he had discarded his gown, was working in shirt and narrow trousers, and Irichels couldn't help admiring the line of his leg. Arak unbuckled her swordbelt, set the weapons clattering in a corner. "Any progress?"

"Some, maybe." Envar straightened, stretching, and gestured to the copy of Zaffara's reading, pinned flat in the center of the table by a pair of book weights, an ephemeris, and an empty cup. "I can confirm that the Tower refers to the Shame of Four Houses, though the only direct reference to the event was in an Avantine text that's—unsurprisingly—banned in Bejanth. Someone among your relatives had a copy, though."

"Also not surprising," Irichels said. "Anything useful in it?"

"It's pretty much the same tale you told me," Envar answered. "A bit more detail about how the Four Houses wanted to take control of the Senate and the Assembly, maybe."

"I'd like to read it," Irichels said.

"I've marked it for you." Envar pointed to one of the books, an octavo volume with rubbed corners and a plain calfskin binding. "What I haven't found, though, is also interesting." He tapped the Death card at the center of the reading. "I haven't seen anything that seems to qualify for this event, the point at which your family fortunes turn around. I don't suppose there's any story you heard that would give me a hint?"

"The house was at low ebb when grandfather inherited," Irichels said. "To give him his due, he changed our fortunes."

"How?" Envar frowned at the drawing.

"There was no single thing," Irichels answered. "That I know of, anyway. But he was mostly just a clever investor, and a good judge of people. They say he made one mistake when he was young, before he was Master, lost money on a barrel of limes that came in spoiled, and he resolved he'd never do that again. And he didn't."

"I wonder," Envar said, still staring at the drawing. "And maybe that's it."

"I don't suppose Death could be the Shame?" Arak said. "And the Tower something further back?"

For a moment, Irichels thought Envar was going to say something cutting, and braced himself to step between, but Envar controlled himself. "It's possible, I suppose. But the Tower is catastrophe, while Death contains renewal within itself. Samar and the other houses weren't supposed to recover from their punishment."

A knock at the door interrupted Arak's answer, and Irichels raised his voice. "Yes? Come in."

It was the boy Tepan, a sheaf of envelopes in his hand. "The keeper said you should have these, Master." His voice was still a little rough but all the words were clear, even if he wouldn't look at Envar. "This one wants an answer right away." He held out a bright blue envelope sealed with a golden wafer. Irichels took it and broke the seal. The neat secretarial hand invited him to a dance the following week at Benoet House. Such requests made to equals included an invitation to the dinner beforehand, and Irichels felt his lips tighten.

"Is the messenger waiting?"

"He is, Master."

"Then give him this." Irichels retrieved pen and paper and copied out the blandest of the formal regrets, then waved the paper in the air to dry the ink before he folded it. "How are you doing, Tepan?"

"I'm fine, thank you, Master."

"Settling in all right?" Irichels kept his voice casual, pretending to focus on the seal and wax, but watched the boy from under his lashes. The color rose in his face, but his voice remained steady.

"Yes, Master."

"Good. Let Marthie know if you need anything." Irichels handed over the sealed response. "Give that to the messenger."

"Yes, Master," Tepan said again, and closed the door gently behind him.

"Another party?" Arak asked.

Irichels nodded, fanning through the other envelopes.

One from Ambros, in Halyssin's sprawling hand—the private dinner Gellis had mentioned, which he would have to attend—a formal note from Gethen, announcing a ball with dinner beforehand, also difficult to refuse, and invitations from Anstellin and Commart for informal dinners.

The final note was dyed deep blue, and the invitation was written in silver ink—and not by a secretary, either, Irichels thought, studying the heavy brush strokes. It invited him and his companions to a private dinner at Manimere House, and was signed simply *Innes Manimere*. He felt his eyebrows rise again. Manimere, the other Senatorial house that had been as good as destroyed along with Samar, and the only house that Tyrn had warned him against. Plus she was acknowledging Envar sight unseen. He tossed the sheet onto the table. "This one we'll attend."

The first set of new clothes had arrived by the evening of the dinner at Manimere House: knee-length brocade gowns for Irichels and Envar; an embossed leather doublet for Arak, supple as velvet, but thick enough to turn a blade. Irichels examined his reflection in the peer-glass in Envar's room, and decided he was pleased. He had chosen blue-on-black for himself, a severe and simple pattern of coiled leaves with black silk braid the only trim, and he thought it made him look as little like a hill country thug as possible. Envar had been persuaded to forego his usual black in favor of a water-toned green in a dot-and-diamond pattern, and the shade brought out the color in his pale skin, and gave life to his light hair. A remarkably handsome effect, Irichels thought, and couldn't help smiling. Envar smiled back.

"You're looking very fine yourself."

"And so am I, and so are we all," Arak said from the doorway, "but if we don't leave now, we will be late."

Manimere House was also on Mercies, not far from the little oratory of Idra-in-Chains, and it was easier to walk than to take a boat. Irichels led them across a string of bridges, crossing the Habest Canal and two smaller ones whose names he couldn't remember, then along the short street to Manimere House. It was a smaller house than Samar, still three stories but with a narrower frontage, and the saffron-painted plaster was peeling away in places to reveal crumbling brick beneath. Still, there was a liveried servant to open the street-side door and bow them into the courtyard, and the patterned tiles of the hall were polished and spotless.

The courtyard was smaller than Samar's, the old-fashioned sort that was open to the sky. Orange trees grew in the beds in all four corners, underplanted with summer flowers, and the air smelled of earth and growing things. Innes Manimere rose from her seat by the fishpond and came forward with both hands outstretched. Irichels accepted the kiss of kinship and introduced his companions, studying her as he did so. She was taller than he remembered, and fuller-figured—though of course she would only have been sixteen or seventeen when he last saw her. Her hair was done up in heavy braids confined by loops of ribbon, and her gown was of oxblood linen open over an underdress figured with multi-colored embroidered flowers.

Another woman emerged from the shadows, followed by a heavyset bearded man in solid merchant's best, and Manimere gestured to them. "My cousin Felisan, and Captain Deion Argerin." Irichels murmured the polite responses, and Manimere waved to a set of iron benches, a table between them set with a platter of fried appetizers and a pitcher and cups. "I thought we might enjoy the evening air before we went in to dinner."

They seated themselves and the cousin poured the wine while Manimere urged everyone to taste the various delicacies. They were mostly rice balls stuffed with various savory fillings, with a handful of blossoms stuffed and fried: inexpensive taverna fare, Irichels thought, but tasty. "These are very good."

Manimere grinned. "I was able to talk our old cook into coming back after I took over, once I promised to make only reasonable demands and pay our bills on delivery. Father had a bad habit of asking for delicacies on a fisherman's budget, and then forgetting the bills."

"I did much the same," Irichels admitted. "Though Aunt Maritsa doesn't seem to have wasted anything. The house was very nearly closed by the time she died. But tell me, how did you come to take over?"

"I was going to ask you the same question," Manimere said. "You first."

"Isn't it ladies first?" Irichels cocked his head, and Argerin laughed.

"Spin a coin." He produced one from his purse and set it on edge on the low tabletop. "Choose, masters."

Manimere gestured to Irichels, who said, "Heads."

"Tails for me, then," Manimere said.

Argerin spun the coin, and it danced across the metal surface to fall clattering against the pitcher. "I see tails, Master Innes."

"Very well, then." Manimere leaned back in her chair. "It's not so much to tell, in truth. My father was a wastrel who gave me the choice of marrying at his direction or taking myself out of the house—to the Oratory was his intention, but I took my mother's jewelry and went into trade. I managed to keep myself, and Felisan here, until at last he died, and I was all that was left of the family. We have that in common, I think, Irichels."

"Certainly." Irichels didn't believe for a moment that was all of the story, but he was in no position to press for details.

"And now your turn," Manimere said.

"I think you must have known I went to University as soon as I was old enough?" Manimere nodded, and Irichels went on, "I did my term there, and took the bond. I have a talent for cursebreaking, and there's always work of that kind. I met Cass four or five years after, and we did some work together. That went well, and we discovered we liked each other, so we've been working together ever since. Seven years ago, we met Arak, up in the hill country west of Bellem, and by then we were doing the sorts of jobs that made a bodyguard handy. We were lucky enough to persuade her to join us. Of course, given that Grandfather had made it very clear he didn't consider me family, I hadn't paid any attention to what was going on in Bejanth until I received a messenger from the family lawyers telling me Aunt Maritsa had died and I was the only heir left."

He could still remember the shock of it, sitting in the parlor of the inn at the foot of the Long Climb that led to Bellem and Galipare and Tol Varthen. It had been raining, the thin, cold rain of early spring that would still be snow in the hills; the fire had split and rolled as he unsealed the letter, and there had been a rush and bustle to get the log back into the hearth before he could read the message. And when he had, it still hadn't made much sense. How could everyone be dead? It hadn't seemed real all the way down the Coast Road to Tarehan, and even less so when he found all the letters waiting. It was only the daemon that had finally made it real.

"Cursebreaking must be interesting work," Felisan said, and Irichels managed a smile.

"I've always found it so."

"Is there much demand for it here?" Argerin asked. "Forgive me if I speak out of turn, but—they say Bejanth is built on curses. Does anyone want them broken here?"

"I never worked here myself," Irichels said, and looked at Manimere.

"Some do, some don't," she answered. "I can't imagine the Senate and Assembly would countenance anyone meddling with the contracts that keep the city safe, but there are always individual curses and contracts that need adjusting."

"We came on a woman who'd called a demon into a boy," Envar said. "So he could prophesy."

"That's a bad business," Manimere said, suddenly serious, and Argerin nodded.

"We—dealt with the matter," Irichels said, and won another of Manimere's flashing smiles.

"That was well done," she said, and sounded as though

she meant it. "But now I believe dinner is ready."

The meal was served in what Irichels suspected was the house's smaller dining room, and even so the table was easily large enough to seat a dozen. Manimere had clustered her guests at one end, as though they were family, and a stout, aproned woman stood ready to serve them from the dishes set on the carved buffet. The spoons and knives and old-fashioned two-tined forks were silver, but the dishes were brightly painted pottery; the wine pitcher was painted pottery as well, though the goblets were gold-bound glass. More indications, if he'd needed them, that Manimere was far poorer than Samar had ever been. And yet there were also signs that the house was rebounding. Manimere's dress was obviously new, neither cheaply made nor made over from some older garment, and the first course was the classic small birds, which had to be brought from the Plana where they were caught. They were perfectly prepared, too, and it was easy to offer the appropriate compliments, which Manimere accepted with becoming grace and promised to pass on to the cook.

"You said you'd gone into trade," Irichels said. "It seems you've done well."

"I've done reasonably," Manimere answered. "The family holds several ship-marks—curses that hold off the sea demons as long as you stay to the regular trade lanes—and once I inherited, I leased their use for a share of the profits. I've an option in three more ships now, and I'm funding up to a third of the cargo in exchange for a third of the profits. And Deion and I have been working together for some time."

"Where do you sail, Captain?" Envar asked, picking up the cue, and the conversation became general. It was, Irichels admitted, the most pleasant meal he'd had outside his own house, and more enjoyable than some of them. Manimere was a convivial host, with a gift for making everyone feel as though they had known each other for years; and by the time the fruit plate was taken away, Envar had peeled a pear for Felisan, and Arak and Argerin had indulged in a cheerful competition to see who could take off the longest unbroken strip of peel.

"In Abesscie, girls toss them over their shoulders to see the initials of the man they'll marry," Argerin said. "But it has to be the whole peel, taken off entire."

"Divination is frowned on in the Hills," Arak said. "Though I know plenty of folk who would have tried it had they known."

Felisan leaned forward. "It's a lovely night, Innes. Perhaps we should take the sweet into the courtyard?"

"An excellent idea," Manimere said, and nodded to the hovering servant. "See to it, please."

"It's getting on toward curfew," Irichels said with real regret. "We mustn't stay too long."

"I'll write you a pass," Manimere said, laughing, and caught his sleeve to keep him from following the others. "I'd like a word with you, Gil, if you don't mind."

Irichels kept his face expressionless. "Of course."

To his surprise, she hoisted herself up onto the unset end of the table, sat swinging her feet in embroidered slippers. "A question, then. Do you know about the Shame of Four Houses?"

"I've heard of it."

"Hmph. My father wouldn't speak of it until his deathbed, and then he wished me the joy of it."

"Hal Ambros told me about it," Irichels said. "I'd heard nothing until then."

"Manimere's version may be a bit different," Manimere said. "Father said Bejanth would have been conquered four times over if it hadn't been for the Four Houses forcing the move to the lagoon. Mind you, he was nearly raving then, so I don't know if that's what he always thought or what his father told him, but..." She shrugged. "In any case, you and I are in much the same boat, and I thought it might serve us both to join forces, so to speak. I expect Samar has a ship-mark or two in its gift, and I learn of far more mercantile opportunities than I can handle; I'd be glad to share them with you, so we can both profit."

"I'm intrigued," Irichels said, "but I'd like more details."

"Of course. I can send you a prospectus tomorrow if you'd like."

"Thank you." Irichels expected her to rise, but she remained sitting, still swinging her feet.

"Also—I know I'm speaking too soon, but I didn't expect to like you and yours this much. And I'm sure everyone and their half brother has already raised the subject."

"Marriage?" Irichels said in spite of himself.

Manimere laughed. "I knew they'd been talking. Yes, marriage. I'm not as young as I might be, but I'm unwed, and I'm Master of Manimere in my own right. And against my age, I've two children already, both strong and healthy, a girl and a boy. There's every chance I could bear you one or two more. I have no objections to your dot're—I quite like him, in fact—though I'll expect comparable liberty. You keep your house, and I keep mine."

"This is...unexpected," Irichels began, and abruptly he was overcome with the desire to laugh. He'd seen this play a dozen times in Tarehan, read it over a long winter in Tol Varthen, heard it sung by wandering balladeers; Manimere had simply switched the sexes. And he was left with the heroine's plea: *I never thought, give me a little time to think it over—*

"Go ahead and laugh," Manimere said good-humoredly, "and of course you'll want time to think. But it's a better offer than you'll get anywhere else, though I say so myself."

"I'm not sure it isn't," Irichels said, and offered his hand to steady her off the table.

Someone had lit flambeaux in the courtyard, and the others had already gathered in the leaping shadows. Felisan had found a lute and was picking out a country tune, and Arak had forgotten herself so far as to join in the chorus, while Envar and Argerin were deep in some discussion. Irichels handed Manimere to her seat, and the aproned server appeared, carrying a shallow silver dish heaped with nuggets of dried

THE MASTER OF SAMAR

fruit drenched in brandy. She set it on the table and Manimere snapped her fingers at it, calling up a spark that burst into blue flame. Even Envar laughed and snatched at the burning fragments, and Irichels had to admit Manimere had chosen wisely. This was a Bejanter treat—no other city built so much in stone, it wasn't safe in the wooden houses of the coast— and he thought she had served it to remind them of their homecoming.

When the flames and the laughter had both died down, he leaned back in his chair, abruptly aware of movement on the third floor, behind the carved stone railings. A child? Two children? Two shapes behind the stone filigree, watching from above. Manimere saw where he was looking and nodded. "Yes, those are mine. Kasia is the elder, she's eight, and Nerin is six."

"And their father?"

Manimere smiled. "I'll tell you the whole long tale someday. Suffice it to say he's no longer in the picture." That was clear enough. Irichels nodded and let her change the subject, and not long after accepted a pass under her seal of the chained and collared dolphin that would allow them to walk home after curfew. The servant let them out onto the alley, and Irichels and Envar called up marsh-lights to light their way back to Samar House.

"Argerin's a pirate," Envar said, once they'd reached the main street.

"Oh?" Irichels lifted an eyebrow, but Arak was nodding in agreement.

"And a successful one, I'd say. I had the impression Master Innes was his banker."

"Does she have the cash for that?" Irichels asked.

Envar shrugged. "That may be where the family money went. It wouldn't be a bad bargain."

"You liked her," Arak said, sounding surprised.

"I did." Envar looked at Irichels. "What did she want from you, my heart?"

"She offered to cut me in on her business," Irichels said, "and she proposed marriage. I said I'd think about both."

"You could do worse," Envar said.

They walked on in silence, taking the longer route that kept to the larger streets, where it would be harder for anyone to set on them unawares. Not that it was likely, Irichels thought, not with three of them and one an obvious bodyguard, but there was no point in taking stupid chances.

"I hear something," Arak said softly. "Footsteps, I think."

"Following us?" Irichels crooked his fingers, shaping the first movement of a spell that could either defend or attack, and Arak frowned.

"I can't tell. It's gone again."

Envar snuffed his marsh-light. "There's a fountain in the next square. We'll drink, you double back and see."

"Yes." Arak faded into the shadows. Irichels held the spell in abeyance and followed Envar across the open paving. The noise of the fountain was loud enough to drown out footsteps, if a person were cautious, and it took all his willpower to keep from looking even casually over his shoulder. Envar found the chained cup and held it under the gushing stream, then finally turned his back to the basin to drink.

"Anything?" Irichels asked quietly.

"Nothing so far." Envar filled the cup again and drank, his eyes roving over the square.

"I don't hear anything," Irichels said.

"I never did." Envar grimaced. "But Arak doesn't imagine things."

"No." Irichels's skin crawled at the thought of someone, something, watching from the shadows. The moon was up at last, but it added little light, and only a few houses still had lanterns lit outside their door. "We should move on."

Envar released the cup, letting it fall with a clatter that sounded ridiculously loud in the quiet, and they walked on together. Arak joined them as they left the square, slipping back out of the shadows as though she'd never left.

"I didn't find anything," she said. "There was something, I'm sure of that, but it spotted me and got away."

"Someone or something?" Envar asked.

"Someone," Arak said. "I don't think I would have seen a sending."

"And one of us surely would," Irichels said. "Let's get home."

The lantern was still burning at the streetside door, and Karan whisked it open almost as soon as Irichels knocked. "Master! It's good you're home."

"What's happened?" Irichels crossed the threshold, a wave of unease rising to meet him. The daemon was restless, swirling from room to room, shadow to shadow, and Karan hastily barred the door again behind them.

"Nothing that we could see," Karan said. "But *it* has been restless." As if in punctuation, something fell and shattered in the kitchen. Irichels started toward it, marshaling his contracts. Arak drew her sword and she and Envar followed.

The kitchen was dark and empty, all the fires banked to nothing. Irichels could feel the daemon's presence—anger, frustration, an obstinate determination—and Envar snapped his fingers to light the lamp. The flame kindled grudgingly, weak and blue, and in its light, Irichels could see a pottery dish in pieces on the flags by the stove. He sketched a sign that should have revealed any arcane presence, but there was only the daemon, a towering column in the corner. It vanished even as he defined it, whisking away like smoke on a strong wind, and he could feel it circling the courtyard before detouring into the ballroom. The light strengthened gradually, and Irichels could see Envar's frown. "Was there something here? Was something trying to enter? That would explain the agitation." As he spoke, he went to one knee to chalk an arc of symbols on the stone floor.

"Maybe?" Irichels released the half-formed sign, working his fingers to ease the stiffness. "It's calmer now." Even as he spoke, it was fading, retreating to its lair in the corner storeroom.

Envar murmured a cantrip, and sparks shot out from his drawing, sweeping across the kitchen floor. They struck the far wall and winked out. He repeated the cantrip, with the same result, and straightened, wiping out the symbols with his foot. "If there was something, it didn't get past the wards. But I'm inclined to think there was."

"It seems better now," Karan said from the door. "Are we all right?"

Irichels looked at Envar, who shrugged one shoulder. "We could spend the rest of the night searching, and not find anything. I think it's gone."

"I'll sweep up, then," Karan said, and went to fetch a broom.

Irichels made the rounds of the first floor and climbed the stairs to his bedroom, the hour finally catching up to him. It was past midnight; even the Oratorians would be in their beds again, for their longer sleep until the dawn service, and the air felt cold and thick with fog. He stopped on the top stair, closing his eyes to assess the feeling. It faded then, slowly enough that he couldn't be fully sure, and Arak said, "Are you all right?"

"Fine. There was just something..." Irichels frowned. "I want you to look around the house again, see if there is any other way out."

"There isn't," Arak said. "Unless you want me to examine the floors? But you said there's nothing under the house but pilings."

"I can't imagine how there could be," Irichels said. "But, yes, check again. We can't keep on like this."

"I agree with you there," Arak said, and closed her bedroom door.

CHAPTER EIGHT

They breakfasted late, and afterward Irichels left Arak to her work and retreated to the workroom, Envar trailing after him with a last slice of toasted bread and cheese. The daemon was back in its usual place, seeming contented enough now, and Irichels wondered if he was overreacting. It had always been touchy, had its moods that no one seemed to understand.

"Are you going to do it?" Envar asked, perching on the edge of the worktable, and Irichels blinked.

"What?"

"Marry Manimere."

"I don't know. I think—I liked her, yes, and I think she'd be better than many of the alternatives. What did you think of her?"

"Oh, I liked her," Envar said. "It was a good evening. Argerin's an interesting man, too, but he's definitely a pirate, my heart."

"As long as she's not backing him to take Bejanter ships," Irichels said. "Innes promised to send me a prospectus for her next voyage. I wonder what that will look like?"

"So respectable it could give oath in court," Envar said. "Not a word anyone could object to, and every boring contingency meticulously covered."

"I expect you're right." Irichels found he was looking forward to reading it. "But I can't do anything until my claim has been accepted. I don't want to antagonize either Gethen or Ambros."

"And what have they got against Manimere, I wonder?" Envar asked.

"An excellent question," Irichels answered, "and one I can't ask—not without raising more questions than I can afford."

"I might be able to find out some of that," Envar said. "And also: when's the Quarter-Court?"

"I think there's six days between the end of the session and the opening of the Court," Irichels answered. "Why—oh."

Envar nodded. "I have a contract coming due."

"Can it be settled here?" Even ferals had to come to the Courts-Between-Worlds to begin and end the contracts that gave them their magic, or at least to do so safely. Of course, they were also supposed to be under bond to one of the schools or to the Oratory, but most courts were prepared to overlook a certain level of irregularity in favor of keeping everyone safe.

"I think so. It was made in Bellem, and I have a passable warrant to that effect. I just don't want to cause you trouble."

"Let's begin as we mean to go on," Irichels answered, and hoped he was choosing wisely.

There was a knock at the door and Arak peered in. "Gil. I understand I need you to let me into the understory."

"Do you?" Irichels blinked, and Martholin pushed past her.

"I beg your pardon, Master, apparently I wasn't clear. The watermen seal the entrance for everyone's safety, and I certainly don't have the authority to unseal it for her." She put her hands on her hips. "Nor do I see why she needs to get under the house, after spending all the morning underfoot, since everyone tells me the wards are secure. And if they're not, I'd be wishful you'd tell me so."

Irichels looked at Arak, who took a deep breath. "As I told you last night, I wanted to check again for some hidden way in or out."

"Of which there is none," Martholin interjected.

"None that I've found," Arak said. "She says there's a way into the foundations, for your watermen and for repairs, and I want to open it."

Envar leaned close. "Ah. The watermen's seals aren't as impermeable as some would like to think."

The watermen were the lowest ranking of the high constable's agents, petty watchmen responsible for keeping the waterways clear. Irichels said, "This is a matter of the house wards, Marthie. I believe I have a right to make things secure."

"Then let me call a waterman, and have it done right," she retorted.

Irichels hesitated—did he really want the watermen overseeing whatever he might find? On the other hand, there was no point in upsetting Martholin without good reason. "Do that, please. As soon as possible."

The waterman arrived within the hour, a gray-bearded, barrel-bellied man in a punt rowed by a pair of teenage apprentices. Irichels explained the situation, the waterman hemmed and hawed and expressed doubts, until finally Envar leaned close to murmur in Irichels's ear. "He's waiting for a bribe."

Irichels feel the color mount to his face. This was the sort of thing he should know, that he should have learned how to do, but all he could think of was how he'd never previously had enough coin in hand to bribe anyone. "Perhaps—"

"Some suitable compensation for the trouble?" Envar suggested, and the waterman's eyes brightened.

"Well, now that you mention it, Master..."

Irichels fished in his purse, found a handful of silver. "And a bit for drink-money." He remembered Bartol saying that, roaring drunk and staggering at the water-alley door, whoever had brought him home waiting behind him in their boat, before he'd escaped to live with his actor. The waterman touched his forehead.

"Won't say no, Master, thank you kindly. If you're wanting to go under yourself, best have your man bring a boat around to the water-alley."

There were three doors on the water-alley, one into the kitchen and the others opening onto the storeroom corridors, the narrow steps leading down to the water exposed by the receding tide. All of them were covered with heavy iron gates, and there were barred doors behind them. The waterman ignored them, ordering his apprentices to bring him alongside the blank plaster wall beyond the two corridor doors. That was just past the cold room, Irichels thought, wondering if it mattered, and the waterman lifted his stick and traced a shape on the pale plaster. The wall seemed to shiver and the illusion rolled away like fog, revealing the outline of a door, its sill a few inches below the canal's surface.

"Tide's going out," the waterman said, and lifted his stick again. He sketched another shape, and then a third, then tapped sharply on the wall. The door sagged backward and he sat down in the boat, rolling up his trousers. "But we won't be dry-footed for another hour."

Irichels and Envar did the same, and Arak copied them with some reluctance. The waterman rose with a grace that belied his bulk and stepped neatly from his boat to the sill and then onto something hidden in the shadows. "This way, Master, if you're coming."

Irichels rose to his feet and picked his way carefully along the length of both boats, feeling them stagger beneath him as Arak caught her balance. There was no splash and he didn't glance back, instead ducking his head to step down onto the sill. There was a platform beyond, ankle-deep in the murky dark, and he grimaced as he stepped onto it. The wood was soggy under his toes, the water cold, and he conjured a marsh-light to float ahead of them. By its light he could see a little way into the forest of tarred pilings, water lapping gently at their bases. The waterman had moved further in, was beckoning from another little platform. "This way, Master, if you'll leave room for the rest."

Irichels followed him, grimacing again at the silt and scum between his toes. Envar joined them, wobbling for a moment before he found his footing, then turned to offer Arak a hand as she stepped down onto the platform. Arak glared but accepted the help, hunching her shoulders under the weight of the house. There was just room to stand upright; at high tide, Irichels guessed, the water would be over his knees.

The waterman snapped his fingers and light bloomed, reflecting from the dark water. "Was there something in particularly you were wanting to see, Master? There's crossbeams that reach under most of the house."

"I wanted to see my wards from beneath," Irichels said, and the waterman shrugged.

"Will you go round the edges first, or see the middle?"

Irichels glanced at Envar, who lifted one shoulder slightly in a shrug. "Start with the edges, I suppose, then back through the middle."

The waterman led them along the outer wall, feeling their way along crossbeams that were sometimes at water level and sometimes dropped a foot or more. Irichels could hear Arak cursing under her breath, and kept a tight grip on the pilings. Here and there loops of rope or leather offered handholds and he clutched at them, fighting for balance on the slippery wood. Something splashed in the distance and then closer, toward the center of the house, and the waterman froze for an instant before directing his light in that direction. The water was brown and murky, ripples moving on its surface.

"What was that?" Arak asked.

"Sanderlings, probably," the waterman answered. He moved his hand, sending the light swaying across the water. Another splash sounded, farther off, and he nodded. "They don't like the light much. But don't ever come down here without a light, they like to hunt in packs."

"Lovely," Arak said, not quite under her breath.

Irichels's toes curled on the soggy beam, digging trenches in the scum that clung to it. He had always known there were sharks in the canals—they scavenged from kitchens and kept the water relatively clean—but he'd never expected to be down here so close to them. He was grateful that the next crossbeam sloped upward, bringing his feet almost out of the water. He could feel the house wards more strongly now, and the daemon floating above them, and in the same moment saw what looked almost like a stretch of sandy beach rising ahead of them. The waterman had stopped well short of it and was starting to turn left to run parallel to it, but Irichels raised his hand.

"Wait. What's that?"

"The end of your wards, Master," the waterman said, with a note of reproof. "Beyond that's the city wards, and none of yours."

"And if I wanted to look further under there?" Irichels asked, setting his hand to his purse, but the waterman shook his head.

"Then you'd need to have a warrant from the high constable, Master, it's more than my place is worth to take you outside your bounds."

"I only wondered," Irichels said. That would be under the street outside the house's back door; he hadn't realized it was built on a ridge of higher ground. There wasn't much clearance between it and the beams that leveled the street, though there were shadowed spaces that suggested it might be possible for someone to crawl through on hands and knees. But if someone had come that way, they would still have had to get through the floor, and he glanced back to see Arak studying the beams above them with wary intensity.

They made the circuit of the house, along the alley-side where the pilings that held the house seemed to merge with the pilings that supported the alley and the house next door. That seemed the most likely way to get in or out, Irichels thought, but there was still no sign of any break in the foundation above them. They crossed back through the middle, wading through deeper water and keeping an eye out for sanderlings, but nothing seemed out of the ordinary.

Back at the water-alley door, Irichels tipped the waterman and his apprentices, then slunk up the stairs under Martholin's disapproving eye to wash off the clinging slime. "I didn't see anything useful," he admitted, scraping mud from between his toes, and Envar shrugged.

"At least we know what's down there now."

Arak reached for the pitcher of warm water and sluiced soap and grime from her feet in a swirl of brown and green, then stopped abruptly. "Where does this go?"

"What?" Irichels cocked his head, considering the question. They were on the second floor, in the bathroom he shared with Envar, all three of them with their feet in the bath and soap and water and towels to hand.

"The water. The drain, more specifically."

"The drain runs into the canal," Irichels said. "The pipe goes down through the wall."

"I wonder," Arak began, but Envar was already shaking his head.

"The drains are always warded. Aren't they?"

"They should be," Irichels answered. "I didn't check separately, but—they should be."

"Better check just in case," Arak said, and Irichels nodded.

"But even if someone was getting under the house, I don't see how they're getting through the wards."

Envar stepped carefully out of the tub, scuffing his feet on a towel. "Flat-boaters—that's what they call thieves who get in through the understories. Flat-boaters usually pick empty houses or warehouses when they know there's only a single watchman on duty."

"So they would have had their eye on this house?" Arak asked.

"I'd think so," Envar answered. "But there was no sign anyone had gotten in. If they had, I think we would have seen it."

Irichels sighed. "I agree. We'll recheck the wards, just to be sure, but I don't think we're any further along."

They dined at Gethen House that night. It had been something of a coin flip whether or not Envar should attend: on the one hand, Irichels was determined to establish him as an integral part of the household; on the other, it might be more politic to wait until he had enough support to guarantee his acknowledgment in the Senate and Assembly. The invitation had been explicitly informal, and that decided him—though as the boat brought them to the canal door of Gethen House, he wondered if he had made the right choice. Envar gave him a sideways smile.

"Too late to back out now, my heart." He was elegant in a new black cope, emphasizing his profession, and Irichels clasped his hand for an instant. It was too late to ask if Envar minded; he hoped the touch would stand for everything they couldn't say, and he let himself be handed out of the boat.

A footman led them into the ballroom, Arak at their heels, and Tyrn Arlechin came quickly to meet them. Irichels accepted the kiss, and let Tyrn bring them down the hall to the low dais where Per Gethen was holding court. He was a round man with a neat white beard, who frequently leaned over to talk to his wife who sat on the dais with one slippered foot propped up on a padded stool, but as they approached Irichels saw his expression harden.

"Irichels." He held out both hands but did not offer the kiss.

"Master Gethen." Irichels bowed to him and to Merete. He thought she had been a Temenon before her marriage, but couldn't quite remember.

She held out her hands as well. "It's lovely to see you again, Irichels. You've grown up very nicely." She nodded to her slippered foot. "I'm only sorry I won't be able to demand a dance with you."

"It's my great regret as well," Irichels answered. "May I present Envar Cassi, my friend and colleague, and my bodyguard Arak min'Aroi?"

Per nodded, still stone-faced, but Merete smiled again. "A pleasure, Dot're, Messida. Do enjoy yourselves." Irichels accepted the dismissal with grace, and they moved together toward the buffet.

"That could have been worse," Envar said under his breath, and Arak laughed softly.

"It may yet be."

It was like being fifteen again, Irichels thought, in the last horrible months before he had left for the University. He was painfully aware of every whisper, every barb slanted in his direction, though at least at forty he was better able to turn a blandly surprised stare on the worst offenders. At dinner he was seated next to the Jeroen widow, who made no bones about her intention to feel him out as a possible husband. She was a sensible woman, and by the end of the first-fish they had agreed they wouldn't suit and were able to move on to other topics. The matron on his other side offered a few complaints about the food and its probable effects on her digestion, but mercifully confined most of her attentions to the man on her other side. Envar had been placed between Oredana Temenon and a fair girl in blue that Irichels couldn't place, and he hoped Oredana would be kind.

It was a relief when the final sweet was cleared away and music sounded from the ballroom. Irichels offered the Jeroen widow his arm, and she allowed herself to be led in; out of the corner of his eye he saw Envar walking with Oredana, head inclined as though listening. Arak hovered on the edges of the room with the other bodyguards, waiting to be summoned, but for the moment, Irichels thought, there was no need. He relinquished the Jeroen widow to a partner more to her taste and turned to look for Envar, but Tyrn Arlechin intercepted him.

"This is going very well, I think."

"I hope so," Irichels answered. "Master Gethen didn't seem so pleased with me."

"I might have advised you to leave the dot're at home," Tyrn answered, "but—done is done. And I'm sure Master Gethen will support your claim."

"I would be duly grateful," Irichels said, and Tyrn nodded.

"Indeed, that's understood. Did you find anything to like in the Jeroen girl?"

"I don't think I'm ambitious enough for her," Irichels said.

"Pity. She might have been useful. But there are plenty of others."

"Evidently," Irichels said, and managed to make his escape. He could see Envar on the other side of the ballroom, sipping at a glass of punch and watching the dancers, Arak a few steps behind him in the shadows beneath the portico. He started toward him but someone jostled him, pushing him toward the edge of the room. He turned, frowning, and Margos Temenon looked down his beaked nose at him.

"I would have thought that even you would have more grace than to bring your catamite into my aunt's house."

"Your aunt has made no objection." Irichels controlled his temper with an effort. If there was a brawl at this party—if there were even raised voices—it wouldn't be the Temenon who was blamed.

"My aunt has more manners than that. And so she is imposed upon by the likes of you."

"And Master Gethen asked you to intervene?" Irichels lifted his eyebrows. Margos was the second son of a second son, of no great importance even among his own family, and he let that knowledge color his voice.

Margos flushed. "Any man with a sense of duty would act in this case."

"You astonish me," Irichels said, his voice flat. "But if you wish to discuss this with Master Gethen—"

"If you want anyone's support in the Senate and Assembly," Margos said, "you'll leave your feral bed-boy at home." He turned on his heel and stalked away.

Irichels swore, loudly enough that a passing couple glanced warily at him, and he had to bow and apologize. But that was more than enough. He'd stayed the requisite minimum, they could leave—except that that would seem to give Margos the victory. He swore again, quietly this time, and let himself be drawn into the next dance.

When the dance ended, he made his way to the other side of the room, and joined Envar and a dark woman in a dashing gown with a twice-slit skirt that showed glimpses of a brocade underdress beneath the plain satin. She gave him a smile, and tapped Envar on the shoulder. "But next time, Dot're, I'm determined you will dance with me."

Envar sketched a bow as she turned away, and Irichels lifted an eyebrow. "Who's she?"

"The special friend of someone called Anthea Valetin," Envar answered. "Sent to assure me that not all parties were this bad."

"I think that was kindly meant," Irichels said.

"Oh, indubitably. But this is not a particularly pleasant party, my heart."

"No," Irichels said with a pang of guilt, "and I'm sorry I dragged you to it. Worse luck, we're going to have to stay a little longer."

"Oh?"

"I had words with Margos Temenon," Irichels said, "and I'm not letting him chase me off."

"Ah."

"The one we met at the Ambros party?" Arak asked.

"The same. I've made an enemy there, I'm afraid." He was aware of several people within earshot, and couldn't resist letting his voice rise just a little. "At least he's not someone of importance."

"Never let him hear that, my heart," Envar said with a grin, and Arak breathed a laugh.

There was more dancing then, and conversation with various members of the Assembly who would probably vote for his acknowledgment if they weren't offended, and the curfew-bell was sounding by the time he rejoined the others. He had not been able to keep an eye on them, and was alarmed to see a faint look of strain on Envar's face. He was holding two goblets and Irichels reached automatically for one, but Envar shook his head.

"I wouldn't, my heart." He set the first one down on the nearest windowsill—it was still nearly full, Irichels saw—and groped in his purse. "You wouldn't have a handkerchief?"

Arak produced one, frowning, and Envar took it. He dipped it into the wine, then emptied both glasses out the open window. The light caught his eyes, reflecting silver for an instant.

"Poison?" Every muscle in Irichels's body tensed. If this was Margos Temenon's idea of retaliation, he would personally flay the little bastard. "Can you handle it?"

"Oh, yes." Several of Envar's contracts involved poisons, Irichels knew, and protected him from most of them. "But I'll want to be sick soon, so—"

"Was it for you, or for him?" Arak asked.

"We can discuss that later," Irichels said. "Both of you, go on and collect the boat, and I'll make our farewells."

It took longer than he'd meant to find Gethen and take his leave in proper style, complete with the pass that would let them travel after curfew. By the time he reached the narrow dock, Antel had brought the boat alongside and the others were aboard, Envar's hands white-knuckled on the gunwales. Irichels stepped into the hull and Antel shoved the boat out into the canal, heading for the dark center of the stream.

"Cass?"

Envar lifted a hand, looked back at Gethen House as though gauging the distance, then leaned over the side to vomit into the black water. Irichels caught his shoulders to steady him, then stroked his hair back out of the way, wishing there were more he could do. Envar vomited again and finally straightened, wiping his mouth with the back of his hand.

"Here's water," Arak said, and passed a bottle. Envar took it gratefully, rinsed his mouth and spat, then finally drank.

"Now," Irichels said. "You're all right?"

Envar nodded. "Flybane, for a guess, a solid dose. I'll need to renew that contract, though, I've only got one rescue left. I wasn't expecting to use any on myself."

"What happened?" Irichels wanted to shake him, demand to know how he could have been so horribly careless, but he knew that was as much reaction as Envar's shaky calm. "Where was it, in the wine?"

"Yes. The servants were bringing around more glasses, some nice spiced wine—ideal for hiding the taste of flybane, I might add, though truly I wasn't expecting this. And if you were, my heart, I'd have appreciated some warning."

Irichels shook his head. "I was not. What happened, Cass?"

"You were finished dancing, I thought—you'd just finished a set. One of the maids had a tray with two glasses left, and offered me one. I said I'd take the other for you and she curtseyed very nicely and left them with me. I took a taste of mine and realized what was in it, and tasted the other as well. And a very good thing that I did, considering."

"Yes." Not that he would have died, Irichels thought, Envar's contracts let him counteract poison in others as well as himself. But there would have been a scene, shouting and sickness and far too much attention, and another reason to oppose his acknowledgment in the Senate and Assembly. And presumably that was what the poisoner was after, unless it was someone like Margos Temenon or even Margos himself, who disapproved of his bringing his lover to a formal party. "Did she say anything to suggest the second glass was for me?"

Envar leaned back against the cushions. "I don't—did she say 'for you and your friend'? I'm not sure. It was loud, and I wasn't paying a lot of attention."

"We both thought you were coming to us," Arak said. "And, no, I didn't hear, either."

Irichels rested his hand on Envar's knee. He didn't want to think about the things that could have happened, would deal with them in the morning. "Take us home, Antel."

He made the rounds of the first floor, taking special care with the locks and bars, and dragged himself upstairs to find his bedroom empty. A light showed under Envar's door, however, and after a moment Irichels let himself into the hidden passage, sliding back the panel at the far end to peer through.

Envar knelt in the center of the room, the carpet pushed aside to leave room for the circle chalked around him on the bare boards. He was speaking quietly, a cantrip Irichels didn't recognize, but as he finished it, his eyes opened, and he nodded slightly. Irichels slipped silently into the room, closing the panel behind him, and Envar drew a thin knife from his sleeve. He pricked his thumb, squeezing drops of blood onto the handkerchief he'd soaked in the poisoned wine, then spoke again. It was one of the demonic tongues, Irichels knew, but not one included in his own bond.

The handkerchief sizzled and smoked, the blood spreading like a spider's web over the surface, and then abruptly vanished. Envar smiled and pricked his thumb again, drawing more blood to stain the handkerchief. Smoke rose again, and then the handkerchief vanished in a flash of silver. He sat back on his heels, pronouncing the Formula of Departures, and Irichels heaved a sigh. Of course Envar had to pay his debts promptly, that was the rule of contract magic, and it was equally certain that he'd confirm the poison in the process.

Envar leaned forward to wipe out one of the glyphs, breaking his circle, and looked up at last. "Definitely flybane."

Irichels wanted to seize him, hold him tight, swear vengeance on whoever had done this, but none of those were things that Envar would appreciate just now. "So you said."

"Well, it's confirmed." Envar pushed himself to his feet and began methodically running his foot over the chalked lines, eliminating the circle. "It's not exactly hard to come by. I imagine most households have some."

"We should leave," Irichels said. "We could leave. I'll tell Tyrn Arlechin in the morning. I'll renounce this whole mess, and we can just walk away."

"But we can't," Envar said. "If someone wants to destroy Samar—and I do think that's the intention here—they'd still have to kill you to succeed. They won't stop just because we've left Bejanth."

That was regrettably true, and Irichels sighed. "We can't go on like this."

"I'd rather not," Envar agreed. "I'd say marry as fast as you can, but I think that would only make it worse."

Because it would increase the pressure to murder him before he could father an heir. Irichels nodded. "Adopt someone, maybe? Some sort of temporary heir, with suitable compensation for taking on the risk? I can't pick you, because everyone knows we're sleeping together, but—Arak?"

"I like that," Envar said. "She's even harder to kill than you are, and I doubt she'll mind the risk. Make it very public—"

"And that should resolve some of the problem." Irichels held out his hand. "I'll talk to her in the morning. In the meantime—come to bed?"

CHAPTER NINE

Irichels made the proposal over breakfast. At first Arak seemed disinclined to take him seriously, but once Irichels had gone over the parameters a second time, the swordswoman shrugged. "I see your point, certainly, and of course I'm willing. But will they let you do it?"

"It's been done before," Irichels answered. "We can only try."

Tyrn Arlechin was not at home, but the daughter who came to greet them volunteered that he was usually at Idra-of-the-Laws at this time of day, and would likely be there until noon. If they hurried, they were sure to find him. Irichels thanked her, and they set off again for Westerly and the Harbor Cut. Idra-of-the-Laws stood almost in the center of Westerly, alone on its plaza, the dome of the sanctuary a thousand shades of verdigris. The plaza was busy, filled with people who had come to consult the lawyers and notaries and book-writers who gathered in the portico, and it took a while for Irichels to find which side Tyrn frequented. An elderly Oratorian finally allowed as how Messire Tyrn was usually on the north side with the other inheritance-brokers. Irichels thanked him and turned away, and nearly collided with Innes Manimere.

"I'm sorry—"

She put a finger to her lips. "We can't talk here. Can you meet me at the Western Harbor—the plaza opposite the Three Gulls?"

It was probably wiser to say no, considering everything that had happened, but Irichels nodded. "When?"

"When you finish your business here?" She was already turning away, as though they were mere strangers. Irichels bowed to her retreating back, and made his way on around the oratory. He was aware of both Envar and Arak's disapproval, and of the sudden movement that was Envar treading on Arak's toes to keep her from speaking, but ignored them both.

He found Tyrn among a flock of lawyers gathered at the shrine of Saint Leonor, and the lawyer broke off his conversation with flattering promptness. "Irichels! Is there anything I can do for you?"

"In fact, there is," Irichels answered. "If I could have a word? It's a bit urgent."

"Of course." Tyrn tucked his arm through Irichels's and drew him away from the other lawyers, pausing at last in a band of sunlight pouring in through the colonnade. Irichels glanced over his shoulder, making sure Arak and Envar were both within sight, and realized that Tyrn's clerk was also following at a respectful distance. "Now, what is it? You look distressed."

"Someone made an attempt to poison either me or Dot're Cassi last night," Irichels said bluntly. "And that's the second time someone's tried to kill one of us. I propose to adopt Arak min'Aroi as temporary heir until I marry or make other arrangements. I know that's been done before."

"Oh, yes." Tyrn nodded. "I think—I'm appalled that this is happening, and I think this is a reasonable solution. Had you settled on terms?"

"We'd discussed it." Irichels laid out the provisions— an allowance from Samar, to compensate for the dangers; a substantial payment when the agreement ended; all the protections he'd been able to think of—and Tyrn listened, making notes on the pair of wax tablets he'd produced from his purse. When Irichels had finished, the lawyer nodded again.

"Very well considered, I believe. You have a legal mind— though of course you must, dealing with curses. There is only one thing I would suggest, which is that Messida Arak be prohibited from renouncing the bequest; otherwise there would be no reason not to continue attacking you, and hoping that she could be persuaded to give up her position. And there is the question of her children."

"She has none now," Irichels said.

"Still, there should be a provision disinheriting any child born before she inherits."

That seemed a bit hard on Arak, but it did make sense. Irichels nodded. "Agreed."

"Let me draw up a document, then," Tyrn said. "I can have it ready for signing in a day or two."

"Would my intention stand in court if anything happened to me in the meantime?"

"If sworn to before a notary," Tyrn answered.

"Then we'll do that, too." Irichels smiled. "There seem to be plenty to choose from."

"And in this case, discretion is hardly a virtue," Tyrn said.

In the end they made a minor production of it, with a notary to record the intention and an Oratorian to certify it. Irichels made no effort to keep his voice down as he answered the notary's questions, and was certain that the story would have flowed through every corner of the city before nightfall.

That done, Irichels returned to the boat, and Antel rowed them down the length of the Harbor Cut, putting them ashore on the southern bank of the Cut where it entered the western harbor. The wharves lined the banks, ships jammed in close so that their masts looked like a forest after a fire, bare black poles against the bright sky. The open plaza between the wharves and the first row of buildings was crowded with tilt-carts, and stevedores humped bags and bundles from ship to barge. Samar had some interests here, Irichels remembered from the house records, but most of the business was handled through brokers. He would have to spend time with them soon, and get to grips with that as well.

The Three Gulls was a brightly painted tavern wedged between what seemed to be a chandlery and a factor's office. The harbor cut in closely here, and a wide expanse of stairs led to a landing suitable for smaller boats, the boatmen jockeying for position by the bollards. Manimere was sitting on a low wall at the top of the stairs, unremarkable in a plain brown tunic and wide-legged trousers, shredding the end of a loaf of bread for the black-headed gulls that gathered at her feet. She was apparently unattended, but Irichels felt certain that some of the idlers were keeping a close eye on her safety. He motioned for the others to stay back, and came to stand beside her, casually resting one foot on the wall. She squinted up at him, shading her eyes, then turned her attention to what was left of the bread.

"Have you had a chance to think, then?"

"I have." Irichels kept his eyes on the harbor mouth, where a three-masted barque was shortening sail for the slow run into its dock. "I'm very much interested in your offer."

"I'm glad to hear that."

"There are some things you should know."

"Besides your handsome dot're?" She didn't look at him, but the corner of her mouth curled in what looked like genuine amusement. "I told you I didn't mind."

"I took you at your word," Irichels answered. "No, this is more—well, first, since I came home, people have tried to kill me at least twice, possibly three times."

"Did you expect everyone to be happy that Samar's not dead?"

"I didn't know anyone was trying to destroy the family," Irichels said. "What can you tell me about that?"

"How could you not think it, after what happened?" This time Manimere did look at him, frowning. "There were too many deaths to be natural."

"I hadn't kept in touch with the family," Irichels said. "My grandfather didn't acknowledge me, and I'd made a career on the mainland. Why would someone want to destroy Samar—and who?"

Manimere looked away again, resuming her casual pose with an effort. "I don't know who. The Temenon or the Ambros? No, you're allied with Ambros, aren't you?"

"Gellis Ambros has agreed to support my claim."

"So probably not him," Manimere agreed. "Could be any number of Assembly houses who'd like to take a share of your family's business."

"They shouldn't find that too hard while I'm finding my feet," Irichels said. "And that's a small thing. Why destroy the house?"

"If I knew that…" Manimere shrugged. "My guess would be that it has something to do with the Shame—that's the only thing Samar and Manimere still have in common, the only reason someone would be pushing both of us."

"You've been attacked, too?"

"Threatened," Manimere said. "My…not all my business undertakings will stand close scrutiny. But I have two children, and a handful of cousins on the Plana. We're harder to get rid of. Also—you're a cursebreaker, and the Shame certainly involved a contract. Maybe there's something in it that you'd see that no one else would."

"That contract," Irichels said. "Even if it was still in effect it would be so overwritten and entangled with other contracts and curses that it would be almost impossible to do anything with it. Or to it."

"You'd know better about that than I would," Manimere said.

"I wish I knew more about it," Irichels said. "I've been looking in our records, but so far I haven't turned up anything useful."

"You'd be welcome to go through Manimere's documents," Manimere said.

"I'd like that," Irichels said. "But. That's the other thing. I've been warned not to make any deals with you, on pain of losing support for my claim. I need to be acknowledged first. And then—yes, I'd very much like to accept your offer."

"I've no problem with that," Manimere answered, scattering the last crumbs to the gulls. She rose to her feet, brushing her hands on her tunic. "I'll look forward to it, then."

The next few days were mercifully quieter. Irichels continued searching through the family's records, but found mostly trading compacts and records of investments. They had been steadily successful, if not spectacularly so, with a definite upturn under his grandfather's supervision. That was no particular surprise—he had always known that his grandfather was a shrewd man of business—but it was a surprise to find that his uncle Galeran had been something of a disaster. From what he remembered, Galeran had been the most successful of the sons, with a business of his own and a solid marriage and four strapping children. The oldest, Bretigil, had been a month younger than Irichels, and they had been friends of sorts, but there had always been a line drawn. Bretigil's gowns were always made new to accommodate his increasing height, while Irichels had been relegated to what his mother and her seamstress Ida could make of second-hand goods and cast-offs. Bretigil had drowned coming back from the Plana, when a sudden storm overturned his boat. That had been the year after Debes was born, the year things really started going wrong.

"And I am wondering," he said that night, over a casual supper enlivened by the presence of Halyssin Ambros, "if that isn't what was meant by the Death card in Zaffara's reading."

Halyssin shrugged one shoulder. "That's outside my ken."

"I think," Envar said slowly, "I think Galeran's inheriting was that event. He brought renewed prosperity and a large family—the Ace of Cups and the Six of Staves—that were overthrown by the Five of Cups and Page of Staves."

"And that's the next question," Irichels said. "The Page of Staves is surely Debes, and the Five of Cups is whatever withered the trading after he was born. But it doesn't answer the question of how that happened."

"Whether he was a cursling or if there was some more focused attack, you mean?" Halyssin reached for a last sliver of tart. They were well into the sweet, with only a few fragments of pastry left on the table and a bit of wine remaining in the pitcher.

"Precisely." Irichels finished his glass, but shook his head when Arak offered more. "I can't find any record that Galeran took advice on the question, not even after Debes died." All the others had died before him: Jilla from her fall, Hafen at University, Jacen in a pointless battle, and finally Bretigil, drowned in the Slackwater. It had to have been clear that there was something wrong with the boy, or Galeran would not have sent his only surviving child to the Oratory, but there was nothing in the house records as to what had happened after that, and Martholin had been gone by then.

"He might have had verbal reports," Halyssin said. "The Oratory would have been willing to handle it discreetly, particularly for an only surviving child."

"Would they have kept records?" Arak asked.

"They're notoriously careful who they let see anything," Envar said.

"I could ask Oredana," Halyssin offered. "She might be able to find something, particularly since it's family business."

"I'd appreciate it," Irichels said. "I wonder if they'd have any documentation about the Shame of Four Houses?"

"They might," Halyssin said, "but I'd advise you to steer clear of that for now. With Manimere—" He stopped. "Forget I said that, please."

Irichels kept his voice as casual as he could manage, careful not to meet Envar's eyes. "What's the trouble with Manimere? Everyone keeps telling me to stay clear."

"Innes Manimere is a thief and a swindler," Halyssin said. "There's every chance she murdered the man who fathered at least one of her children. And she acts as broker for any number of captains who make their living more by piracy than by honest trade."

No wonder I like her. Irichels swallowed the words, said mildly, "I'm surprised the Senate and Assembly haven't taken action."

"They will," Halyssin said. "They are." He hesitated, his expression troubled. "I don't know what she's done now, but the high constable is moving against her."

"What, tonight?" Envar's voice was lightly amused.

"Most likely." Halyssin sounded grim. "I'm not—I don't think it's a wise move, but no one's asking me."

"Why now?" Irichels asked, and Halyssin shook his head.

"I don't know. I'm not supposed to know this much."

Irichels forced a shrug. "Hardly my business."

"Though Debes is," Envar said. "Would it be acceptable to ask Sister Oredana for a meeting, do you think? I think that's very relevant to your troubles, Gil."

"I wouldn't think it would be an issue," Halyssin said, and Irichels let the conversation turn. His mind wasn't fully involved, a part of it focused on Manimere, on the high constable's men who could be surrounding her house, and he was grateful when Halyssin took his leave. He walked him to the waiting boat and waved him off into the dark water, careful not to look toward Manimere House until the boat was out of sight. Envar caught his sleeve.

"You can't go. You know that."

"I can't send a message, either. And I can't ask the boy to go, it's not safe."

"You don't send a servant," Envar said. "I'll go."

Irichels look a deep breath, and went back into the house, letting Karan close the door behind him. "I want you to mind the street door for now," he said. "I may be receiving messages before curfew."

Karan bowed and withdrew. Envar said, "You know I'm right."

He was, that was the problem. A feral mage had any number of reasons to be out and about in the hours between sundown and curfew—if he encountered the constables, they'd be suspicious but they wouldn't necessarily make any connection to Manimere. Irichels wanted to send Arak as well, but that would only complicate matters. At the back of his mind, he could feel the house daemon stirring, roused by his own unease, and he took a deep breath, controlling his feelings. "All right. But just pass the word and come straight back here."

Envar nodded. "If I can. If what Halyssin said is right, we may be too late."

"I know." Irichels led him to the ballroom, unbarred one of the doors that led to the alley. "I'll leave this door open for you, or Karan will be at the street door. Be careful." Envar nodded again, and let himself out into the night.

Irichels returned to the parlor and the remains of the meal, calling for more candles. He was unsurprised when Martholin herself came in with the box of everyday candles. She refilled the candlesticks on the table, stowing the stubs carefully away, and Irichels shook his head when she would have lowered the wheel candelabrum to refill it. "Let them burn out for now."

"Are we expecting trouble, Master?" Martholin fiddled with the candle box, not meeting his eyes. "I only ask because *it* is nervous."

"I know. I'm sorry." Irichels took a deep breath, trying to calm his own nerves. "I don't—it's possible there may be some trouble, though I hope not. I've asked Karan to mind the street door just in case, and we'll be staying up a little longer. You can send the rest of the staff to bed, though."

"Very good, Master."

"Also, would you make a pot of kaf for me, and tea for Messida Arak?"

"Of course, Master." She bobbed a curtsey and disappeared. Irichels opened the door that connected the parlor to the ballroom. He could just see the door he had left unbarred for Envar, though of course it was far too early to expect his return. He would barely be across the first bridge by now, or not even that far if the constables were out and he had to go roundabout.

"He'll be all right," Arak said.

"I know." This was hardly the first time that Irichels had had to rely on Envar to act alone, but this felt different. It didn't help that the daemon was restless, and it was impossible to tell if it was reflecting his own unease or worrying at something on its own accord. He took more slow breaths, controlling his emotion, but the daemon remained uneasy, a roiling presence in the corner of the house. Martholin returned with a tray, kaf and its fixings on one serving plate, a pot of tea and a plate of small cakes on another, and disappeared back into the kitchen. Irichels concentrated on the ritual of preparation, the spices, the coarse dark sugar, the stream of kaf poured from on high to create a layer of foam; but when he had finished, he was hardly aware of the taste. He sipped at the cup, broke a cake in half and nibbled at it, but his attention was on the ballroom door.

A bell sounded at the back of the house, and both he and Arak shot to their feet. "The street door?" Arak asked, and Irichels nodded. "I'll go."

"No. You watch for Cass." Irichels put down his cup and hurried across the courtyard. He emerged in the dim lobby to find Karan closing the door behind a cloaked woman who had a small boy at her side. As he watched, she lowered the cloak's hood, and he recognized Manimere's cousin Felisan. "Dona?"

"No, don't bar it, I can't stay." Felisan looked back at Irichels, her face drawn and pale in the flickering light. "We're in trouble, Master. Manimere is under siege, the constables are at the door, and I can't get Nerin back to his mother. Can you take him? Please?"

"Yes." He hadn't thought about his answer, but once given, he had no desire to take it back. "What's wrong, what do the constables want?"

"There's a warrant out, accusing her of funding an attack on a Bejanter ship," Felisan said. "It doesn't matter whether it's true or not, because they can arrest her and throw her into the cells under the Assembly and without her the house will fall apart. We almost found out too late. Nerin had a dancing lesson, I came to fetch him, but I couldn't bring him home without running into the constables. You will take him?"

"Yes," Irichels said again. "I'll keep him safe until Manimere comes for him. Or you, of course."

"Yes. Thank you." Felisan drew up her hood again. "Now let me out, please, I mustn't be seen anywhere near Samar House."

"Will you be all right?" Irichels asked, as Karan moved to unbar the door.

"I'll manage," she answered, and slipped out into the night.

CHAPTER TEN

Karan barred the door again, his expression carefully neutral. Irichels said, "Stay at the door for now, this is likely to be a busy night." He looked down at the boy, who hadn't made a sound since he'd arrived. "You're—Dona Felisan said your name was Nerin?"

For a moment, he wasn't sure he was going to get an answer, but the boy's lips parted. "Yes. You're—Mama said she might marry you."

"Yes. I'm Gil Irichels di Samar. But you mustn't repeat that, about your mother and me marrying."

"Mama said I mustn't, too."

"Come in the dining room," Irichels said. "There are cakes—"

He heard sounds from the ballroom, hoped that it was only Envar coming home but focused on the boy, leading him through the courtyard and into the small parlor. Arak was there ahead of them, and Envar with him, shedding his black cope to toss it onto a side chair.

"—constables are up throughout the city," Envar was saying. "I couldn't get anywhere near Manimere House."

He stopped, seeing the boy, and Irichels said, "Innes was warned. This is her son Nerin. He'll be staying with us for a while."

"You'll need to disguise him," Envar said. "If they come for you—"

"Why would they?" Arak demanded, and Irichels shook his head.

"Better not to take chances. Nerin, you heard what Dot're Cassi said. We need to disguise you so that it seems as though you belong to Samar House. Are you willing?"

For a moment, he thought the boy hadn't understood him, but finally he gave an infinitesimal nod. "Aunt Felisan said I should do what you said."

Thank Idra for that. Irichels looked at Envar. "You have something in mind."

"I can mask his Manimere blood, make it seem as though he belongs to Samar," Envar said. "Some child of one of your uncles, perhaps, whom we've just uncovered?"

"That runs the boy into danger," Arak said.

"Safer than belonging to Manimere, I think," Envar said.

"We're going to pretend that you belong to my Uncle Hamel," Irichels said. "He's dead, and I just found out you existed. Your mother was a dancer."

"He can't remember all that," Arak said, and Nerin looked up sharply.

"Can too."

"Hopefully you won't have to," Irichels said. "There's no need to say anything unless we're asked. Are you willing?"

"Yes."

"Good boy." Irichels found the plate of cakes and offered one. Nerin took it hungrily.

Envar said, "Best we get on with it."

"Tell me what you need."

Envar was already moving chairs to create an open space by the hearth. "A drop or two of blood, though not just yet." He produced a piece of chalk and went to his knees to scribe a circle, laying out symbols in careful haste. "Here, Nerin, step to the center." The boy hesitated, and Envar gave him a quick smile. "You can keep the cake."

Encouraged, the boy stepped into the center of the markings and Envar sat back on his heels, closing his eyes. "Gil, join him. When I tell you, prick your thumb and mark his forehead with the blood."

Irichels nodded. He felt the air shiver as Envar spoke,

a skein of words that drew power from the water beneath the house and from the stones of the house itself, from the common stock of magic and the contracts that bound Envar to the other worlds. The daemon shifted, aware but not alarmed, perhaps even approving, and Envar said, "Now, please, Gil."

Irichels drew his penknife and stabbed his thumb, squeezing it to draw up a bead of blood before touching it to Nerin's forehead. Envar spoke again, and Irichels felt a spark leap between them. Nerin's eyes flashed open, startled, and Envar began the Formula of Departures, hurrying through the phrases. Irichels frowned, and then he heard it, too: voices on the canal, and the thump of a boat pulling up against the house's dock. Envar finished, rubbed out a symbol.

"Go. Hide him. I'll deal with this."

"We will," Arak said, and stepped out into the hall.

Irichels took Nerin's hand, hurrying him across the courtyard. Martholin would protect him, would lie for Samar without question—and she wouldn't have to lie if he told her to repeat the story Envar had proposed, that Nerin was Hamel's child.

The kitchen was empty, the fires banked and the doors locked and barred. There was no time to get him upstairs, and no place to hide him if the house was searched. Unless in the passage between his room and Envar's? But there was no time to take him here, he could hear the bell ringing at the street door, and Karan's voice raised in challenge. The daemon roused, swirling out into the corridor between the storage rooms, and Irichels caught his breath. That was all he needed, to have to control that, while hiding the boy and dealing with the constables. The daemon surged into the kitchen, the shadows thickening in front of the great hearth, and Nerin edged closer.

"Stop," Irichels said, putting all his will behind the word, and the daemon hesitated.

Give. Safe. Hide. Safe.

The constables would certainly fear the daemon, but could it be trusted? There was knocking at the canal door now as well, and he knew he was out of time. He looked down at Nerin. "Does your house have a spirit?"

Nerin looked even more uneasy. "I'm not supposed to talk about it."

"Then you know about them." Irichels took a breath. "That's it there, it's come to hide you. It will keep you safe. It may seem frightening, but it won't harm you." *And Idra send that's not a lie.* "Hear me, spirit! Nerin is under my protection, under the protection of Samar. Hide him, keep him safe here, let none touch him except by my leave."

He felt the daemon shiver, shying like a horse, and then it flowed over them, wrapping them in air that felt like cool silk. Nerin closed his eyes, hunching his shoulders a little, but didn't move. "Go with it," Irichels said. He could hear voices in the hall, in the lobby, shouts and orders and the clatter of arms. "You'll be safe. Don't be afraid."

"I won't be," Nerin said, but his voice wobbled. The daemon enshrouded him, concealing him, and Irichels sprinted for the courtyard. He reached its center just as the first constables spilled out of the entrance hall, Arak following empty-handed. He could hear more men in the lobby behind the stairs, Karan arguing, and he lifted his voice, hoping to prevent a fight. "What is this? What are you doing in my house?"

"Gilmyssin Irichels di Samar?" That was the leader, a man who wore the gilded gorget of a senior constable. There were at least ten men with him, and more pouring in from the lobby behind the stairs.

"That's me." For a moment, Irichels was tempted to insist on the title, but thought better of it. "What's this about?"

"We're here on a warrant from the high constable," the senior constable said. "We are commanded to search the house for any sign of or messages from Innes Manimere, and to escort you to the Assembly hall to answer to the high constable."

"What has Innes Manimere to do with me?" Irichels asked. The birds were twittering nervously in their cages, roused from sleep, and he could see Martholin and the other servants peering over the railing on the third floor. "I've no business with her."

"There are sworn statements that contradict that, Messire," the senior constable said. "Have your people stand aside and let us search."

"Absolutely not," Irichels said. He would have to give in, he couldn't fight twenty men, but he could buy some time. "Show me this warrant."

The senior constable flourished a scroll, letting it unroll in his hand, seals dangling from its lower edge like a fringe. Irichels took it, scanning the clear clerkly writing. He could feel the daemon gathering its strength, a weight pressing on the edges of the room. At least one of the waiting men seemed to be a bonded mage, and Irichels saw him edge up the senior constable, murmuring something in his ear. The senior constable frowned. "You'll control your daemon, Irichels."

"What you feel is the house spirit," Irichels answered. "It is—naturally!—unhappy at all of this."

"Control it," the senior constable said more sharply.

Irichels re-rolled the warrant, handed it back. "As much as I can. As you know, the Senate and Assembly haven't yet acknowledged me—"

"Control it," the senior constable said, "or we will be forced to control it for you. And that would certainly be counted against you."

Irichels spread his hands. "As far as I can." He closed his eyes, made a show of concentrating, settling his feet firmly against the courtyard's stones. "Hear me, spirit! I permit these men to search my house. You will not harm them."

"Or obstruct them," the senior constable suggested.

Irichels sighed. "Or obstruct them." The daemon reared out of the stone, a sudden wall of shadow that reached to the courtyard roof and then collapsed, a black wind sweeping through the first floor. The marsh-lights dimmed, and the unshielded candles winked out, but then it retreated to the edges of the building, present but not quite threatening.

Hinder.

If you can, Irichels thought, and looked up at the servants huddling at the top of the stairs. "That of course goes for you as well."

Martholin bobbed a shaky curtsey, Tepan and the youngest maid clutched close to her side. "Yes, Master."

Irichels looked back at the senior constable. "Then I'm at your disposal."

The senior constable detached a sergeant and ten men for an escort, and Irichels let them lead him out onto the dock. He was aware of Envar staring after him, of Arak carefully keeping her hands away from her knives, but there was no time to speak to either of them. The waiting barge was twice as large as the usual punts that carried traffic through the residential canals, with lanterns flaring on bow and stern and a dozen oarsmen at the ready. The sergeant led him to the seats in the stern, beneath the steersman's high platform, and the soldiers scrambled after. An oarsman released the anchor lines and shoved them away from the dock, leaping after them to take his place.

As they made the shape turn onto the wider Dawan Canal, Irichels realized that the entire city seemed to be roused and awake. There were lighted lanterns at the doors of the great houses, and even the smaller buildings were flying strings of paper lampions from their upper stories. There were groups with torches on the bridges, and they pointed and catcalled as the boat passed them.

The rowers picked up the pace as the barge turned onto the Eastern Water, and someone in the bow began ringing a heavy bell, warning any other traffic to give way. They were heading for Lawgivers' Isle, not the usual landing spot at the Water Stair, but further along the Isle's northern edge, where the shore curved in closer to the Assembly building. There was a watchpost there, and the entrance to the enclosed walkway—the Prisoner's Walk that led to the lower levels of the Assembly—and Irichels was unsurprised to see another detachment of guards waiting there. He had underestimated the trouble Manimere would bring, and the thought chilled him to the bone.

The barge came alongside with a minimum of shouted orders, dockmen in the constables' livery bustling to catch the mooring ropes. The sergeant motioned for him to step ashore and Irichels obeyed, aware again of eyes watching from the Assembly and from every vantage point along the channel's edge. He kept his back straight, his movements calm, and hoped that would buy him some support. And then they were out of the torchlight and through the arch of the Prisoner's Walk, and his world narrowed to the passage, gray stone and wavering marsh-light.

He had not been in the Assembly since he was a boy, and then only in the public levels, full of gilding and marble panels. The Prisoner's Walk came in at the building's narrow end, a level below the grand Assembly rooms themselves, and emptied into a windowless corridor that led to an equally featureless stair. At its top more lanterns blazed, brighter than the marsh-lights, and still in silence the sergeant motioned for Irichels to climb. He did as he was told, the only sound the noise of boots on stone and the creak of leather armor and the occasional clink of metal from someone's scabbard, and emerged in a narrow lobby. There were three doors but only the one on the left was guarded, and the sergeant motioned him toward it. The guards opened it at their approach, and the sergeant said, "Gilmyssin Irichels di Samar."

By comparison to the halls outside, the room was brightly lit, with a great wheel-candelabrum suspended in the center of the ceiling, branched candlesticks set at intervals around the ring-shaped table that dominated the room and more candles in mirrored sconces along the walls, casting shimmering light on the frescos that covered them. From every panel, a phase of the moon supervised a scene of night's secret life, from a lover serenading his lady to thieves hauling goods through a broken window. A frieze of lobsters and shellfish ran along the base of the panels, picked out in silver and ground glass to catch the light.

Irichels's breath caught in his throat. Now he knew where he was: this was one of the rooms where the Assembly or its representatives could sit in judgment. There were three of them, each decorated with motifs from the cards: the Sun, Judgment, and the Moon. This was the Moon, where private decisions could be made. He had badly underestimated the dangers of Manimere's advances.

About two thirds of the chairs around the table's outer edge were occupied, but he couldn't make out the faces. The candles illuminated the central space within the table's ring, and the paintings on the wall, but left the judges in shadow.

"Irichels di Samar. Come forward, please." Irichels didn't recognize the voice, but obeyed cautiously. "Into the center, please." He blinked, then saw the gap in the table and stepped through into the center. There might be eight or ten people at the table, but he couldn't be sure, with the lights placed deliberately to blind him.

"Gilmyssin Irichels di Samar," a different voice said. "You stand accused of conspiring with Innes Manimere to prey upon the merchant fleets of Bejanth and her houses, and to sell those goods in other states along the shore. How do you plead?"

"Not guilty," Irichels answered promptly. The room was not warm, but he could feel himself sweating beneath the plain tunic and narrow trousers he'd worn for an evening at home. He looked like a pirate, he knew, bearded and broad-shouldered, wished too late that he'd dressed more carefully for his dinner with Halyssin.

"You are known to have met with Innes Manimere," another voice said. "To have had intimate dinners with her and your households."

"I dined with her once," Irichels said. "As you know, I did not expect to inherit Samar. I've been looking for friends where I can find them."

"And what did she offer you?"

Irichels said carefully, "She offered friendship and her vote in the Assembly when I was to be acknowledged."

"And in exchange?"

"She said she wanted friendship and nebulous future favors." Irichels was determined not to mention the marriage unless he had to. "She also suggested I might be interested in one of her commercial ventures, and promised to send me a prospectus. I have not yet received it."

The second voice said, "What did you understand her to mean by a 'commercial venture'?"

"We had discussed various trading ventures, investments in cargos for other cities—cash paid to captains and factors." Irichels hesitated, decided it was worth expanding. If Manimere had escaped—and surely she had—he wasn't harming her. "I got the impression that she was short of cash herself, and hoped to persuade me to make up the difference."

"She did not suggest that there was greater profit to be made from raiding than from trade?"

The voice was almost familiar—Per Gethen's, perhaps? Irichels shook his head. "She did not."

"Nor express ill-will toward the Senate and Assembly?"

"She did not."

"Perhaps 'ill will' is too strong a phrase," the third voice said. "Did she say anything that would make you think she opposed any policies of the Senate and Assembly—that she perhaps wished your support for that opposition?"

Irichels shook his head again. "No. We talked about trade."

"You were told to stay away from her." That voice Irichels did recognize: Gellis Ambros. And that meant this was a joint court, with members of both the Senate and the Assembly in attendance: not a good sign. "Explain why you defied that advice."

"I—in retrospect, I think I misunderstood what I was told." Irichels chose his words carefully. The Courts-Between-Worlds had contracts that constrained witnesses to tell the truth; he didn't think the Senate and Assembly had any such—they were expensive and difficult and required active cooperation from spirits and demons to maintain them—but he didn't want to take chances. "I thought—the question arose when Tyrn Arlechin and I were discussing my marriage, I thought I was not to marry her, not that I was to stay away from her entirely." He paused. "I regret my error."

"Did she suggest marriage?" That was Gethen again.

Irichels braced himself for the lie. "She did not." Nothing happened. He kept his face expressionless with an effort, breathing through the wave of relief that washed over him. There was no truth-contract in effect here.

"Tell us about this dinner," Ambros said.

"There's very little to tell," Irichels said. "She invited me to an informal dinner—me and my household. I didn't think I could refuse any offer of friendship, so we went."

"Who was at the dinner?" Gethen asked.

"Of her house?"

"Both your houses."

Irichels took a breath. "Of my house: myself, my colleague Dot're Cassi, my bodyguard Arak min'Aroi. From Manimere, Innes herself, a cousin—Felisan, I didn't hear a byname—and one of her captains. I think his name was Argerin."

"What did you make of this captain Argerin?" Ambros asked, and Irichels shrugged.

"Very little, to be honest. We didn't speak much except generally. He told a few sea tales, made himself agreeable. I had a vague idea he was the captain she wanted me to invest in."

"Did anyone say so?" a new voice cut in.

Irichels shook his head. "No. I just assumed."

"Tell us what Manimere wanted," the second voice said, and the questions began again. They took him through everything twice more, different voices from behind the ring of light, and by the time they were done, his legs were aching from standing so long in one position. The sweat was long dried; the room was cold now, the candles burning low enough that he could almost see the shapes of his questioners. They spoke briefly among themselves, low not-quite whispers intended to intimidate without informing, and then at last Gethen spoke.

"It is agreed that there is no immediate evidence of involvement, but neither is there evidence to acquit. Therefore the defendant will be held in the Assembly cells until a decision can be reached."

"Masters," Irichels began, and there was a flash of movement as someone raised a hand.

"Be silent. There is no more to be said." For an instant, Irichels was tempted to shout, to protest, but he knew it would do no good. Better to obey, and hope that earned him chances for the future. He inclined his head, and let himself be led away.

The Assembly cells were reached by a series of windowless stairs that led down into the depths of the island. Irichels guessed that they were below the water table, held back by stone and spell, and couldn't help shivering as he was escorted down a line of barred doors. The cells he passed were utterly empty; the one opened for him at least had a cot with a blanket, and a chamber pot in the corner. One of the escort set a marsh-light floating in the corridor while another locked the door, and then they retreated the way they'd come, leaving Irichels alone in the dim light.

It was late, painfully so, and he was shaking, reaction, fear, and exhaustion combining to weaken his muscles. When the footsteps had died away, he made himself move to the door and peer out into the corridor. The other cells had all been empty and there was no sign of a guard at the far end of the corridor, just the locked door that gave onto the stairway. That was unexpected, and he considered his options. Left to his own devices, he could probably open the cell door and even the door to the stairs; what lay beyond that was a jumble in his memory, stairs and more stairs. If there had been guard posts—and surely there must have been—he didn't remember them. But perhaps he could investigate just a little.

He rested his hand on the lock, tasting iron and oil and cold dirt. The spells he knew under the University's bond could be stretched to manipulate the tumblers, and he closed his eyes, feeling his way into the pattern of the cantrip. Yes, just there...

There was something sour on his tongue, something that swelled, thick and vile. He flinched away, the thing taking shape and weight, soft and fleshy and tasting of low tide and death. It wriggled against his teeth, scrabbling on his tongue. He clawed at it, stretching his jaws as wide as they would go, hooked a finger behind the thing, and a toad leaped free, landing on the stones with a wet plop. He shook his head, working up spit to clear his mouth, pounding one fist against the bars. There was no water, nothing to rinse his mouth; he wiped his tongue with the back of his hand, but the disgusting taste remained. He gagged, managed to spit at last, gagged again, and made it to the chamberpot just before he vomited.

When he was sure he could stand again, he retreated to the cot, wrapping the blanket around himself. The toad glared at him from the stones, then hopped slowly into the shadows. He'd known of such spells, of course, spells that took and twisted subsequent magic to produce toads or maggots or beetles instead of the desired outcome, but they were Great Works, created by dozens of mages and their spirit and demon helpers under strict contract. Rumor said that the University's Examination Hall in Tarehan was so warded, but mages weren't tested there, for obvious reasons. It had not occurred to him that the Assembly's cells would be under such a spell.

Probably it should have. The lack of guards should have made him think. He leaned his head back against the cold wall, closing his eyes. If he couldn't use any of his spells, he had no chance of contacting Envar, would have to wait until the constables came back for him. The only sensible thing to do was to wait, but his thoughts darted from one thing to another, from whatever Manimere was actually doing, and whether she'd escaped or not—and surely she had, or they wouldn't be wasting time with him—to her son, left in the dubious protection of the house daemon. Envar would handle that, he told himself, Envar and Arak between them could take care of the daemon and of the boy. He would tell the Assembly what they wanted to hear, talk his way out of this somehow as soon as he was brought back before them. In the meantime, he would wait. Eventually he slept.

He woke again cold and confused, the cell unchanged from when he had fallen asleep. The blanket was doing him no good; he made himself get up and walk, swinging his arms and then performing calisthenics until the worst of the chill was gone. That left him hungry, and, worse, thirsty, but the hours passed, and no one appeared. There was no way to judge the time, except that the immediate hunger eased, overridden by thirst. He slept again, perhaps briefly, woke bleary-eyed and miserable to huddle in his blanket and wish for water. No one came, and after a while he went to the bars and shouted.

"Hey! Hello! Anyone there? Hello?"

There was no answer, not even the sound of someone moving beyond the closed door, and he retreated to the cot, wondering if he had been abandoned. Surely not, though if they wanted Samar destroyed, this would be the way to begin. But Arak was his heir, and Envar's spell to hide Nerin made it seem as though he, too, was part of the family—surely that would make it impossible to be rid of all of them. Eventually, he fell asleep worrying at the problem, and dreamed of blood flowing over the stones of the courtyard, Envar's body hanging from the balcony.

He woke at the sound of noises from the stairs, dragged himself upright as the door opened and a group of constables entered the corridor. There were half a dozen of them, constables in livery with halberds, and one with a sergeant's collar who carried what looked like a ceremonial boarding axe.

"Irichels di Samar," the sergeant said. "You'll come with us."

Irichels let the blanket slide off his shoulders, drawing up what was left of his dignity. "Water?"

The word came out a cracking whisper, and the sergeant and the leading guard exchanged glances. The guard produced a leather bottle and offered it through the bars. Irichels took it and drank deeply. It took all his willpower to keep from emptying the bottle in frantic gulps. It was lukewarm and tasted of the wax waterproofing, and he welcomed the way it erased the last lingering flavor of the toad he had inadvertently created. He handed it back, and the sergeant said, "Step back from the door." Irichels obeyed, tightening his muscles to keep from shivering. "This way."

They brought him back up the winding, windowless stairs and through the tangled corridors, to emerge again in the lobby where the three doors led to the judgment rooms. There were windows in the lobby, letting in what might be afternoon light, but the sergeant turned him toward Moon before he could get his bearings. "Irichels di Samar," he announced, and Irichels stepped through the door.

There were small windows at the very top of the walls above the murals, each round of glass shaped with the face of the full moon and the phases of the moon painted between them; but the wheel-candelabrum was still needed, its candles casting light on what he thought was a smaller group than before. He recognized Gethen and Ambros, and the high constable himself at the fulcrum of the table, but the other four were strangers.

"Into the center, please," Gethen said. Irichels did as he was told, bracing himself inwardly for whatever was to come. He was trained never to show surprise or shock; that could be deadly with demons and was likely to be just as dangerous here. He let his face settle into the neutral mask he had perfected for the Courts Between, and waited. Gellis Ambros eyed him with an equally stony face.

"Irichels di Samar. After considerable discussion, we have agreed that you are not guilty of conscious collaboration with Innes Manimere. However, we believe that your contacts with her have brought danger to the city of Bejanth, and therefore we impose sanctions on you, to extend until it pleases the Senate and Assembly to cancel them. Formal acknowledgment as Master of Samar will be withheld; you will remain on probation until such time as it pleases the Senate and Assembly to receive you. You are barred from voting in the Assembly, and from speaking before the Assembly or Senate unless by the agreement of a majority of the Assembly. You will place yourself under the tutelage of House Gethen and will abide by their decisions regarding Samar's actions. Is this clear?"

"Pellucidly." Irichels shut his teeth hard on further protest. He knew what would happen if he refused: back to the cells, and more threats to make him obey. He would not risk Envar and the others—and he would gain nothing by stubbornness. Better to accept quietly, and see how he could wiggle out later.

"Do you accept the judgment of this council?"

"Yes."

"Then this council is ended." Ambros lifted the bell that sat before him and rang it once, the note heavy and discordant in the dull air. "Master Gethen, I give him into your care."

"Thank you, Master Ambros."

The council members were all in motion, scraping back their chairs and turning to each other in rising conversation as they moved toward the door. A tall, fair man hung back with Gethen, a collared cormorant, wings spread, clasping the neck of his gown. A pearl nearly as big as a grape descended from it, lustrous against the plain wool. Irichels knew he should recognize the house sign, but it eluded him.

"Young fool," Gethen said without heat. "I'd have thought you'd have better sense." A door had opened in one of the painted walls, and he led them through into an inner lobby. It overlooked a space Irichels did recognize, the long antechamber where assemblors and senators gathered before and after their sessions. He had been taken there as a schoolboy, gawking with the rest of the class at the fine fittings. It was mostly empty now, the long line of padded benches unattended, the pattern of the mosaic floor uninterrupted lines of stylized waves. "It's cost us a pretty penny to get you out of this."

"Then I'm duly grateful," Irichels said.

"And will pay us back," Gethen said pointedly.

Irichels managed a bow. "Of course."

"There is one more concession," Gethen said. "Master Cambryse here has a daughter who is of age and of suitable station. Her name is Alaissou. You will marry her."

Irichels blinked, remembering the fair, frail child he'd seen at the Ambros dinner. "Isn't she a little young?"

"She's sixteen," Cambryse said. "Certainly old enough to marry."

Young enough to be my daughter. Irichels looked at Gethen. "If it's required."

"It is."

"I'll look forward to your visit, then," Cambryse said, and nodded to Gethen. "Sooner would be better than later."

"Yes," Gethen said tight-lipped, and shook his head when Irichels would have spoken. "My barge is waiting. I'll take you home so you can rest—I am aware that this has been an ordeal for you—and tomorrow we will call on Master Cambryse."

CHAPTER ELEVEN

Cethen's barge deposited Irichels on the dock of Samar House and Arak opened the door to him, offering her hand over the threshold. Irichels took it rather than risk stumbling, his eyes on Envar further back in the shadows of the entrance hall, and Arak said, "We've been—concerned."

"So was I." Irichels held out a hand to Envar, and the two embraced, Envar pressing hard against him. "How long?"

"This is the second day." Envar's voice was muffled, his face pressed against Irichels's shoulder. "They took you night before last."

No wonder he felt strange. Irichels nodded, and Arak said, "We still have guests."

"Constables?"

Arak nodded. "Three of them. For our protection, they said."

"In the courtyard," Envar said in his ear.

"Right." Irichels felt his smile twist out of true.

Envar released him reluctantly. "You're all right?"

"Yes." Irichels took a deep breath, marshaling his strength. "Is everyone all right here?"

"We're fine," Envar said. Behind him, Irichels could see movement, a constable moving closer, to watch and listen.

"And—Hamel's boy?"

"Also fine," Envar said. "The house spirit was very protective of him, but Marthie has him in hand now."

"Good." Irichels closed his eyes, trying not to think about the weight of the toad on his tongue. "I want—a bath first, and drink, and something to eat."

"I'll see to that," Arak said, and Irichels started for the stairs, Envar at his side. The constables bowed politely enough as he passed and he made himself respond in kind, but couldn't help breathing a sigh of relief as Envar closed the bedroom door behind them.

"I'm all at sea," he said apologetically, as Envar turned the taps that filled the narrow tub. "There were no windows, no way to tell how long it had been."

"And they didn't feed you, I would guess."

"Nor was there water."

"My heart." Envar scowled. "Maybe I was wrong. We might have done better to run."

"Too late now," Irichels said, and caught water in his cupped hands. He drank noisily, and Envar disappeared, to return with a pottery cup. Irichels filled that as well and drank again, less frantically, and Envar stirred the water in the tub, murmuring a cantrip that made the water steam. He added a bag of herbs, the soft scent driving back memory, and Irichels set the cup aside to begin undressing. "There was a bond on the cells. One of the twisters."

Envar made a face like an unhappy cat's. "That's extremely unpleasant."

"Yes. It was."

"You're free of it now." Envar took his gown to set it aside for cleaning and Irichels stepped into the steaming water. He wanted to tell Envar to burn every stitch he'd worn, every thread that had been contaminated by that magic, but common sense prevailed. He let himself sink into the scented water, stayed soaking until he heard the door open again, and Envar stuck his head into the bathroom to say that the food was here. Martholin had brought a tray, the boy Nerin at her side. Irichels frowned, drawing his dressing gown tighter around himself, and she said, "He's been worried about you."

"I imagine so." Irichels forced a smile. "Are you all right, then? Settling in?"

"Yes." Nerin's voice was very small.

"Good. Marthie, thank you for taking care of him—"

"Please," Nerin said. "Is Mama all right?"

"She hadn't been caught when they let me go," Irichels said.

To his surprise, the boy nodded. "She'll be all right, then. *Daphneis* is the fastest ship in the Narrow Sea."

"I'm not surprised," Irichels said. "Go with Marthie, now."

Martholin took Nerin's hand and led him out again, closing the door behind her. Envar said, "He's been worried something had happened to you. As were we all."

"I'm all right," Irichels said again. Martholin had brought bread and butter and a wedge of soft cheese as well as a bowl of broth brimming with vegetables, and he wolfed the first slice of bread before reaching for the soup.

"What's the price?" Envar asked.

Irichels stopped, the brief good feeling draining from him. "I'm on probation—the Senate and Assembly will accept me, they say, but for now I'm to do what Gethen tells me. And I'm to marry Alaissou Cambryse."

"Who's she?"

"The sickly sixteen-year-old daughter of the Master of Cambryse," Irichels said.

Envar blinked. "Why?"

Irichels paused. "That's not a bad question. I thought, to keep me from marrying Manimere—but, first, they didn't know about that, and, second, there are enough eligible women within Ambros's faction who'd put me even further in Gethen's debt. So Cambryse must have demanded this as the price of his support. But, again, why?"

Envar nodded. "Someone's been trying to destroy Samar. What happens if you die after you marry her?"

"If there's no child, Samar goes to Arak," Irichels said. "If there's a child, then, yes, that child inherits."

"And if that child dies?"

"That would be the end of Samar," Irichels said.

"And the girl would be young enough to marry again,"

Envar said.

"You're implying that Cambryse would kill his own grandchild," Irichels said.

"Can you say he wouldn't?" Envar asked. "You're very trusting, my heart."

Irichels made a face. He had known since he could walk that his own grandfather would have preferred him dead; it wasn't such a great step from that to arranging a child's death. If his mother hadn't lived... He thrust the thought away. "Cambryse and my grandfather seem to have had a falling out, and Galeran never made it up. So they're certainly not a friend to this house. They're definitely a part of this. But what does it get them?"

"Money?" Envar refilled their glasses, and Irichels took his gratefully. "More power in the Assembly? If they can compel you to vote with their faction?"

"That only works if I'm alive," Irichels said. "What do they get if I'm dead—if Samar ceases to exist? They're one of the Four Houses, anyway." Envar looked up sharply at that and Irichels paused, considering his own words. There had been four houses involved in the Shame, Manimere and Samar from the Senate, and Cambryse and Morellin from the Assembly. "It always comes back to the Shame, doesn't it?"

"The reason for the Shame—for the punishment of the four houses, for the demotions and the fines—was that the Senate and Assembly couldn't undo their contract without destroying the city," Envar said. "Yes? Presumably that restriction still applies, but—"

"But it might not," Irichels said. "It's been hundreds of years, and who knows how many contracts have been piled on top of it, what sort of linkages have been created. It might be superseded, or rendered moot, or even already broken." He stopped, shaking his head. "No, that can't be right, or there wouldn't be any need to bother with us."

"There are always reasons to break a contract," Envar said.

"To get a better one," Irichels agreed. "To tidy up an

impossibly tangled skein of contracts. The Senate and Assembly are always talking about that, though as far as I know, no one ever really does anything. Every time someone proposes an alteration, it always means doing damage to something important, and no one wants to take that risk."

"The Senate and Assembly wouldn't," Envar said. "But a faction within them might."

"We need to know what the contract was," Irichels said. "And how it's woven into the fabric of the city." He shook his head in frustration. "But that's the last thing anyone's going to tell me right now. They're not going to let me into the Chamber of Records while I'm on probation, either."

"The Oratory?" Envar said doubtfully.

"If they have records, I doubt they'd share," Irichels said. "It's going to be hard enough to get them to tell me about Debes." He sighed, and Envar nodded.

"That leaves the Court Between Worlds, then. Not an easy option, my heart."

Irichels reached for the last crust of bread. "No, but— Cass, it might actually be the best way to do it. I have standing, and I have the right to know what contracts I'm now party to. The Court can compel the demon-side to give me the details."

"That's assuming that it was a contract with the sea-demons," Envar said. "If it wasn't—"

"If it wasn't, I'll stand the fine," Irichels said impatiently. "Whatever it may be. It can't be worse than what the Senate and Assembly are doing."

"It certainly can," Envar said, and Irichels waved the words away.

"It won't come to that. If the story is at all accurate, the contract has to have been between the Four Houses and the sea demons."

"You'll want more than Arak at your back if you're going to walk into the Court Between and toss this on the bench," Envar said. "The Senate won't put up with it."

"Between us, you and I have the bonds to demand a private session," Irichels said. "To invoke and enforce it."

Envar laughed softly. "I'm willing if you are, my heart. But we'll have to be rid of the constables first."

Irichels grimaced. "Leave that to me. I'll be meek as a lamb, do everything they tell me, and see if we can't get rid of them."

"Will you marry the girl?" Envar asked.

"If I must," Irichels answered, and drowned regret in another glass of wine.

Gethen was as good as his word, arriving in the house barge to take them to Cambryse House. Irichels dressed in his sober best, his beard and hair newly trimmed, and made no complaint when Gethen ordered him to leave Arak at home. He would be safe enough in Gethen's company, he thought, and it was important to show himself compliant.

Cambryse House stood on the north-east edge of Weepers' Isle, almost within the shadow of the great oratory of Idra-of-Sorrows. Unusually for an Assembly family, the house fronted on the natural channel between Weepers and the Boot, and someone had added a long dock that ran the length of the frontage. Columns at each end were topped by the chained and collared cormorant that was the house symbol, their wings lifted as though they were drying themselves in the sun, and the house itself was decorated with pink stucco and saffron trim. Gethen glanced at him as the steersman maneuvered the barge alongside the dock.

"You'll let me do the talking, Irichels."

"Very well." Irichels dipped his head and tried to look obedient.

"You're prepared to propose to the girl?"

"Have I a choice?"

"You do not."

"Yes, then."

Gethen nodded. "Don't take it out on her. It's not her fault."

"I've no intention of doing so," Irichels said, stung. "And if you're that worried about her—" He broke off, knowing he was being foolish.

Gethen's mouth tightened. "This was Cambryse's price for his cooperation—without which, I hardly need add, you would not be walking free. I am not particularly pleased with the choice."

And you think I am? Irichels swallowed the words, said, "I understand the situation."

"Good," Gethen said. "I expect you to act accordingly."

"Of course."

The dockmen were in spotless livery, and as they secured the barge, the house door opened to admit an older man who wore a heavy livery collar draped across his shoulders, the silver links alternately anchor-knots and roses. The collared bird hung from its central point, the enamel bright against sober black velvet.

"Master Gethen," he said with a bow. "Master Samar."

"Sanni," Gethen said. "Master Cambryse is expecting us."

"Indeed." The majordomo bowed again. "If you'd follow me."

Either Cambryse House was larger than Samar, or it was laid out on a different axis, or possibly both. The main door opened not onto a hallway but onto shallow steps that led up into a loggia opening onto a garden courtyard. Birds were singing in half a dozen gilded cages, and a fountain spilled water into shallow stone channels; when Irichels glanced down, he saw that these were stocked with bright silver fish as long as his thumb. Someone on an upper floor was plucking idly at a cittern, and was abruptly silenced.

The majordomo led them across the courtyard, the stones underfoot worn to soft shades of blue and gray and rust, where once there had been a bright diamond pattern. Cambryse himself emerged from beneath the loggia opposite, holding out his hands. Gethen took them, and they exchanged the kiss; Cambryse did not offer the same courtesy to Irichels, who bowed instead.

"The contract is waiting." Cambryse waved toward the shadows of the loggia. "If you'll come with me, Per, we can leave Irichels to make himself agreeable to Alaissou."

"I would like a look at the contract myself," Irichels said in his mildest voice. Inwardly, he was seething—he should not be treated like a boy at his time of life—but he knew better than to show it. "I should like to know my obligations."

"That's only reasonable," Gethen said.

Cambryse shrugged. "As you will. This way, then."

The workroom opened off the loggia, a long, book-walled room not much different from the one in Samar House. The contract lay on display on the largest of the tables, the main document with the ribbons and wax laid ready, the copies to be certified beside it. At Gethen's gesture, Irichels took one of the copies into the shaft of light from the half-open shutters and skimmed through it. It was much as he'd expected, promises of maintenance and the outline of a merely nominal dowry, the naming of his children and Alaissou's as heirs to Samar, superseding any other claims. If Alaissou and he separated, he was responsible for her maintenance as well as her children's; if the separation was at his insistence, there was a fine as well, and the loss of her dowry. He skimmed through the rest, relieved to see that there was no demand that he give up Envar, and returned the paper to the table. Gethen lifted an eyebrow, and Irichels nodded.

"You should be grateful," Cambryse said bluntly. "I wanted your catamite excluded, but he said that was too much to ask."

"I appreciate your forbearance," Irichels said, and thought Gethen approved.

"Now." Cambryse looked at Gethen. "Time he spoke to Alaissou, and you and I can discuss the details. Sanni!"

The majordomo appeared almost instantly, as though he'd been waiting for the summons. "Master?"

"Take Master Samar to my daughter. I believe she's in the music room."

"Yes, Master," Sanni murmured, and beckoned to Irichels.

"This way, please."

The music room was on the corner of the house, a small room with a row of chairs lined up against the one windowless wall beneath the stylized sprays of flowers, and what looked like a copyist's stand in the center of the room. There was a small sofa as well, covered in pale brocade, and a set of shelves held monochords, a cittern and a lute, and a small virginal. A larger virginal sat on its stand between two windows, the shutters folded back to reveal translucent silk half-screens, the Cambryse cormorant stenciled on them so that they cast shaped shadows across the worn carpet. A woman was sitting on the sofa, back very straight as though she were balancing her plain cap on the top of her skull, and the girl he had seen at the party was standing beside the virginal.

"Master Samar, Dona," Sanni said, and disappeared.

"Dona Alaissou," Irichels said and bowed to Alaissou, and then to the chaperone sitting silent in the corner.

"Samar," Alaissou said. She was not as pale today as she had been at the party, though she was small and painfully thin. Someone—the girl herself?—had had the wit to dress her in plain sea-green satin, a color that showed off her red hair and made the most of her ivory complexion. Pearl-trimmed slippers showed beneath the wide legs of her trousers, and a heavy collar of pearls emphasized the length of her fragile neck.

Irichels moved cautiously closer. "I hope you don't find the situation too difficult."

"No more so than you do, I'm sure." Her voice was high and childish, but the words carried a definite sting. She hooked her hand through his elbow, turning him toward the farther wall. Irichels let her draw him on, revising his first impressions, and she looked up at him guilelessly. "Would you open the shutters, please?"

"Of course." Irichels undid the latch and folded back the wooden doors, letting in a bar of sunlight that stretched almost the length of the room. It caught a bit of metal embedded in the wood of the floor, and Irichels recognized one of the glyphs used to cast a standard circle. His attention sharpened, and he traced the rest of the circle that nearly filled that end of the room.

"It's to dampen the sound of my practice," Alaissou said.

"You're a musician, then?" Irichels's attention was still on the glyphs. Silence, certainly, but also containment, and more powerful than he would have expected.

"Yes. And a good one."

"What do you play?"

"Rebec and small vielle, for preference. But of course I can make my way on a monochord or at the virginals." Those were all professionals' instruments, and Irichels regarded her with new respect. She met his eyes gravely. "I must give you notice that I will not give up my practice."

"I see no reason that you should," Irichels answered. "There's currently no music room in Samar House, but you can choose a space that suits you."

"Thank you. That is generous."

"I suspect this is not what either of us would have chosen," Irichels said carefully, "but there's no reason we can't make things comfortable for both of us."

"I'm glad to hear you say so," Alaissou answered. She didn't look at her chaperone, still sitting bolt upright on the sofa. "Catrin is more deaf than she realizes, so she can't hear us as long as we keep our voices down. And she won't care as long as we don't do anything scandalous."

"Will she accompany you after we're married?" The word was uncomfortable on his tongue, but Irichels managed to pronounce it without stumbling.

"I would like to choose my own attendants." That was an ambiguous statement and Irichels opened his mouth to ask a clarifying question, but the door opened instead.

"Dona Alaissou, Master Samar," Sanni said. "The contract is ready for you to sign."

Alaissou looked at Irichels. "If you see anything—please don't say anything."

"See anything," Irichels said. "Such as?"

She was already walking away, the chaperone rising to cluck over her and twitch hair and tunic into more perfect shape. Irichels felt his mouth tighten but followed meekly. They were both trapped; the least he could do was give her the benefit of the doubt.

The carpet had been rolled back in Cambryse's workroom to allow the family's contract lawyer to chalk a circle around the worktable and the contract itself. Candles were lit on the table, and the pot of sealing wax was heating on the little burner; Gethen and Cambryse stood facing each other, the blue-gowned lawyer between them while an apprentice stood ready to close the circle.

"Master Samar." The lawyer bowed. "Dona Alaissou. Are you prepared to sign the contract of marriage between your persons and houses?"

Irichels couldn't help glancing at Alaissou, but she was looking straight ahead, her expression severe and unmoving. "I am."

"Dona Alaissou?"

"I am."

At least her voice was steady, Irichels thought, as he offered her his hand so they could step together into the circle. He couldn't have borne to sign the contract with a weeping bride. The lawyer bowed to both of them. "Master, Dona, have you had the chance to review the contract?"

"I have." This time it was Alaissou who spoke first, and Irichels nodded.

"I have also."

"Do you wish the provisions reviewed again?"

For a moment, Irichels was tempted to say yes, if only to annoy Cambryse who was looking impatient, but better sense prevailed. "Not I."

"Nor I," Alaissou said.

"You may close the circle," the lawyer said to his apprentice, who immediately began to fill in the last symbols. Irichels felt the air thicken, the peculiar heaviness that came when the circle was complete and the practitioner was ready to draw the attention of the Worlds Beyond. The lawyer murmured the first invocation, sealing the circle and warding it from all unfriendly forces, and then the second, calling the spirits with which his teachers had established their contract to witness and enforce the terms of this one. Irichels's skin prickled, hairs rising at the nape of his neck, and he saw the shadows of his own contracts appear like lines of ink spreading down from his wrists across the backs of his hands.

Something moved at the edge of his vision, and he glanced sideways to see shadows retreating beneath Alaissou's pearl collar. Had there been another mark across her chest? If there had been, it was gone now. At least he was sure of the mark on her neck, the sign of some contract of her own, and he wanted to kick himself for having failed to ask about her obligations. Certainly she was very young to have made any agreements, but clearly she was capable of surprising everyone. For an instant he was tempted to stop the rite, demand an explanation—but this was obviously what she'd meant there at the end, when she'd asked him not to speak. That suggested this was none of her father's doing, and he found himself unwilling to betray her to Cambryse.

"Master Samar," the lawyer said, and he dragged himself back to the moment. "You will sign and seal the contract."

Pen and ink were waiting, the latter shimmering slightly, with the odd oiliness that meant it was made with blood and bone and a touch of mercury. He dipped the pen and signed his name, then waited while the lawyer formed the wax over the first ribbon and set Samar's seal firmly in place. Alaissou signed next, adding her personal seal, and then Gethen and Cambryse placed their family seals as witnesses and patrons. The lawyer lifted his hands, calling his spirits to witness and bind, and Irichels felt the obligation wind itself around him, settling among the other contracts that bound him.

He glanced at Alaissou then and saw her sway, eyes flickering shut, but she straightened, skin paling even further. Irichels offered his hand in support—it would pass for formal acknowledgment—and she rested her hand on his as though it grounded her. The lawyer pronounced the contract complete, and then the dismissal, and the apprentice hastened to rub away the glyphs and release them from the circle.

"Well, that's done," Cambryse said and frowned at his daughter. "And you, if you're going to faint, do it elsewhere."

Alaissou looked at Irichels. "If you'll excuse me?"

"Of course." Irichels watched as she curtseyed to her father and slowly left the room. "If she is unwell—"

"She's oversensitive," Cambryse said. "You'd be wise to ignore her airs and graces, Samar, else you'll be catering to them the rest of your life. Now. We need to set the date for the marriage procession."

"As you know, I'm still establishing my household," Irichels began, "and I don't want to give your daughter any less than her due."

"My steward and staff will be happy to help with the feast," Gethen said. "And with anything else you need."

"I'll need at least five days to make ready," Irichels parried. "Even with your kind offers."

Gethen looked at Cambryse, who nodded briskly. "Five days. Then we'll have the procession to Samar House and the wedding feast. I'll send you a list of who you should invite."

Irichels nodded, and looked at Gethen. "And I trust you'll do the same."

That earned a small smile. "I will do so."

"Good." Cambryse waved to his lawyer. "And you, Dorick, make sure the contract is properly submitted."

"Of course, Master." The lawyer bowed, his apprentice busily packing up their tools behind him.

"I think I'd like to see that done myself," Gethen said. "If you'd like, I can give you a ride to the Assembly building."

"That's very kind of you, Master Gethen."

"I'll join you," Irichels said, and thought Gethen, at least, approved.

He followed Gethen and the lawyers aboard Gethen's barge, and then when they docked on the Lawgivers' Isle followed them into the Assembly building itself. They did not go up to the chambers on the second floor, but instead crossed the echoing lobby to reach the Hall of Records. There a clerk in gray robes accepted the primary copy and added the Recorder's seal to the copy that would be burned for the Court Between. The lawyer led them into the smaller chamber where a permanent circle had been inscribed around a stone replica of the Court Between's bench.

The tablets of the contract hung on the wall behind it, and a banked brazier stood ready. The apprentice fed the fire while the lawyer activated the circle, then passed a long sliver of cedar through the flame. The lawyer laid the contract on the replica of the bench, murmuring the invocation, and Irichels felt the circle close, as easy as an old lock sliding home. The lawyer touched the burning cedar to the contract, which blazed up in bright blue flames and then vanished completely: the contract was now on record among the spirits as well as in the mortal world. The lawyer spoke the Formula of Departures, and the circle collapsed as smoothly as it had closed. Gethen thanked him, slipping a small purse into his hand, and the lawyer bowed again.

"So," Gethen said, as they emerged into the lobby. "That's settled. I'll send my steward to consult with you. What else will you need to pull this off?"

"As I said to Cambryse, I'm nowhere near to having set up my household," Irichels answered. "So, people first. I may need an advance of cash for the gifts and the charity-boat. Most of Samar's income is still tied up in its investments, and I wasn't expecting to have to make such an outlay so quickly."

Gethen nodded. "My steward will be happy to loan you staff, and to advise you if you need help hiring quickly. I can certainly help with the cash, and Ambros will contribute, as a patron of your house. I'm pleased that you're taking this seriously."

"I know what I owe my house," Irichels said, and was startled to find that he meant it. "And it would be unkind to Dona Alaissou to do any less."

"She's been through hard times," Gethen said. "She was a sickly child, no one thought she'd live to marry. Her mother went to the Oratory and Cambryse remarried, got himself two fine boys in quick succession. I'm surprised he wanted this marriage, but he insisted."

"Was he trying to get the girl out of his house?" Irichels said tentatively, and Gethen shrugged.

"Or perhaps his new wife was. She's a Temenon, they tend to cling to what's theirs. I'm damned if I know."

Back at Samar House, Irichels informed Martholin of the marriage and the upcoming processional. After a token protest, the housekeeper promised she would have a list of everything needed to present to Gethen's steward. "Though you'll never have new clothes made in time, not without spending something outrageous."

"I have a gown I've not yet worn," Irichels answered, and hoped it would be good enough. "Send for the noon meal from the taverna, you've work enough on your plate."

"The day I can't feed the household and plan a reception is the day I retire," Martholin retorted, and proved her point by sending in a meal of a cheese tart with ham and olives.

Irichels shared the morning's events with Envar and Arak over the plates, and Arak frowned. "So are you married, Gil? Or is this procession the ceremony?"

"The contract is the marriage," Irichels answered. "If we were to separate now, all the provisions of the contract would be in force. But the procession and the feast is the public acknowledgment."

"It would be a shame and a scandal for a woman to move to her husband's house—or vice versa—without at least the procession," Envar said. "Even the poorest folk make a holiday of it." His tone suggested any memories were ambiguous. "What about this contract you thought you saw?"

"You know exactly as much as I do," Irichels answered.

"That will bear watching," Arak said, and Irichels had to nod.

Chapter Twelve

The next days passed in a blur of activity. Irichels refused to move Envar out of the consort's room, ordering instead that the best guest suite at the front of the house be made ready for Alaissou and her attendants. Even Martholin knew better than to protest, though she achieved her revenge by moving the nicest pieces of furniture into the new rooms. Irichels signed orders for staggering amounts of food, brought the rest of the silver out of the bank, distributed livery badges to his own household and ribbons to the people borrowed from Gethen, and tried not to wince too visibly at either the mounting costs or the contents of the guest list. At least Halyssin Ambros had agreed to take the brother's place in the ceremony, and Oredana Temenon would offer the prayers: it would have been better to have closer friends—if he had been marrying Manimere, Envar would have stood with him and no one would have dared say a word—but at least they were not active enemies.

And then at last the day arrived. Banners hung from every window of Samar House, the collared salamander coiling in flames, and the fireworks-man was ready on the roof to set off pots of colored smoke. Carpet was laid from the dock into the hall, and a garland of flowers arched over the door. Just before sunset, Cambryse's biggest barge made its way ponderously down the canal, festooned with banners and bright lanterns, a brass consort playing from the stern, the cormorant figurehead newly gilded. A flotilla of smaller boats followed, hoping for a share in the coins that would be tossed from the end of

Samar's dock, or even the scraps from the tables.

Alaissou and her parents waited amidships under a canopy of cloth-of-gold, and when the borrowed steward handed her ashore, Irichels could see that her overdress was also golden. He greeted her, his words drowned by the brass consort and the bangs from the roof as the smoke pots went off, and led her to the end of the dock where Karan and a handful of well-armed retainers supervised the boat-shaped charity chest. Irichels opened it with a flourish, seeing the boats swoop closer, and the retainers crossed their halberds in front of the chest, warding off any grasping hands. He took a handful of coins and tossed them into the nearest boats, trying to scatter them as randomly as possible. Alaissou did the same, and then reached into her sleeve to produce a small sealed purse. She flung it out into the heaving mass of boats, and a tall girl plucked it out of the air. The boy working her oar never faltered, but another boy put two fingers in his mouth to give a long shrill whistle, and Irichels saw her smile for the first time that day. He tossed another handful of coins to the crowd and stepped back to let Karan wave away the boats that had already received their share of the largesse.

"Who was that?"

Alaissou gave him a sidelong glance. "Musicians. Friends of mine."

"If I'd known, I'd have invited them to play."

"My father would not have approved."

There was no good answer to that. Irichels reached for more coin, tossed it toward the waiting boats. Alaissou did the same, and there was another flurry of movement as the crowding boats bobbed and shifted. A few more handfuls would fulfill their obligation, and the coin was the same regardless of whether it came from their hands or from Karan's. That done, he caught her hand before she could throw again and turned her toward the door, decked with a great garland of flowers. For a moment, he thought he'd offended her, but she managed a smile as he led her under the flowered arch. As she stepped into the hall, he felt the daemon gather, a thickening of shadow that made her stumble, but Irichels forced it back. He led her between the lines of bowing servants though the courtyard and into the ballroom. A dais had been set up at the end of the hall, with two chairs each beneath its house canopy, and he lifted her up the step, wishing she were Manimere. That would at least have been a bargain both sides understood.

They took their places beneath the canopies and Oredana came forward to invoke the Oratory's blessing on their newly-joined houses. It was not precisely a contract itself but it reflected the marriage contract, and Irichels felt it tug at the new strands woven into the network of his contracts. He saw Alaissou's eyes widen as though she felt the same thing, and then Oredana took the pledge-cup from a waiting servant and handed it to Alaissou. She drank and Irichels drank in turn, hearing further dull thuds from the roof as the fireworks-man ignited more smoke pots. Beyond the row of doors that looked out onto the alley the light was fading, and he could see a servant hurrying to light the next row of torches, while more servants bustled through the hall, making sure all the guests had glasses.

Oredana pronounced a final blessing and Halyssin took her place, a gilded cup in his hand. It was the traditional brother-gift, and Irichels was glad to see that it pleased him as well as he had hoped. "A toast to the union of Gilmyssin and Alaissou! We wish them health and wealth, and may they live long in harmony, secure in the sanctity of their contract and in the loving-kindness of their friends. *Salvasit!*"

The guests echoed the traditional cry, and there was another salvo from the roof. Tepan materialized from the shadows with a tray and two of Samar's best goblets, and Irichels took his gratefully. There was still the dancing to get through, but mostly he and Alaissou would spend the rest of the evening receiving congratulations and probing comments until curfew arrived. He had spent the previous evening signing several hundred excuses for his guests' use, and thought they would want them. Halyssin came to stand with them, offering smiling good wishes to Alaissou and genteel protection for both of them, and Irichels braced himself for the first of the long line of well-wishers.

The tables along the courtyard wall were heaped with food and Martholin sent servants to bring them plates, but there was never time to eat. Instead, Irichels led Alaissou through the figures of the first dance, feeling like a fairgrounds bear by comparison with her diminutive grace. Alaissou was looking pale by the end, and he brought them back to their chairs, waving away the traditionalists who would have insisted on another dance. For a moment he thought Cambryse was going to make a scene, but Ambros intercepted him, and the moment passed.

Then at last the curfew bell sounded and the last guests made their farewells, Halyssin herding them away with a wink over his shoulder and the promise to visit in the morning. Left to himself, Irichels flung himself back in his chair and reached for his glass only to find it empty. And he shouldn't drink any more until he'd had something to eat, he thought. Alaissou probably needed food, too, but he couldn't seem to make himself move. The servants were already beginning to clear, and Arak stepped out of the shadows, the jeweled salamander glittering at the base of her throat.

"You should be off to bed," she said. "I can lock up tonight."

"Thank you," Irichels said with real relief, and hauled himself to his feet. "Alaissou—"

"Master Gil." Martholin came bustling over, wiping her hands on her apron. "Dona Alaissou. Congratulations, late as they are."

"Thank you, Marthie," Irichels said, and Alaissou managed a wordless but agreeable murmur.

"I've saved a bit of the best of everything for you upstairs," Martholin said, "because I know you'll never have had a chance to eat. And there's more wine, too, and a fire and all."

Irichels stooped to kiss her cheek. "You're a life-saver, Marthie. Thank you."

"And my woman?" Alaissou asked. There had been a maid, Irichels remembered, sent over from Cambryse to supervise the fitting out of the guest room.

"Waiting for you in your room, Dona," Martholin said with a curtsey. "No harm in a bite to eat first, though."

"I am hungry," Alaissou admitted, and Irichels led her from the ballroom. The courtyard was quiet and already well on its way to being tidied, only a few plates and glasses stacked neatly on the edge of the loggia. The birds were silent, settling down to sleep, and Irichels looked up to see the moon bright beyond the glass ceiling. It occurred to him that he hadn't seen Envar all evening, and hoped he had found something to eat. What he really wanted was to share a late meal with him, but that was beyond wishing for. With the house emptying, he could feel the daemon restless again, and pushed it away. He led them up the stairs to the master's rooms, the door standing open to welcome them, and felt her hesitate at the threshold.

"This is yours?"

"It is." Irichels paused. "Marthie said she had a meal for us, and I could certainly do with something. After that—you have a suite at the front of the house that's yours."

For a moment he thought she was going to say something—probably about consummating the marriage, which he didn't actually want to think about—but then she nodded. "Yes, thanks," she said, and came warily into the room.

There were three trays on the sideboard, along with a decanter and glasses. Irichels filled one of the waiting plates with savories—tiny puffs filled with cheese and onion, miniature tarts that held a single sliver of ham or sausage, stuffed mushrooms, pastry pyramids that would be filled with peas—and took a careful bite of one of the mushrooms. The rich flavors reminded him that he was starving, and he wolfed down two more before he managed to put the plate down and move to stir the fire back to life. It blazed up under his attentions, bringing more light and driving back the night's damp. Out of the corner of his eye, he could see Alaissou helping herself to a wedge of almond tart, and in that moment of inattention, the daemon surged up and into the room.

Alaissou made a small strangled noise and dropped her tart, curse-marks darkening beneath the pearl collar that encircled her neck and rising from under the bodice of her gown. Irichels swung around, hands lifted and fingers already curled to ward it off, but he stopped himself with a painful effort. "Stop!" He put all his will into the word, and felt the daemon hesitate. "This is Samar's bride."

Blighted. Tainted.

The daemon rose further, not quite visible except as a thickening of shadow, filling the other half of the room. Blocking them from the bed, Irichels realized, power coiling violet-black in its folds like lightning buried in mountain clouds.

"Make it stop!" Alaissou cried. "Make it go away!"

Tainted. Bound.

"What is the contract?" Irichels demanded. There was no time left for subtlety. "Tell me!" The daemon rose over them like a wave, and he fought it to a stop.

Blighted. Barren. Unworthy.

"The contract!" It was taking all his strength to hold back the daemon, and he heard Alaissou sob.

"I don't know—"

"The truth!"

"This one—" She touched her breastbone above the bodice edge. "I swear, I don't know, it's always been there, as long as I can remember."

"The other?" Irichels wrestled the daemon back another foot, took a gasping breath. He heard the door open behind him, prayed it was Envar, but couldn't spare the strength to look.

"Mine." Alaissou drew herself up with desperate dignity. "It counters the other. I told you, I'm a musician. I called a demon with my music and we made a bargain. The more I play, the more it protects me."

Feral, Irichels thought. A natural talent, completely untrained—and a powerful one, to have created this. *Hold off*, he told the daemon, *stand back and let me work*. He felt it hesitate and then give way, retreating slightly. He risked a glance over his shoulder then to see Envar just inside the door, Arak behind him. She'd closed the door after them, and Irichels turned his attention back to Alaissou. "You say this first contract has always been there?"

"As long as I can remember."

Irichels moved closer, working his shoulders to push back the daemon's presence so that he could feel the parameters of the contract wound around Alaissou's chest. "Do you know what it does?"

She hesitated. "It—I think it makes me sick."

And that was, at best, unusual: the children of the Assembly houses were usually well warded against malignant contracts. Even poor parents would save their pennies for curses to protect their cradles, blue beads and braided thread to ward off wandering demons.

"Someone is not taking good care," Envar said softly, and Irichels allowed himself a nod.

"I'm going to touch you," he said, and Alaissou bowed her head. He laid his fingertips against the ridge of her collarbone, calling up the patterns he'd memorized at University. The shape was crude but strong, like the wooden yoke they put on felons in the highlands, clumsy and hindering, woven deep into the fiber of muscles and bone. It had been there a long time, the pattern warping her growth, leaving her small and thin and vulnerable, but it was crisscrossed with brighter strands, sharp and strong as wire, as tough as the strings of a vielle. They wound through the older curse, here pulling back a section that wanted to close like a vise on the liver, there tangling two sections so that they contradicted each other, in several places supporting an old injury, and always constraining what had been done. The demon who wove it hadn't been very strong, but it had been clever, or well-guided. "Your contract. What does it do?"

Alaissou took a deep breath, her chest heaving under his touch. "I learned a summoning song, and when it came, I told it I wanted to be well again. The one thing I had that was my own was the music, so as long as I practice, this contract pushes back on the other one, counterpoises it. The longer I play, the more effective it is. I'm not nearly as sick as I was."

"Yes." Irichels lifted his hand and turned his attention to the daemon, which had retreated further in what felt like confusion. *It's not her fault*, he told it. *She's fought this well, she has earned our respect.*

Barren. Blighted. This time the words carried grief, not anger.

Perhaps not. Give me time.

There was a pause, a moment of stillness, and then the daemon vanished, whisking back to its place beneath the stones. Alaissou caught her breath in a sound that might almost have been a sob, then stooped to retrieve her shattered piece of tart.

"You're as feral as I am," Envar said with delight, and she turned, startled, only to blush as she realized who he must be. "Sister! That's clever work, Gil."

"It is," Irichels agreed. "What teaching did you have?"

Alaissou's blush deepened. "I read some books."

"Very clever," Envar said, and Irichels nodded in agreement.

Alaissou hesitated. "When I got better—better at summoning and shaping, and feeling better, too—I tried to get rid of it entirely, but I couldn't figure out how. You're a cursebreaker. Can you?"

Irichels closed his eyes, remembering weight and structure. "Maybe. I'll need time to study it. To figure out what exactly it is, and how not to interfere too much with your contract—I assume you don't want to alter that?"

"I'd rather not," Alaissou admitted. "It's made my music better."

"That'll take time," Irichels said again. "And now is not the night to begin, I think." He looked past her to Envar, who nodded.

"Since all's well, I'll excuse myself," he said. "But—Gil, we should all talk in the morning."

He was right, there were any number of questions to be answered, Irichels thought, from the nature of Alaissou's original curse to how she had maintained her contract to whether the daemon was right when he called her barren. "Yes, of course," he said, and the others withdrew. He took a breath. "You should sleep here tonight. It's expected. But I won't—there's no need to consummate the marriage tonight. I'll sleep on the couch."

Alaissou glanced over her shoulder, the high spots of color vivid in her cheeks. "The bed is big enough. Let's not disappoint your daemon any more than I already have."

There wasn't much to say to that. Irichels refilled their cups and chose another plate of little treats, then came to sit by the fire. He was tired and still hungry, and for a moment he let himself concentrate on the food and the fire, hunching his shoulders against the chill that came from wrangling contracts on an empty stomach. He rested his head against the sofa's high side, half hypnotized by the flames, and Alaissou said, "I'll go change. Then I'll be back."

"Yes." He knew he should get up and change into his own nightshirt, but it felt so good to rest. He wished again that he would be sleeping with Envar—and he still could, of course, he could slip away into the spouse's bedroom and leave the master's room for Alaissou and for an instant he almost had the strength to do it. But it would be unkind to leave her without an explanation, and he shifted against the sofa's cushions. They would have to consummate the marriage at some point, but this was not the night.

The door opened, and he hauled himself to his feet to find Alaissou standing just inside the doorway, a rawboned, gray-haired woman at her back. She had discarded the cloth-of-gold for sheer linen and trimmings of lace as wide as a man's hand, with a wrapper of pale peach silk over it: suitable wear for a young bride but embarrassing to both of them, judging by the color still standing high on her cheeks. The maid gave him a disapproving glance—he should, of course, be ready to receive his bride—but Irichels met her eyes squarely. "Thank you. Good night."

For a moment, he thought she was going to ignore him, but Alaissou managed a smile for her. "Yes, good night, Barabal."

She sniffed loudly, but made a reluctant curtsey. "Good night, Dona," she said, and closed the door behind her.

"I'm sorry," Irichels said. "This—I doubt it's what you wanted."

"No more than you did," Alaissou answered. "And I am tired."

Irichels nodded. "The bath is through there," he said, pointing to the painted door, "and next to it is the dressing room." He paused. "I usually sleep on the left side." He went on into the dressing room without waiting for her answer. The unshuttered window looked out on the water alley, bright in the setting moon; the wall of the building opposite turned a blind face to the house, plain pale stucco from waterline to roof. He had no idea what was appropriate for a bridegroom, settled instead for the nightshirt with the fewest patches, and a loose wrapper over that. Alaissou had doused most of the candles; he called up a wisp and snuffed the last branch of candles, then shed the wrapper and climbed into the cold sheets. He ought to say something, he thought, but fell asleep before he could think what.

He woke late and alone, and lay for a moment listening to the distant shouts of boatmen from the canal before he could drag himself out of bed. There was no sign Alaissou had ever been there, and he slipped through the secret passage before he could change his mind. Envar was sitting at the table he'd had brought up from a lower room, several books spread open in front of him, but he looked up with a smile as he heard the latch open. "Good morning."

"And to you." Irichels came to join him, and Envar leaned back to look up at him, letting his head rest against Irichels's ribs. Irichels allowed himself a sigh—he hadn't realized until that moment how afraid he'd been that things would change—and rested his hand on Envar's shoulder. "What's all this?"

"She's clever, the little sister," Envar answered. "I wanted to work out how she'd arranged her contract, with nothing more than a book of summoning songs to go on, and she's put it together very neatly. She's not very strong, nor was the demon she called, but they leveraged what they had as well as anyone could have done."

"You're sure she did it herself?"

"You have a reason to doubt her?"

Irichels shook his head. "No more than I'm doubting everything about the situation."

Envar gave a wry smile. "I suppose there's that. But, no, I think it's her work alone, hers and the demon's. Otherwise I doubt it would be tied so thoroughly to her music."

That made sense, and Irichels nodded. "What's required?"

"For her to practice daily," Envar answered. "Or as near to daily as possible. She and Marthie were talking at breakfast about turning one of the rooms in that guest suite into a practice room. Or maybe one of the bedrooms overlooking the canal."

"Whichever she'd prefer," Irichels said. "A room with a window, surely."

"One would think." Envar looked back at his books. "Will you attempt to break it?"

"The original curse?" Envar nodded. "Up to her, of course." Irichels found the second chair and seated himself. Envar pushed the kaf pot toward him, and Irichels filled the emptied cup. For a moment, it was like every morning they had shared, from the Bitter Sea to the hills of Bellem, and he wished he had never come back to Bejanth. It was too late for that regret, and he focused on the question at hand. "From what I've seen, it would be a tricky business, particularly since she wants to preserve her own curse—it improves her music," he added, and Envar nodded again. "Her work is unorthodox but solid. I'm inclined to leave it alone for now."

"I agree," Envar said. "And it buys us time." Irichels raised an eyebrow. "If the whole point of this is to weaken or destroy Samar, they have to wait until there's a child, yes?

And even if you quicken her on the first try, which isn't likely, there's still nine months before the child is born."

"True enough," Irichels said. "I wish—I want to find out what I can about Manimere."

"I may be able to ask some questions," Envar said.

"Thank you."

"We also ought to inquire of the Oratory," Envar went on. "Whatever was wrong with Debes—that's part of this, I'm sure of it."

"I'll write Oredana," Irichels said. "I owe her a nice note anyway. And Hal, too."

Before he could say anything more, there was a knock at the door. Envar looked over his shoulder. "Yes, come in?"

The door opened to reveal Tepan, who managed a jerky bow. "I'm sorry to disturb you, but Dona Alaissou says her mother's here and you should please come down."

"That's not me," Envar said, and Irichels sighed.

"Tell Dona Alaissou that I'm just dressing. I'll be down directly."

"Yes, Master." Tepan bowed again and disappeared.

"Wear something nice," Envar said with a wry smile, and Irichels sighed again.

"Only the best for my mother-in-law." It was his second-best gown, actually, expensive Bellem wool in a rich, deep brown a shade darker than his eyes, trimmed with matching silk braid that required a second glance to recognize its intricacies and its worth. He hoped it made him look younger and less like a thug, but as soon as he came into the family parlor he realized his mistake.

The table had been cleared and set to one side, and Alaissou and her stepmother sat facing each other in front of the empty fireplace. A kaf service sat on the small table between them—Irichels recognized his grandfather's guest set with its blue glaze and gold trimmings—and Arak stood very straight behind Alaissou's chair. Dona Cambryse had brought her own escort, an elderly maid who sat against the wall behind her, busy with her spindle. They were both in carefully informal tunics and wide trousers, and the whole tableau had the look of a scene from a melodrama, the barbarian's child bride facing down the representative of true justice. Irichels put on a polite smile and came to join them, bowing to Cambryse's consort.

"A pleasure, Dona. To what do we owe the honor?"

"I've come to see how my daughter is adjusting to her change of station."

"I don't believe you've met my stepmother, Gil," Alaissou interposed. "May I present Seresinha Temenon, Dona Cambryse? She has raised me since I was a child."

"Honored," Irichels said with another bow, and Seresinha extended a graceful hand for him to kiss. He complied and came to lean on Alaissou's chair, hoping to look possessive. Alaissou smiled up at him.

"I'm glad to see that the experience wasn't too much for you," Seresinha said, and Irichels saw Alaissou blush.

"I have no complaints," she said.

"I am very glad to hear it," Seresinha answered. She gave no signal that Irichels could see, but the maid abruptly stopped her spinning, winding the thread neatly onto the spindle. Seresinha rose gracefully to her feet. "Alaissou, I have no desire to keep you from your day. Now that I know you're well, I'll leave you to your husband."

"Very kind," Alaissou murmured, rising with her. They walked in a group to the canal door, where a large Cambryse punt was drawn up against the dock, gilded livery gleaming in the sun. Across the canal, Irichels could see people gathered in their windows and along the walks, enjoying the show. *Very well*, he thought, *we'll do this properly*, and offered his arm to Seresinha. She took it, looking up at him from under long lashes.

"I hope you won't take it amiss," she said, "but you should know that Alaissou has always been a fragile child. I know you'll take due care of her."

"I assure you," Irichels said. The words touched him on the raw, and he added, "I have some hope I may be able to restore her health, with time."

Her eyes flicked up at him, and then away. "Idra send her blessing. I would be glad to see her well."

"As would we all," Irichels answered, and handed her into the punt. The maid hurried after, adjusting Seresinha's cushions as she settled in the seats at the stern, and the oarsman poled away. Irichels watched them go, aware of the faces still watching, and only turned away once they were out of sight. Alaissou was waiting in the doorway, Arak at her side.

"I'm sorry," she began, and Irichels shook his head.

"No need."

"She would try to get all the details," Alaissou said, ducking back into the hall. "She's not even my mother."

"We can find a way for you to avoid her," Irichels said.

Alaissou sighed and shook her head. "That would probably be worse. No, I'll just keep ignoring her. There's breakfast left, if you want it." Irichels accepted the change of subject, and let himself be steered away.

CHAPTER THIRTEEN

The next few days were spent sorting out the aftermath of the reception—returning servants and borrowed goods and drawing cash from various accounts to pay back Gellis Ambros. The bulk of the silver went back to the bank, though Irichels kept enough to host a respectable dinner, and Envar slipped out on various errands while Irichels wrote the necessary letters of thanks and drafted a request for Oredana. Alaissou took over one of the second floor guest rooms above the dock and Irichels inscribed a permanent circle for her, ostensibly to damp the sound of her practice, but also to allow her to work her magic. The sounds of rebec and vielle spilled out occasionally anyway, and Irichels found he liked their presence. The high constable withdrew his men, though Envar reported that the house was still watched, and life returned to something more like normal.

He and Envar lingered over a late lunch, the faint sounds of a vielle drifting down from above while Arak ran through her exercises in the courtyard, and Irichels found himself wishing that the seeming peace was real. But it wasn't, and he couldn't risk believing that it was, and he carved a last sliver of meat off the roasted chicken. "Any news of Manimere?"

"Nothing of significance," Envar answered. He was still in the worn, unobtrusive clothes he wore when he went in search of news, and Irichels could feel the curses that clung to them, inactive here in the house, but ready, diverting eye and ear and blurring memory. "She's not been caught, though supposedly the city fleet caught sight of her pennon two days ago, and sent a patrol out after her. They've not returned, and there's a certain smug pleasure circling round the docks. Manimere and her captains paid well and treated their people fairly, and no one seems sorry that the city captains are showing poorly. Nothing more than that, though, at least not in the circles I know." He paused. "There is a new tune making the rounds, with a chorus of 'strike the bell'. I can't make much sense of it, but the ones who sing it seem to dodge the city sailors. I don't know so many people on the docks."

"Ask Alaissou," Irichels suggested, and Envar nodded.

"I'd thought of that. At least you can tell the boy there's no bad news."

"I'm glad of that."

"So am I," Envar said. "You'll need to figure out what to do with him, my heart. The longer he passes for yours, the more dangerous it is for him."

"I know. But he'll be safer passing as Samar for at least a little while longer." Irichels looked up as the door opened, admitting Tepan.

"Beg pardon, Master, but there's a letter from the Oratory. You said I should bring it right away."

"Yes, thanks." Irichels took the folded paper and broke the seal, scanning the elegant formal hand. "Finally. Oredana says she can get me an interview with the Oratorian who ruled on Debes's case."

"That may be very helpful," Envar said. "Do you go by yourself, or do you want to make a party of it? You're still being watched, you know."

"I know. Let me think. I don't suppose you'd come with me?"

"I'd rather not draw the attention," Envar said, and Irichels nodded. Ferals generally stayed away from the Scholastica, and the Oratorians turned a blind eye to their presence on the other islands.

"I'll take Arak, then." Irichels glanced at the paper. "They'll see me tomorrow afternoon."

It was easier to walk to the Scholastica than to go by boat. Envar accompanied them as far as the edges of the Palinade, then vanished into its depths in search of someone who might know more about Manimere. They would meet afterward at a kaf house at the foot of the Middle Bridge, and Irichels hoped they would all have news to share.

The Oratory was less built-up than most of the other islands. Even the crowded streets of the Scholastica were punctuated with pocket gardens, and nearly every house had garden boxes at the windows or curtains of vines running up the sunnier walls. Arak eyed them thoughtfully, obviously considering the amount of weight they'd bear, and Irichels was grateful that she made no comment. But then, even Arak had to be able to feel the curses that protected these houses, the intricate lacework that bound them one to another and to the Oratory above all. He could hardly blame Envar for wanting to stay clear of their tendrils.

The twin bell towers of Idra Redeemer rose above the rooftops, and he steered toward them, following the wide avenues. The Oratory had fewer canals, too, and they didn't enter the Scholastica; it felt strange to see so many people on foot and to hear no sound of water, and Irichels was surprised to realize how quickly he'd adjusted to the city.

They passed under the arched Southgate into the immaculately tended lawn that surrounded Idra Redeemer. The white stone gleamed in the afternoon sun, and the dome's gilded ribs looked almost molten in the strong light. It was the oldest of the oratories, older even than Idra Mistress of the World on Lawgivers' Isle, and Irichels could feel the presence within the walls, strong and serene and as indifferent as the stone that contained it. There were curses, too, though the Oratorians wouldn't call them that, woven into the stone and the ground beneath and reaching up toward the zenith, a delicate web surrounding the central building, containing and enhancing its power.

Oredana was waiting on the steps of Academicians, her hands folded in her wide sleeves, the red of her gown clashing with the ruddy brick. Irichels made his best bow and she offered her hands, but her smile was forced. "My apologies for the formality, Irichels, but my brother is being a nuisance."

"That would be him watching?" Arak asked. "From the gray building over there?"

It took most of Irichels's self control not to look. Oredana nodded. "In the doorway of Memories, yes. He's making himself ridiculous. But that's not your problem."

Not unless he makes it mine. Irichels swallowed the words and bowed again. "I'm sorry to have caused you difficulties."

"No, what you're asking is entirely reasonable, and I'm glad to help." Oredana turned, leading them up the stairs. "My brother is a fool."

Irichels followed her up the stairs and into the dimly lit lobby. Once inside, he couldn't resist looking back. Sure enough, three men had come out from under the pillared portico of the building called Memories, one in fine clothes and the other two in the red-and-white Temenon livery. Arak gave him an eloquent look and Irichels nodded back: best to walk carefully on the way home.

Another Oratorian in red was waiting for them on the far side of the lobby, a short, round man with thinning gray hair and a deceptively mild smile. Oredana bent her head in acknowledgment, and gestured to the people at her side. "Brother Leonor. May I present Irichels di Samar? He's here to inquire about his kinsman Debes. Also Arak min'Aroi. Brother Leonor had charge of the case in question."

Irichels made his most respectful bow, feeling his own curses flare and tighten as he came within arm's reach of the Oratorian. Not just a teacher or even one of the technicians who were the Oratorians' own cursebreakers, but a searcher and an exorcist, one of that elite group trained to find and vanquish those unfortunates who'd succumbed to a demon's power. He saw Leonor's expression flicker as he assessed

Irichels's bonds, and was profoundly grateful Envar had stayed away.

"I won't say it's a pleasure to meet you, Master, not under these circumstances," Leonor said, "but I am glad to have the chance to speak with you. Perhaps you would care to come into my workroom? We can have kaf, and speak privately."

"Thank you, Brother," Irichels said. His skin crawled at the thought of entering a closed space with the man, but he controlled himself rigidly.

"Then I will leave you here," Oredana said, "and have a word with my brother. Give my regards to Hal when next you see him."

"Of course," Irichels said, bowing, then turned to follow Leonor.

The workroom was small and plainly furnished but pleasant, smelling strongly of beeswax and lavender. A servant was setting up a kaf service, taking delicate painted cups down from a place of honor; she set them in a shaft of sunlight where their colors glowed like jewels, then curtseyed silently and let herself out, closing the door behind her.

"Please, Master," Leonor said, waving Irichels toward the table. "And you, Messida?"

"Thank you, no," Arak murmured.

Irichels filled his own cup, adding the condiments in tiny spoonfuls: candied orange peel, cardamom, coarse crystals of honey. Leonor did the same and led him to the chairs that waited in the shadows. "I had hoped to speak again with someone from Samar. I was never satisfied about that matter."

Irichels managed to keep his hands steady as he sipped the kaf. It was perfectly made, as he had expected, but this was clearly not the moment for social compliments. "That wasn't the impression I had from the report the house received."

"Mine was the minority view."

Irichels said carefully, "The majority held that Debes's death was an unfortunate accident, unrelated to the concerns that had caused my uncle to send him to your care."

"I believe we were mistaken." Leonor set his cup aside.

"What were you told of this?"

"I was told nothing," Irichels said. "I was not expected to inherit—all Bejanth knows the story. All I know is what I read in the Oratory's report to my uncle Galeran." He paused. "And one or two things I was told by an old servant of the house. Thus I come to you."

"The boy Debes was first brought to our attention when he was twelve," Leonor said. "His father said he had shown signs of a mage's talent, and asked us to examine him. A brother was sent, and he reported that Master Galeran was correct. I believe there has always been a strain of talent among the Samar." He smiled politely, and Irichels bowed in acknowledgment. "He recommended that Debes join one of the Academies—I believe you yourself attended one?"

"Yes."

"Just so. It was presumed that would resolve the matter."

"I haven't found any record of this visit," Irichels said.

"Quite probably not," Leonor answered. "It was handled as a favor rather than as a matter of real concern. I regret to say that happens too often, when a family of importance is involved. And, to be fair, nine times out of ten no harm's done."

"But this was the tenth," Irichels said.

Leonor bent his head. "Just so. The boy behaved himself at the Academy and before his father, but he couldn't resist tormenting the weakest of the household's servants. Finally he went too far, and left injuries that couldn't be explained away. The cook brought the girl to Idra-in-Chains, and I was sent to speak to Master Galeran. The boy did his best to hide what he was, but he was still young. I was able to show that he was a cursling, fully acquiescent in what he had become, and Master Galeran gave him into our custody."

Irichels couldn't repress a shiver. Even believing Martholin, even agreeing with the verdict, the idea of being handed over to the Oratory had been—was still—one of his oldest nightmares, one of the weapons in the long battle between his mother and his grandfather. He knew Leonor had seen, but the Oratorian's expression was sympathetic. "I had some of the story from Marthie—the cook you mentioned. She said he made a maid dance until her feet bled."

Leonor nodded. "The woman's testimony was conclusive for all of us, including to the family. I take it she was well known to everyone?"

"She was with us as long as I can remember," Irichels answered. "Even my grandfather respected her—and listened to her, which is more to the point. Even in his day, she kept the kitchen accounts."

"I wondered at the time," Leonor said. "Usually it's not so clear when the servant is telling the family a thing they haven't wanted to admit they see."

It was unexpected honesty, and Irichels found himself answering in kind. "She's a good woman, kind and generous. She'd never lie, not about a thing like this. And from everything I've read, Uncle Galeran must have had some concerns already."

"The sister's death, you mean?" Leonor reached for his kaf again, but his expression was intent. "You weren't there yourself then."

"I went to the University in Tarehan before my grandfather died." Irichels smiled. "I'd lay money neither my name nor my mother's was mentioned when you dealt with the family."

"You'd be right, but only on a technicality." Leonor returned the smile. "Master Galeran said there was a nephew who had shown talent and had gone away to study. I always wondered what had happened there."

Irichels kept his smile steady. He had no particular desire to let Leonor probe further, but at the same time he couldn't afford to draw too much attention. "My mother married against her father's wishes. She was a teaching preceptress in the royal household in Bellem, and left the Oratory to become a third-rank wife of the tarmynor of Cal'Innis, Ystelas min'Yver. He died when I was four, and my mother brought me back to Bejanth with her. Grandfather did not approve, and he made it clear I wasn't really part of the family."

"But the marriage was legal," Leonor said.

"Under canon and civil law and in every city and kingdom, or I wouldn't be here," Irichels answered. "But we were speaking of Debes."

"Of course. My apologies, curiosity is my besetting sin. What more can I tell you?"

"The document sent to Galeran said that he had been possessed, and his death was an unfortunate accident," Irichels said. "But you said he was a cursling. As far as I know, there's no cure for that."

Leonor's expression hardened. "Misplaced consideration. Samar—Galeran had lost all his children and was ill himself. It was decided that the simplest explanation was the best. But the boy was a cursling. I am certain of that."

Irichels nodded slowly. "And what did the Oratory plan for him, seeing he couldn't be cured? He could never be allowed to inherit."

"There are provisions here for housing such souls," Leonor said. "Ones such as he, possessed at birth or even before, cannot be said to be at fault for what they do, any more than a sanderling can be arraigned for murder. But nor can they live among ordinary people. We keep them within the towers of the Scholastica, where we can prevent them from harming anyone. Some can, with care and effort, be taught to abstain from harm and do a few useful things, and we count them our successes. The rest..." He sighed. "We do what we can. They are fed and housed and cared for as best we can. Idra be praised, there are never many of them. There are many things that look like curslings, but are comparatively harmless."

"And you're certain Debes was one?"

"I'm sorry. There was no question. And had there been doubt, his death would have confirmed it."

"Oh?"

"Idra's bells are holy, and they are also bound and spelled to protect the city, both the bells of the oratories and the bells of the watchtowers. They will strike a cursling who comes too close to their presence."

"I understood that he hanged himself," Irichels said.

"The bells took him," Leonor said. "As is their purpose."

Irichels had expected that answer. "He was a cursling from birth, you said?"

Leonor nodded. "Every indication pointed that way. It happens, if rarely—sheer mischance, no blame to your family." He hesitated. "Though—if you'll forgive my speaking frankly?"

"That's why I'm here."

"Your grandfather—by all accounts, he was a difficult man, and one who had wound himself into a tangle of obligations by the time he died. That can open doors." Leonor fixed him with a sudden sharp stare. "I wonder if you have any insight into that."

"I don't," Irichels said. "I hadn't considered it." But it might make sense, might fit with the reading Zaffara had done: not something he wanted to say to Leonor, and he schooled his expression to show only surprise.

"You've seen nothing since you've taken over?" Leonor asked.

"Grandfather died twenty-three years ago," Irichels answered. "Galeran was master longest, but there were two more uncles and an aunt who held the title before it came to me. And I was raised believing I would have no inheritance. I've barely made my way through Galeran's records, never mind Grandfather's."

"If you would like my advice," Leonor began, and Irichels spread his hands.

"Please. It's what I've come for."

"I would look into your grandfather's affairs. It may be nothing, of course, but that seemed the most likely place that a cursling could find a foothold."

"Thank you." Irichels nodded. "I will bear that in mind."

"One other thing," Leonor said, and there was a new hard note in his voice. "I can tell that your own contracts are solid and maintained as they should be, and I am glad. Curslings are a rare danger; much more common—and more dangerous—are the ferals who refuse to bind themselves to any tested Rule. They cannot be tolerated."

"That's a change for Bejanth," Irichels said cautiously.

"A necessary one," Leonor said. "We—the Oratory, Senate and Assembly—have been too tolerant for too long. The tangle of contracts and outright curses that muddy our waters must be resolved for the sake of the city. Every new layer of magic, every new contract, only makes the situation worse. It cannot continue." He stopped, and managed a wry smile. "And I do know that there are good people who have not submitted to Rule, but they must, before it's too late."

Irichels dipped his head. He understood the message all too clearly: if he wanted to protect Envar, persuade him to accept a Rule. Envar would never do it, and Irichels would never ask. "I'll bear that in mind," he said aloud.

"That's all anyone can ask," Leonor said.

They walked back across Oratory in silence, aiming for the Middle Bridge and their rendezvous beyond it. There was no sign of Margos Temenon, and Irichels hoped the man had given up and gone home long before. The sun had sunk below the rooftops, and the usual thin evening clouds were sweeping in from the east. The Middle Bridge loomed ahead of them, a high arch better suited to pedestrians than the Cart Bridge to the west, and they joined the crowd flowing back toward the Palinade. The shops were beginning to close, hawkers crying last minute bargains while beggars clustered in search of discards, and someone was tuning a rebec in a tavern while a boy swept the day's debris into the gutters.

Envar was waiting as promised, tucked into the corner of a rundown kaf house, a service already in front of him along with a stack of twice-baked fruit breads. He lifted a hand, seeing them, two fingers curled in the old signal that all was well, and Irichels slid into the seat next to him. Arak took the corner, where she had her back to the wall and a clear view of the entire room, and Envar gave her a curious look.

"Expecting trouble?"

"Margos Temenon was at the oratory," Arak said. "He was gone when we left, but..." She let the words trail off, and Envar nodded.

"A lovely creature. What did you do to him, Gil, steal his schoolbooks?"

"Our paths never crossed," Irichels answered. "I didn't even know he existed. Did you have any luck?"

"Some." Envar filled their cups, and Irichels added condiments to his cup. It wasn't as good as the kaf he had been served at the oratory, but he felt safer drinking it. "Manimere is definitely well, and her fleet's been seen outside the bay. There's a whisper that she's sent agents back to the city by landing them at Teller's Point, but that's so specific, I think it's distraction." Irichels nodded.

"But she certainly is getting agents in," Envar continued. "A man brushed up against me in the crowd, and left me with a note under her sign." His hand moved beneath the table, and Irichels accepted the rolled bit of paper. It looked like the sort of fortune you bought from a bottle-woman, and Irichels made himself unfold it with the same idle curiosity. The writing was in a bland, untraceable secretarial hand: *Keep the boy a little longer,* and an elaborately drawn M.

"Her mark?" Irichels twisted the slip of paper into a long spill and held it in the flame that heated the kaf pot.

"Oh, yes."

"Well. Easily enough done." The paper had burned out; Irichels crushed the ashes to nothing.

"Good to know she can reach you," Arak said.

"There's also a rumor that she's raising ships to blockade the city," Envar said, "but I think that's just a rumor."

It was probably the thing that the Senate and Assembly feared most, Irichels thought, but it would also be almost impossible to pull off. "We'll keep an ear out anyway. And I won't be investing in any trading ventures."

Envar laughed. "Probably best to be conservative, my

heart." He poured himself another cup of kaf, added a heaping spoonful of coarse sugar. "Did you get what you wanted?"

"Some information, at least," Irichels said. "I spoke to the searcher who managed the case."

"A dangerous man," Arak said.

Envar gave her a sharp look, and Irichels said reluctantly, "He's opposed to ferals."

"Most searchers are," Envar said.

"More than most, I'd say," Arak said.

Irichels nodded. "He's one of the ones who wants to bring order to everything. Everything should be under a Rule."

"Then we'd best stay clear of him." Envar's voice was not as light as his words. "And the boy?"

"Leonor said he was a cursling from birth," Irichels said, "and blamed it on some contract of my grandfather's."

"Interesting," Envar said. "That would fit with the reading."

"I thought so, too," Irichels said.

"I wonder if your daemon might be of any help."

"How?" Irichels asked, and Envar shrugged.

"A cursling must have challenged it, upset it—surely there's some way to tell?"

"Maybe." Irichels knew he sounded doubtful. "I'll see if I can figure out some way to ask, or at least see if there are any indications in the records. I've been spending most of my time looking at Galeran's business, but I can certainly look further back. The records all seem to be there."

"I'll help if I can," Envar said.

"Believe me, I'll let you." Irichels paused. "It's not just Leonor pushing to bring everyone under Rule, he's got support in the Senate and Assembly. This makes it more important that you get your contracts renewed."

"I know."

"Did you have a plan?" Arak asked.

Envar gave her an annoyed glance. "There are always options—always places the Court meets that are outside the Oratory's notice."

"I'm not sure that's such a good idea this year," Irichels said.

"I know," Envar said again. "I'd also considered going to the Plana."

"You shouldn't go alone," Irichels said. "And I'm not sure I'd be allowed to go with you. I could send Arak—"

"That would be ill-advised," Arak said, and Envar nodded.

"Arak's right, my heart, you're hardly safe right now. Anyway, there are a lot of places where the Court can be called. The Oratory can't watch all of them."

"We hope," Arak said.

"How much support does this Leonor actually have?" Envar asked. "The Senate and Assembly always say they want to bring everyone under Rule, but they don't generally mean it."

"It sounded serious, but I can't be entirely sure," Irichels said. "I'll see if Hal can find out."

"That's a thought," Envar said. "Then we can decide what to do."

They finished the kaf pot and the rest of the fruitbreads, and made their way back out into the emptying streets. It was heavy twilight now, the first stars showing against the purple sky with its wisps of cloud, and the street lamps were mostly lit. The shortest way led through the Palinade, but by mutual agreement they took the longer route, skirting the now-closed Palinade Market and following the course of the Saltan Canal. Irichels could see the lanterns at the foot of the Barnaban Bridge, and said, "Almost home."

"Someone's following us," Arak said.

"You're sure?" Envar didn't look back but his right hand curled, and Irichels felt the tug of energies as he prepared a cantrip.

Arak didn't bother with a direct answer. "Four of them, maybe six? Behind us and in the alley."

Irichels swallowed a curse of his own. 'In the alley' meant they were cut off from the Palinade, trapped with the canal at their back. He looked toward the bridge, and saw three more figures gathered at its foot. "I don't think they're friendly either."

"No." Arak's hand was close to the hilt of her sword, but she didn't draw or change her steady pace. "Is there a boat?"

"Two tied up at the next bollard," Envar said. "Little ones."

That wasn't much help, and the next bollard was a dozen yards away. Once in the boat, Irichels thought, he and Envar could shield them—and shield the hull—but Arak was no sailor. Still, it was better than holding off nine or more, might buy time for someone to call the constables. On the edges of the Palinade it was even odds whether anyone would try, but it was better than nothing. "Go for the boats."

They kept walking, hearing the footsteps closer now. Irichels reached for his own contracts, preparing cantrips for attack and defense, and saw the men at the foot of the bridge move slowly toward them. Ten steps, twenty...they had covered half the distance to the boats when a pair of men stepped out from between two tall houses, steel gleaming in their hands. Envar unleashed his first cantrip, a blaze of blue light intended to blind as well as stun, and Arak swung around, drawing her sword and countering the first attack in a single smooth movement.

Irichels spared a glance for the men by the bridge—starting toward them, still too far off—and slung a cantrip across the stones. In its wake the shadows took on substance, writhing like vines to catch the attackers' ankles, and two of them went down, the shadows rolling over them. He turned to face the men from the bridge, reaching for another cantrip, and saw almost too late that one of them held a crossbow. He slammed his shield into place, both hands crooked to catch the bolt, and the force of it struck him in the solar plexus, flinging him backward. He fought for breath, aware of nothing but the pain and the struggle to breathe. Light flared, Envar again, and Arak shouted something unintelligible, metal clashing on metal. Irichels knew he needed to get to his feet, needed to help, but he only managed to get to one knee before someone caught him under the shoulder.

"Go," Envar said, and there was a rumble of stone on stone as a paving stone rose in the air and shattered. Irichels saw him direct the debris with a sweeping gesture, and then Arak bundled him over the edge of the canal and into the battered boat that was tied up there. Irichels crouched in the bottom of the boat, automatically balancing on the center line, while Arak reached for the mooring line, ready to cut them loose.

"Envar!" There was a hiss and a shiver and the air filled suddenly with clouds of dust, enough to send Irichels back into a paroxysm of choking. Envar dropped into the boat beside him and Arak cut them free, the boat wobbling dangerously before she got it done.

"Sit down, in Idra's name!" Envar said furiously, and the swordswoman obeyed. Envar found the boatman's oar and dug deep, speeding them toward the bridge.

"Bowman," Arak said, and Envar released one hand to shape a shield of his own. Irichels heard the snap of the spring and Envar's grunt as he absorbed the energy, and then Arak flung one of her knives and sank back into the bottom of the boat. Ahead, the canal swung south, and Envar steered them around the corner, picking up speed with every stroke of the oar.

"Gil." Arak crawled toward him, and Irichels managed to straighten, both fists still thrust hard against the point of his breastbone. "Gil, are you all right? Let me see."

Irichels tried to speak, but it was all he could do to breathe at all. Arak reached for him, pried his hand away, and sat back with a sigh of relief. "It's just the wind knocked out of him. He's all right."

"Idra's mercy." Envar's voice was very quiet. "Right. We're clean away, I think—"

"It looks that way," Arak agreed. "How much trouble will there be over bodies in the street?"

"More trouble over the magic," Envar said. "But we got away clean."

Irichels struggled to sit up, and Arak supported him until he could brace himself against the side of the boat. His breath was coming easier now, no longer whooping in his throat, and he said, "Did you see who?"

The words were rasping but clear. Arak said, "Two of them were in red and white, so—Temenon, I'd guess."

"I saw—" Envar paused, leaning hard on the oar to turn them into a narrow cut that would bring them back to Samar by the quickest route. "I would swear I saw Cambryse's badge on one of them."

Neither one made any sense, Irichels thought. No matter how jealous Margos Temenon might be of his sister's honor, it had been very clear that they had no business with her— she had left as soon as they met with Leonor. And Cambryse had wanted him to marry Alaissou badly enough to force the wedding. What possible purpose could it serve to kill him before Alaissou had borne a child? Now that he could breathe again, his hands and his chest were throbbing from the effort of stopping the bolt, making it hard to think. "We should use this," he managed, and Arak frowned.

"Use it?"

"The ones who got away," Irichels said. "They couldn't see how badly I was hurt."

"All they saw was us dragging you into the boat," Envar said. "I begin to see what you're after, my heart."

"Let them think it's worse than it is," Irichels said. "Carry me into the house and put me to bed, and see what happens."

"A good thought," Arak said.

Irichels nodded and let himself sink back against the unpadded seat. His trousers and gown were wet, and dark enough that they would only show an indeterminate stain: he would make a suitably pitiful figure carried into the house. It was definitely worth the attempt.

Chapter Fourteen

Irichels lay back in the boat as they approached the house, feeling Arak shift to support him. "Let me do the talking," Arak said, and Envar gave a shaky nod.

"Hail the house, then."

"Karan!" Arak raised her voice. "Ay, Samar! Karan!"

There was a noise from the dock and then the sound of the door opening, and Irichels closed his eyes, letting himself lie boneless. There was a babble of voices, Arak's rising above the rest to give orders, and then he was lifted from the boat and carried awkwardly through the hall and up the stairs into his own bedroom. They laid him gently on the enormous bed, and he heard Arak herding the servants out again. Envar's hand closed on his, and he dared to peek out under his lashes. "They're gone," Envar said. "Alaissou is coming."

And there was the first question: to trust her or not? Irichels propped himself up on one elbow, wincing at the pain in his ribs. "She'll have to know. And Marthie."

Envar looked as though he might have protested, but Arak came to join him. "Agreed. I've sent Karan to deal with the boat. I assume you want the story to spread?"

"Yes—"

Irichels broke off as the door opened, and Arak turned to block the newcomer's view. "Yes?"

"Marthie is coming with water and bandages." Alaissou's voice was only slightly unsteady. "And then you must let me send for a physicker."

"Envar can care for him," Arak said, and motioned for

her to shut the door. Irichels heard it close and sat up, Envar's hand at his back.

"Yes, but—" Alaissou stopped abruptly, halfway into the room. "You're not hurt?"

"Not as badly as I pretended." Irichels heard his own voice weaker than he would have liked, and managed a wry smile. "I'd like to see what happens if whoever attacked me thinks they succeeded."

"But—" She stopped again, shaking her head. "Do you think that will work?"

It was not the question he had expected, and he was both surprised by and grateful for her quick grasp of the situation. But then, she was feral, and only the quick survived their first encounter with their demons. "I'm thinking it will tell me more than I know now. Will you help?"

"Of course." She paused. "Are you hurt?"

"Bruised." Irichels looked at his hands, each one crossed with a red weal where he had caught and controlled the bolt's energy. "Nothing serious."

"What am I to tell people?"

"We were attacked on our way back from Oratory, and Gil was wounded," Arak said. "They'll know he was hit by a crossbow bolt, but we won't want to say that."

Irichels nodded. "The less you say, the worse they'll think it is."

"All right." There was a sound at the door and Alaissou whirled to answer it, admitting Martholin with a basin and a bundle of bandages draped over her shoulder. She shut it again quickly, and Arak moved to take the basin as Martholin's mouth dropped open.

"They had you at death's door, Master. I'll have a word with them—"

"That's what I wanted," Irichels said. "I'm laying a trap for whoever's behind this."

It took a little longer to convince her, but she soon agreed and promised to return with food 'for the dot're'. Alaissou went with her, promising to make sure no one disturbed him without her permission, and Irichels leaned forward as the door closed behind her. "Idra, I'm sore," he said. "And you, Cass?"

Envar turned his hands palm out, showing bruises along both palms. "You have it worse, I think."

"Best you both take care of it," Arak said. She stationed herself by the door. "The water's gone cold."

"Easily fixed." Envar sketched a glyph over the basin and stirred it to steaming, then dipped one hand in it with a grimace. "Take your shirt off, Gil—if you can?" Irichels undid the buttons of his gown and shrugged it off, then pulled his shirt gingerly over his head. There was a spreading bruise at the base of his breastbone, black at the center, as though he'd been kicked by a horse. Envar brought the pot of ointment, grimacing as he saw the damage. "No wonder you couldn't breathe."

If the bolt had broken his shield, he would have been dead long since: neither one of them would say the words, but Irichels knew he was shaking. Envar sat beside him on the bed, warming the ointment with a quiet word, and Arak said, "I'll be outside."

Irichels nodded, grateful for the swordswoman's discretion, and felt Envar's hands trembling as he applied the ointment. "And you?"

"I'm well enough."

Irichels let him finish, but caught his sleeve before he could leave. "Let me see."

"Not as bad, I told you." Envar discarded his gown, and opened his shirt to show a welted bruise crossing the top of his left shoulder. Irichels reached for the ointment and spread it gently over the mark, calling on a contract as he did so. He wasn't much of a healer, but this contract was enough to ease some of the soreness, and Envar nodded. "Thanks."

They leaned against each other then, not needing to say more, until at last Envar pulled away. "I should bandage you. We want this to be convincing. And then you'll need to stay abed a few days."

"With my devoted dot're at my side," Irichels said with a smile, and Envar laughed softly.

"You needn't go to such lengths to get my company."

Irichels matched his smile and let himself be wrapped in the lint and linen Martholin had brought, settling himself back among the pillows just in time for her to reappear with the promised tray. They ate in silence, sitting close enough to touch, and when Envar would have moved away, Irichels caught his wrist. "Don't go."

"Only to put the tray aside," Envar promised.

Irichels spent the next few days in bed, watched over by Envar while Arak and Alaissou guarded the door to be sure he wasn't caught out and Martholin added extra food to Envar's trays to keep them from going hungry. As he'd expected, the news of the attack spread widely and brought a stream of concerned visitors. Tyrn Arlechin paid a call, on behalf of both himself and House Gethen; Gellis Ambros came on the second day, gravely concerned, and it took some effort on Envar's part to ward off the visit from another chirurgeon.

Halyssin came that same afternoon, bringing fruit from the family glass-house and Oredana Temenon. Irichels feigned exhaustion, lay with closed eyes and slack breath while they talked with Envar: he had expected Halyssin, but not the Oratorian, and he wondered what had caught her attention. She listened to Envar explain that the injury was far from fatal but required time and patience to heal well, then spoke quietly with Alaissou while Halyssin demanded to know who was behind the attack. After they had gone, Alaissou reported that Oredana had wanted to know much the same thing, but there was little enough to tell her. The Oratory was taking an interest, Irichels thought, but that was hardly news.

The fourth day brought both a delegation from the high constable and word from Martholin that a stranger had been sniffing around the kitchen door, ostensibly looking for scullery work but actually prying into Irichels's health. "I sent him off with a flea in his ear," she said, clashing plates as she cleared away another tray, "but not before I saw the chained dolphin tattooed on his wrist. So Manimere's still sticking her nose in."

Also not unexpected, Irichels thought, any more than the high constable's men had been. Envar propped him up on an impressive stack of pillows to answer their questions—what had happened, where had they been attacked, could they identify any of the attackers—and chased them out again before they could see too much. Left to himself, Irichels stretched, feeling the tug of healing muscles, and tried to find a comfortable spot in the big bed. So far, he hadn't learned as much as he had hoped; it might be time to try his luck with the Court Between, and then declare himself healed.

The door opened, and he looked up to see Envar close it hastily behind him. "Cambryse is here," he said.

"To see Alaissou?" Irichels submitted to being rearranged, the sheets pulled up to his shoulders, pillows propping one side higher than the other, so that his face lay in shadow.

"To inquire about you." Envar set a basin of artfully dirtied linen against the wall, glanced around to be sure the scene was properly set. "Was this what you were waiting for?"

"Maybe."

"Best you be asleep." Envar rolled up one sleeve and went to answer the knock at the door. Irichels relaxed against the pillows, eyes slitted so that he could just see through his lashes as Envar opened the door.

"Dona Alaissou."

"Dot're. Can we see him?"

"He's sleeping," Envar said softly. "The high constable's men wore him out, I'm afraid."

Cambryse brushed past his daughter and was halfway down the room before Envar interposed himself. "I'm sorry, Master—"

"Get out. If you have no shame, I do." Cambryse's voice was low enough for a sick room, but the venom was unmistakable.

"I'm the chirurgeon here," Envar answered with a hint of steel, and Alaissou lifted a hand.

"Please, Dot're. I'll make sure no harm is done."

"As the dona wishes." Envar had himself well under control. "Arak will be at the door, should you need her."

The door closed behind him and Cambryse took a step forward, but Alaissou caught his sleeve. "Don't wake him. The high constable's men were here for a good hour, and he needs to rest."

"So the catamite said."

"Envar knows his business," Alaissou answered.

"Then why is he dying? Or is that not true after all?"

There was new wariness in Alaissou's voice when she answered. "Not so far as I know. And I believe Envar has been honest with me. Irichels is injured, but he should recover."

Irichels thought Cambryse relaxed visibly. "So. That's better news than I expected."

"I'm not sure why it should matter to you," Alaissou said cautiously, and Cambryse rounded on her.

"He's your husband, you had better care. And as far as that goes—has he bedded you yet?"

Through lowered lashes, Irichels could see the color flooding Alaissou's face, though her voice was steady enough. "He has. Though such activities will be out of bounds for some time yet, thanks to this attack."

Cambryse grunted. "And he has no idea who did this?"

"None." Alaissou paused. "The high constable's man suggested it might be some of Manimere's people."

"Not likely. They've got other things to worry about."

"There's talk in the kitchens that Margos Temenon has added him to his quarrel with Halyssin Ambros," Alaissou said.

"That fool," Cambryse said. "Well, if that's the case—I may be able to do something about that."

"That would be kind," Alaissou said, in her most colorless voice.

"Nothing of the sort," Cambryse said. "He has to—it's inconvenient. And you, my girl, need to make every effort to get a child from him, as quickly as possible."

"But why?" Alaissou's voice was high and innocent.

"Because it's your duty, to our house and to his," Cambryse snapped. "With that swordswoman as his heir, with Idra knows how many ill-bred cousins loose in the hills—the line of descent must be clear."

"If I were pregnant today, there wouldn't be a child for months," Alaissou said. "And no guarantees even then."

"Do you think I don't know that?" Cambryse kept his voice down with an effort. "But there's not a lot of time."

"I don't understand," Alaissou began, and Cambryse cut her off.

"You don't need to. Just do as you're told." He stopped, eyeing the bed, and Irichels let himself relax even further. "There's a curse on this house, and he's not long for this world. Are you happy now?"

"It's better to know," Alaissou said after a moment.

Cambryse snorted. "Just give him a child. That's all you need to do. And send word if his condition changes."

"As you wish," Alaissou said, and led him from the room. Irichels lay still for a hundred heartbeats, until he was sure they wouldn't return, then opened his eyes fully and pushed himself up on one elbow. In almost the same moment, the secret door slid open and Envar emerged.

"I can't say I much like your father-in-law, my heart."

"That makes two of us." Irichels sat up, dragging the pillows to a more comfortable position. "A curse on this house and not long for this world. Not cheerful news."

"But not strictly true, I think," Envar said, and Irichels nodded.

"Agreed. I don't see a curse on the house—nothing that doesn't belong here, anyway, nothing that I can't identify as Samar's own work. But it does argue that Cambryse knows someone who wants me dead."

"Though not the people who attacked you this time,"

Envar said. "He seemed distinctly unhappy at the thought of someone else killing you."

"That was interesting, wasn't it? Do you suppose it was Margos after all?"

"Arak did say he saw red and white livery," Envar agreed. "But I swear I saw a Cambryse badge."

Irichels frowned. "Wasn't Cambryse's wife a Temenon before the marriage?"

"Was she?" Envar paused. "If you're right that she's behind the curse on Alaissou—"

"Idra's mercy," Irichels said. "It's my own fault. When she was leaving, I said I was sure I could restore Alaissou to health. If she's behind it—well, that's the last thing she wants. Particularly if Cambryse doesn't know she did it."

"I can find whoever did it," Envar said. "Just give me time."

Irichels nodded. "Yes. I want proof. That would be a very nice lever to use against both of them."

"I'd still like to know what Cambryse is after," Envar said. "To eliminate the line altogether? Though if Alaissou has a child—but he could easily be rid of that, too, I suppose."

"His own grandchild?" Irichels said again, and Envar shrugged.

"Would you put it past him?"

"No," Irichels said. "So, to eliminate Samar. Or to control it? But that still doesn't say why. What does Samar have— what are Samar's contracts, if he's right about a curse, and do they go back as far as the Shame? We need the Courts Between."

"And I have contracts needing renewal," Envar said. "Can we do it from here?"

"It depends on the daemon," Irichels said.

Irichels performed the calculations to determine the best time to enter the Courts Between, and felt the daemon stir as he sketched the preliminary circles. It didn't seem hostile, however, just watchful, and Irichels watched it in return, wondering which of them had changed. It no longer hated him, no longer felt like an extension of his grandfather's anger; he was getting used to its presence, to its willingness to watch and ward. At night, it haunted the first floor, its shadows moving against the moonlight. Martholin kept the servants upstairs and out of harm's way, with only Antel to sleep beside the street door. He claimed not to be afraid, and if Irichels didn't quite believe him, he did believe that the man understood how to coexist with it.

With Irichels reported on the mend, Envar took time to consult his old friends and came back with a promise of a name for Dona Seresinha's practitioner—and a warning that the Oratory was paying closer attention to the ferals' dealings with the Courts Between. Most ferals were taking themselves to the Plana or even further afield, even into the neighboring states' territories, to renew their contracts.

"And I grant that may be the wisest course," Envar said, over brandy in Irichels's bedroom, "but it's not possible."

"Sadly, no."

"Is it possible here?"

"I think so." Irichels unrolled the paper that held his calculations, and Envar came to look over his shoulder. "Tomorrow night the proper hour is just before midnight, which gives us extra privacy. And I believe the daemon won't object as long as we set proper wards."

"We can double the circle," Envar said, eyeing the space between the bed and the sitting area by the fireplace. "An inner and an outer. If your Marthie can find me a carpet to cover the marks, I can start constructing them." Martholin sent up a solid roll of rush matting, and Envar brought water to give the boards a ceremonial washing. Irichels watched as he added the herbs and powders, then sat back abruptly, frowning.

"What's wrong?"

"There's something—" Envar dried his fingers and splayed them delicately on the boards, the frown deepening. "There's been a circle here before, I think."

"Oh?" Irichels joined him, feeling cautiously along the painted wood. He could feel something beneath his fingertips, as though the grain of the wood was raised and roughened, but when he scraped his nail over it, the wood was smooth. "It's very old, whatever it is."

"Yes." Envar was making his way across the floor, hands outstretched to follow the faint traces. "Not actually a circle, but a square." He pulled out chalk and marked the corners, then sat back on his heels.

"That's a very old form," Irichels said. Only the oldest contracts were built on squares rather than the more familiar circle; he had seen diagrams in books, but never encountered one in the world.

Envar nodded. "And it must have been very powerful, if there's any trace of it left. I wonder..." He ran his fingers over the invisible lines again. "I can't tell what it was used for."

"Or why it was in the master's bedroom," Irichels said. He laid one hand flat on the floor, but he couldn't feel anything himself. "Blood?"

"Your blood might wake it," Envar agreed. "It's in the master's room, that implies it's for the master's use. But I'm reluctant to try without a better idea of what it was meant for."

"Could we contain it?" Irichels eyed the chalk marks warily. He had gotten comfortable in the master's bedroom, but the ghost of someone else's magic woke all his earlier misgivings.

"I think we ought," Envar said. "Something passive, just to warn us if it wakes—and I wonder that we didn't feel it when the fetch got in."

"It must not be defensive, then," Irichels said. "And what person works magic where they sleep?"

"You were about to do just that, my heart," Envar said, with a grin.

"Yes, but you know why. And I wouldn't have done it if I had a better choice."

"It may be so old that it can't be woken," Envar said. "We'd never have known it was there if I hadn't been going to wash the floor."

That was also possible. Neither magic nor magic's tools lasted for long without regular infusions of power, and this one hadn't been fed in some considerable time. Perhaps the master who'd used it had never intended to pass it on, and some quirk of the house, of the family, had let it linger. Or perhaps someone had failed to pass along its presence, dying before the secret could be shared. That was the stuff of legend, but also far from impossible. It was too old to have belonged to his grandfather, but the family stretched back to the founding of the city. It was easy to imagine that something could be lost between generations. "Let's ward it anyway," he said. "And then figure out where to put the new circle. We can't miss the Courts."

In the end they drew the new circle in Envar's room, the working circle within a warding band, and then waited as the house stilled and the bells of Idra-of-Mercies tolled the hours. Alaissou had been warned of their plans and waited with Arak, ready to fend off any social intrusion while Arak stood ready in case of a more direct attack. Inside the room, Irichels lit more candles while Envar rolled back the matting to expose the doubled circle, then came to join him inside the first ring. "Ready?"

"Certainly." Envar stooped to inscribe the final symbols, speaking the formula that sealed the circle. Irichels felt the symbols catch and hold, and the daemon rose from its resting place, filling the room. It didn't feel threatening, however, or even hostile, and Irichels focused his attention on it.

"We're going to the Courts Between. You see that we have laid protection."

Wait. Watch. Ward.

That was not the answer he had expected, but he didn't think the daemon was capable of lying. "Yes. Watch and ward." He paused, decided courtesy never hurt. "Thank you."

The daemon shifted, its shadows thinning as it surrounded the circles. Envar eyed it warily. "That's helpful, I think."

"Best get on with it," Irichels answered. They stepped into the inner circle, and once again Envar sketched the final symbols and spoke the formula that sealed it. This time, rather than closing out forces, the center of the circle shivered and then expanded, a cylinder of bluish haze that grew until it filled the circle. It quivered against the skin, as though Irichels could feel the touch of a thousand conversations, a rush of wind from a world he could not see. He glanced at Envar, who straightened, nodding, and spoke the opening incantation.

The rush of sensations slowed and steadied, became a murmur of voices and an arch of carved stone that opened into a corridor lined with stone roses. That was a good sign, recognition both of their presence and their right to speak, and Irichels stepped forward into the illusion. It thickened around him, and together he and Envar moved toward the shimmer of light at the end of the corridor. As they drew closer, it resolved into another carved arch, the frozen roses twining up the pillars, and beyond it the light strengthened further, revealing the four pillars and the central flame that was the Court Between.

"Envar Cassi." The voice came from one of the figures that materialized on the far side of the blue-toned fire, a tall creature mostly human in shape and feature, but with curved tusks that jutted up out of the corners of its mouth. The tips were sheathed in gold, Irichels saw, and its fingers were tipped with golden claws.

"Altibeledon," Envar said.

"Have you come to pay or to renew?" the demon asked, and Envar smiled.

"To renew."

"The price grows ever higher."

"But the rewards are ever sweeter," Envar answered, and Irichels thought there was almost laughter in his tone.

A chime sounded, and another figure stepped forward. This one was also roughly human in shape, with two arms and two legs, but its skin was dark green and its ears rose like bat's wings from its hairless skull. The planes of its face were bulbous, almost a caricature of a human shape, and little flames danced where eyes should have been. A judgment-spirit, Irichels knew, and bent his head in acknowledgment.

Envar did the same, as did Altibeledon, and Judgment waved a gnarled hand. Envar's clothes vanished and he stood naked before the fire, his body wound in a tangle of black lines, some thick, some thin, some fading toward gray while others looked deep and new. His left hand was entirely black, tendrils reaching up his arm to his elbow; a wide swirl crowned the opposite shoulder and there were more broad splashes down his thighs, fading into a delicate tracery that covered half his body. Irichels knew some of them—the hand was a complex of the chirurgeon's contracts—but as always he was taken aback by the sheer number. Envar had balanced them one against the other, so that no one demon could revoke its contract or demand payment without provoking retaliation from at least some of the others, but it was sobering to see them all at once.

"You wish to renew this contract," Judgment said, and Envar bowed again.

"I do."

"And you?" Judgment looked at Altibeledon.

"I also wish it." It bowed its head.

"So be it. The contract is renewed in all the worlds." Judgment lifted a hand, and Irichels heard Envar hiss as one of the twists of lines darkened further. Then he stepped back, clothed again, the marks once again invisible, and Irichels felt the floor tremble beneath his feet as Judgment turned its attention to him.

"Gilmyssin Irichels." It waved its hand, bringing forward a winged figure with a serene motionless face like one of the masks the senators wore. "The bond of Tarehan claims no obligations."

"My name and station have changed," Irichels said. He felt his own clothing vanish, the familiar hatchmarks of the contracts he claimed from the University dark beneath his skin. "I am Gilmyssin Irichels di Samar—Master of Samar."

There was the faintest of touches against his skin, little more than a breath of air, as though someone, somewhere had been startled into some reaction. Not Judgment, Irichels thought, and not the University's demon, but he could see no one else among the shadows.

"Duly noted," Judgment said. "The bond is so amended."

Irichels felt its attention beginning to fade, and spoke quickly, "As master, I wish to know what other contracts bind me—and my house."

"That is surely outside the jurisdiction of this meeting."

Irichels could not see who spoke, just that it came from the shimmering shadows beyond Judgment. The voice was unfamiliar, too: not a class of demon that he recognized. "This is the season for affirming contracts. I'm entitled to know what my house has bound me to, just as I'd be entitled to know if the University had expanded its bond."

There was a moment of silence, the world stilled around them, and then Judgment inclined its head. "Fairly put. I will allow it."

A figure coalesced from the shimmer, darkening from glimmering silver to the pale blue of a spring sky. Like the others, it showed itself roughly human, though it had no nose and its mouth was too wide, showing a doubled row of pointed teeth. Its hands were webbed, and sand-colored hair cascaded down its back, wound with strands of what might be pearls the size of grapes: a sea demon. Irichels studied it cautiously, keeping his face expressionless with an effort. He hadn't had any dealing with their kind—they had no power on land, and he had never worked at sea.

"Samekhysenmere," Judgment said. "You speak to this."

"I am the responding party," the sea demon said. Its words were entirely clear, in spite of the teeth crowding its mouth.

"I have said that he is within his rights," Judgment said. "You will tell him what your contract requires."

"The contract is very old," Samekhysenmere said. "Its terms were long ago fulfilled. The city stands on water as it would on land. We may not touch it or its ships under mark on the agreed-upon roads."

So that much of the story was true. Irichels held himself immobile with an effort. "What must be done to maintain it?"

"You must exist," Samekhysenmere said. "As long as the pillars stand, the contract holds. We have no quarrel with its effects."

"And if Samar ceases to exist?" Irichels asked.

Samekhysenmere showed all its teeth. "Then the city is open for our taking, and all the sea is ours again. That is the contract."

"Does that apply to all the houses?" Irichels knew he was pushing his luck, and was unsurprised when Samekhysenmere shook its head.

"That has nothing to do with your contract, Samar. I am not obliged to answer."

"That is so," Judgment said. It lifted a hand, a blue-white light brighter then the sun caught in its palm. "This session is ended."

The light flared, blinding them, and abruptly they were back in the double circle, the daemon circling them like fog. Irichels's heart was pounding as though he'd run a mile, and he drew a deep breath. "Well."

Envar shook himself, stretching as though that would help his contracts resettle themselves, then stooped to break the inner circle. "Well, indeed. It's an answer, my heart."

"An answer," Irichels said, "but I wanted more."

CHAPTER FIFTEEN

"But why would anyone—any human—want to destroy the city?" Alaissou asked. They were sitting in the parlor over a late breakfast, kaf and bacon and boiled eggs along with slices of a currant-studded twice-baked loaf. Irichels caught himself looking at the half-emptied plates with new eyes, a reminder not of wealth but of the city's fragility. The eggs and honey might come from the city proper, there were houses on Orangery and Weepers and parts of the Quadrata that had yards large enough to keep poultry, and the Orangery certainly had bee-keepers; but the rest came from the Plana and its farms, or from even farther away. Arak's tea came from the high hills, the kaf from Abesscie, the currants from Daluse across the sea, like a thousand other luxuries. Bejanth depended on trade for everything—depended on the forbearance of the sea demons, which the contract produced by the Shame had at least ensured.

"That would be the question," Arak agreed.

"The sea demons might have tired of it," Envar said. "Of leaving Bejanth alone, I mean. Or perhaps someone wants to make a different contract? Though I can't imagine what would be better terms."

"If I understood the demon—Samekhysenmere—correctly, the terms are remarkably easy," Irichels said. "The four houses simply have to exist."

"That seems awfully little," Arak said. "Are you sure that's the contract?"

"It couldn't lie in the Courts Between," Envar said. "So

that part's certainly true."

"It said the terms were fulfilled." Irichels ticked the points off on his fingers. "It said that to maintain the contract, the four houses had to exist. And it said that if Samar ceased to exist, the contract would be broken. It refused to say if that applied to the other houses, but I think we can assume so."

"Why?" Alaissou looked up. "There's no reason you couldn't require different things from different houses, is there?"

"The sea demons could ask," Irichels said, "but I don't think the houses would agree. I'd expect the burdens to be shared equally and exactly."

Envar nodded. "Presumably they planned to share the rewards the same way."

"Yes." It was easier to guess what the four masters had originally planned: build new neighborhoods on the sea, on the few tiny islands for a start and then build out from there, sinking pilings in the shallow water. Whether or not they then provoked a demonic attack, as the story of the Shame said, they could reasonably expect to end up controlling the city.

"Maybe someone's tired of sharing," Alaissou said.

Arak laughed. "Wouldn't surprise me."

"Yes, but sharing what?" Irichels shook his head. "The Senate and Assembly took away all the gains—surely that's what the Tower tells us. What I need is a copy of the contract."

"And it's here?" Envar cocked his head to one side.

"Not that I've found." Irichels sighed, thinking of the last crumbling boxes he hadn't yet investigated. So far, half of them stank of mice or even less salubrious things, and the rest had proved unhelpful.

"Could you see if one of the other houses has a copy?" Arak asked. "Not Cambryse, obviously—"

"Or Manimere," Envar said.

"Or Manimere, no, but—who's the fourth house?" Arak looked at Irichels, who frowned.

"Morellin."

Alaissou looked embarrassed. "They're—I'd call them

under Father's thumb, myself. And we're cousins about five different ways. My mother was a Morellin."

"Ah." Irichels sighed, and Envar breathed a laugh.

"Never mind, then."

Irichels spent the rest of the morning sorting through another mouse-rotted box of papers, wondering why it had been necessary to keep seventy-five years of receipts for trades in pepper and galengale. He briefly entertained the idea that there might be some sort of code involved, but it rapidly became clear that wasn't the case. Envar had lasted until the first urine-soaked nest, and then announced that he wanted to see if he could make contact with Manimere's people. Irichels could hardly blame him: at this point, the fear of arrest was nothing to his desire to get away from the mouse leavings.

He finished at last, still without turning up anything useful, and turned the mess over to Karan to dispose of. He scrubbed his hands at the kitchen boiler, and then returned to the courtyard to trail fingers in the fountain, grateful for the smells of greenery and the sunlight pouring in through the skylights. It was still too soon to show himself, not after the rumors he had spread, and he felt abruptly at loose ends. There had to be a way to get the details of the contract that didn't involve paying a further price to the Courts Between. What had Samekhysenmere called the contract holders? Pillars: *As long as the pillars hold, the contract stands.* Though whether those pillars were physical, metaphorical, or some combination of the two…

He pushed himself to his feet, frowning. Might the circle they had discovered have something to do with the contract? It was possibly old enough, if it had been placed when the house was built. And if the houses were pillars—well, that should be easy enough to establish. Samar House had always stood on this site, from the founding of the city; he thought the same was true of Manimere. As for Cambryse and Morellin… He climbed to the next floor, tapped at the door of Alaissou's music room. The faint sound of scales stopped, and the door opened.

"Yes?"

"An odd question," Irichels said. "Has Cambryse House always been where it is? I mean, is that the original site?"

"I think so." Alaissou blinked, one hand on the neck of her vielle, the other holding the taut-strung bow. "As far as I know, anyway."

"Do you know about Morellin House?"

"Sorry. I don't."

He could find that out later, when he checked on Manimere House. "Thanks," Irichels said, and she retreated to her practice.

In his room, he rolled back the carpet to reveal the faint marks, and stood studying them for a long moment. If this was related to the curse, it would make sense to place it in the room where the head of the family slept, where the next generations were most likely engendered—where it touched most closely on the person who symbolized the family. He went to one knee, running his fingers over the lines, but he still couldn't feel more than the faintest prickle of past power.

The daemon flowed up from the storage room, coalescing in the corner by the head of the bed, not hostile, but certainly present. If anything, it felt curious, and Irichels sat back on his heels. "And what do you know about this, I wonder?"

Circle.

"Do you know what it's for?" Irichels felt its confusion, and tried again. "What its purpose was?"

Spike. Pin. Finished, long ago.

"How long ago?"

Long.

"Has it always been here?" That was another way to get at the question: the daemon had not always been part of the house, was a created thing, however inadvertent that creation had been.

Always. Don't touch.

"Why not?"

Finished. Over. Don't touch.

Irichels eyed the corner where it lurked, a shadow not

quite at the edge of sight. It was less frightening than it had been, less hostile. Maybe Envar was right, not trying to block it out was the key—well, that and the fact that he was the last surviving heir. When he was a boy, his grandfather had made it clear he didn't belong, he was unwanted, and the daemon had followed that lead. That, at least, was gone. And it had been more than twenty years and four masters since his grandfather had ruled here. Samar was his own now, for better or worse.

He touched the lines again, trying one more time to trace the glyphs, and once again there was nothing he could read. He took a breath and closed his eyes, calling up the daemon's words, *spike, pin*, holding them in his thoughts as he reached for the elusive magic. For a long time, he felt nothing, just his own heartbeat and the presence of the daemon, neither aroused nor distressed, and each time he pushed thought away, reaching for the ghost of the circle. And then, just for an instant, it came clear: a spike indeed, like the central pier that held the foundation of a house, a pillar of flame driven deep into not just the bedrock but through the veil between worlds and into the fabric of the worlds both Above and Below. Salamanders darted in and out of the fires, but they were faint and thin, vanishing even before he lost the overall image. Then it all disappeared, leaving him gasping and deflated. The daemon rumbled like distant thunder and vanished.

Envar returned in the slack of the afternoon, carrying a respectable-looking basket as though he'd been out on errands. Irichels, who had seen that act many times, retreated to his workroom and shortly Envar joined him, trailed by Martholin bearing a tray of kaf and all its fixings. She set it on the sideboard, curtseyed, and departed, closing the door gently behind her. For a brief moment, it was like all the jobs they'd had before, a hundred well-worn rooms smelling of ink and beeswax, and Irichels could almost imagine that he could walk out the door and find himself in the Hills, or Abesscie, or the cobbled streets of Salandram. Envar met his eyes with a wry smile, as though he'd guessed what Irichels was thinking, and Irichels said, "Do you mind terribly? Coming back here, I mean."

Envar's smile widened slightly. "Too late for that, my heart."

That was unfortunately true, and also honest enough to bring pain, and Irichels said, "I'm sorry."

"It's not like you had a choice." Envar stirred honey into his kaf with a stick of candied orange peel. "If you hadn't come back, I suspect we'd have been dodging assassins around every corner. People have been trying hard enough to kill you here, my heart. And you and I and Arak are very good, I'll grant it, but being on guard like that would have been exhausting. No, one way or another, we'd have ended up here."

That was also true—Envar had a gift for laying things out—and Irichels nodded. "Still."

"I have no intention of leaving you," Envar said lightly. "Now. I have some interesting news to share."

"Oh?" Consoled, Irichels fixed his own cup and came back to the worktable. He'd exchanged his grandfather's enormous carved greatchair for a lighter chair, something he could tip back against the wall when he needed to stare at the ceiling, and he leaned back now to cross his ankles on the table.

"I had a long conversation with one of Manimere's agents," Envar said. He added a pillow to the greatchair and settled himself cross-legged in it. "A woman calling herself Canamun. A very respectable person to look at, all dark wool and fine linen. She says she's Manimere's factor, and it may even be true."

"And if she's not Manimere's factor?" Irichels sipped his kaf.

"Oh, I'm sure she's a factor," Envar said. "Just not necessarily for the legal goods. She's also certainly spent some time at sea."

"So she's one of Manimere's pirates."

"She was, anyway," Envar said. "She says Manimere has made an appeal to the Senate and Assembly—in writing, of course, delivered by a neutral third party—and is cruising off the mouth of the bay waiting for an answer. Manimere would like to know if she could expect your support for that appeal."

"I would if I could," Irichels said. "What did you tell her?"

"Exactly that. Your ability to act independently is considerably curtailed these days."

"And she said?"

"That she certainly understood that, but hoped you'd use what influence you had."

Irichels nodded. "I can do that. And would anyway, which I expect she knows."

"I agree. She also hinted Manimere would like your support if things took a more...active turn."

"It's not like I have an army to loan her," Irichels said.

"But you could raise—well, not an army, but help. And you have influence."

"Less than I had before she fled."

"Canamun says she's authorized to offer you the access to documents that Manimere promised."

"That makes a difference," Irichels admitted. "Though—is there a house daemon? I didn't feel one, but I wasn't looking."

"I didn't feel one either," Envar said. "Though the boy seemed to know about them, which would suggest there's something there. And there's staff, of course. And I'd assume the constables have people watching the house, whether or not they have someone on the inside."

"I'd like to get a look at the house," Irichels said. "While you were gone, I took another look at the circle in my bedroom." He went through what he had found, including the strange almost-conversation with the daemon. "I'd be very interested in knowing if there was a similar circle in Manimere's bedroom."

Envar nodded. "I'll tell Canamun. She swears she can get us in unseen."

"I'll hold her to that," Irichels said.

It took several days to arrange the visit. Irichels spent the time tracing the ghost of the circle and the pillar it had raised. It pierced the house and drove deep into the bedrock, just as the builders' pillars did, but drove through the barriers between worlds as well, reaching most strongly into the world Below. The storeroom with the daemon's stele lay directly below his bedroom, and he followed the traces of the pillar there, wondering if whoever had sent the fetch had known about the pillar. It would be a weak point in the house wards, and might explain why the fetch had fled this way, and why all traces seemed to lead beneath the house. It might also explain why the family had welcomed the daemon as one more level of defense. He learned its shape and sensations, too, though the connections remained more insubstantial than a ghost: it was enough to identify another such in Manimere House, but not much more.

"If anyone wants me, tell them I've suffered a relapse," Irichels said. They were gathered in the hall between the storage areas, the door that gave onto the water alley already folded back behind the heavy iron grille. "But no one's likely to come."

"Yes." Alaissou's voice was taut.

"I should come with you," Arak said.

They had argued this out three times already. "I want you to be here to back up Alaissou," Irichels said.

"And people will notice three of us more than two," Envar said. "We've discussed this."

There was the soft splash of a pole in the water alley, and then wood ground against the wooden fenders nailed to the wall beside the door. Envar looked out, then unlocked the grill. "Canamun."

"Dot're."

Alaissou caught the grill, holding it open as Envar stepped

down into the boat. Irichels followed, glancing back only after he had seated himself. Arak looked down at him, her face set. "We'll be waiting for you," she said softly, and closed the doors.

Irichels looked at Canamun, perched at the poleman's feet. She was older than he, or at least more weather-worn, and in the evening shadow it was hard to make out any details of her features. She was plainly dressed, a sailor's short breeches showing bare legs and dirty feet: no one you'd look at twice. Then again, he'd worn his oldest tunic, and boots worn so thin he might as well have gone barefoot; and Envar was once again dressed like the street rat he'd been born, so he supposed they were all doing their best. He just hoped they didn't look so disreputable as to attract attention from the constables.

They worked their way through the emptying canals, taking what Irichels knew was a roundabout approach to Manimere House. There was no sign that they were being followed, or indeed that anyone was at all interested in them, and at last the narrow boat fetched up at the back door of the house. Canamun tapped twice, then twice again, and the door folded back behind another set of bars.

A stocky man peered out, then hauled the grill aside. Canamun steadied the boat and nodded for the others to go ahead. Envar took the lead, fingers crooked and ready, and then Irichels stepped carefully into the darkened hall. A moment later Canamun followed them, and there was a soft splash as the boatman moved away. The servant closed the door behind them, and Envar snapped his fingers for a light. In the same moment, someone else did the same and they stood frozen in the doubled light, facing a graying man in the neat suit of a senior servant.

"No need for that," he said, sounding irritable. Canamun breathed something like a laugh, and he looked down his long nose at her. "Were you followed?"

"Not that I could see. We came the long way, I'd have seen if we were."

"Let us hope so."

Canamun bared teeth in what was not quite a smile. "Samar, this is Estavellan, Manimere's steward."

"Manimere has bidden me to put myself at your disposal," Estavellan said.

"Manimere offered to let me look at documents in her possession," Irichels said. "Relating to the Shame."

Estavellan's lips tightened but he managed a bow. "So I understand. I'll ask you to come with me, and to speak to no one. The household is loyal, but there's no point in trying anyone too far."

"No, indeed," Envar said, not quite under his breath, and Canamun grinned again.

"I want to see the papers," Irichels said, "and one thing more. And then I won't trouble you further."

Estavellan bowed a second time. "This way."

He led them down a darkened servants' hall. Irichels guessed it gave onto storage rooms and work spaces and perhaps ran under the main stair. Everything was clearly closed up for the night, the servants who remained in the house withdrawn to the top floors, and he stretched his nerves for any sign of a daemon. He felt nothing, only the weight of an old house and its history, and thought from Envar's expression, poised and attentive, that he felt the same.

Estavellan stopped at a door covered in cracking leather, Manimere's collared dolphin displayed on a worn brass at its center. He knocked twice, and twice again, and pushed open the door. "Your visitors."

It was a small workroom, as Irichels had expected, half the size of his grandfather's but similarly furnished, with bookcases and cabinets and a long table. The shutters were closed and barred against the night, and a sailor's lantern rested on one end of the table. A woman was sitting on the table's other end, swinging bare feet above the polished floor, and Irichels couldn't repress a grin. "Manimere."

"Samar." She held out both hands and he took them, watching her expression change to the smug smile of a woman who's pulled off a coup against the odds. Out of the corner of his eye he saw shock and admiration chase each other across Canamun's face.

"If I'd known you'd be here, I'd have brought your son," Irichels said.

"I wish you could have," Manimere answered. "But he's safer with you a while longer."

"Master," Canamun said. "This is a risk."

Manimere waved the words away. "I'll be gone before dawn. And it's necessary. Irichels, you know what I want from you."

"I told your agent I'd do what I could," Irichels said. "But I don't have an army."

"And if I handed you one?" Manimere cocked her head to one side.

"I don't think that's how this is going to be resolved," Irichels said. "This is part of something—more complicated."

"Explain, then." Manimere slid off the table. "No, wait. Canamun, watch the door. Estavellan, make sure everything stays quiet. It seems we need to have a talk."

There was a murmur of agreement and the servants left, closing the door behind them. Irichels said, "The Shame— the four houses involved created a contract with the sea demons. We're all agreed on that, yes?" Manimere nodded. "Someone is trying to destroy one of the houses. I've spoken to the Courts Between, and the contract is held together by the existence of the four houses. If any one of them ceases to exist, the contract is broken."

"Who?" Manimere frowned. "And why?"

"I'm still working on that," Irichels said. "I suspect Cambryse—he forced me to marry his daughter, by the way."

"So I heard," Manimere said. "Pity, that."

"She's clever," Irichels said. "And not under her father's thumb. But that's not the point. The point is that I can see that someone's trying to break the contract, but I can't see what they—what he, if it's Cambryse—gains from it. So I'm looking for a copy of the contract."

"That I don't have," Manimere said. "After we spoke, I looked through the family records, and I found some early references that seem to paraphrase some clauses. But it's not complete."

"It's better than what I have," Irichels said.

"Shall I?" Envar asked, and Manimere nodded.

"Yes, go ahead, it's the scroll there. Good luck with it, it's old Chancery script and all abbreviations. In the meantime, Irichels and I can discuss the price."

Envar settled himself at the table, drawing the lamp closer as he unrolled the scroll. Manimere gave Irichels a look, hard to read in the shadows. "I will not be driven under."

"Nor should you be. It's a danger to the city, on the most basic level." Irichels took a breath. "If the contract is broken, the sea demons are no longer obliged to protect Bejanth, and we'll drown in the first storm. And starting a war in the city isn't going to change that."

"That makes no sense," Manimere said. "Breaking the contract, I mean. It's served us all for centuries. What can anyone possibly gain?"

"I don't know," Irichels said. "I can think of possibilities, and I'm sure you can, too."

"Try me."

"One of us wants a better deal," Irichels said. "That would explain Cambryse, I think. I gather the family has already absorbed Morellin?"

"They've intermarried considerably," Manimere said. "All right, yes. But why would Cambryse think he could get a better deal from the sea demons?"

"I don't know. I don't know what he could offer, and I certainly couldn't guess what they might offer him." Irichels paused. "Also—and this is less true of Cambryse, I think—someone might want to regularize the city's contracts. Someone's always complaining about what a tangled mess it is."

"But no one ever does anything because it's too complicated," Manimere said. "I suppose someone might be trying to force the Senate and Assembly to act? It's just—it's a demon's chance to take."

"So was the original contract," Irichels said. "But, yes, I think that's less likely."

"All right," Manimere said after a moment. "But that still doesn't solve my problem."

"I know. I'm sorry." Irichels paused. "Are you appealing to the Senate and Assembly?"

"Of course. I just don't expect to get anywhere."

"But that buys us some time."

Manimere folded her arms. "Not enough."

"I'm not asking you to give up your house," Irichels said. "Samar's in as much danger, and I don't intend to go down, either. But if it's Cambryse, I may be able to force him to act before he's ready."

"If and may," Manimere said. "Not reassuring."

"If I can't make it work, or if it's not him, then yes, I'll side with you," Irichels said. "And otherwise you'll back me?"

"As far as I can," Manimere said. She looked toward the table where Envar was bent over the scroll, scribbling in his copybook. "Are you finding what you need?"

"I'm finding useful things," Envar answered, his attention clearly elsewhere, and Irichels cleared his throat.

"There's one more thing I'd like to see while I'm here. Samekhysenmere—the sea demon representing this contract—called the houses of the Shame the pillars of the contract, and there's at least a metaphysical pillar in Samar House. This is the original site of Manimere House?"

Manimere nodded. "In fact, there's a family covenant forbidding us to move."

"Oh, that's very interesting," Irichels said. "I'd like to see if there's a pillar here as well."

"It depends on where you want to look," Manimere said.

"In our house, it's in the master's rooms," Irichels said.

Manimere grinned. "From anyone else, I'd be suspicious. But—yes, I think we can slip upstairs without anyone taking undue notice. The dot're will be all right here?"

"Yes," Envar said without looking up, and Irichels nodded. "This way, then."

As Irichels had suspected, the workroom was under the main staircase. It was dark in the courtyard, the moon not yet up, and there was a faint sound of singing from the top of the house. There were lights there, too, behind the latticework of the balconies, but the floor between was dark. Manimere put a finger to her lips and led him up the first flight of stairs, their feet silent on the stones. Halfway up, they heard a door open and both froze, Manimere with her hand on Irichels's arm. For a moment, the household sounds were louder, then the door closed again. Manimere mimed relief, and tugged him on after her.

The master's room was smaller than in Samar House, though there were more windows. Those were shuttered now, and when Manimere shut the door behind them, it was very dark. She snapped her fingers to light a lamp, and in the wavering flame Irichels could make out the shape of an enormous canopied bed that filled one end of the room like the prow of a ship. There was a faint scent of perfume, and he wondered if Manimere had dared to sleep in her own bed.

"What are you looking for?" she asked, and he dragged his attention back to the business at hand.

"There was a circle—well, a square, the old style—set in the floor." Irichels went to hands and knees as he spoke, sweeping his hands across the bare boards. There weren't many carpets here, just woven rush matting by the empty fireplace, and he focused on the space between it and the foot of the bed. The paint was chipped in places, the wood dented, everything you'd expect in an old house—and then he felt it, the odd roughness that wasn't actually there. He traced it, slowly: another square like the one in Samar House, carved into the wood and then sanded away, so that only the ghosts of the symbols remained. It felt the same, and he sat back on his heels, closing his eyes.

For a long moment there was nothing but the sound of his heartbeat and Manimere's breathing, the lamplight quivering against his eyelids. Then he saw it, the same slender spike running from bedrock and beyond up into the ethereal. Its silver surface was covered with fish, every size and shape and kind, and strands of netting spun out from it here and there, but trailed off into a haze of fog. He held the image for an instant, frantically committing detail to memory, and then it slid away.

"Idra's mercy," Manimere said. "Has that always been here?"

Irichels caught his breath, pushed himself to his feet. "You saw that?"

"You made it clear."

Well, she was the Master of Manimere, and it was her pillar. "It looked as though it was in good shape."

"For which I suppose we must all be grateful," Manimere said. "What do I do with it?"

"Leave it alone," Irichels answered. "Let's see what Cass has found."

They made their way back down the stairs without attracting attention, and returned to the workroom. Envar was still bent over the scroll, but looked up at their approach. "Did you find it?"

Irichels nodded. "Yes. In the same place as in Samar, too."

"Interesting." Envar returned his attention to the scroll.

"So," Manimere began, and the door slammed open.

"Master! The constables!" Canamun beckoned from the doorway. "Estavellan will stand them off, but—"

Manimere swore. Envar swept away the book weights and began to roll the scroll to fit it back into its case. "Take it with you," Manimere said. "There's no time." Envar tucked case and tattered roll under his arm, and she nodded. "Quickly, this way."

She led them back through the corridor beneath the stairs, but instead of heading for the water door, she turned into a storeroom. Canamun closed the door behind them and turned a key in the lock, while Manimere stooped over one of the flagstones. It rose under her touch and slid sideways, and Irichels could just make out a ladder dropping into darkness. "Light?" he asked, and Manimere nodded.

"Please. But not too much."

Irichels snapped his fingers for a wisp and sent it ahead of her down the ladder. In its wavering light, he could see water and the darker shapes of the piling crossbeams just below the water's surface.

"Canamun," Manimere said. "You first. I'll close the trap behind us."

Canamun nodded and obeyed. Envar had managed to get the scroll crammed into its case, and slung it around his neck before following her down the ladder. Irichels followed him and found himself balancing uncomfortably on slick wood, half stooped to keep from cracking his head on the enormous house beams above him. To either side, the water looked dark and very deep.

"This way," Canamun said, and he edged out onto the beam after her, making room for Manimere to drop down beside him.

"They may or may not find that," she said, "but it'll take a while. Cana, you've left a boat?"

"This way," Canamun said. "The tide's up, Master."

"I know," Manimere said. "We'll just have to wade a bit."

Irichels looked down at the lapping water, black as a scryer's mirror. He had no desire to dip even a toe into it, much less wade any deeper, and he caught a look on Envar's face that said the other man was thinking the same thing. He made himself follow Canamun, one hand bracing himself on the beams above and beside him, the other directing the wisp to light their way. The water was cold even through his boots, and there was a coating of slime on the beams that threatened to send him flailing. Both Canamun and Manimere were barefoot, but that had its own hazards.

They reached the edge of the house pillars and a broader path loomed out of the shadows, several boards laid across the beams. They led under a brickwork arch, and Irichels hesitated, feeling old wards under them. Canamun fished under her tunic and pulled out a brass medallion, which she kissed and held ahead of her. The wards relaxed, and Manimere said, "We're under the street here."

A city ward, then, Irichels thought. At least the boards were fully above the water, though he had to keep in the very center to prevent his head from striking the bricks above him. They passed a crossroad, where the platform had been built out a little and a second walkway ran parallel to the road, but Canamun ignored it, kept walking toward the end of the arch where it loomed out of the shadows ahead. Irichels fed the wisp a little more strength, hoping to see the promised boat, but instead there was only another maze of pilings and crossbeams. An old contract whispered against his skin, faded but still a definite warning, and he lifted his hand. "Wait."

"It'll let us pass as long as we stay to the edge," Manimere said.

"All right." Irichels ducked under the arch and stepped awkwardly down onto another submerged beam. The water here was over his ankles, and he heard Envar make a noise of disgust ahead of him. A moment later, he himself stepped into the nest of seaweed and swallowed a curse of his own. The contract sang against his skin, a dull buzz like the note of a badly tuned viol, and he quickened his step, eager to get out of its reach before they triggered a stronger reaction. He could see a change in the pattern of pillars ahead of them, another tunnel opening up through the tangle, and behind him Manimere swore. Canamun looked back. "Master?"

"I've cut my foot," Manimere said, her voice tight. "It's nothing serious."

"How deep is that passage?" Envar asked.

"Above the knee," Canamun answered. "The tide's high, there's nothing we can do."

"Is there another way?" Irichels asked. They had reached the edge of the house pillars, clung precariously together on a single wide beam. To either side there were more pillars and crossbeams, and the constant shimmer of curses; the tunnel stretched ahead of them, a clear path, but the dark water rippled uneasily. There were sanderlings in the spaces beneath the city's buildings, and other things, too, trap-jaw eels and flatfish with their barbed tails. No one with any sense went wading in Bejanth's waters, especially not when they were bleeding.

"You might could get out that way," Canamun said, gesturing to her right. "I think it comes up on someone's dock. But I don't know for sure."

"Our boat is waiting at the end of the tunnel," Manimere said. "It opens into what looks like an ordinary water alley. It's not even far."

"Are you bleeding?" Irichels asked, and she looked away.

"Yes."

"We could carry her," Envar said dubiously, and Irichels sighed.

"I could. If you'll let me," he added, and Manimere gave a crooked smile.

"Not quite what I'd had in mind, but yes. We don't want to attract sanderlings."

"Let me see your foot," Envar said. She caught Irichels' shoulder for balance and lifted her left foot, the fabric of her trousers falling back in wet folds, and flexed it with a grimace. There was a cut across the ball of her foot, blood still seeping sluggishly from it. Not that deep, Irichels thought, but the water kept it from closing. Envar considered for a moment, then crooked his fingers, holding his hands a finger-length apart. A shadow grew between them, gray and dusty and spangled with tiny flecks of darkness. He flicked his fingers and it flew from them, lodging against the wound. Manimere winced but made no sound. "That'll hold a while, and you won't be dripping blood. It will probably wash away once you get it wet again."

"It'll do," Manimere said.

"On my back, I think," Irichels said, and she nodded. He stepped down onto the walkway, feeling it solid and not too slick underfoot. She wrapped her arms around his neck and he tucked his arms under her legs, grunting as he took her solid weight. "All right?" he asked, and felt her nod. "Cass, more light, if you can."

"Yes." Envar closed his eyes, his fingers working, and then opened his hand to release a glowing white sphere. It settled just below the overhead beams, casting a circle of bright light across the submerged walkway, and the water ahead of them churned for a moment as something fled into deeper shadow. "Ah. That's good, I hope."

"Let's hope so," Canamun muttered, and hitched up her trousers. "Come on."

She stepped out confidently and Envar followed, the light hovering over him. Irichels could see that his hands were poised and ready, a spell in each, and wished he could do the same. Manimere was heavy, despite her efforts to make herself an easy burden; he couldn't help splashing, the water rippling like a boat's wake, and he could see movement in the shadows to either side. Sanderlings were drawn to the scent of blood and offal, but too much movement drew them as well.

"Not much further," Canamun called softly, but Irichels didn't dare move any faster. Something broke the surface to his left, a flash of spray and the flick of a tail, and was gone again. Envar gestured to the right, loosing a flash of light, and there was more splashing. Irichels could feel the grain of the wood through the soft soles of his boots: the leather would be no protection at all if the sanderlings attacked. If he moved any faster, he would just upset them more—and then a heavier beam loomed out of the water, rising a solid foot above the tide. A stone wall stood on top of it, the foundation of some building, and a narrow wooden door was set into the stones. Canamun gave a sigh of relief and scrambled up onto it. "Here, Master, let me help—"

Irichels turned sideways so that Manimere could step from his back to the beam, and Canamun steadied her as she reached safety. The water behind them churned and flashed, sanderlings gathering outside the circle of Envar's light. Irichels pulled himself up onto the beam and offered a hand to Envar, who crouched beside him. There was not quite room enough to stand. "Well?"

"The dot're will need to douse the lights," Canamun said. "There's a door here that opens on the water alley, and we don't want to draw attention."

"I'm not sure that's such a good idea," Irichels said, eying the thrashing water.

"No, but we really can't be seen," Manimere said.

"You're sure that boat is there?" Envar asked.

"I left it there twelve hours ago," Canamun answered. "Master, we need to keep moving."

"Cana's right," Manimere said, and Envar sighed.

"Be ready, then."

"Ready," Canamun said, and Envar clenched his fist, dousing the light. The noise increased, advancing rapidly, and Irichels flattened himself against the stone. Something jumped up at him, slapping against his shin, and next to him Manimere swore. He grabbed her arm to keep her from overbalancing, and at last Canamun got the door open. In the relative brightness, Irichels caught a glimpse of a dozen sanderlings thrashing and leaping at the end of the causeway, and then Envar was tugging at his sleeve.

"This way, there's a boat—"

"There had better be," Manimere muttered, but she accepted his hands to steady her down into the hull. Her trousers were torn, and there was a new cut along her shin, where a leaping sanderling had struck her. Envar made a worried noise.

"Better let me see to that, Master."

"Gladly." She leaned back against a thwart, and Irichels settled himself behind her. Canamun unshipped the oar and pushed away from the mooring ring. She had closed the door behind her, and they might just pass for late-returning workers, Irichels thought—if they hadn't already passed curfew. But no, there were still a few figures on the banks as they pulled out into the larger canal, and he unclenched a little. Envar sat back, his hands relaxing, and Manimere wrapped her arms around her body. "We'll drop you at the Eastern Bridge."

They'd have to hurry to make it back to Samar before curfew, but that was nothing compared to either hiding or leaving the city, as Manimere would have to do. Irichels nodded. "Thank you."

"I'll try to make things less exciting next time," Manimere said.

CHAPTER SIXTEEN

They crossed the Eastern Bridge back to Mercies, staying at the edges of the lantern-light. It was late enough that even the taverns were closing, which offered some cover if anyone was looking for them. Envar had managed to tuck the scroll case under his cloak, Irichels saw, and in the dim light it was unlikely anyone would notice that their clothes were wet. Still, it was a relief to reach the street door of Samar House. Envar turned around to survey the street while Irichels pulled the chain that sounded the porter's bell. A few moments later, Antel drew back the bolts and they slipped inside. "Well?" Irichels looked at Envar, who shook his head.

"Nothing that I saw."

"Good." Irichels started for the stairs, and intercepted one of the maids as she crossed the courtyard. "Tell Marthie I'd like a supper tray in my bedroom, please—for two."

"Yes, Master." The girl dropped a curtsey. "Dona Alaissou is waiting for you there, I think."

"Thank you."

Alaissou and Arak were sitting in front of the fireplace, a tables board between them, and Arak rose as the door opened. "Trouble?"

"Nothing serious," Irichels answered, and heard Envar grunt in disagreement. "Nothing too serious, anyway."

"You're wet," Alaissou said.

"The constables raided Manimere House," Envar said. "Probably because Manimere herself was there. We got out by the flat-boaters' road."

"Through the pilings?" Alaissou sounded scandalized.

Irichels nodded. "Yes, and I'd like dry clothes. I'm sure Cass would, too."

"I daresay," Arak said, "but then we should hear what's happened."

"Once I'm dry," Irichels said firmly, and retreated into the dressing room. He peeled off his boots, grimacing at the stains, and Envar did the same.

"We'd best get these cleaned right away, my heart."

Irichels nodded. The rest of his clothes weren't so badly marked, could be left tumbled in the corner as though he'd straggled in after curfew, and he wrapped himself in a dressing gown. Envar pulled on dry trousers, though he left his shirt loose over them, and followed him out into the bedroom.

Martholin had brought the tray by then and was unloading it onto the sideboard, a mix of bread and cheese and cold ham and a crock of pottage that had clearly been warming in the fire for some hours. Envar reached for that hungrily, and Irichels held up their boots. "Marthie, I'm sorry to ask, but can you clean these tonight? They don't have to be dry, just clean."

"Maybe that'll teach you to stay out of places you shouldn't be," she answered, but took the boots. "These are disgraceful, Master Gil, you need a new pair. And the dot're, too."

"I'll get to that," Irichels promised. "And thank you, Marthie."

"I'll fetch the dishes in the morning," she said, and closed the door behind her.

"Were you seen?" Arak asked.

"Not that I could tell," Envar answered.

Irichels said, "If we were seen, I think we'd know about it already."

"Did you say that Manimere herself was here?" Alaissou asked, and Irichels nodded.

"Rallying her folk, I expect. She's determined not to lose her place, nor do I blame her."

"And she wants your help," Arak said.

"Yes," Irichels said, and in the same moment Envar said, "Of course."

Irichels glanced sideways at him. "You disapprove?"

"Not disapprove, precisely, but she's asking a great deal on very short acquaintance."

Irichels grimaced. There was a little too much truth to that for comfort. "You say that with Manimere's scrolls under your coat?"

"Point." Envar made a face himself. "And I am grateful, what she's given us should be useful. But I don't think you should raise an army for her."

"Is that what she wants?" Alaissou asked with some alarm.

"As a last resort," Irichels said. "And I needn't remind you that none of this must leave this room."

She looked momentarily offended, but nodded. "I don't see how you can."

"No more do I," Irichels answered. "And I think there's more going on here than just Manimere's banishment. Or than bringing me to heel. I think someone is trying to destroy the contracts that keep Bejanth safe, and they're somehow using the Shame to do it."

There was a little silence then, Alaissou pale and worried, Arak scowling, Envar with the crooked smile he used to hide his thoughts. It was, of course, Envar who spoke first, "Granting that, and I think you're right, my heart—what do we do?"

"You have that scroll to work with," Irichels said. "Manimere said it at least quoted some of the provisions of the contract, was that right?"

"Seems to be." Envar nodded.

"I want to know everything you can find out about the Shame and its contract. Then I want to know what quarrel Grandfather had with everyone, and what contracts he'd made at the end of his life, since that Oratorian, Leonor, suggested that was what brought us a cursling, and I'm thinking it might be the Death card in Zaffara's reading." Irichels paused, considering. "And also—Alaissou, you said your father was determined for you to get pregnant as soon as possible?"

The ready color swept up from her bodice, but her voice was steady. "Yes. He said you were cursed to die soon."

"We need to find out exactly what your first curse does—among other things, if it affects fertility."

The color deepened, but she nodded again. "Tell me what you need."

"Cass and I can assess the curse," Irichels said.

"And I know some folk who may be able to say who made it, and who they sold it too," Envar interjected.

"You think it's my stepmother," Alaissou said flatly.

Irichels nodded. "Yes. If there's a reason I shouldn't suspect her—"

Alaissou shook her head. "No. I can't say that there is."

"If I can prove it," Irichels said, "and if the curse does what I think it might, I think I can use it against your father. If I go to him, say that someone has cursed you, that you cannot bear a child—I am in a position to undo whatever he wanted done by this marriage, and fear of that should force his hand."

"That's not a bad idea," Envar said, and Arak nodded.

Alaissou said, "He won't back down."

"I can't see that he'll have a choice," Arak said.

"He'll make one," Alaissou said. She looked at Irichels. "When he wants a thing—he's very determined."

"I'll keep that in mind," Irichels said.

Even with Envar's help, it was a morning's solid work to analyze Alaissou's curse, and the bells of Idra-of-Mercies had sounded noontide long before they had finished. And they'd not gotten as much as he'd hoped, Irichels admitted, as they hurried through a cold luncheon under Martholin's disapproving eye. Envar thought he could identify the feral who'd created it, which was something, but otherwise... Otherwise, they'd been able to determine that it was intended to bring a wasting death, shriveling the internal organs and stopping breath, and that Alaissou's counter-curse, tied as it was to her music, had been remarkably successful in holding the stronger curse at bay.

"Which was what we knew going in," Irichels said, when he and Envar had retreated to the library, and Alaissou had disappeared to her rooms to practice.

"Certainly, my heart," Envar agreed, sorting through the contents of his shabby satchel. The scroll he'd taken from Manimere House lay on the worktable, ready to be examined in more detail, and he gave it a regretful look. "But now I've got the feel of the work, I think I can find whoever did it."

"Unless the stepmother's a feral herself," Arak said.

"I'd think we'd have heard," Envar said. "At least rumors."

"It felt professional," Irichels said. "As though someone with formal training had made it, anyway."

"Doesn't that rule out most ferals?" Arak asked.

"Not here," Envar said, and Irichels spoke in the same moment.

"Not in Bejanth. Anyone who survives long enough to make it a profession has had some teaching."

"But that doesn't mean looking for them is safe," Envar said. "Which is why I want company."

Arak looked at Irichels. "Is it safe, do you think?"

"Leaving me, or going with him?"

"Both."

"I'll be safe enough here in the house," Irichels said. "And if Cass says he needs you to watch his back, I want you there."

Arak nodded, and the pair took themselves off, Arak dropping into the faintly defeated slouch that marked less successful hired swords and that seemed to guarantee her invisibility. Irichels watched them make their way up the street, taking the long way to the Orangery, and wished he could go with them. But he was the noticeable one these days, and in any case he had Manimere's scroll to look at.

He eased it out of the case, wincing as the antique paper cracked under his touch, edges flaking away. He laid it out on the worktable, setting the polished weights to hold it flat, and began to work his way through the earlier entries. As Manimere had warned, the scribe had used a particularly crabbed version of the old-fashioned Chancery hand, and it took about an hour to get his eye in, so that he could read it with reasonable fluency. Most of the entries were the same sorts of things that he'd been reading in Samar's records: monies invested in cargoes or on the Plana, household accounts, the occasional birth or death or wedding deemed significant, all added on as they happened and with only minimal commentary.

And then, between a list of the Year-End gifts to the household and a scratched-out calculation that seemed to involve an exchange of pine-nuts for peppercorns that had not come off, he found the first entry. It involved a court case—the Senate and Assembly's commercial court, not the Court Between Worlds—apparently disputing the payment of a transit-fee to the Supervisor of the Sea-Roads. Irichels didn't recognize the title, and his grandfather's Chancery-book was no help, but the question seemed to be whether Manimere's ship had to pay this fee or if it was exempt under a prior contract.

The family clerk had transcribed a section of what seemed to be the relevant contract, which was an agreement between parties not named in the excerpt to allow safe passage between Bejanth and certain specified harbors, both along the coast and across the Narrow Sea. Irichels copied it out, his eyebrows rising. If that was part of the original contract, then the houses of the Shame had not merely moved to control the city but to dominate its trade as well: it was no wonder the Senate and Assembly had acted to punish them, but it was no reason to break the contract.

He moved on, muttering under his breath as the crabbed hand gave way to one that was flamboyantly beautiful and equally illegible, stopping at last on what seemed to be another excerpt. No, it was the same clause, but summarized rather than copied, and with a notation about licenses for fishing rights: again, proof that the houses of the Shame had done their best to dominate their new city, but no reason to undo what they'd wrought. A little further on, there was the record of the purchase of a new house, and the notation that it was not and never could be the family seat, as that would invalidate the requirement that the Four Points remain fixed. That would be the circles he had found, he guessed, and the invisible pillars that pierced them: again, useful information, but he doubted anyone would risk the destruction of the city to get a larger house.

By the time he'd worked his way through the rest of the roll, the muscles in the small of his back were pinched and aching, and his eyes were gritty from deciphering the antique script. He had copies of all the references, and rolled the scroll carefully back into its case and locked it into the family strongbox. He stretched, wincing, and looked again at his pile of papers. Most of the references were to trade, which made sense, but he couldn't quite see how that fit. It was possible he had missed something in Samar's records, but he found it hard to muster the energy to start that search all over again. He only hoped Envar had had better luck.

"Gil?" That was Alaissou's voice at the door, and he lifted his head.

"Come in."

"Marthie says, will the dot're and Messida Arak be home to dinner?"

"I expect so," Irichels said, and she came to stand by the table.

"Have you found anything?"

"Not as much as I'd have liked," Irichels admitted. "There's one clause that gets referred to several times, but it seems to be about trade routes. It looks as though the four houses made an agreement with the sea demons about safe passage—safe routes, I suppose—as well as protecting the city."

To his surprise, Alaissou nodded. "That would make sense. I suppose that's where the ship-marks come from."

"Ship-marks?" Manimere had mentioned them, he remembered: curses that provided safe travel along certain trading routes. And that had to have been what Manimere had been fighting over in the cases referenced in the scroll. And the sea demon had said something about them as well.

It was Alaissou's turn to look surprised. "Surely you know about them."

"I wasn't raised to the family business," Irichels said. "And then I spent most of my life on the mainland."

"All the trading ships have them," Alaissou said. "Well, most of them. Nobody wants to risk a long voyage in a ship that doesn't carry one."

"Manimere said they protected ships at sea as long as they stayed on certain trade routes,"

"That's the theory. And certainly they work, but..." Alaissou shrugged. "There's only a certain number available, I don't know how many, and the Senate and Assembly hand them out, for a fee, of course. There's always grumbling because not everyone who wants one can have one, and you have to pay a tithe of the profits from every voyage as long as you keep them. And then with the trade opening up with Hyppola, there's no direct route on the approved list—you have to go by way of the Skattans, so there's always someone trying to make a quick profit by going straight across." She paused, considering what she'd just said. "Do you think that's what this is about? I know it's been an issue in the Assembly for a while now."

"So the Senate and Assembly issue these ship-marks that protect traders using the agreed-upon routes." Irichels rooted through his notes, found the first section he'd copied. "That would match with this piece of the contract. But if there's a limit to the number of ship-marks—"

"And if the safe sea-roads aren't as profitable as they used to be," Alaissou said. "Hyppola is the biggest one, but there are half a dozen new ports on both sides of the Narrow Sea that don't lie on the old courses. To trade with them, you have to take your chances, and that means everyone else can compete with us. Father complained about that all the time."

"Which would be the first good reason I've heard to meddle with this contract," Irichels said. "Thank you. That's—this has been extremely helpful."

She flashed a sudden smile. "I'm glad. I just assumed everyone knew."

"Not me," Irichels said, and there was a knock at the door. "Yes?"

"Pardon, Master," Tepan said, "but Marthie was wanting an answer from Dona Alaissou."

"I'd best go," Alaissou said, and Irichels nodded.

Envar and Arak returned in time for dinner, though not in time to change beforehand. Martholin allowed herself one comprehensive look of disapproval, and served the meal without further complaint. There was even a sweet, little balls of fried dough in a crackling sugar sauce, and when that was picked over, Envar leaned back in his chair, licking his fingers.

"Can I take it you were successful?" Irichels asked. There had been no time to talk before the meal, and it had seemed unwise to have this conversation within earshot of the maids, but now they would have some minutes before Martholin herself came to remove the sweet and the kaf service. Even so, Envar glanced quickly at the door, and Arak sighed.

"Surely we can talk now."

"Yes," Envar said. "And yes, we were successful. I've found the feral who wrote the curse and brokered the contract, and he's agreed he'll speak to you, confirm the identity of the person who commissioned it. Who is the person you expected, by the way."

"I say it's a trap," Arak said.

"Why?" Envar asked. "He's respectable, as these things go. And it was a long time ago."

"Not long enough," Arak said.

"It's been rumored I've been asking questions," Irichels said. "Alaissou?"

"I have trouble imagining my stepmother hiring assassins," she said, "but that doesn't mean she wouldn't."

Irichels poured himself another cup of kaf, taking his time over the condiments. "Where does this person live?"

"Orangery. The Limmerwil." Envar's voice was without inflection, for all that the Limmerwil on the sea-facing side of the Orangery was one of Bejanth's least salubrious warrens. "And, yes, where you'd think. But all the more reason not to want to see their clients murdered."

"Or to take good coin for murdering them," Arak muttered.

They were both right, and Irichels sighed. "Will he name names?"

"He said so," Envar answered.

"Then there's not much choice," Irichels said. "It's worth the risk."

But not worth visiting the Limmerwil at night. Instead, they left Samar House a little after the third hour, with Irichels himself managing the family's smallest punt. Envar perched in the bow, his gown bundled at his feet, while Arak clung unhappily to the single cracked seat in the center of the boat. She was well armed, sword and dagger and a small crossbow, plus a doublet lined with iron plates, which Irichels hoped would be enough to discourage any trouble. The early hour would help, too, as would Envar's presence.

For himself, Irichels had worn his heaviest hill-country leather jerkin in spite of the weather, and carried a sword as well as his curses. He steered the punt through the crowded canals, dodging the traffic around Lawgivers' Isle to cross the wider expanse of the Serenna before ducking under the Soliman Bridge that connected the Orangery to the Boot. The Limmerwil lay not far beyond, and he grimaced as he turned the boat into Doth's Cut. He could feel the tangle of curses that held the rotting buildings together, prickling on his skin like heat rash. "How far in?"

Envar glanced back at him. "Take the first cross-cut. Then it's a few hundred yards."

Irichels dug the oar deeper into the slack water, the movements still familiar after all these years. On the seaward side of the Cut, crumbling houses showed heavy doors and shuttered windows to the water; on the inland side, a narrow walkway widened abruptly into a plaza, with shops set back from the edge. Only a few of them seemed to be open yet, and most of those were eating houses, the smell of frying fish mixing with the sour scent of the canal. It was not so different from the Quadrata or the worst parts of the Palinade, but Irichels found himself glancing warily into the shadows where an assassin might hide.

"Here," Envar said, and Irichels swung the boat obediently into the narrower canal. The houses pressed close, cutting off the watery sunlight, and Arak shifted her position, reaching for the crossbow by her feet to set it across her knees. There were few windows at canal level, and the ones on the higher floors were tightly shuttered; there had been occasional boats on the Cut and tied by the plaza, but there were none here.

"It's not as bad as it looks," Envar said, and Arak grunted. "Let's hope not."

There was another cut ahead, and a gap in the houses where a building had collapsed and not been repaired, letting in a wedge of sunlight. A couple of small boats were tied up in the ruin, and there was a makeshift dock on the far side, giving onto a slightly wider alley. "Is this it?" Irichels asked, and was unsurprised when Envar nodded.

They left their boat tied up with the others and climbed out onto the dock. It was more secure underfoot than Irichels had expected, and the houses along this street seemed to be in better repair. Envar led the way toward one of the smaller buildings, where the plaster had been recently patched but the painted woodwork was fading from a brilliant pink. The shutters were open on the topmost floor, and Irichels shaded his eyes to peer up at them, wondering if that was where the feral lived. Envar knocked on the door, and Irichels heard his sharp intake of breath as the door swung back at his touch.

"That's not good," Arak said, and brought the crossbow

out from under her cloak.

"Wait," Envar said, and pushed the door open the rest of the way. He sketched a sign in the air between himself and the dark interior. Sparks flashed and vanished, and he looked back at Irichels with a shrug. "No trap."

"At least not here," Irichels said, and followed him into the hallway. Arak pulled the door closed behind them, and Envar sketched another sign, sending it floating ahead of them. It reached the sunlight where the hall opened into the courtyard and disappeared.

"Nor here." Nor likely anywhere until they reached the feral, Irichels thought. He made his way cautiously into the courtyard, where the air smelled of ash and old cooking and the catch basin beneath the open skylight was green with drying slime.

"The second floor," Envar said and Irichels nodded, sending a sign of his own ahead to test the stairs. They were clear, too, and he made his way up as quietly as he could, grimacing as the wood creaked under his weight.

"Did you speak to him here before?" Arak asked softly.

"I spoke to his brother," Envar said, matching her tone, "who's also his broker. But not here."

Irichels stepped out onto the narrow landing, frowning as he saw a half-open door ahead of him. "Cass. Is that—?"

Envar nodded, fingers curling in a defensive spell. Irichels called up an attack of his own and followed, grimacing again as he caught the first faint whiff of blood and urine. Behind him, Arak swore under her breath. Envar pushed the door all the way open, though he didn't enter the room, and over his shoulder Irichels caught a glimpse of the body huddled on the floor, flies feasting on the blood that overspread the cracked tiles. He sketched a testing sign, let it drift into the room to hover above the body until it faded into nothing.

"Clear," he said, and Envar nodded.

"That's him," he said, and went to one knee beside the body, careful to avoid the blood. "Falguera." The body lay on its side, and when he tugged the shoulder, it rolled all in one piece, the arm that had been outstretched pointing toward the ceiling. The front of his gown was soaked in blood, and more flies swarmed up. Envar waved impatiently at them and loosened the front of the gown to reveal first the bloodied shirt and then two great gashes in the man's chest. "Stabbed."

"A solid day ago, too," Irichels said, looking at the extended arm.

"I spoke to his brother a bit after noontide," Envar said. "Stiff as he is, he can't have been killed long after."

Irichels looked around the room. It was sparsely furnished, just a table and a brace of stools and an open cabinet with empty shelves hung on the far wall. There was a door that had to lead to an inner room and he crossed to it, fingers shaping another sign as he pushed it open with his other hand. The figure sparked and died, leaving him looking at a tumbled bed, the blankets in a heap at one side, and a snowstorm scatter of papers drifted across the boards. A bookpress had been opened and plundered, one door broken half off its hinges, and he realized abruptly that what he had taken for blankets was another body. "Cass."

Envar came to join him, his face twisting in an unhappy grimace. "Not another—"

Irichels knelt beside the crumpled body. It had stiffened, too, couldn't be turned onto its back, but he drew the torn blanket away from the face, then craned his neck to examine the torso. It was hard to tell, given the way it was contorted, the arms crossed tight over the chest, but he thought this man had been stabbed as well.

"It's the brother," Envar said. "He's the one I spoke to." He shook his head. "I was careful, I swear."

"Not careful enough," Arak said, from the doorway. "We shouldn't linger."

"I made sure I wasn't followed," Envar said. "And Laure seemed calm enough. He thought they were safe, I swear it."

"He was wrong," Arak muttered, and Irichels reached for the nearest scrap of paper. It was half a horoscope, crossed out and overwritten by an entirely different set of calculations;

the next paper had the details of a curse laid out in multi-colored ink, and the one beneath it had notes for what looked like a contract for poisons.

"We need to search this," he began, and realized instantly that it would be pointless.

"They've already done that, my heart," Envar said, but he, too, was picking up papers as though there might be something left.

"They might have missed something."

"Not likely," Arak said. "More to the point, they likely know you were coming here. We should leave."

She was right, Irichels knew, but couldn't stop himself from picking up another two, three fragments. They were nothing useful—more contract notes, part of a recipe, a chandler's bill—and he pushed himself to his feet. "Arak's right."

Envar sighed. "I know."

They turned toward the door, and Irichels laid a hand carefully on Envar's shoulder. The feral shook his head, but didn't move away. "I thought—I should have been more careful."

"None of us expected this," Irichels said. Possibly it was a sign that he was on the right track, but with the bodies behind him that was no consolation. They reached the main door, and he pulled it back into the half-open position it had occupied when they arrived.

"We should leave," Arak said again. "Now."

"There were people upstairs," Envar said. "Other lodgers."

Irichels suppressed a groan. Arak said, "They will have fled. Or else they're dead, too."

"I want to know which," Envar said, and started up the next flight of stairs.

Irichels swore under his breath, and followed.

There were three doors at the top of the stairs; one stood open, letting in sunlight and a breeze that smelled strongly of the canal, and the rest were closed. Envar opened them one after the other, let out a sigh of relief when both gave onto nearly empty rooms. Whoever had lived there had left and taken the best of their goods with them; all that remained was some bits of wooden tableware and a stool with a short leg. "Satisfied?" Arak asked, and Envar nodded.

"I had to know," he said, as they made their way back down the stairs.

"I know." Irichels glanced over his shoulder. "This is not your fault."

"I should have been more careful." Envar sighed again. "I thought I was."

They had reached the courtyard, and Irichels put a hand on the chirurgeon's shoulder. He was rewarded with the twist of a smile, and Arak said, "It's not safe to stay."

"No," Irichels agreed, and was pleased when Envar nodded.

The street was still empty, the other houses closed and shuttered. The boat was untouched where they had left it and Irichels shoved them away from the dock, turning not to retrace their passage but to follow this canal to the Burnt Cut and out into the Sundrin Passage. To his relief, no one followed, nor did they draw any particular attention as he steered them along the Burnt, dodging barges loaded with compost as they left the Limmerwil and drew closer to the better parts of the Orangery. The tide was with them as he turned into the Sundrin and the wind was out of the east, setting up a chop that jostled the shallow boat and had Arak clutching the gunwales with both hands. Irichels kept the boat close to shore in spite of the traffic, and didn't try to cross to the far side of the canal until they'd turned into the shelter of the Orangery. Arak sat up straighter, her expression less grim than it had been. "What do we do now?"

"An excellent question." Envar turned so that his back was resting against the upcurved bow-piece. "I heard Falguera's word, and Laure's, but with them both dead, that's second-hand at best."

"And you'd be a biased witness," Irichels agreed. "Still. It may be worth trying anyway."

"If Dona Alaissou says her father won't take the bait," Arak said, "I'd believe her."

"He'll bite," Irichels said, and hoped it was true.

At Samar House he changed into better clothes, considering his options. The Senate and Assembly were in informal session, the series of meetings that preceded the formal sessions, and he guessed that Cambryse would be present, at least as an observer. He himself should not be, strictly speaking, but no one had actually forbidden him to attend. And certainly he could wait for Cambryse when he left the session—that might be the most effective way to find him, and safer than trying to arrange a meeting on less neutral ground.

He took the larger boat this time, with Antel handling the oar, and Arak and Envar accompanying him. The meetings were still in session, though an usher allowed that it was winding down; Irichels found a spot in the shade of the portico where he could watch the Assembly's doors, and waited.

It wasn't long before the members of the Assembly began to emerge. At this informal session most of them had left off their robes and masks, and it didn't take long to spot Cambryse among them, very elegant in chestnut-brown brocade. Irichels stepped out from under the portico and headed toward him, aiming to intercept his course before he reached the crowd of boats waiting at the foot of the steps that led down to the water.

Cambryse saw him coming and turned to meet him, frowning slightly. "Samar." There was a tall man at his side, with a high forehead and weatherworn skin. There was something familiar about his face but Irichels couldn't place it, focused his attention on Cambryse instead.

"Cambryse. If I might have a word."

Cambryse's frown deepened fractionally, and then he smoothed his expression. "Is it urgent? But I'm remiss. You must know Fane Temenon."

"I don't believe we've met." Irichels quelled his own impatience. He couldn't quite place the name, and the man smiled sourly.

"You've met my son Margos."

This was the younger brother, then, not the master. Irichels dipped his head, and kept his tone scrupulously neutral. "I've had that pleasure." He looked back at Cambryse. "I'm afraid the matter's somewhat urgent."

Fane's eyebrows flicked up, but he nodded to Cambryse. "I'll leave you then. We can talk later."

"Certainly," Cambryse agreed. He waited as the other man turned away, then waved for Irichels to walk ahead of him, away from the crowd proceeding to their boats. "If it's so important we must talk now—"

"It's about Alaissou," Irichels said.

Cambryse looked from him to Envar and then to Arak. "In that case, I don't see why you need your household."

"In case I need their testimony," Irichels said.

"Let's wait and see if you do," Cambryse answered, and drew him on out of earshot. "Now. What is it?"

"She's been cursed," Irichels said. "This wasting sickness—it's the result of a curse, and you're lucky she's still alive. Frankly, I'm surprised you didn't see it."

There was a moment of silence, of utter stillness, the color draining from Cambryse's face. "I don't—no, you wouldn't say it without proof."

"I can prove it."

Cambryse nodded. "Who? And have you broken it?"

"It's stable," Irichels said. He hadn't expected that moment of shock, made himself focus again. "But I fear she will not be able to bear a child."

"What?" Cambryse controlled himself instantly. "I assure you, Samar, I did not know of this. Can you break the curse? Or will I need to find someone who can?"

"I can," Irichels said. "But I can't know how much damage has already been done, or whether I can fix it. And that is a problem."

Cambryse nodded. "Who? Who did it?"

Irichels hesitated, but there was no turning back. "Your wife."

"I don't believe you."

"Dot're Cassi found the feral she paid for the curse," Irichels said. "Give me a reason I should not bring this case before the courts and demand both that your lady be punished and that this marriage should be annulled."

"If you could do that, you'd already be there," Cambryse said. "And if you had witnesses—you don't, do you?"

"I have more than enough to go before the courts."

"No." Cambryse shook his head. "This is a family matter, Samar, between me and my wife—I will speak with her myself, find out what's going on, and deal with it. And you will leave it to me."

"Why should I do that?" Irichels countered. "I have done your bidding this far, and what has it gotten me?"

"Make a case of this, and I assure you, it will not stand. Your only witness is your catamite—if you had the feral, you'd have gone to Ambros first—and that's not nearly enough. Bring a suit, and I'll claim you're trying to get out of our agreement."

"Any Oratorian would testify to the curse," Irichels said.

"But they couldn't prove who placed it, any more than you can. Accuse my wife, and I'll accuse you. The Senate and Assembly would be glad to find a reason to put you back in a cell." Cambryse drew a deep breath. "We will speak further regarding Alaissou. But you'll leave this to me." He turned on his heel without waiting for an answer and stalked away.

Envar and Arak moved closer and Irichels sighed. "That didn't go the way I'd planned."

"I told you you should have listened to Alaissou," Arak said.

CHAPTER SEVENTEEN

Irichels stared after Cambryse's departing figure, watching him make his way down the steps and into the painted boat with the bow-piece of the Cambryse cormorant. Though it hadn't gone as well as he had hoped, perhaps it would still be enough to make Cambryse act injudiciously. He shook himself, looking now for his own boat, and a familiar voice spoke behind him.

"Samar. What are you doing here?"

He turned to see Gellis Ambros frowning at him, Per Gethen at his side. "I needed a word with Cambryse, Master Ambros. That's all." He sounded defensive and knew it, and Ambros's frown deepened.

"What do you know about the letter?"

"What letter?"

"Manimere's letter," Gethen said. "If you were part of this—"

"I have no idea what you're talking about," Irichels said, and put all the sincerity he could muster into the words. "I'll swear on anything you like."

Ambros paused, visibly considering. "You've heard nothing at all."

"I spent the morning on the Orangery dealing with a family matter," Irichels said. "I went home and changed my clothes and came here to see Cambryse. Will you tell me what's happened?"

He could see it hanging in the balance, saw the moment when Ambros conceded. "A captain of her fleet came into the harbor under flag of truce. He had a letter from her saying that she had seen strange signs and portents while she cruised offshore, and asking for permission to return to share what she's seen."

"The Assembly refused, of course," Gethen said.

"If she was serious, she could have authorized her captain to give the details," Ambros said. "He's been sent to the cells in the hopes he'll think better of it."

"And now we find you here." Gethen glared.

"I knew nothing of this," Irichels said. "I give you my word, if you'll take it. I've had no dealings with her since she left the city." And that was literally true, even though he fully intended to mislead them.

Ambros shook his head. "It's a bad business."

"It sounds it," Irichels said. "The captain gave no hint at all?"

"He spoke of lights on the water, and a heavy, oily swell— like a storm was coming, but lasting for days, and no sign of clouds or wind."

"He swore Manimere had more to tell," Gethen said, "but he denied knowing details, and said he couldn't speak further for her."

"Not that you could blame him," Envar muttered, but softly enough that he could be ignored.

Irichels said, "I doubt she'd risk sending a warning if there wasn't something there."

"Can you think of a better way for her to worm her way back into the city?" Gethen answered. "No, the Assembly was right to refuse her."

Ambros looked less certain. "I hope the captain will reconsider. Or that Manimere gave him more room to bargain. If even a part of this is true..."

"What do the city's captains say?" Irichels asked. Trouble at sea could just as easily mean trouble with the sea demons, and it seemed entirely too coincidental to think it wasn't related to the Shame and whatever Cambryse was doing there. For a moment, he considered telling Ambros everything he had found, but that seemed more likely to confirm he was in league with Manimere than to get the Senate and Assembly to act. "Or anyone else who's come home recently."

"We've heard nothing from our captains," Ambros said. "Though that doesn't mean much; they're patrolling closer in than Manimere's fleet. We've sent a dispatch-boat to make inquiries, and questions are being asked along the docks. We'll see what they say before we consider further action."

"It's a worrisome thing," Irichels said, and Gethen gave him a suspicious look.

"If it's true," Ambros said, and Irichels nodded. "Go home, Samar. Stay out of trouble."

Irichels bowed. "As you wish."

The canals were crowded, boats making their way from Lawgivers' back toward their masters' houses, and Antel struggled to make way across the open water. Irichels leaned back against the cushions, barely aware of the chop that made Arak hunch her shoulders and sent plumes of spray into the boat. He supposed it was possible that this was some trick of Manimere's, but that didn't seem like her, and if it wasn't... If these were signs that the sea demons were rousing, in defiance of the contract, that was something the Senate and Assembly needed to hear, from Manimere if not from him.

The contract should still prevent a direct assault, but if Cambryse was trying to break the contract, the city could be vulnerable. Even if he and the sea demons were intending to make some new contract—and surely that had to be part of the plan; there was no advantage to be gained by destroying Bejanth—there would be a moment when the old was gone and the new was not yet formed. And that assumed that this was not some trick to get Cambryse to break the contract so that the sea demons could bring down the city. No, he had to share his suspicions—with Ambros, for preference, and maybe Hal could help with that.

They tied up at the Samar House dock, the boat knocking against the fenders in the uneasy waves until Antel had it secured. Irichels made his way into the courtyard, to find

Alaissou coming down the stairs. She gave him a sharp look and said, "No luck, I take it."

"No." It was slightly better than *I told you so*, but not much. "Would you ask Marthie to bring me a pot of kaf? I'll be in the workroom."

"Of course." She drifted across the courtyard and Irichels went on into the workroom, leaving the door open behind him. After a bit Envar joined him, settling into the cushions that now padded the greatchair, knees drawn up like a boy.

"What do you think he'll do?"

"I don't know. I hoped he'd be willing to bargain, but..." Irichels shrugged. "I suppose I should have listened to Alaissou."

"I'd like to ask a few questions about Falguera's death," Envar said. "I'm sure it was her—Seresinha, I mean, her or some of her household. The Temenons seem to be an aggressive family. But I'll wait if you tell me to."

"What I want is for you to be careful," Irichels said. "Ask if you think you can get useful answers, but don't take any risks."

"It's a risk breathing in this city," Envar said lightly.

"You know what I mean." Irichels looked up as the door opened again and Martholin herself appeared, carrying a kaf service. She set it on the sideboard, and held out a sheet of cheap paper.

"Have you seen these, Master Gil?"

Irichels took it warily. It was cheaply printed, too, the ink smeared and the type barely serviceable, but Manimere's collared dolphin was at the top and bottom of the notice. *Trouble on the Waters*, the largest line read, and beneath it was a letter purporting to be from Manimere, warning of strange happenings in the deeps and urging readers to question newly-returned sailors if they didn't believe her. "I had not."

"They're saying in the market that Master Manimere sent the same letter to the Senate and Assembly, a warning, they say. But the Senate ignored her."

"Apparently she sent them a letter with much the same

warning, and one of her captains as well," Irichels said carefully, "but what they turned down was her asking to return."

"They should let her come," Martholin said. "If she has news for the city, they should let her in."

"I gather they don't believe her," Irichels said. He set the broadsheet on his worktable. "May I keep that?"

"Certainly. There are plenty about," Martholin said.

"What are people saying?" Irichels asked. "Has anyone else seen these signs, or heard that anyone has?"

Martholin shrugged. "They say that a crew from Abesscie saw the lights she mentions, flickering on the horizon all the way north. They thought it was heat lightning at first, but it never broke, and the color changed as they got closer to us, turned more green than blue. And Karan says he spoke to our baker, and she said the last grain shipment was delayed by contrary winds."

"That happens," Irichels said.

"But not much this time of year," Martholin answered. "And they saw the lights, too." She paused. "What do I say to the household, then?"

Irichels glanced at Envar, but the chirurgeon didn't meet his eyes. "Tell them the Senate and Assembly have the letter, yes, and that Manimere wants to come home on the strength of it. I don't know what they'll decide."

"That won't keep them happy long," Martholin said, and Irichels sighed.

"It's the best I have."

"What are you going to do?" Envar asked, after the door had closed behind her.

"Write a note to Hal," Irichels said, "and see if he'll persuade his father to talk to me."

Envar's eyebrows rose. "What will you tell him?"

"What I suspect about my family, and about the Shame," Irichels said, after a moment.

"Will you name Cambryse?"

"I don't know." Irichels poured himself a cup of kaf and

began adding condiments. "It depends on how he takes it, I suppose."

Envar uncoiled himself from the chair and came to pour a cup of his own. "Be careful, my heart."

"I intend to be."

It took several days to arrange a meeting with Ambros, even with Hal's help. Over those days, more broadsheets appeared sharing Manimere's warning, and Martholin reported that more sailors were confirming that they, too, had seen the ominous signs. Another round of posters appeared, tacked up on tavern walls and on the sides of shuttered businesses, demanding that the Senate and Assembly allow Manimere to return. The constables attempted to arrest a bill-poster, only to be charged by a gang of dockworkers, who freed the girl and spirited her into hiding while the fishwives threw shells and garbage.

"That's the worst of it so far," Hal said, greeting him and Arak at the side door of Ambros House, "But part of that is that the constables have been pulled back to protect the warehouses. Even the middling folk are starting to ask questions."

"The weather isn't helping," Irichels said, and saw Arak nod. Not that it was bad, but the sky was hazed white, a thin layer of cloud hiding the sun and stars, and the wind rose to gusts out of the southwest, then died, perpetually on the edge of breaking into something worse.

"No." Hal led the way down a side hall, brought them into one of the small parlors. A dining table had been laid, and an array of cold dishes waited on the sideboard, while Ambros himself refilled his glass from the waiting pitcher and Hal's brother Valens kicked moodily at the ashes in the cold fireplace. "Samar's here, Father."

Arak paused at the door, but Irichels beckoned her in. "I may want your testimony," he said, over his shoulder, and bowed to Ambros. "Thank you for seeing me."

"I've things to talk to you about, as well," Ambros said. "But we'll serve ourselves first."

"If you'll permit, Master Ambros?" Arak asked, tipping her head toward the wine, and Ambros blinked once before he nodded.

"Thank you, Messida."

Arak filled the glasses with the grace she'd learned in the courts of the hill country, then came to stand behind Irichels's chair as the others took their places. Irichels gave her a nod of thanks, and looked at Ambros. "What was it you wanted, Master?"

"I'd rather hear you first," Ambros said. His tone brooked no argument, and Irichels bowed again.

"As you wish." Irichels took a careful sip of wine. "Since I came back to Bejanth, I've been—concerned—about my family's run of, at best, extremely bad luck. I wondered about a curse, given everything that had happened—"

"But that was disproven. Wasn't it?" Valens said, and waved a hand in apology. "I'm sorry, Samar, go on."

"There was no negligence from the executors," Irichels said quickly. "I've no complaints there. But something wasn't right, and the further I've dug into the matter, the more reason I've had to think that someone is trying to meddle with the city's contracts, and mostly likely the contract that founded the city."

"You're referring to the Shame," Ambros said, expressionless, and Hal breathed a laugh.

"Who has more right?"

"I think so," Irichels said and matched Hal's wry smile.

"But why would anyone do that?" Valens asked. Irichels hesitated, not sure how much he wanted to say on that subject, and Ambros shook his head.

"More to the point, what's your proof?"

That was easier to answer. Irichels set his wine aside and began to lay out what he had found about the Shame, from the card reading after Maritsa's death to his own researches and his visit to the Courts Beyond. He left out his discussions with Manimere and with Cambryse, stressing instead the unlikeliness of Samar's decline. Ambros was visibly unimpressed, however, and he finished, "In any case, there's no question that someone has been acting against Samar, and I can find no other reason to want to eliminate the family entirely."

There was a little silence when he had finished, and then Ambros shook his head. "No," he said slowly. "No, I can't— no one would meddle with the foundational contracts, and not with that one in particular."

"The deaths," Irichels said, and Ambros shook his head again.

"Oh, I'll admit that it looks very much as though someone was trying to destroy the family, and I would back you if you wanted to bring that before the Senate and Assembly, but no one wants to see the city fall."

"Destroying Samar will break the contract," Irichels said.

"They can't have known," Ambros answered. "Your grandfather had enemies, especially at the end of his life— even Galeran had a few enemies by the end. But you'd have to be mad to bring down the city."

There was no point in arguing, at least not without more evidence. Irichels said, "I'll think about coming before the Assembly—when I'm allowed, of course."

"Which brings me to the other matter I wanted to discuss with you," Ambros said. "You'll have seen the broadsheets." Irichels nodded. "The Senate and Assembly are meeting tomorrow to vote on allowing Manimere to address the Senate. It's been agreed that you'll be reinstated for the vote."

As long as I vote the way you tell me to, Irichels thought. He said, "I don't have gown or mask."

"Find some if you can, but you'll be admitted without," Ambros answered. "We need to know what Manimere has seen, but we can't just let her back. We need to bring her back under escort, and she needs to surrender to our authority."

"Is that the only choice?" Irichels asked.

"Of course not. There's a considerable party that says we should keep her out, that she has nothing useful to say." Ambros speared a slice of the chicken that he had neglected until now. "And there are those who want to bring her back without conditions, though they're a smaller party."

Hal lifted his head. "Has anyone considered that everything Manimere has reported—everything that's being talked of on the docks—might be a sign that Gil's right? If the contract is hanging by a thread, and the sea demons are gathering..."

"How would they know?" Valens demanded, and Ambros shook his head.

"Manimere wants us to believe it's the sea demons, and I'll grant you the signs are worrisome. They've tried before to cut off our trade, and that's what this sounds like, the way they're massing at the edge of the deeps."

"And if she's right, she's doing the city a good turn," Irichels said, in spite of himself.

"Yes," Ambros said, "and herself as well. There are some who are saying she's made some contract with them just to get herself home." He lifted a hand before either Irichels or Hal could speak. "Which I don't believe, but that's the talk. You'll receive a summons to the Assembly, Samar."

"I understand," Irichels said, and turned his attention to the meal.

It was another long day before the summons arrived, coupled with the formal charter allowing him to take his place. Martholin found a gown and mask somewhere in the boxes that cluttered the third floor storerooms and managed to mend the spots where moths had nibbled at the hem, while Karan blacked and waxed the leather mask until it looked new-made. Irichels tried them on in front of the mirror in Envar's bedroom, and had to repress the urge to rip them off his body. This was everything he had never wanted to be, everything he had been told he wasn't and could never be, and his skin crawled at the sight of his grandfather in the tarnished mirror. The house daemon stirred, disturbed by his reaction, and

Envar said, "Gil?"

Irichels snatched off the mask, then made himself stop and lay it gently on the nearest shelf. "I'm all right."

"What if we left?" Envar said. "Packed up the household and took everyone to the Plana. We can still get ahead of whatever's coming."

"And then what?" Irichels shrugged out of the gown, tossed it over the back of a chair.

"Let the Senate and Assembly tend to the city," Envar said. "You warned them, they didn't listen. You've done what you could."

It was tempting. And it might even work: whatever Cambryse was doing, the sea demons seemed to have separate plans, might even have figured out a way to void the contract on their own. He could at least save the household. Except that there were only ten of them, and a thousand times their number left in the city. If there was any chance at all of stopping this, he was bound to try. "You know I can't."

Envar sighed. "Send the boys, then. And maybe Alaissou."

"And who would I send to protect them?" Irichels asked.

"Send Arak."

Irichels narrowed his eyes. "You are worried."

"I am." Envar moved closer, laid a hand on Irichels's arm. "I'm afraid, my heart. If the contract is broken, the city will drown. That was the bargain, and the sea demons haven't forgotten it. It's what they're waiting for. If we stay—"

"You don't have to."

Envar ignored him. "If we stay, at least we can save Arak. And the household."

"I'd rather see you safe, too," Irichels said.

"You'll need me if you're going to do anything," Envar answered. "But Arak's another matter."

"Why am I another matter?" Arak asked, from the doorway. "Forgive the interruption, but you didn't hear me knock."

"We were talking about having you take the household to the Plana," Irichels said.

Arak shook her head. "Antel and Karan can protect them if it comes to that. As Envar said, you'll both need me."

"You know my contracts," Irichels said. He was speaking more to Envar than to Arak, but hoped the hillwoman would listen, too. "I'm sworn to act."

"You're not sworn to kill yourself," Envar said.

"But I am." Irichels took the other man's hand. "Not in so many words, but that's the bargain. That's the core of the University contract. We protect, against men and demons alike, regardless of cost."

"I know." Envar closed his eyes. "I know."

"If you want to send anyone away," Arak said, "we'd better start now. But I won't be among them."

"No more will I," Envar said, briskly. "But the children—"

Irichels went to the window, folded back the shutters so that he could see out into the water alley. The wind had died again, and the sky was pale as milk; the water below was dark and still. He was sure he wouldn't be the only person sending family and household into safety, and that made it harder to guarantee Nerin's safety, never mind about Alaissou and the others. Alaissou was skilled, but her knowledge was narrowly focused; there had been no time to teach her defense. Antel and Karan were competent enough swordsmen, but they were only two men, and Karan wasn't young. Romello might use a club if pressed, but Irichels wouldn't bet on him hitting only the right people. "We'll wait until after the Senate meets," he said, and hoped he wasn't leaving it too long.

The bells of Idra Mistress began tolling an hour before the Senate and Assembly were to meet. Irichels reluctantly took his place in the larger punt, gown and mask bundled at his side, Arak in her best leather behind him, and joined the procession of boats approaching Lawgivers' Isle. Antel took his place in the line of boats waiting to discharge their passengers as Irichels shrugged on his gown, then held them close to the steps while Irichels stepped ashore. Arak followed, and Irichels paused, unwilling to put on his mask just yet.

Nothing seemed to have changed—if anything, the water was smoother than it had been, only the breath of a breeze ruffling the agate-brown surface. The sun was a paler spot behind the clouds, and the air was heavy with salt. The contract was holding, then, Irichels thought. And maybe that was the key, to keep the contract intact, because surely the sea demons couldn't attack the city while it was still in force. At least they couldn't attack directly, he amended, but that would have to be enough.

"Samar!" He recognized Cambryse's voice, and turned to see him coming up the steps from the water, his barge just pulling away. "I want a word with you."

Irichels spread his hands. "Here I am."

"You will vote against the return," Cambryse said. "Otherwise—anything you allege about my daughter, I will turn against you. I will ruin you and your catamite utterly. Do you understand?"

"I understand," Irichels answered, and Cambryse stalked away.

"Does he really think that's going to work?" Arak asked with what sounded like genuine curiosity.

"Damned if I know," Irichels answered and turned toward the Assembly, joining the stream of robed and masked figures making their way up the broad steps and through the triple doors. At the entrance to the chamber he had to show the charter with its multiple seals, but the ushers passed him through with only minimum hesitation.

He hadn't been in the Assembly chamber since he was a boy at school, and he paused uncertainly at the top of the entrance ramp. The tiers of benches stretched along both sides of the long hall, rose in a curving bank behind him, carved stone imported from the Plana as white as the sky outside. He found his way to a place in the middle tier, behind and to the left of Gethen's party. Irichels left Arak to mark their place and obeyed Gethen's wave, stepping cautiously over the seats to stand beside the older man.

"Ambros spoke to you?" Gethen asked.

"He did."

"And?"

"He said you want Manimere to return."

"With conditions," Gethen said.

"I think we need to hear what she's seen," Irichels said, and was not surprised when Gethen shook his head.

"That's as may be, but we can't let her think she's won."

"Do you know what conditions are proposed?" Irichels asked, but before Gethen could answer, a trumpet sounded from the far end of the hall.

"Time to take your place," Gethen said. "You'll hear soon enough."

Irichels returned to his seat, leaning forward slightly to see past his neighbors as the Assembly's speaker entered the hall, escorted by men carrying boathooks and boarding axes, and followed by a quintet of Oratorians with torch and censer. He made himself sit still through the long invocation, then through the ceremonious calling of the roll, remembering to answer to the family name just in time. And then finally the speaker took his place at the rostrum, looking out over the Assembly.

"Masters. We are met to discuss rescinding the banishment of one of our own, in exchange for information she claims to have gathered about a threat to our city. Three solutions have been proposed: rise and speak now, if you have another option to share."

There was a heartbeat's silence, and then a clamor of voices. The speaker sorted them out expertly, and they came one by one to the petitioner's square, porphyry dark as old wine against the pale gray marble. Irichels listened, but soon was lost in the tangle of proposals and arguments and veiled insults passed between factions. Arak leaned down to murmur in his ear, "I think they're all saying the same thing."

"I'm not sure what they're saying." Irichels looked at his left-hand neighbor, a graying woman who had removed her mask as though that would help her hear better, and she gave him a wry smile.

"Your swordswoman's not wrong. There are only three choices, and everyone ought to know it."

"Refuse to send for her, send for her, and send for her with conditions," Irichels said. "Is it the conditions they're arguing over?"

"We should be so lucky." She shook her head. "The only conditions that make sense are that she brings a single ship, under escort, and submits to the Senate and Assembly. That way, if she refuses, she can still send a ship to bargain. And, yes, I think she'd do that. I've had dealings with Manimere, she's loyal to the city."

"I agree," Irichels said, and wondered too late if he should have held his tongue.

An hour crept by, and then another, the bells of Idra Mistress punctuating the debate. Irichels braced his foot against the base of the bench in front of him, wishing it was over. His neighbor was right, there were only three choices, and only one set of conditions that made any sense. And then he would have to vote. There was no real choice there, either: he owed Manimere that much, after the help she'd given him, and he was reasonably sure Ambros and Gethen would forgive him. Cambryse would carry through on his threat, but he had never been anything but an enemy. He just wished it would be over. He could feel the contracts that bound the city, a faint tremor along the marks of his own bonds, waiting as breathlessly as the weather for something to break.

Finally the speaker called the hall to order, and people settled grumbling into their seats. The speaker rested both hands on the rostrum, looking out over the Assembly for a moment before he spoke. Irichels wondered whether the Senate had voted yet, and what their decision had been if they had. "Members of the Assembly," the speaker said. "There are three proposals before us, in answer to the letter sent us by Innes Manimere, whose title is in abeyance. Those proposals are: first, to accept her offer and allow her to return to Bejanth. Second, to allow her to return, but with only one ship and only escorted by ships and captains under contract to the Senate and Assembly, with the further promise that she will submit to our judgment once she has returned. Third, to refuse her offer. Discussion having concluded, the vote is called." He paused, and Irichels was aware of the ushers fanning out around the hall to count the votes. "Those in favor of the first proposal, to allow Innes Manimere to return to Bejanth as she requested, rise now."

Irichels pushed himself upright, the shuffling of feet and rustle of heavy silk gowns suddenly loud. Perhaps a third of the hall was standing: not enough to carry the vote. He should probably have expected that and voted the way Gethen wanted, but he owed Manimere at least this support. And he owed the city. He saw Gethen look up, scowling, but pretended he didn't see.

"The count is complete," the speaker said. "Those in favor of the second proposal, to allow Innes Manimere to return under condition, rise now."

More people rose for this, Irichels thought, craning his neck to try to get his own count. More than a third, maybe as much as half, which surely meant that proposal would carry.

"The count is complete," the speaker said again. "Those in favor of the third proposal, to refuse Innes Manimere's offer, rise now."

Again there was a great shuffling of feet on stone, and Irichels leaned forward. Not as many as before—there was a knot of supporters clustered on the far side, around Cambryse himself, and pockets here and there, but not as many as had voted for return with conditions, maybe not even as many had voted for unconditional return. That was better than nothing.

"The vote is tallied," the speaker announced. "The Assembly agrees that Innes Manimere may return as requested, subject to conditions." A steward stepped up to him, spoke quietly, and the speaker nodded. "This is in agreement with the vote of the Senate." There was an immediate outcry, voices colliding in approval and protest, and the speaker raised his voice to carry over them. "The high constable has dispatched his flagship as escort, leaving immediately. This session is now ended."

"And that's that?" Arak asked, as they joined the groups moving toward the heavy doors. About half the Assembly seemed inclined to stay and argue, Irichels saw, but he wanted out.

"That's it for now. I hope they reach her in time."

"Samar!"

Irichels paused. "Gethen."

"You were to vote with us. We needed to be sure some form of return could pass."

Irichels sighed. "You could have told me that."

"I didn't think it was necessary." Gethen glared at him.

"Gethen," Irichels said again. "You can feel what's coming—how do your contracts feel? Are they twitching? Something's stirring in the foundations, and Manimere knows about it. She has to return before this breaks."

Gethen shook his head. "I'm not University-trained."

"Then look to the weather," Irichels said, and turned away.

CHAPTER EIGHTEEN

I t was better outside on the wide plaza, though the clouds had thickened. Irichels snatched off his mask and took a deep breath, tasting the air. Salt and mud, nothing but the familiar tidal smell, and still his skin prickled, and he looked south, half expecting to see storm clouds rising over the roofs of the Orangery. There was nothing, of course, just the same white sky, and he handed Arak the mask so that he could undo the clasps of the heavy robe. There was a crowd at the base of the steps, senators in black and assemblors in white all struggling to reach their boats and seeing that, he slowed his steps.

"No point in hurrying," Arak said in the same moment and Irichels nodded agreement, handing her the robe as well.

"Samar!" Irichels turned, to see Margos Temenon striding toward him, one hand already on the hilt of his sword. "You were told how to vote—"

Irichels curled fingers into a protective shape, and out of the corner of his eye saw Arak juggling the awkward gown. "I chose differently—"

Margos drew his sword and slashed at him, aiming for his face. Irichels leaned away from the blow, bringing up his shield, and felt the impact on it and along his jaw. Arak flung aside the gown, drawing her own sword, and there was a clatter of boots on the stone.

"Hold! Hold in the high constable's name!"

Irichels snuffed his counter-curse, but kept his shield ready as three constables skidded to a stop just out of sword range.

Arak stepped up beside him, and Margos sheathed his sword with a contemptuous oath. "You'll regret this," he said, and stalked away. Irichels stared after him, and Arak slowly shook her head.

"Your sword, Messida," the constable's leader said, and Arak returned it to its scabbard. More constables were joining them and Irichels heaved a sigh.

"This was none of my doing," he said.

"No, Master, we saw what happened." The constable seemed disinclined to go further, and Irichels saw Arak's eyebrows rise. The hillwoman said nothing, however, and Irichels chose his words carefully.

"Then I trust there will be no repercussions for me."

"I see no need," the leader said.

"And for him?"

The leader looked uncomfortable. "He's a known hothead, and we have other things to worry about. Your forbearance would be greatly appreciated."

Irichels laughed, releasing the shield. "Do I have a choice?"

"It would be appreciated," the leader said again, red-faced. "Greatly."

"Understood." Irichels looked over his shoulder, but Margos was nowhere in sight.

"There was a boat waiting," Arak said.

Irichels nodded. "Under the circumstances, Messire, might I ask for an escort home?"

"Of course," the leader said, and gestured to two of his men. "We'll take you there ourselves."

Perhaps thanks to the escort, the return to Samar House was uneventful. Irichels offered the usual tip, and was meanly pleased to see the leader blush again. He took the coin, though, and Irichels watched them pole away, while Karan secured their own boat to the pilings.

"What now?" Arak asked.

"I wish I knew." Irichels gave the sky a wary look and stepped inside.

Alaissou was sitting in the courtyard, tearing the last of a loaf into crumbs for the birds. "Is it true they've recalled Manimere?"

"Under condition," Irichels answered.

She nodded. "So we heard. A crowd came by shouting for her an hour ago, and Dot're Cassi went out to see the ship launched."

Irichels grimaced. He would rather have had Envar safe inside the walls, but he had to trust that the chirurgeon knew what he was doing. "No trouble, though?"

"None so far, but everyone's on edge." Alaissou brushed the last of the crumbs into the waiting dish, then rose to scatter them in the first of the cages. The birds bounced and fluttered, but did not land. "Even the birds."

"The household?"

"Marthie has them in hand." Alaissou turned away from the second cage, fixing him with a minatory stare. "If you're planning to send them away, you should know I won't go with them."

"It would probably be safer."

"Only probably. And if the city falls, it won't be any safer on the Plana."

"I don't think the city will fall," Irichels said and stopped, hearing the lack of conviction in his own voice.

"There's something very wrong," Alaissou said. "I'd rather meet it here."

"If I asked you to take Nerin to the Plana—" Irichels began.

She shook her head. "Too conspicuous. Send him with Marthie and Dot're Cassi."

"He says he won't leave either," Irichels answered.

"No, I suppose not." Alaissou frowned at the birds, still clustered at the tops of their cages. "I think we're safer here anyway. Bejanth has stood against the sea demons before, and against ordinary fleets."

But not with the contract broken. There was no point in saying that, she knew it as well as he did, and he said instead,

"Did Cass say when he thought he'd be back?"

"He said he wanted to see the city's ship depart, and to hear the news. That's all I know."

Irichels nodded, wishing the answer had been different, and made himself turn away. Maybe he could find something useful in his grandfather's records, or at least provide himself with a distraction.

Envar returned a little before sunset, looking tired but none the worse for wear. He had seen the city's ship set sail, the crowd cheering from the docks, and watched it until the scarlet banners vanished below the horizon. There had been no sign of Manimere's ships, nor of any incoming weather, but he had come home by way of the Boot and the northern edge of Mercies, and even walked to the point where Idra-in-Chains overlooked the Slackwater before turning back to Samar House.

"And the short of it is, it looks as though half the city is trying to cross the Slackwater just now," he said, curled up in the greatchair in Irichels's workroom with his hands wrapped around a cup of kaf. "If you had it in mind to send the household away, this is not the moment."

"How bad is it?" Irichels glanced at the tide chart pinned beside the calendar.

"Dozens of small boats, punts and haugs, and only a few large enough to belong to houses, or to defend themselves," Envar answered. "I saw fights already, when a boatman wanted double pay, and once when a larger party wanted a boat that was already claimed." He paused. "I dealt with that one, but there will be more. The freebooters will be waiting, too."

The tide was high now, would be going out before he could get the household to move, and that meant any boat he sent would have to pick its way through the smaller network of channels available at low tide before they could reach any of the Plana's settlements. Or they'd have to wait on the water for the tide to turn, and that had its own dangers, as did the dark. "Better we wait until tomorrow, then," he said, and hoped there would be time enough.

He spoke to Martholin after dinner had been cleared away, drawing her out of the bright kitchen into the hall where the lanterns burned low in the heavy air. "I want to send our people to the Plana in the morning. Can you have them ready?"

"Will you be going, Master?" she asked, and snorted when he shook his head. "And the mistress will be staying, too, I expect."

"Not if I can persuade her to leave," Irichels answered.

"I wouldn't waste your time trying," Martholin answered. "We could leave by the afternoon, maybe, depending on what we take—and I'm thinking we'd want to take supplies, everyone and their half-brother will be trying to get ashore, and by the time we get there, you won't be able to buy goods at any price. And where would we go?"

Irichels considered. The closest towns, Lueta and Pujola and Capete, would be overrun by now; Boneme and Dalmas were half a day's journey further inland, but Boneme, at least, was larger, might have more room to spare. "Boneme. I'll give you money for lodgings. And you'll have Karan and Antel to protect you."

"With all respect," Martholin said, "I'd rather stay, and I think the rest would, too. It'd be one thing if we were going to a family house—or if you were coming with us, Master. But this is too chancy. Especially if Nerin's coming with us."

The trouble was, she wasn't entirely wrong, but he couldn't bring himself to leave the city. "Talk to the household, tell them that I'll help anyone who wants to leave. And I hope you'll reconsider. It's not safe here."

Martholin smiled. "Idra's mercy, Master Gil, it never was."

Irichels woke to the clamor of bells, Idra-of-Mercies and then Idra-in-Chains ringing an urgent peal, picking up and amplifying the bells of the other oratories. He sat up in the dark, automatically calling a wisp of light, and Envar rolled over beside him. "Trouble."

Irichels threw back the covers, pushed open the shutters of the street-side window, then went into the dressing room to look out on the water alley. Lights bloomed in the neighboring buildings, but the streets were empty and he could see no sign of whatever was causing the alarm. "An attack?"

"Fire," Arak said from the hall door, and Irichels took a deep breath. Yes, there was a hint of smoke in the air, strengthening as he tasted it, and Envar shoved himself out of bed.

"Should we rouse the house?"

"They won't sleep through this," Arak said, and Envar made a face.

"You know what I meant." He sniffed, too. "It's not close."

"Get dressed," Irichels said, "and we'll go up to the roof. We can see better from there."

He pulled on shirt and trousers, the others copying him, and stepped out into the hall. There were lights on the third floor—none of the household had slept through the bells— and Alaissou came striding out of her bedroom wrapped in a belted gown, her maidservant scurrying behind her with a lamp. "What is it?"

"I don't know," Irichels said.

Arak said, "I smell smoke, but—"

Irichels started up the steps to the third floor. Martholin met him at the stairhead, a shawl thrown over her shift, Karan in shirt and drawers but with his sword ready to hand. "Master Gil—"

"I don't know," Irichels said again. "I'm going up to see."

He turned to the narrow stair, very nearly a ladder, that led to the roof, letting the wisp float ahead of him until it bumped against the trapdoor. He dispelled the protective curse and freed the bolt, pushing the heavy wood up and over until it fell with a crash onto the narrow walkway that ran along the perimeter of the house. The smell of smoke was stronger here, and the starless sky showed light to the west, the orange glow of a rising fire.

He edged further along the walkway, one hand on the rail, the glass that covered the courtyard black under the cloudy sky, then turned the corner by the smallest of the cisterns and made his way toward the front of the house. Envar followed, and then Alaissou, Arak trailing behind her.

The view was better from the front, the canal opening in the right direction so that he could see the plume of smoke, darker than the clouds, and the tongues of flame licking at its base. The tower of Idra-of-Mercies split the flames, but the bells were silent now: the fire hadn't crossed the canal to reach Mercies. "Looks like it's on the Boot," Envar said, leaning precariously over the rail.

Irichels grabbed his belt to steady him. "Yes. I don't think it's as far as Westerly."

"Is there something we need to do?" Arak asked. "Send people to help?"

"Not yet," Irichels said. Most of the bells had stopped ringing, except for a steady tolling that had to come from Idra-of-the-Laws, since there was no oratory on the Boot. "If they need more bodies, they'll ring the bells at Idra-of-Mercies."

Alaissou cupped her hands, shaping something, and Irichels felt the prickle of a contract invoked. She held her hand to her eyes, frowning, and said, "I think—I think that's Morellin House."

Envar leaned out even further and Irichels tightened his grip on the other man's belt, saying, "Are you sure?"

"Not sure, but—" She paused, peering through the cantrip she had shaped. "They have a very distinctive weathervane, the chained hare. It's in line with Idra-of-Mercies when you look that way."

If she was right... Irichels chewed his bottom lip. If Morellin House burned, would that break the contract? Probably not if there were still members of the family left alive, but it would certainly weaken the contract's structure. It might be enough to let Cambryse undo the contract himself, unless it could be defended at its source. "We need to go to Lawgivers' Isle."

Envar slid back off the rail, looking at him oddly. "So you think this is an attack, my heart?"

"I'd like to be wrong," Irichels answered. "But we can't take the chance."

He sent the others ahead of him, then slid down the stairs himself, pausing only long enough to reestablish the protective curse. Martholin was waiting, dressed now, and Irichels nodded in approval. "The dot're and I will be going to Lawgivers'," he said. "I want you to keep an eye on things. Send our people to help if they're called for, but otherwise keep the house locked up."

"In that case, I'm coming with you," Alaissou said. "You'll need all the help you can muster."

"Unfortunately," Irichels said.

Martholin nodded. "I've sent the boys back to bed, and the younger maids. Not that I expect they'll sleep, but we'll all be better for it later. What door will you be using?"

"Bar everything," Irichels answered. "And have Antel and Karan take turns watching the doors. I'll shout when we return." *If we return.* If they were going into the Senate and Assembly building—into the sections that gave access to the Courts Between—there was every chance that Cambryse would be there before them. It could even be a trap to bring him there, to a place that Cambryse could attack, though that was unlikely. On the other hand, if this was an attack on the city's originating contract, the Senate and Assembly was the best place from which to defend it, though that would be no less dangerous. "Alaissou, get dressed—something dark and practical, if you have it. Arak, I'll want you, too."

"Of course," Alaissou murmured with a demure smile, and turned away.

Irichels retreated to his own room to dress in haste, pulling on the worn familiar clothes that he kept for cursebreaking, plain dark wool beneath a leather coat that would at least slow a knife-thrust. His satchel of tools lay ready, untouched since he'd arrived in Bejanth, and its weight was a comfort against his hip. Envar emerged from his own room, all in black, his fair hair hidden beneath a sailor's knitted cap, the long tail flung over his shoulder. He looked more like a climbing-thief than a feral, and Irichels smiled in spite of himself. Envar smiled back and caught him by the wrist. "You will be careful, my heart."

"I fully intend to be," Irichels said.

"That's not a promise," Envar said, shaking his head, but let him go.

Alaissou emerged from her room in dark blue wide-legged trousers and a knee-length tunic, her maid following unhappily carrying the cased vielle. Arak eyed her thoughtfully and said, "Wait a moment." She vanished into her own room, and returned with a stiff leather vest. Alaissou shrugged it on, and took the vielle from her maid.

"Thank you."

"It'll turn a blade in a pinch," Arak said. She was in her heaviest leathers, sword and dagger at her side, her crossbow in her hand.

Karan had brought the smaller boat around to the dock, and held it close as they climbed aboard. "You should let me come with you, Master Gil. You'll need someone to mind the boat."

"I need you to guard the house," Irichels answered, and thought he saw a flicker of relief in the older man's eyes. He stepped into the stern, hoisted the oar, and Karan shoved them out into the channel.

Even in the narrow canals that crisscrossed Mercies, the water had a distinct chop. The tide was running out, almost at its lowest point, but the wind was from the southwest, and stronger than it had been during the day. To either side, the houses showed lights at their windows and shapes moved on the roofs: watching the fire and waiting to see if help would be needed, Irichels knew. A few people clustered on the docks and at the intersections, and more than once someone called after them, asking for news. "We're finding out," Envar shouted back and Irichels leaned harder on his oar, driving the boat onward.

The chop was worse as they made the turn into the wider expanse of the Eastern Water. Irichels kept the boat close to the northern bank, creeping cautiously along the edge of Mercies until he reached the point where the channel narrowed. The tide was slower there, trapped by multiple islands, and Irichels brought them safely across the channel, fetching up at the base of the stairs that led up to the Senate and Assembly. Envar leaped ashore, drawing the boat up against the nearest mooring post, and Irichels stowed his oar before climbing out onto the wet stone. Ahead, the spire of Idra Mistress of the World showed pale against the sky; when he looked to his right, down the Eastern Water and toward the top of the Boot, flames still leaped above the rooftops. The scent of smoke was stronger here, bitter with tarred wood and burnt fabric.

A handful of boats were tied to the mooring posts along the stairs, perhaps half a dozen in all. None of them bore a house marking, and none of them had a boatman in attendance: they could belong to constables still on duty or to Cambryse, Irichels thought, and glanced up at the sky again. The clouds were solid, though it was hard to tell if they were thicker than before. The wind was more definite but it still wasn't a storm. Alaissou produced a wisp, holding it low to light the stairs. The vielle was ready at her shoulder, as much a weapon for her as Arak's sword and crossbow or Envar's weighted quarterstaff.

Nothing moved on the plaza or by the Assembly doors, though Irichels was sure there would be constables watching somewhere. Unless they'd all been called to the fire, which was both possible and an excellent reason for setting it, and he shrugged his worry away. "Let's go."

No one called out as they crossed the plaza, though Irichels's spine tingled as they made their way across the bare expanse of stone, and he allowed himself a sigh of relief once they were in the shadows of the portico. There was no one there, either, and the great doors were closed. As Irichels started to push gently on the inner portion, Alaissou said, "Over here."

It was a smaller door, hidden in the shadows, already opening to her touch. Irichels nodded his thanks and slipped inside, holding still and silent in the shadows to see what would happen. For a long moment, he could hear nothing but his own heartbeat, and slowly allowed himself to relax, calling the faintest of wisps to add a little light. Nothing changed, and he eased forward, letting the others follow him in. He let his own wisp grow brighter, and Envar and Alaissou added theirs.

They were in the inner portico, the colonnaded walkway that ran along three sides of the entrance hall. To right and left it had doors that gave access to the various ancillary offices, recorders and clerks and tax officials, while the doors at the end of the hall opened onto the Assembly hall itself. One of those doors was open, but there was nothing to be seen but darkness. Irichels took a deep breath, the small of incense overriding the distant fire, and Envar said quietly, "You said there were circles on the lower level?"

"Yes."

"Where contracts are sent to the Courts Between," Alaissou said. "There must be four or five of them."

Irichels closed his eyes for an instant, feeling for the ebb and flow of power through the building, shaped by centuries of curses and contracts. His feet tingled, a thicket of curses reaching up through the stones of the floor; the air that touched his face was alternately cool and warm, currents stirred by a circle at work somewhere in the building. "To the left," he said, "and down."

"The doors are that way," Alaissou said, pointing across the open hall, and Irichels stepped out into the lighter space. He could feel the power more strongly now, a subtle shifting beneath his feet, as though the stones themselves were not quite steady in their beds.

"Someone has a circle open," Envar said quietly at his shoulder, and Irichels nodded.

"The second door, I think—" Before he could finish his sentence, he felt the air thicken and stopped abruptly, flinging out one arm to halt Alaissou as a blast of heat and light erupted from under the portico. He raised both hands, fingers curled, got his shields open just in time to intercept a second blast. Arak's crossbow thumped, the bolt singing past him into the dark to clatter against stone. The ratchet crackled as she reloaded. Envar flicked one hand to release a sheet of light, hovering overhead to illuminate the space ahead of them.

A shadow moved under the portico, dodging from column to column, and Envar pointed at it, then gestured. Curse-marks darkened on his fingers, and the air rippled. The figure dodged away, and Arak fired her second bolt. There was a yelp and a curse, smoke slithering across the stones, and Irichels reached for a curse of his own, sending it skidding toward the figure. He felt it strike and grab, clinging like bindweed, and Envar conjured weight from nothing, pinning the man to the ground.

"I have him."

"Good man." Irichels moved closer, the light overhead just beginning to fade, and shook his head as he recognized Margos Temenon. "Idra's—what are you doing here?"

Margos glared up at him, straining against the invisible barrier. "He said you'd come. But you can't stop him—I won't let you."

"Cambryse?" Envar said.

Irichels nodded. "Cambryse is trying to bring down the city, to destroy the contract with the sea demons. Are you sure you want to be part of that?"

"Liar!" Margos spat toward Irichels's feet. "I know what you and Manimere were planning."

Arak worked the crossbow's draw again, the sound of the ratchet loud in the silence. "Kill him, I say."

It was painfully tempting. No one would know, and it would ensure they'd never have to deal with Margos again. Irichels took a deep breath. "Tie him up. Gag him, too."

"Better to kill him," Arak said.

"No."

Arak grimaced, but replaced the crossbow's safety and set it carefully aside before bending to strip Margos of his belt. Alaissou offered her kerchief and Arak finished their work, leaving Margos trussed against the base of the column.

"We should have asked him where Father was," Alaissou said, looking down at him.

"I think we can feel that," Envar said.

"That way," Irichels said, and started for the middle door. It gave onto a shallow spiral stair made of pale stone that seemed to glow faintly in the light of their wisps. As they made their way down, Irichels thought he saw light ahead, the flicker of a lantern, and stopped to listen, but heard neither voices nor movement. Probably Cambryse had already opened the circle and was gone ahead into the Courts Between, or perhaps even further. The real question was whether he'd left anyone behind to guard his way. A sensible practitioner would, but there was no knowing how many people he had, or how much strength he would need when he reached his destination.

Further down the stairs took on an almost organic look, as though they had been shaped like clay or sand—pale and fine-grained, the edge of the stairs curving sinuously around the central post. The post itself looked as though it had an odd twist, and when Irichels touched it cautiously, it was warmer than it should be. Envar copied him, then snatched his fingers back, wincing, and displayed a blister already rising on the tip of his forefinger. "It burned me."

"It doesn't like your contracts," Irichels said, and Envar nodded.

"This is not a place that loves ferals."

"No," Alaissou said, in a small voice. She was keeping to the middle of the stairs, stepping very carefully. Arak offered her a hand, and she smiled but shook her head. "I'm all right."

"We're nearly there," Irichels said. He could definitely see lantern-light now, where the stairs ended in a vaulted corridor.

The air was heavy, and warmer than it should be; there was a definite smell of tar and salt. For a moment, he wondered if the city itself had a daemon, like so many of the houses, but brushed the thought away. If it had, it would already have manifested itself, and none of them would have made it this far into the spaces beneath the Senate and Assembly.

At his gesture Arak slipped past him, releasing the safety of her crossbow, and edged along the wall until she could peer into the chamber where the lantern burned. She paused there for a moment, then turned back, shaking her head. "Someone's been here: there's the light, but the room's empty."

"Gone on through," Envar said. "Do we follow?"

Irichels moved to join Arak, flicking his fingers to send a cantrip skittering across the floor in search of traps or alarms. There was nothing, just the stone circle permanently carved into the floor, and the faint shimmering of the air within it to warn that it was open. "We have to," he said. "But not, I think, through here. There's another circle in this hall."

"Over here," said Alaissou, and pointed. It was another stone room, with a vaulted ceiling that met in a decorative finial above the center of the circle. Irichels allowed his wisp to drift upward to hover at the point of the finial, and studied the circle.

"How can you be sure you'll end up in the same place?" Arak asked. "Or is it all the Courts Between?"

"It's all the Courts Between," Envar said.

"It's not exactly a place," Irichels qualified, "but yes, we can follow where Cambryse went. With your help," he added, looking at Alaissou.

She nodded, already fumbling with her tunic to find her purse. She pulled it out, vielle tucked under her arm, and found a wooden needle case. She pricked her thumb, squeezing it to make the blood well up, and held it out to Irichels. He dipped his finger in it, murmuring a formula, and touched the blood to the back of his left wrist. He could feel it instantly, a spot of warmth that waxed and waned as he turned toward and away from the door.

"You'd better open the circle," Envar said. "I'm not sure I trust it." And that might be a problem, if the magic here was antithetical to ferals, but it was too late to worry about that. Irichels took a breath, steadying himself, and began to walk the circumference of the circle. He felt the deeply carved symbols spring to life as he crossed over them, a door so well-used that it practically opened itself, and the air in the center of the circle hazed and shimmered as the circle formed.

"How do we play this?" Arak asked. She held out her little dark-lantern, and Envar snapped his fingers to light the wick.

"You'll be our anchor," Irichels said. "Inside the circle, but no further into the Courts. We'll go forward—"

"I can fiddle a thread for us," Alaissou said, lifting her vielle. "To make sure we don't lose the way."

They would be safer with some external means of retracing their steps. Irichels nodded. "Do that. Cass?"

Envar nodded, the curse marks standing out black against his skin. "Ready when you are."

"Then let's begin." Irichels waited for the others to enter, and took the last step that sealed it behind them.

CHAPTER NINETEEN

Irichels turned back to the center of the circle, seeing the air haze and thicken. It was warmer than usual, smelling strongly of salt, but he stepped into it without a backward glance, Envar at his side. Alaissou followed a heartbeat later, looking around curiously as they passed through the hedges with their stone roses. The Court opened before them, but the pearl-shadowed space was empty; the four pillars were mere shadows, and the flame was out.

Irichels paused, half expecting something to change, some being to appear, but there was no response. He considered his contracts, chose a curse that drew directly from a demonic bargain—to call winter's snow out of season—but when he invoked it, he felt the power bounce back against him, a dull thud against his heart. A single snowflake fell, melting to nothing before it hit the ground. The Courts were closed, or at best unresponsive, all attention drawn elsewhere. Presumably toward whatever Cambryse was doing, he thought, and reached for a more direct summoning spell. It slapped back as well, hard enough to make him gasp, and Envar said, "No one's here, my heart."

"No." Irichels eyed the opening on the far side of the Court, a triple arch that gave onto fractured scenes that might resolve once he drew closer, or might diverge entirely.

"I've never been beyond the Court," Alaissou said. "What's—can we even go there?"

"Oh, yes," Envar said, eying the arches.

Irichels said, "It's not a single place, it's a doorway. And a maze. What we want are the contracts attached to the city's heart, which should be this building, and that should be possible to find."

"Cambryse is likely there ahead of us," Envar said.

"Or he's still searching," Irichels said. "There's no way to tell until we start. Alaissou, you said you could spin us a thread?"

Alaissou nodded. "But I've only done it in the real world before."

"It's very much the same," Irichels said. It was mostly true, and she could stand the confidence. "Anchor it here, and we'll go on."

Alaissou tucked the vielle against her shoulder, produced the bow and drew it across the strings. For a moment, music sounded, rough and irregular, and then it faded, became a glittering strand of scarlet, bright as blood in the hazy air. It rose, looped itself into an elaborate knot around some invisible point, and Alaissou nodded. "I'm ready."

"Then let's begin." Irichels walked toward the triple arch, Envar half a step behind, Alaissou trailing him as she tried to play and walk at the same time. The thread unreeled behind her, first in fits and starts and then more smoothly.

To his surprise, the area visible beyond the arch moved closer together as he got closer, became a forest of pale-barked trees, the ground beneath them drifted with the wispy dark skeletons of leaves. There were paths between them, and he could feel the heat strengthen where Alaissou's blood had touched his wrist as he faced the one that led away from the center arch. "This way."

It was darker under the strange trees, though when he looked up the canopy was lost in shadow. The air was sticky with salt, and when he scuffed the skeletal leaves away from the path, he felt sand beneath. The bones of a fish lay half buried in a pile of leaves, needle-sharp teeth still visible in the gaping mouth. He glanced over his shoulder and saw Alaissou's thread unreeling behind them, still seemingly secure. He swung his hand again, feeling for the warmest spot, and took a smaller path through a stand of even larger trees, a thicker carpet of leaves brushing against his feet.

The further they went, the less tree-like they became and more like stone columns, rough-hewn at first, with stiff straight lines that weren't quite like bark, and then curved and fluted, with bands of carving spiraling up the pale stone. "Curses?" Alaissou asked, bending closer to see without slowing the movement of her bow.

"Contracts," Envar said. He kept scrupulously to the center of the path, his hands held tight to his body. Irichels looked more closely. Some of the marks he recognized, and some were unfamiliar; still others writhed under his gaze, changing their shapes in ways that made his stomach roil, and he looked hastily away.

Ahead the path widened, the shadows retreating—not driven back by light from above, he realized, but by a faint glow from the columns themselves. These were larger, more heavily carved, some covered with faces, some curved and coiled as though the stone itself had been braided. Here a line of skeletons danced hand-in-hand up the twists of one column, while a line of boys and girls danced back down again; on another, bands of eyeless faces ringed the column at regular intervals, mouths open as though they spoke or sang. One column had no figures at all, but the stone itself was shaped like a twisted length of chain, its upper end disappearing into the dark. Envar was right, these were the contracts that bound the city and its people. The trick now was to find the contract that had begun the Shame.

He lifted his hand again, letting the air touch the smudged spot where he'd wiped Alaissou's blood. He felt the warmth flare again, pulling him deeper into the columns, and Alaissou made a small, distressed sound. "I can't—I'm losing my grip on the Court."

Envar lifted his hand. "Give me a note."

She nodded, bow working, and Envar drew a second strand from the air, pale gold this time, tugged it gently toward him. "Can you sustain that?"

"I think—yes."

Envar nodded. "I have it, then."

"This way," Irichels said.

More paths split off ahead of him, like fingers on a hand. He chose the farthest right, between two leaning columns that were carved like stylized stooping birds and hummed like bees. The spot on his hand was definitely warmer now, almost hot, and he winced as he wove his way through a patch of crooked columns banded with broken crowns caught on the narrow curves. He gave them a sharp look, wondering if they could be part of the Shame, but there were too many of them.

Then he heard it, a rushing like fire or falling water, growing rapidly louder as he turned toward it. Envar caught his shoulder and he nodded, peering between columns into a sudden break in the maze. Where all the other stone had been pale and sandy, the ground here was streaked with vivid color, bands of blue and gold and crimson crisscrossing each other in a figure so complex it turned the gaze. A single column rose from its center, the thickest he had seen so far and the most thickly carved, though at this distance it was impossible to tell what the figures were. It shimmered and shivered—no, Irichels realized, it was on fire, though the flames were so pale and weak as to be almost invisible. Cambryse and another man stood before it, their hands upturned, urging the fire to rise, while a third man lay sprawled on the stones behind them, hands outstretched. He looked unconscious or dead, Irichels thought, and couldn't tell which. Beyond them, half hidden by the pillar, stood a sea demon, wide mouth gaping to show its triple row of teeth.

"I know Cambryse," Envar said softly. "The others?"

"The one standing I think is Fane Temenon," Irichels answered. "The other—Cambryse's feral?"

"Very likely." Envar nodded. "He's spent, anyway. I can take the demon, my heart, if you'll handle Cambryse and Temenon."

It would be a stretch, Irichels knew, but he could see the flames thickening, taking on more substance even as he watched. The sea demon flinched back from them, shading its face with one webbed hand, and Temenon gasped something. Cambryse ignored him, all his focus on the flames, and they rose higher, licking at the figures. It was very nearly too late; he had to act now, Irichels thought, before the fire strengthened any further. "Agreed."

Envar stooped, anchoring Alaissou's thread with a gesture. Irichels considered the range of his contracts. They were biased toward suppression, toward breaking and disrupting and damping: useful for stopping what Cambryse was doing, but not the most potent of weapons. Envar had a wider range of aggressive contracts, but he would need all of them against the sea demon. "Ready?"

"As I will ever be," Envar answered, with a crooked smile.

Irichels sketched a sign in the air ahead of him. "Go." He clenched his fists, seeing the curse marks darken suddenly on Envar's hands and face, and focused on the fire climbing he column. Damp coalesced from the air around him, from the memory of night and fog, fell like a blanket on the flames at the base of the column. He felt the fire falter, and Cambryse swung to face him, fingers working. Irichels flung up his shield, but the blast of wind knocked him back a step.

"Leave him," Fane shouted. "Tend the fire, I'll deal with this." In the same moment, the sea demon shrieked, words in a language like steel on stone. Envar answered, but Irichels couldn't risk a look. Instead, he concentrated on his shield, one he could hold for hours if needed, then called a counter-curse that ripped Fane's half-formed cantrip to shreds and sent the man staggering sideways into Cambryse. Cambryse fended him off and Irichels struck again, pouring his strength into a curse intended to break through shields and end the struggle. Fane stumbled again, blood starting from his nose, and Irichels called invisible vines to catch and tangle. Fane fell but Cambryse turned, hands curling to turn the flames on Irichels. Irichels caught them, his eyebrows scorching, damped and then extinguished them, but the flames on the column leaped up, the pale stone beginning to char.

Out of the corner of his eye he could see curses weaving through the air, lines of light and shadow, glitter and smoke that sparked where they touched, heard Envar gasp a familiar curse, and the sea demon's snarl in response. There was nothing Irichels could do to help, not without abandoning his own fight, and he focused on the column instead, calling up another suppressive curse. The flames faltered, the air momentarily cooler, and in that moment Cambryse struck again, conjuring lightning from the shivering air.

Irichels caught it, the weight of the blow thudding against his heart, but his shield held back the worst of it. He answered with his own fire, leashed and shaped, but Cambryse deflected it. He was tiring already—and so, surely, was Cambryse, but he didn't dare make this into a battle of pure attrition. The column was smoking again, flames solidifying; he needed to make an end to Cambryse so that he could preserve the contract. He held his shield, struck fire again as he sorted through his remaining curses, looking for some combination that would bring Cambryse down. Another tangle, slung high to catch Cambryse's arms, and then the hammer strike, air turned momentarily solid. The first caught, but failed to hold, sliding off Cambryse's shields; the second knocked him back, but the shield still held, and Irichels braced himself for the counter.

"Cambryse!" The voice came from a point a quarter of the way around the circle. Irichels dodged away from it, losing his grip momentarily on the tangle, and Cambryse wrenched his other arm free before Irichels could reestablish his hold. Cambryse gestured toward the fire, and the flames intensified, taking on new shape and color. The stone blackened, pieces flaking from the images.

"Cambryse, what in Idra's Name?" Margos Temenon stumbled out from among the maze of columns, blood on his sleeve where Arak's crossbow bolt had grazed him. There was more blood on his wrists where he'd fought free of his bonds. Irichels risked a glance over his shoulder, saw nothing, and realized that Margos must have used Cambryse's circle.

"It's Samar," Cambryse said, gasping. "He's destroying the contract—"

"It's not my fire," Irichels answered, and risked the damping curse again. Cambryse had been waiting for the attempt, and he barely managed to catch the counterblow on his shield, the heat washing over him.

"Liar!" Irichels flinched, but Margos was glaring at Cambryse, his own hands raised in a crude conjuration. There was a sudden breath of cold air and a hailstorm pounded the open space, needles and knives of ice mixed with lumps like stones.

Irichels ducked, pulling his own shield close, and the storm beat over and through Cambryse, flattening him against the bands of stone, blood running from mouth and nose and ears. It struck the burning pillar, and the stone cracked under the sudden change of temperature. A curling edge swept over Envar and the sea demon, still locked in combat, and the rest swung back at Margos, sweeping over him and burying him beneath a shroud of jagged ice. Irichels reached automatically to rescue, but the sound of more stone cracking spun him back to face the column.

The fire was out but the stone was black and crumbling, larger and larger pieces falling away. Only the top of the column seemed intact, and it was darkening rapidly. Cracks were visible at the base, and as he watched they rose through the stone, widening as they went. He reached for his curses, unsure what he knew that would restore something so badly broken, and behind the column Envar stumbled, went to one knee under the pressure of the sea demon's attack. The web of curses closed in, the sea demon's curses riding up and over Envar's. He raised both hands in defense, and Irichels seized his own best counter-curse and launched it into the maelstrom. There was a sound like wire breaking. Envar shoved himself upright and the sea demon leaped backward, mouth open in a soundless wail.

The column shattered. Irichels raised an arm to protect himself but a shard broke through his faltering shield, drew a line of blood along his cheek. Envar dodged toward the nearest intact column, and the sea demon keened aloud. An instant later it was gone, leaving behind a tangle of seaweed and shell, and Irichels felt the ground tremble underfoot. "The contract's broken."

"Yes." Envar snatched up a shell and a hank of weed. "We can't stay."

Irichels stared at the gap where the column had been. The colors were leaching from the floor, fading and dissolving into pale sand, and on every side the other columns had begun to sway like trees in a rising wind. There had to be a way to mend the contract, he thought, some way to pull it all back together, but when he touched the nearest flake of stone, it lay dead in his hand. If this contract went, the city fell, and he could see no way to prop it up again.

"Gil." Envar caught his sleeve. "Gil, we can't stay."

"The contract."

"Is broken," Envar said. "You can't mend it. We have to get away."

Why? If the contract was broken, and the city fell, what point was there in fleeing? He had failed, and he might as well die here in whatever vain attempt he could muster to restore the contract. Irichels reached for the strongest of his own contracts, looking for a way to weave it into the broken remains, but there was nothing left to hold.

"Gil," Envar said again, pulling harder. "We have to get back to the house."

That cut through the fog, fatigue and fear and despair. Yes, they could get back to the house, and he might even be able to get the household to safety. If he couldn't do anything else, at least he could do that much. "Yes," he said, and turned into Envar's hold.

Envar snatched loose the end of Alaissou's thread, and let it tug them forward between the quaking pillars. "We need to hurry."

Irichels stumbled in his wake, the light fading around them until they were following the golden thread almost blindly. All around them, there were strange sounds, cracks and the sounds of stone falling, once or twice a high sweet sound like a harp string breaking: there were other curses tied to the Shame, woven into the fabric of the city itself, and while they might not fail entirely, they were certainly affected by the destruction of the core. If he'd acted sooner, he might have saved it—or he might have lost Envar, and seen the city fall anyway. He wouldn't think about that, not now.

Ahead a trio of columns leaned drunkenly together, pressing on the golden thread, so that they had to stoop to get past them. Irichels risked a glance behind them and saw only thickening dark, rolling up out of the central space, the columns vanishing into its shadow. He tapped Envar's shoulder in warning and they both quickened their steps, until they were almost running. Alaissou was waiting where they had left her, vielle still pressed to her chest, bow rising and falling as she kept playing her silent tune. "What happened?"

"We failed," Irichels said. "The contract is broken."

"We need to get out of here," Envar said, in the same moment, and Alaissou gave a jerky nod. She caught her thread with one hand, tucking the vielle under her arm, and tugged lightly.

"This way."

Irichels staggered as the ground shifted under him, regained his balance with an effort. It felt less like solid stone, more like sand, so that he had to fight to make any progress. Envar reached back, his hand black with curses, and Irichels seized it, felt some of his strength return. Even so, it was a struggle to walk in the deepening sand, his breath coming hard in the hot air.

Alaissou's thread was unraveling, fraying into disjointed notes, shrill and off-key and unsettling. She scowled, grasping it more firmly, and a length dissolved with a screech, leaving her to snatch for the fraying end.

"Gently," Envar said. "My heart, can you move faster?"

If I must, Irichels thought, but he had no breath left to answer. He put his head down, feeling the ground tilt beneath him, his feet sliding in deepening sand. He was climbing up an endless dune, surrounded on all sides by the ghosts of trees, skeletal branches reaching to trip him. Behind him stone ripped and fell, and he went to one knee as the ground tilted further.

"We're almost there," Alaissou panted, and Irichels lifted his head to see the triple arch at the top of the long slope. It wasn't so far, except that it was steeply uphill and the sand was sliding away beneath them. He dragged himself another few steps, digging his fingers into sand that was both hot and damp. Beside him, Envar murmured something, and for an instant the slope eased. Irichels managed three quick steps, reached back to catch Envar's outstretched hand, and then they were at the arches, Alaissou one step ahead of them. Irichels dragged himself up onto the solid stone, hauling Envar with him, then sprawled panting. The ground was warm beneath him, when always before the Court had been unnaturally chilled, and he forced himself to his feet.

"This way," Alaissou said, pointing.

Irichels started after her, wobbling like a drunk. Envar caught him around the waist, pulling one arm over his shoulders. "Come on."

Ahead of them the hedges were closing in, thorny branches reaching out to clog the path. Alaissou reached for her vielle, sawing out a tune that turned to gouts of flame, singing the encroaching branches. A rose fell at her feet, shattering, and she flinched back from the shards. Another, larger branch swept toward them and Irichels raised his shield, pouring the last of his strength into it. The branch cracked and fell, but he took the weight of it on his shoulder, his arm dangling useless. Envar steadied him, the curses on his hands blackening again, and then at last the air wavered and they were back in the circle beneath the Assembly.

Arak swung to face them, sword in one hand, lantern in the other. The stones of the chamber creaked alarmingly. "What's happening? There was an almighty crash not a quarter-hour ago. From the other circle, I think, but I didn't dare leave to go see."

"You didn't see anyone?" Irichels forced himself to stand upright. Whether it was Envar's curses or being out of the maze, he felt a little stronger, though his arm still tingled where his shield had failed.

"No."

"We should keep moving," Envar said, glancing up at the ceiling. Irichels followed his gaze, but saw nothing but shadow. He stooped instead, opening the circle, and a whirl of dust surrounded them, carried on a sudden hot breeze.

"Not good," Envar said, under his breath, and stepped out of the circle. The others followed, Arak opening the lantern's shutter all the way.

More light showed the hall, spilling from the first chamber, the one that Cambryse had used. Irichels worked his shoulders, trying to find some reserve of strength. The light was flickering, brightening, and two figures stumbled out into the corridor. Arak put herself between them and the rest of her party, and the pair swung to face them, one holding the other up: Cambryse's feral, Irichels realized, and the semi-conscious man was Margos Temenon.

"You're not dead," he said, and too late realized he'd spoken aloud.

The feral gave a wry grin. "Not yet. But we'd better hurry, I don't think this place will stand much longer."

"Agreed," Envar said, pushing Alaissou toward the stairs. The stones were trembling underfoot, as though something enormous was rolling over them, coming closer with every step. Irichels started up the long spiral of the stairs, dragging himself along behind Alaissou and Arak. Every step seemed mired in sand, and he looked back at the halfway point to see Envar helping the other feral drag Margos up the long stairs. He took a step back but Envar looked up. "Keep going."

Irichels obeyed, too exhausted to do anything but trust him. At last they reached the main floor, only to be greeted by a crack of lightning that shook the high dome. Thunder boomed, echoing through the hall, and in the light of the next flash, Irichels could see more dust sifting down out of the upper levels. There was a strange sharp smell in the air. "Stay under the portico."

They made it out through the heavy doors just as the thunder boomed again, hurrying down the long stairs and out onto the plaza. Overhead the sky was thick with cloud, the boiling towers lightning-lit, and the thunder was a constant mutter punctuated by louder crashes. At the edge of the plaza, waves were breaking halfway up the steps, sending little plumes of spray into the night; the boats were rocking frantically at the mooring poles, and even as Irichels watched, one tore loose and was whirled away into the canal. "We won't get out that way."

The wind strengthened, and a gust of rain blew over them, gone almost as quickly as it had appeared. Irichels shivered, and saw Margos stir in the feral's hold. "I didn't know," he said.

No, not even you would be that foolish. Irichels said, "What did you do? Where's Cambryse? And—that was Fane Temenon?"

"Yes," Margos said. "My father." His ankle gave way and the feral caught him, eased him gently to the ground. The feral went to his knees beside him, curses darkening on his fingers, then looked up at Irichels.

"He'll live, I think. Though he's hurt bad."

"Where's Cambryse?" Irichels asked again.

"Dead." Margos closed his eyes. "Father too. He killed my aunt."

"My stepmother?" Alaissou said sharply, but Margos didn't answer.

The feral said, "Cambryse set fire to Morellin House. He killed his wife, too—I don't know why, he was in a killing fury, but I don't know what about. Then he came here, to break the curse. I swear, I didn't know which curse he meant—"

Lightning struck again, across the Eastern Water among the houses of the Quadrata, the thunder shaking the stones underfoot. Arak said, "We need shelter—"

"Not in the Assembly," Irichels said, and there was a

deep groan from the building, the stone of the plaza rising and falling as though lifted by the waves. "The Processional Bridge."

He turned toward the broad arch that joined Lawgivers' Isle to Mercies, unable to stop himself from looking west toward the Boot. The fire seemed to be under control; at least he saw no more flames, and the smoke was paler than the roiling cloud. But a darker line of cloud was rising in the southwest, rushing toward the city, and at its base there was a flicker of yellow light, paler than the lightning. He counted, and as he reached thirty, there was a distant rolling rumble— not thunder, he was sure of that, but he couldn't place it.

"Samar!" A squad of constables poured off the bridge, the high constable himself at their head. "What are you doing here? What's going on?"

"Don't go in," Irichels said quickly. That seemed like the most important thing, to keep everyone outside. "The foundation curse is broken, the sea demons are coming—"

"We knew that," one of the constables said, with a look to the west, and Irichels realized that the distant rumbling was cannon fire.

"Our ships are engaged," Jeroen said. "The city's and Manimere's against the sea demons. You said the foundation curse is broken? What in Idra's Name?"

"Cambryse did it," the feral said. "They tried to stop him, but—he's dead, and the contract is broken."

Jeroen swore under his breath. "Is that right, Samar?"

Irichels nodded. "That's Margos Temenon there. His father was part of this, Margos tried to stop them."

"Right." Jeroen looked at the Assembly building, its bulk vanishing into the darkness. "Right, we'll have to go in—"

"No." Irichels caught his shoulder. "No, the building's unstable, it's not safe—" As he spoke, the plaza rippled again, and one of the gables above the steps suddenly crumbled, the statue of some long-dead high constable crashing down among the pieces. A head and a hand tumbled free, went bouncing across the stones.

"Idra's mercy." Jeroen rubbed at the stubble on his chin. "Can it be restored?" He looked over his shoulder, and a woman in the Oratorians' scarlet stepped out from among the constables. Irichels was unsurprised to recognize Oredana.

"Perhaps, but not by me alone."

"Samar?" Jeroen began, but Oredana shook her head.

"This is a matter for the Oratory, if anyone. And look at him, he's spent." Behind them in the Assembly, stone split with a crack as sharp as lightning, and there was a crash from somewhere inside. "No, go home, Samar, see to your people. We'll summon you if you can be of help."

Jeroen nodded. "Yes. There's a lot to see to." He looked at the feral. "Not you, however. I'll want more of a word with you and Margos."

Irichels considered protesting but his arm ached, and he couldn't tell if the ground was swaying or if he was no longer steady on his feet. His curses were mostly spent; he would need rest and ritual to restore them, and Envar was in no better shape. "All right," he said, and let Alaissou tug him toward the bridge.

CHAPTER TWENTY

Water was licking at the foot of the Processional Bridge, not so deep yet that they couldn't risk wading, but deeper than any but the highest tides. Another breath of rain washed over them, and Irichels hunched his shoulders, trying to find some reserve of strength. It wasn't so far to the house—it would be quicker by water, of course, but their boat would founder in the waves already rolling up the Eastern Water. And that was one of the more protected waterways; he shuddered to think what conditions would be like on the wide bays to either side of the Weepers, entirely exposed to the oncoming storm. Or on the Sundern, or among the already-battered houses of the Limmerwil.

He paused at the top of the arch to catch his breath, looking west toward the wider water of the Serenna. It belied its name, waves showing white-capped with every flash of lightning, and water was already rolling up against doors and over docks on the outer edge of the Boot. He stared, transfixed, and Envar pulled him on.

There was more water running over the stones at the Mercies end of the bridge, only a few fingers deep, but running hard and rising. Arak opened her lantern all the way, lifting it high, and Alaissou pointed to the north. "The Mason's Walk is a little higher than some others."

Irichels nodded, the water sucking at his boots, and they splashed across the plaza to climb two steps to the Walk. In the distance a tide-bell began sounding, and a few moments later was picked up by Idra-of-Mercy and then by Idra-in-

Chains. Shutters opened, voices calling from house to house: every house on Mercies, every house in Bejanth, knew what it needed to move when the tides rose. This time, though, it might not be enough.

The Walk turned to run along a cross-canal, and Irichels was relieved to see that the water had not yet overtopped the bank, though it was choppy enough that the few boats still at their moorings were bouncing off the stones. Wood splintered somewhere, but he made himself follow Arak's lantern. A few yards on, Alaissou turned onto a cross street and stopped abruptly. Over her shoulder, Irichels could see lamplight, shadows swaying as the wind tossed hanging lanterns, and a small crowd was splashing in ankle-deep water, hauling a small boat up onto higher ground. The low bridge was already half under water, waves breaking against its rails.

"Not that way," Envar said, and drew them back toward the Walk. They were coming up on the Dawan, Mercies's main canal, and Irichels hoped the bridges there would still be above water. They were taller, built to allow larger boats to pass; there was every chance they'd be passable.

Arak stopped again, the lantern swinging in her hands, and Irichels stumbled to a halt behind her. The Dawan was over its banks already, the water running strongly over the stones of the street, waves churning in the center of the canal. The bridge was only a little way ahead, the lanterns at each end still lit, but the one that hung from beneath the central span had vanished, and the water was clearly on the rise.

"We can make it if we stick to the edge," Envar said, and grabbed Irichels's good arm. "Come on, my heart, it's not much further now."

They stumbled along the street, clinging close to the houses. Doors and windows were shut fast, though there were lights within, and occasionally a shout or a crash as households struggled to move valuables off the lower floors. Martholin would be seeing to the same precautions, Irichels thought, splashing through the deepening puddles, only there was no certainty this time that they would work. The contract was broken, the sea demons could raise the waters unchecked, and Bejanth would finally sink beneath the waves. And maybe he could have prevented it, if he'd protected the contract instead of Envar.

He shoved that thought aside, furious that he'd even acknowledged it, and splashed down into ankle-deep water. His boots were thoroughly soaked, water squelching between his toes, and Alaissou's trousers clung to her calves, hampering her steps. They'd have to wade to reach the bridge, but then they'd be across, and there would be only a few smaller canals to cross before they reached the house. The current plucked at him, mere pressure at first, and then stronger, so that he and Envar braced each other against its pull. Ahead of him, Alaissou gave a muted shriek as a bigger wave slapped her off balance, but Arak caught and steadied her up onto the bridge itself.

Irichels followed, the water calf-deep now, and climbed the stairs to the bridge. The stones were trembling gently, but he couldn't resist a quick look down the Dawan's length, toward the Eastern Water. He could just make out the canal's end, a distant lighter patch between the rows of houses, but the water was over the banks of the canal as far as he could see, a confused wash of foam and floating debris. The prow of a boat swept past him, and something else crashed against the arch before breaking free. This was not the time or place to stop, and he made himself move along.

This part of Mercies was higher than others and the streets were mostly dry, though the cross-canals and water alleys were as full as at high tide. They skirted the southern edge of the Palinade, crossed the Paradis Cut, and came out at last on the street that fronted Samar House. Arak seized the bell-knob beside the door, and gave it a hard pull. She did it again and again, while Irichels stared into the alley. There was a faint curl of white about a third of the way along its length, foam and debris pushed up by the water.

The spy-hole beside the door opened and Irichels heard Antel swear under his breath, and then the sound of bars and locks being undone. "Master. We're just clearing the lower floor."

"As much as we can," Martholin said, as they filed into the space beneath the stairs. "There's not enough of us to move the heaviest pieces, and they're more likely to stand a wetting. Everything delicate has been moved, though."

Irichels moved on into the courtyard. All the lamps were lit, their flames flickering slightly with the gusts, and by their light he could see a slowly spreading puddle at the end of the hall by the front door. "The library?"

"We moved the chests of papers to your rooms, and the books that were in the presses," Martholin answered. "Also the silver and the kitchen goods, though we couldn't clear the storerooms completely." She paused. "How bad is it?"

Irichels hesitated, but she deserved the truth. "Bad. Cambryse has broken the contract that held the city together, and I don't know what will happen. The high constable and the Oratory are doing what they can, and Manimere and the city fleet are out against the sea demons, but—" He stopped, shaking his head. "I don't know, Marthie, I'm dead on my feet."

He saw her take a deep breath, her medallion of Idra-in-Chains winking in the lamplight. "Well. That's bad, indeed." She looked over her shoulder at the water creeping up the hall. "We'll have kitchen fires for a few more hours yet, I think, and then it'll be cold food or what we can heat on the upstairs braziers. Go upstairs, get some rest. This won't be over quickly, whatever happens."

That was probably true, and it was certainly true that he was exhausted. He could feel his curses sinking into his skin, as tight as though they'd been soaked in salt water: he would have to repair them soon, but perhaps he could rest just a little first. "Thank you," he managed, and dragged himself up the stairs.

The bedroom was crowded with chests, both from his workroom and from the strongroom where they kept the silver. Irichels dropped into one of the chairs beside the empty fireplace, too tired to undo the straps of his boots. In a moment, he told himself, and rested his head against the chair's high back. *In just a moment I'll change my clothes...*

"Gil."

That was Envar's voice, soft but insistent, and Irichels dragged himself awake. "What—how long—?"

"Not so long," Envar said, his voice soothing. "It's just dawn. Let me get those boots off before they stiffen any further."

Irichels blinked hard, trying to pull his thoughts together. His hands ached, his chest felt bruised, and the muscles at the small of his back pinched painfully with every movement. And surely it wasn't dawn already? The room seemed lighter than before.

"Drink this." Envar held out a cordial glass filled with something dark and sticky. Irichels sniffed it, grimacing at the unpleasant salty sweetness. He recognized the tonic, one of Envar's restorative potions, and drank it off. His boots were stiff with salt water and it took an effort to get them off, but he and Envar managed it at last. "There's dry clothes waiting, and Marthie brought a tray."

I'm not hungry. Irichels swallowed the words, knowing he needed to eat, and made himself put on the dry shirt and trousers. He tore a piece off the loaf and made himself spread cheese on it, chewed and swallowed, his eyes returning to Envar. The chirurgeon looked half-dead himself, the color leached from his already pale skin, a bloodied bandage wrapped around one hand. Payment for his contracts, Irichels knew, and for the tonics that were giving both of them a temporary measure of strength, and he stuffed the last of the bread in his mouth. "Let me," he said, indistinctly, and took Envar's hand to re-fasten the bandage.

"Thanks," Envar said, and leaned against him. That more than anything brought home how exhausted they both still were, and Irichels tightened his hold.

"So. What now?" he asked, and felt Envar's breathy laugh against his neck.

"I wish I knew." He paused. "Food, I suppose, and then—we'll think of something. And thank you, by the way. I couldn't have held off the sea demon much longer. I never had any desire to die for this city."

And quite probably I should have let you die, Irichels thought. *Grandfather would have said so, and probably all my ancestors. But—no. That is not a fair price.* "I wish I'd never come back. We should have stayed inland, renounced the inheritance—at the very least, I should never have let you come with me."

"Do you think you could have stopped me, my heart?" Envar asked. "I wouldn't let you come back here alone."

Irichels rested his cheek against the other man's hair. "We have to do something."

"Agreed," Envar said. "I'm just not sure what."

"Eat first."

The food on the sideboard was cold now, but still palatable. Irichels made himself finish his share of the loaf, hunger returning as he ate, and together they finished off what was left of the cheese and sausage and olives. There was kaf as well, not the usual elaborate service but tall glasses already mixed with sugar and spices. Irichels downed that as well, and there was a knock at the door. Envar moved to open it and Arak slipped inside. She looked better than Envar, Irichels thought: well, she was younger, and there'd been less call for her talents at the Assembly. "Well?"

"Antel's been to Idra-in-Chains and back," Arak said. "They say that between the fleet and the towers at the harbor mouths and the contracts that bind them, the sea demons haven't been able to enter the city. But the water's still rising, and the storm's getting worse."

Irichels cocked his head, listening. Maybe the wind was stronger than it had been; certainly the rain was heavier, and steady, rattling against the windows. He went into the dressing room and eased back the sliding shutter there. The rain swept past at a near-horizontal angle, churning the water alley to foam-streaked waves. The water lapped at the walls of the house opposite, already well above the tide-mark. He slid the shutter closed again. It was too late to try to get his people away—had been too late before he left for the Assembly, but he wouldn't think about that. There had to be something he could do to protect the household if not the house, but he couldn't seem to think of anything. "I'd better take a look," he said, to no one in particular, and shrugged an old gown over shirt and trousers.

It was lighter on the balcony, though the roar of the rain was louder on the roof, and water was dripping down into the courtyard where the seams of the glass panels had given way. Irichels leaned over the balcony, seeing water covering the stones. The leaks from the roof raised a steady splashing, making it hard to see if the water was still rising, but it was already over the second step, nearly knee-deep. The bird cages were open, and he looked up to see some of the birds huddling in the spaces of the third-floor railings. He could feel the house daemon's agitation, ricocheting from one wall to another, and tried to project calm.

"Master Gil!" Martholin came hurrying down the stairs from the third floor, her hair bound tight beneath a scarf, trousers rolled to her knees in case she needed to brave the kitchen.

"How are things upstairs?"

"Not so bad. A few leaks in the roof, most of them in places that have always leaked, and some windows broken in the front of the house. We've nailed the shutters closed over them, so that's stopped the rain getting in, but one of them was in Lady Alaissou's music room. We've got all her things moved into the bedroom, so that should be all right."

"Good work." Irichels wondered what more he should say. There should be something, he knew, but he couldn't seem to think of it. "If you need to move people down from the third floor, there are plenty of empty rooms."

"Already thought of," Martholin said, "though there's no need just yet." She lowered her voice. "Antel went to Idra-in-Chains for the news, did they tell you?" Irichels nodded. "We won't be leaving the city any time soon, from what he says."

"I left it too late."

"I still say we're safer here," Martholin said. "Though if you could persuade *it* to settle, we'd all be easier."

"I'll do what I can," Irichels said.

"There's plenty of food, if you're hungry."

Irichels shook his head. "No, thank you, but if there's more kaf? Like you made last night?"

"I'll make you a glass," Martholin said, and started back up the stairs.

Irichels made his way down the next set of stairs to the landing. It was mostly dry, though there was a growing leak that fell just at the top of the stairs that led down to the courtyard. He looked up, trying to spot the gap in the glass and leading, but could see only a smear of rain and the featureless gray of the clouds. He sat down in the niche at the top of the stairs, conscious that this had been a forbidden thing throughout his childhood. But in those days the niche had housed an enormous painted urn, brought at ridiculous expense from across the Narrow Sea; where it had gone, he neither knew nor particularly cared. His back pinched again and he stretched, trying to loosen abused muscles.

Antel appeared, carrying the glass of kaf, and Irichels braced himself to listen as the man described what he had seen. He'd made it to Idra-in-Chains and back, yes, following the more sheltered streets, but doubted he could do it again, unless the low tide brought some relief. The Oratorians were sheltering perhaps a hundred people in the raised galleries, folks flooded out of the houses along the Dawan; the young Oratorian who'd climbed the bell tower claimed to have seen some of the city's ships still engaged, firing into the storm, and the tower at the mouth of the Eastern Water was still lit. All good, Irichels thought, but at some point the ships would run out of spelled shot and powder, and the sea demons would close with the towers— He shoved the thought away, thanked Antel and sent him off to rest, then drained the glass, barely tasting the syrupy sweetness. Presumably Jeroen had some plan in mind, but he hadn't shared it if he did.

He felt the daemon again, swirling through the kitchen

and into the rooms at the front of the house, as offended as a cat at the water covering the stones. It swung back through the ballroom, and then under the stairs, restless and fretting as it pressed against the walls. Trying to hold the water back, Irichels thought. About as useless as trying to bail the courtyard: there was no place for the water to go except in, and even the daemon wasn't strong enough to seal the stone.

Unless... He straightened, wincing as his back twinged again. The daemon was unguided, untaught. If it were given a curse, if it was asked to enforce a curse, would it be strong enough to hold the house together? He started up the stairs. "Cass? I've got an idea."

They settled in the chairs beside the empty fireplace, lamps lit and brought close until they sat in a ring of light. Irichels found paper and ink and a board to rest them on, and Envar leaned close, frowning slightly as he watched the other man work.

"The house-daemon's restless," Irichels began, and Envar laughed softly.

"So are we all, my heart."

Irichels smiled in spite of everything. "True. But I was thinking, if we could channel that energy to protect the house—"

"Not into the wards," Envar said. "They're not strong enough, to start."

"And not designed for this, no," Irichels agreed. "But if we could create a curse that would do that, it might be strong enough to maintain it."

"Protect it how?" Envar asked, and Irichels sighed.

"I don't know." He shook his head. "Maybe I'm looking at it wrong. Can we mend the part of the contract that protected this house?"

"It was a contract," Envar said, "not a curse. Essentially a two-sided bargain, and one side clearly doesn't want to rebuild it. Though it's been in place so long, and so many other curses were built on top of it—"

"Maybe we could pull the pieces back together," Irichels

said. "Not a contract—not an agreement, but a barrier."

"A proper curse," Envar agreed.

It might be possible, Irichels thought. In theory, at least, if the pieces still lingered, held by the later layers of curses, it might just be possible to create new curses to fill the gaps, to knit the structure back together, though the amount of power it would take would be prodigious... He put that aside, focusing instead on the problem of transforming a broken contract into a one-sided curse. If anything, it was a matter of grammar, shifting from agreement to ban: recasting clauses that existed by consent to ones imposed by fiat. It would be easier if he knew exactly which sections had been destroyed, but if the ends of the structure remained, he thought he could shape a curse that would fit that gap. His charcoal moved almost of its own accord, sketching the familiar symbols, nulls standing for the pieces that would have to be added on the fly. Envar leaned over his shoulder, nodding.

"That would work. Perhaps an elemental sign there, not lunar?"

Irichels nodded, rubbed out the lunar invocata and substituted the null that meant the appropriate element. "We'd need the agreement of the four houses, or at least their proxy."

"Well, you can get three of them," Envar said. "Samar, Manimere, and Cambryse."

"And Morellin," Irichels said. "Alaissou said her mother was a Morellin."

"That's thin," Envar said, "but it might work."

"Blood from each of us to consent to changing the bargain."

"Shell and seaweed from a sea demon." Envar pushed himself away from the chair, came back a moment later with a bleached dish-like shell, only a little cracked along the edges, and a twist of something stringy and black that smelled of low tide. "To define the beings warded against."

"I saw you grab that," Irichels said.

"I hoped I might call this one to account," Envar said, "but this is a better use of it."

Irichels nodded again, looking at his notes. It would work, he was reasonably sure of that—if he could reach the broken bits of the contract where they were still entangled with the rest of the city's curses, but he was fairly confident of that as well. What was missing was the power: this was a simple curse, could only be a simple curse, given what he was trying to do with it, and there was no room in it for any of the tricks and cantrips generally used to multiply the caster's power. He had worked for decades to build his strength, it was a cursebreaker's stock in trade; but even thoroughly rested, he wouldn't have enough for this.

Envar frowned. "Don't even think of sacrificing yourself for this."

"That wasn't my plan." But it would take someone's life, Irichels thought, as least as it was written, and preferably a life already intimately connected to the curse. He studied the symbols again, hoping for a way out, but he could see no way to reduce the strength that would be needed. Even just to protect this house would take more than he had, and probably more than he could draw from Envar and Alaissou. "I'd thought—my first thought was to harness the house-daemon somehow, persuade it to act. But now I'm not sure."

"It might be enough," Envar said. "But persuading it might be tricky, my heart."

And if it's strong enough to do any good, it would be too strong for me to force it. Even if I thought forcing it would work. "I know," Irichels said. "But I haven't got anything else."

"Surely the high constable is doing something," Envar said, but his tone belied his words. "It might even work."

"He doesn't have the keys. I do." Irichels looked at the bare spot in the center of the room where the circle had once been carved. "Will you get blood from Nerin and Alaissou?"

Envar nodded. "Are you going to open this circle?"

"I want whatever it can give me. And I want to see the pillar."

"All right." Envar disappeared into this room, returned with a tiny silver bowl and a knife with a wickedly pointed blade. He lifted his eyebrows, and Irichels held out his hand, wincing as the point pierced the ball of his thumb. He squeezed it, drawing up a fat bead of blood, and turned to the circle as Envar moved away.

The circle was the ghost of what it had been, the symbols barely more than rough spots on the boards, tangible only when they ran against the grain of the wood. He knelt at its edge, holding his left hand carefully to keep from spilling the blood before he was ready, and felt for the symbols with his other hand. He had traced it out before, but he made sure he had fixed it in memory before he turned his hand and let the blood drop fall. It hissed and smoked, and the daemon swirled up out of the floor, radiating shock and uncertainty. The shutters rattled under another gust of wind.

Irichels ignored it all, focusing instead on the pillar he had seen before. A spike, a pin, salamanders running in the flames... He breathed deeply as it grudgingly took shape. Before it had been bright, translucent, pale shapes darting among even paler flames. Now the shapes were still, the brightness quenched, so that it seemed to be carved from smoke, a frozen shadow of what it had been. It felt brittle, fragile, as though the wrong touch would shatter it—but at the same time, it still reached from beyond bedrock up to the ethereal.

Irichels sat back on his heels. The pillar would lead him straight into the maze that lay beyond the Courts, and from there he could reach the pieces of the shattered contract. Whether he would have the strength to repair them was another matter, but it was worth the attempt. He could feel the daemon edging closer, its uncertainty changing to sorrow and anger.

Broken. All? All gone?

"Not all of it," Irichels said. "It can be mended, but I need your help. Can you come with me?"

There? Into that? There was a pause. *Don't know...*

"Will you try?"

There was another long silence, the daemon shrinking back into the shadows. *Can't...*

"For the house," Irichels said, and there was a shiver like a sigh.

For Samar.

The door opened again, and the daemon retreated. Irichels turned, seeing Envar's eyes flick toward it, but he held out the bowl without comment. There was a smear of blood in its depths, one or two drops from each of the others, and Irichels was unsurprised to see Alaissou following in Envar's wake. Arak was behind her, glancing warily at the shutters as another gust of wind-driven rain struck the building. "The water's up to the fourth step now."

Up to mid thigh, and still rising. Irichels said, "I can see a way out, maybe. If we're lucky, and if I can manage it."

"You could let us help," Alaissou said.

"If this were Cambryse house, you'd have to do it," Irichels said. "But this is Samar. I'm the only one of us who can manipulate this circle, and the pillar it holds."

Alaissou gave Envar a look, as though expecting him to protest, but the chirurgeon only sighed. "Will the pillar hold you, my heart?"

"I don't know," Irichels admitted. "I hope so."

"And will—*that*—" Alaissou gestured to the corner where the daemon hovered. "Will *it* help you?"

"Yes." Irichels spoke with more confidence than he felt, and was surprised to feel faint agreement from the daemon.

Alaissou looked at Arak. "Fetch my vielle, would you? Please."

Arak ducked away. Envar said, "The circle still feels solid. That's good. What do you propose?"

"To follow the pillar down into the maze," Irichels answered. "Create the curse from there if I can."

"I should go with you."

"I can't spare the strength," Irichels said. "I'd have to clear the way for you, all the way down, when I can walk it by right. You know I can't."

Envar closed his eyes. "I know. Will you let me inside the circle? I can be your anchor."

"Yes. Gladly."

"Your vielle," Arak said, to Alaissou. She took it, began adjusting the tuning, and Arak said, "What can I do?"

"Keep people out, keep people calm," Irichels said. "If things go badly—" He stopped, not having a better answer than to bar the doors from the outside and hope for the best, but Arak nodded as though she'd heard the words and they made sense.

"Let me play you a line," Alaissou said. "The way we did before."

Irichels wasn't sure that would make much difference— the pillar struck deep into the heart of the maze; when he reached its foot, he should be where he needed to be—but he nodded anyway. "Thank you." Envar handed him the bowl of blood, already starting to congeal, and then the shell and the fragments of seaweed. Irichels stepped into the circle, Envar on his heels, and the daemon swarmed over and around them before retreating to the far side of the pillar. Irichels hunched his shoulders against the daemon's chill, remembering its touch in childhood, then put that thought aside.

"Here." Envar handed him the small knife, and Irichels stabbed his thumb again, milking out two drops of blood to join the liquid in the bowl. He swirled it twice, then braced himself, facing the pillar, and spoke the words that closed the circle. The light thickened around him, blotting out the room beyond the circle, but the pillar stayed frustratingly indistinct. He invoked a contract, and felt the circle shift around him; the pillar shimmered, but remained unchanged. He closed his eyes, focusing on making it come clear, and felt the daemon shift around him, probing and then withdrawing in little darting movements.

Broken...

"No." *No, I won't let it be, there has to be a way—* Irichels stilled those thoughts, forcing calm and control. He moved closer to the pillar, willing it to solidify, and in that moment heard Alaissou began to play. This time, he could hear the music, a weirdly familiar tune that he abruptly identified as a children's song. Even he had learned it, scuffling in the courtyard of the day-school: *Up and down the Founders' Well, on a cold and frosty morning.* A spark flared, fizzing like the fire at the end of a fuse, and struck the pillar. Around it, the shadows solidified and the spark began to spiral slowly down, stairs appearing as it sank. Irichels took a deep breath and followed it, bowl and shell and seaweed still in hand. The daemon followed him like his own vast shadow.

The spark wound down and down, tracing the shape of the pillars, drawing an endless stair. Motionless flames shaped the walls, studded with salamanders frozen in every possible posture, coiling, leaping, mating, fighting. The song's chorus echoed in his ears even as the tune screeched and wavered; he concentrated on that memory and the spark steadied again, leading him ever downward. Behind him the daemon swelled and thickened, until he didn't dare look back.

Then at last the air brightened, the base of the pillar returning almost to normal, and he looked out through the slowly waving flames into a clearing that was surely part of the maze beyond the Courts. Irichels braced himself, the music still whispering in his ears, and stepped out of the pillar into a vast expanse of pale sand. It rose slightly toward the apparent horizon, as though he was at the bottom of a shallow bowl, a fitful wind scribbling nonsense across the shifting ground. Three pillars rose in the distance, dark against the sand and the faintly paler sky: the pillars that belonged to the other houses, he guessed, still standing, but not as securely as he had hoped. One was leaning at a definite angle, as though the wind that was a breeze where he stood was a gale strong enough to uproot trees. Another seemed to be fraying, its edges blurred and shivering: he was just in time, if he could pull it off.

He put doubt aside, and lifted the bowl, marshaling the new curse. Instantly, a blast of wind struck him, heavy with sand. He turned his shoulder to it, protecting the things he held, but a scrap of the seaweed tore away, vanishing into nothing. He found a counter-curse, spoke it aloud, and the wind dropped reluctantly. A few gusts swirled around his knees like water, but the rest were deflected. That was good, gave him space to work, but it had taken strength he didn't have to spare.

He could hear bells ringing, far in the distance, a discordant clamor that beat against the thread of Alaissou's song, hammering it to a new rhythm. It was the rhythm of the Founders' Day hymn, slow and weighty, every syllable beaten home by a bell, and he realized that the children's song ran in counterpoint, wound through and with it to form another shape, scaffolding that could shore up the crumbling towers. The bells were all around him, coming from all directions; and as he focused on them, he realized that he could just make out the thin fingers of the bell towers, eight of them spaced equally around the sandy circle.

A circle, and the pillars forming a square within it, while the bells and Alaissou's song cried out to the broken structure: he would never have a better chance to mend it. He went to one knee in the sand, sheltering the bowl with its thickened blood and the bits of sea demon from the wind. He formed the curse carefully, holding each component firmly in mind before he dipped his finger in the blood and drew each symbol on the shell, piling them one on top of the other as though he were laying stones in a wall. He felt the correspondences catch and hold, but the connections were fragile, too weak to take the strain of the completed curse. He slashed the heel of his hand to pour more blood onto the shell and into the curse, but it was nowhere near enough.

He looked over his shoulder, but the daemon was gone. It had come all this way, come down to the base of the pillar, but it had not left it—maybe couldn't leave it. Maybe his gamble had failed, and there was nothing the daemon could do to help him, drawn outside its proper domain. And he was so close... The blood had helped; if he spent his life, bled himself dry, would it be enough? Could he live with himself if he didn't try? He cut his hand again, aware of the veins two fingers' width away from the cuts. There was the blood, there was the power; the curse tightened, feeding on what he gave it, but it was still too ragged to hold. Envar would never forgive him. Envar would also understand, more than anyone else. He pushed back his cuff, and drew the knife across the veins before he could change his mind.

It hurt more than he had expected, so that it took an effort to turn his arm so that the blood fell where it should. The bells beat against him, tangled with the thread of Alaissou's song, and he reached for them both, riding the flare of strength that came with the sacrifice. The curse to mend the towers, to make the square whole: he could feel it taking shape, coalescing with each heartbeat, but too slowly, not enough, and he had nothing more to give.

He bent his head, stripping power from his contracts, pouring that out with the blood: there was no point in conserving anything now, he could only spend what he had and hope it would be enough. The wind roared, sweeping sand over him, blotting out the sound of the bells, and he could only huddle against the ground and endure.

The ground shook beneath him, and abruptly he was engulfed in familiar cold shadow, the daemon wrapping itself around him. He reached for it blindly, meaning to channel its strength into the curse, and recoiled as he felt another daemon with it. And another, and yet another, dozens of them, some as old and as strong as Samar's, some new and small and uncertain, but all willing to be guided into the shape of the curse. He clutched at his wrist, slowing the bleeding, and made himself focus, laying out the pieces of the curse one by one. The structure was simple enough, and the daemons seized on it, pouring themselves into it.

He felt the pieces slot into place, pulling the broken bits together, mending gaps. The leaning tower slowly moved upright, with a groan that he felt in his bones. The fraying tower ceased to fade, solidifying against the pale sky, and along the horizon the bell towers rose like sentinels. A square in a circle, the oldest protective shape, the manifold curse that now held the city together... It was all part of him, and he was part of it, spreading out into the structure so that he felt the moment it locked and held. He caught a glimpse of Manimere, drenched and powder-blackened, screaming over the wind to bring another broadside to bear. In the wreck of the Assembly hall, the high constable lifted his head where he stood at the center of a circle of Oratorians, and from him rose the shape of Idra-in-Chains, wielding her broken links like a flail against the thrashing water.

He felt the sea demons break and run, one last tired wave washing up the canals barely half a foot high, and then he was falling back into his body, found himself sprawled on the floor of his bedroom, the lines of the circle smoldering around him, while Envar clutched his bleeding wrist and Arak flung water to damp the marks. The daemon was there, hovering pleased and wary and worried, and he managed a smile for it before he turned his face to Envar's chest and let himself collapse.

CHAPTER TWENTY-ONE

He woke more slowly this time, to lamplight and the smell of low tide and limewash. His wrist and hand ached sharply, with the throbbing warmth that hinted at infection, and he propped himself up on his other elbow, squinting as he tried to judge the time of day. The bedcurtains were open, and Envar rose from his seat by the fire, catching up a bottle as he passed the sideboard.

"You're awake, then."

"I think so."

"That's better than you were." Envar seated himself beside him, ready to offer support, and held out the bottle. "Drink."

"What is it?" Irichels sniffed warily, recognizing bitter herbs.

"A tonic. Which you need."

There was no arguing with that. "All of it?"

"Yes." Irichels grimaced, but drank it off. Envar took the emptied bottle and set it aside, then reached for the other's bandaged arm. "What were you thinking?" Irichels winced as Envar unwound the bandages, revealing the angry red lines of the healing cuts. The one on his wrist bore the black dots of stitches, and he looked away as Envar redid the wrappings. "You said you wouldn't do that."

"I didn't have a choice," Irichels said. "And it wasn't for the city, it was for the people."

That was one of the mercies of having been together so long: they knew each other well enough to skip the actual recriminations. Envar shook his head. "Don't do that again, my heart. I don't think I could bear it."

"I never meant to do it even once," Irichels said. He looked around, frowning. "How long—have I been out long?"

"Three days," Envar said. "The high constable wants a word with you, Innes Manimere has been restored—and she's collected Nerin, with thanks. Cambryse is very dead, so there's a new heir, though I'm not sure who, and Marthie has hired extra maids to scrub down the floors and the furniture where the water came in."

"And the rest of the city?"

"Cleaning up, making repairs. There are some bridges down, and some houses in the Limmerwil and on the southern edge of Weepers collapsed. But not as bad as it could have been."

"Well."

"Do you know what you did?" Envar set the old bandages aside.

"I mended the contract."

"Don't play games. I told you, the high constable wants a word, and I won't be able to put him off once he hears you're awake."

Irichels sighed. "I'm entangled, aren't I? Enmeshed in it." If he closed his eyes, he could feel the tide draining from the city, the shift of the wind as it swung to the southeast, the damaged bridges and the cracked and shifted pilings not just in the Limmerwil and Weepers but on Westerly as well. He could feel the gap where Morellin House had been, burned to the waterline, the broken towers of the Assembly, and even the tiles blown from the roofs all across the city, swept here and there into untidy piles.

"Gil." Envar laid a hand on his good wrist, and Irichels blinked himself back to this room.

"Bound to the city," he said, and couldn't quite keep the bitterness from the words.

"You gave your life to it," Envar said. "It's not something you can take back, my heart. I'm just grateful for your daemon."

"It knew it wasn't strong enough," Irichels said. "But it knew there were others like it, all as determined to protect their houses as it was to protect Samar. And they all gave bits of themselves to shape the curse." He paused. "Is it all right?"

He felt it then, secure and almost somnolent in its niche beneath the bedchamber, aware of his touch but in no hurry to respond. Envar said, "It's been quieter than before, but it's certainly there. It let me feed it, though it hasn't let Marthie clean that back storeroom." That would have to be dealt with, Irichels thought, and struggled to sit up. Envar stuffed a pillow behind his back, and Irichels leaned gratefully against it. "But I'm more concerned about you, my heart."

Irichels shrugged one shoulder. If this was what he suspected, he could never leave the city—at the very best, he might cross to the Plana and the cities there, but never for very long. He had left gladly at seventeen, never felt any urge to return, and he'd never wanted more. He had taken up Samar because it was necessary, not expecting to be changed, but now... He could feel the city again, the tide race slowing, fugitive strands of beach appearing along the shores; could feel, too, the circle-and-square that held it all together, deep beneath the shifting sands. The city stood, and its people were safe—Martholin was safe, and the rest of the household, and all the city, when he'd been sure they were all going to drown. That was worth the sacrifice. "I'll be all right," he said, and hoped that it was true.

The high constable arrived the next morning, trailed by a pair of guards and carrying a leather scroll case. Irichels met him in the courtyard, where the sunlight poured in only occasionally broken by a passing cloud, while the guards retreated to the kitchen. Most of the birds had been lured back to their cages, though a single bright-green warbler still fluttered around the top of the house, not yet ready to return. Irichels could hear it calling as he welcomed Jeroen, waving him to a seat beside the slow-running fountain. Martholin brought kaf and little cakes, and Envar leaned on the back of Irichels's chair. Jeroen gave him one quick look, and visibly decided to say nothing. "I came to thank you personally. The Senate and Assembly will have their own say, of course, but I felt what you did."

"My family was in danger," Irichels said.

Jeroen nodded. "I trust they're all well?"

That was not the response Irichels had expected. "Yes, thank you."

"I also came because our curses now intersect," Jeroen said, and reached for the scroll case. "This—these are the bonds that appertain to the high constable's office. I can tell you how they used to interact with the foundational contract, but in return I'd like you to tell me how the new curse is made."

That was also unexpected, but not unreasonable. "I can do that," Irichels said, "but it'll be easier in my workroom. Cass and I haven't yet drawn out the results, but I can at least show you what we planned to do."

"Thank you," Jeroen said and added, almost without visible effort, "and you, Dot're."

They unrolled the diagram on Irichels's worktable, weighting the corners with the polished stones. The room smelled of herbs and oil, and beneath that of limewash, but there was no whiff of mold. The scroll itself was clearly a copy of a much older document, though if it had been as elaborately decorated as such things usually were, the copyist hadn't bothered to copy the decorations. Instead, a map of the city had been laid out in silverpoint, and the web of curses that bound the high constable was drawn in over it, centering on Lawgivers' and the Senate and Assembly building.

"Oh, that's cleverly done," Envar said, and Irichels nodded in agreement.

"This is what we did." He rummaged through the papers that had been brought back down from his bedroom, found the square with his scrawled notes and laid it on top of the scroll.

Jeroen considered it. "That's not all you did."

"No. Things had changed when I got there." Irichels looked around. "Cass, is there any fine paper left?"

"Here." Envar brought a sheet of the translucent paper and laid it over the scroll, replacing the weights. It was easy to see the penmarks through it, though the silverpoint was more elusive.

"The structure of the Shame was a square," Irichels said, "with each of the houses making a corner." He marked them lightly with a stick of charcoal, and saw Jeroen nod. "And then the towers at the harbormouths, they form a circle that encloses it, but it was made later, and not part of the original contract."

"But they are tied to the high constable's office," Jeroen observed.

"Which I didn't know at the time," Irichels said, adding the towers to his own drawing. "But that fundamentally is what was done: rewrite the contract as a simple curse, and tie it to the later circle."

Jeroen looked from the drawing to the notes, watching as Irichels drew in the rest of the symbols that represented what he had done. "But you're only one house. How did you compel the others?"

"I had members of the other houses here as well," Irichels said.

"Cambryse's daughter," Jeroen said. "And her mother was a Morellin. But what about Manimere?"

Irichels hesitated, and Envar said, "She's a hero now, my heart. I think you can say."

Irichels laughed in spite of himself. "Manimere left her son with me. And that makes four."

"Of course she did," Jeroen said, shaking his head. "And just as well." He looked at the drawing again. "The Oratorians will be pushing to regularize all the city's curses. I'm not sure how far they'll get, but they'll have more support than usual after all of this."

"I'll cooperate as far as I can," Irichels said, answering the unspoken question, "but I won't weaken the curse."

"Idra forbid!" Jeroen made a propitiatory gesture. "You've saved us all, the last thing we need is to interfere with that. And if there is anything I can do…"

"What are the limits?" Envar asked. "If this curse binds him to the city—how close must he stay? Can he leave and come back? What are the rules?"

Jeroen paused. "If it's like the high constable's bond of office, then he can't leave the city limits. You can stretch it as far as the shore of the Plana, to Lueta and Capete, they're almost part of the city, but no further. And even then, you can't stay long. You start to feel it, and it's—not pleasant."

"That's useful," Irichels said.

"I hope so," Jeroen said. "The Senate and Assembly will want to recognize what you've done, but that will probably need to wait until the buildings are repaired."

That sparked a memory. "Cambryse is dead, and Fane Temenon. What's going to happen to Margos?"

"Not my decision," Jeroen said. "For which he should be grateful. There will be a tribunal, but most likely he won't be too severely punished. Since he did the right thing at the end."

"They won't reduce the family to the Assembly?" Envar asked, almost innocently, and Irichels frowned.

"That was never a good idea."

"Nor is it likely," Jeroen said. "Radulph Temenon wasn't involved in any of this, as far as I can tell, and he's master, so nothing should change. Though we'll be keeping an eye on them just in case."

"And the feral?" Envar asked.

Jeroen met his gaze squarely. "What feral?"

"Ah."

Jeroen looked at Irichels. "The man was punished enough, I saw no reason to pursue the matter."

"I expect the Oratory thought differently," Irichels said.

"The Oratory wasn't asked," Jeroen answered, and Irichels nodded. He looked back at the scroll, the lines of the old curses showing faintly through the fine paper, meeting and matching the curse he had created.

"I'd like some time to study this."

"The copy's yours," Jeroen said. "And if you have questions, I'll do my best to answer."

The next days were filled with visitors, to the point where Irichels pleaded exhaustion and fled to the sanctuary of his bedroom. That let him avoid some of the crowd but there was no way to put off Hal, voluble in his relief and carrying unofficial messages from his father and from Gethen, all promising future support. Nor was it possible to avoid Oredana Temenon, arriving in a barge flying the Oratory's colors from a sterncastle newly repaired and repainted after the storm's damage. Her messages were official, backed up by a formal escort of armed guards and a pair of lower-ranking Oratorians, and Irichels took a certain pleasure in receiving her in the courtyard with Envar at his side. He thought he caught a matching flicker of amusement in her expression, but she confined herself to the formal compliments and thanks, and the reminder that Samar still needed an heir.

"Which was not a thing I needed to be told," Irichels said, after she had left and he and Envar had retreated to the workroom. "The curse still depends on the four houses."

Envar nodded, his eyes on the chart he had unrolled on the worktable again. "Samar's more important than the others, but yes. And I don't see a way to change that. At least not easily."

"We should work on it," Irichels said. "Not that I'm eager to meddle with what we have, but it would be better if everything didn't depend on the families."

"It will be different when you're dead," Envar said. Irichels lifted his eyebrows, and Envar had the grace to look sheepish. "Not that I'm eager for that to happen! But right now your life is bound into the curse, which complicates things. Once you're dead, you become a stable point, the price paid, and it should be easier to make changes."

"Do you know, I think I'll leave that to someone else," Irichels said, after a moment.

"And may it be a long way off." Envar sketched a propitiatory sign in the air between them. "Do you have a plan, my heart?"

Irichels hesitated. "I like Alaissou. She's good and brave and clever, and we wouldn't have survived without her at least twice that I can name—but if I must be married, I'd still rather it were Manimere. Not to mention that Alaissou's father betrayed the city. However, I don't want to leave her without support."

"Have you thought of asking her what she wants?" Envar cocked his head to one side.

"Of course, but it's not an easy question to raise—"

Envar sighed. "Have you seen her and Arak lately?"

Irichels blinked. Yes, he had seen them together more often than not. Just this morning, they'd been in the courtyard, setting out seeded bread to try to lure the last warbler back to its cage. The bird had dropped down but soared away again before Alaissou could cast the tiny net, and they'd leaned together laughing as it scolded them from the balconies. "She's too old for her," he said, and felt himself blush.

"Oh, my heart." Envar gave him the look that deserved. "She's twenty years younger than either of us. Alaissou's old for her age, too, as if it matters. And I'd say it's what she wants, at least for now."

"I'll talk to her," Irichels said. He could feel the city slumbering in the sun, a soothing presence the back of his mind.

The chance didn't arise until that evening, when the last visitor had left, and they were finally all able to sit down to dinner. It was still plain cooking, bread and cheese and a ragout of ham and onions, and the wine had been decanted from a bottle splashed with mud, but things were demonstrably returning to normal. There were even sweet, thin friable sugar wafers from the just-reopened bakery three streets up, and Irichels watched Alaissou scour the last crumbs from the platter. "I think—now that your father is dead, there are things we need to talk about."

She froze for an instant, shooting him a wary look, and then made herself resume dabbing up the last bits of sugar. Out of the corner of his eye Irichels saw Arak look up sharply, but was careful to pretend he didn't see. The hill folk had strong ideas about honor; this had to be between himself and Alaissou, if he wasn't to make things worse. "I suppose we must," she said.

Irichels allowed himself a wry smile. "It's a tangle, I know. But we can get out of it, and without much trouble. Since the marriage wasn't consummated."

"I told my stepmother that it was." Alaissou's voice was admirably steady, though she was blushing. "But she's dead, too, and if she told anyone, I can always say I lied to make her leave me alone. Which is ironically the truth." She paused. "Do you want to end it?"

"Yes." Irichels lifted a hand. "No blame to you, and I hope you'll stay my friend—stay here in the house as long as you wish, call on me like family. But I don't want to marry." And that, he realized, was more truth than he'd meant. What he wanted was Envar, and a child, preferably with Manimere, who he thought would understand; he was bound enough by the city.

Alaissou nodded slowly, as though she were putting pieces together. "And if—when—I choose to look elsewhere myself?"

"I'll raise the wedding toast myself," Irichels said, though if it was Arak she wanted that would not be an option. In the hills, Arak could have an acknowledged place; here in Bejanth they would have to invent something else, but he didn't doubt they could.

She nodded again. "So be it. I agree. And I will also stay here for now, since you've offered."

"You're entirely welcome," Irichels said.

After dinner, he made the rounds of the ground floor, checking the doors and windows: a pleasantly ordinary task, after everything that had happened. Arak followed, carrying a branch of candles. It was quiet, after the bustle of the day; Irichels could feel the city around him, the flooding tide and a shift in the wind that promised good weather to come, the spires of the oratories silent and waiting in the hours between esperin and the midnight bell. Something swarmed in the canal, darting beneath the house as a larger fish came by, and the daemon watched from its corner. If he just made a little effort, he could feel another daemon four houses away—a small one, newly raised, and still recovering from the power it had shared. It would recover, though, and grow, if its family took even moderate care, and it would secure the city when he was gone.

"Gil?"

He realized that he had stopped, was standing in the middle of the kitchen looking at the barred door, and shook his head in apology. "Woolgathering."

"As long as you're all right."

"Yes. I promise."

Arak frowned at the candles as though she was concentrating on not spilling the wax. "You meant it? About letting her go?"

"Alaissou?" Irichels kept his voice casual. To say the wrong thing was to offend, when what he wanted was for everything to end well. "Yes, I meant it. You know me, Arak. I can't give her what she deserves, never mind what she wants. It's good to have an excuse to untangle ourselves from a marriage neither one of us wanted."

There was a little silence. Irichels waited, and saw the swordswoman sigh. "When she's free—I intend to court her. If she'll have me."

"She could do far worse," Irichels said.

"Or better." Arak's voice was sharp.

"Do you love her?"

"Yes. She's—well. You've seen."

Irichels nodded. "She's not had much love, I think. But she knows her own mind."

"And well I know it," Arak said, with a quick smile. "It's one reason I like her. I'd like to stay on, regardless—"

"You'd be welcome," Irichels said, and they turned toward the stairs.

His door was open, light spilling onto the landing, and Arak moved past him, heading for her own room. Irichels quickened his step, expecting Envar, but instead it was Alaissou who waited by the fireplace. "I wanted to talk to you."

Irichels swallowed a pang of disappointment. "Of course." He closed the door behind him, grateful to see that Martholin had restored the decanters on the sideboard, and crossed to it to pour a glass of brandy. He held out the decanter in invitation, but Alaissou shook her head.

"No, thank you." Irichels seated himself beside the fireplace and waited.

"I realized I should tell you something," she said, after a moment. Her expression was closed, unreadable, and Irichels guessed she wasn't used to sharing confidences. "I'm glad to end the marriage—not because I dislike you, or because you've done anything wrong—"

"It wasn't what either of us would have chosen," Irichels said, when she seemed unable to go on.

"That." She nodded. "But also—I have grown fond of Arak, and once I'm free, I can say so without offending her. I thought you should know."

"She's a good woman and a good friend," Irichels said. "You'd have a hard time finding a better."

"I've read that in the hills ladies sometimes take their swordswomen for their lovers. That it's not just not forbidden, but acceptable. I don't want to offend her."

"It's the happy ending to the story, more often than not," Irichels said. "You won't offend. It'll be harder here, of course, but—"

"You manage."

"So far."

She cocked her head. "You don't mind, then?"

"I'd hate for her to leave the household," Irichels said.

"But I'd dislike you leaving, too."

"They'll say I made a fool of you," Alaissou said. "That I took a lover under your nose and now I'm flaunting it."

"They're more likely to say that I corrupted you, and try to rescue you," Irichels said. "Or that I'm a sodomite, and that you're well rid of me."

"And you don't mind that?"

"They owe me the city," Irichels said. "I feel I have leverage."

She grinned. "I just didn't want you to be surprised."

"I think the two of you could make a good match," Irichels answered, and felt ridiculously old. She nodded again and let herself out, closing the door softly behind her. Irichels drained the rest of his brandy, and the secret door clicked open.

"You had to have expected confessions," Envar said, his voice trembling with laughter.

"Just tell me you're not here to make one," Irichels answered. Envar shook his head, and crossed to the sideboard. He poured a glass for himself and held out the decanter. Irichels accepted a second glass and took another drink, letting the sweet heat burn its way to his belly. "Is—are you all right with this? Staying here, I mean."

"I want to be with you," Envar said. "If ever that changes, I'll let you know."

That had always been the terms of their bargain. Irichels nodded, satisfied, and felt the city shift around him, almost as though it approved.

He wrote to Manimere the next morning, inviting her to luncheon. She arrived a little behind the noon bells, leaning on a stick, Nerin at her side. "The boy wanted to visit his friend," she said, before Irichels could say anything, "and he's promised to be no trouble."

"I'm sure he won't be," Irichels agreed. "Tepan's in the kitchen, I think."

"Thank you." Nerin bobbed a kind of bow, and scurried off.

Irichels nodded to the cane. "No one told me you'd been wounded. I'm sorry."

Manimere rolled her eyes. "That's because I wasn't wounded. I slipped on wet stairs once I got home, twisted my knee. Pure farce, after everything we'd been through! But it's getting better."

"I'm glad to hear that." Irichels led them into the formal dining room, the upper windows open to let in a breeze from the alley. The table had been reduced to its smallest size, but was still larger than necessary; Martholin had set places at one end and garnished the empty end with an enormous bowl of flowers.

Manimere seated herself, stretching the injured leg carefully, and looked up as he poured the wine. "So. Did you really remake the contract?"

"I did." Irichels hesitated. "I took blood from Nerin to do it. There wasn't any other way."

She waved a hand. "I'm not so worried about that. It's more—what's it done to you? I've heard a dozen stories."

"I'm tied to the city." As he said it, Irichels could feel the hitch and pull of the waves, the tide running in through the Sundern and the Weeper's bays, the fall of hammers as masons worked to rebuild the bridges. He put that aside, went on as normally as he could manage, "It's like the high constable's bond, except it's personal, not tied to the office."

"They say you traded your life."

"Not exactly." Irichels hesitated, but she would need to know the whole story. "It's more of a deferred payment. I belong to the city now, and when I die what's left of my soul goes into it. There are far worse fates." She nodded thoughtfully, and he said, "What I've not heard is what happened to you and your fleet."

"Oh, nothing so exciting as your adventure." Manimere grinned. "I suppose you were at the Assembly to vote on my return?"

"I was."

"Then you know the gist of it. We could see the sea demons massing, driving a storm ahead of them the likes of which I'd never seen." Her smile faded. "We all had ship-marks, of course, and that was some protection, but, Idra's Breath, the waves were tall as my foremast. We had powder and shot, and ferals to curse them, and the city fleet had Oratorians once they came out to join us, but there's only so much you can do. We didn't dare turn broadside to the waves, so we could only bring the bow or stern guns to bear at first, and you could never be sure whether you would be firing into wave or cloud. They drove us back onto the southern approach, and that's got curses of its own to deflect the waves, so we were able to make a stand there.

"But there were hardly enough of us to guard each entrance and each tower, and we were running low on shot by then. Our feral was cursing every scrap of metal on board as fast as we could fire it off into the storm. And it just kept coming, clouds rising blacker and blacker over the horizon, and you could see the lights of the sea demons flickering just under the surface..." She shook her head. "I thought we were done for, and the city with us. We could hear the bells warning everyone, and I thought, well, maybe Samar can get his people out, maybe they've got a chance on the Slackwater. And then the wind shifted, the bells got louder, and it was like a door closing, almost. The sea demons disappeared, and the storm became—just a storm. Bad enough, but we've ridden out worse than that. And then we came back in, and the high constable told us what you'd done." Her smile returned. "And then I went home, and slipped on the stairs, and spent three days in bed myself."

"That was well done," Irichels said. "If you hadn't kept them off, I'd never have been able to mend the curse."

"I'm glad to have been of service," Manimere said, not entirely lightly.

Martholin appeared then, trailed by two of the kitchen maids to serve, and laid out the meal with grave formality.

Irichels thanked her with equal gravity, and they retreated, leaving him to serve. He filled their plates, then lifted his glass. "To surviving."

"To surviving," she echoed, and drank deep.

They talked of other things then: Assembly politics, gossip, the repairs going on across the city, the shortage of luxury goods and Manimere's plans to supply that lack once her ships were repaired and reprovisioned. She was easy to talk to, and Irichels found himself relaxing into laughter. When the last plates were cleared, she reached for her stick, but Irichels raised his hand. "The last time we ate together, you made me an offer."

She raised her eyebrows. "But you're married, Samar."

"Alaissou and I have agreed to end it," Irichels said. "But I still need an heir."

"True enough."

Irichels hesitated. "The truth is, I don't want to marry. This curse—I'm bound enough as it is, I don't want more. Would you be willing to have me on those terms?"

Manimere leaned back in her chair, considering. "That's not unappealing," she said, after a moment. "I'm fond of my freedom, too. And I can't see the Senate and Assembly challenging us, not after what you did."

"That would be my hope," Irichels said.

"Very well, I'll agree."

"Thank you." Irichels paused again. "We should draw up a proper contract, get everything in writing."

"Oh, certainly." Manimere reached for her stick again, and this time he didn't stop her. "But we'd best not take too long, I'm not getting any younger."

"Nor am I," Irichels answered, and offered his arm.

They collected Nerin from the kitchen, and he walked them to their waiting boat, steadying Manimere when her injured knee threatened to give way. Her maid gave him an eloquent glance and settled her on the cushions, but Manimere looked up at him undaunted. "I'll have my man-at-law call on yours, shall I?"

"I'd welcome that." Irichels watched them pull away, and turned back to the house only when the boat had turned the corner. Envar was standing by the fountain, staring up at the warbler still fluttering around the third floor balconies, but he turned at Irichels's approach.

"Did you sort everything out, then?"

"I think so." Irichels looked up at the skylight, a few strands of cloud bright against the blue: the sky was always clear after a storm like that, even one unnaturally fed by the sea demons. The city closed in, wrapping him in sun-warmed stone and the smells of salt and tar and tide, the broken stonework tugging at his skin. "I want to go up on the roof. Come with me?"

"Of course." Envar followed him up the stairs to the ladder, and then out through the trapdoor onto the roof. The cisterns rose at the four corners of the building, familiar and solid and brimming full after the storm: one fewer thing to worry about as summer approached. Irichels moved along the walkway, peered west and south to see the gap where Morellin House had been. The pillar was still firmly in place, piercing sand and sea; Morellin would have no choice but to rebuild, and he hoped whoever inherited would find some pleasure in it.

To the south, scaffolding already enclosed the Senate and Assembly buildings. The sun was warm on his skin and he closed his eyes, letting the city wash over him. He could feel it all around, the flow of the canals, the wind that swept out of the west and left the taste of salt on his lips, the stones and the pilings and the piled sand beneath the waves. He could feel the daemon, still somnolent but omnipresent, could feel other daemons, too, each in its own house like some sea-creature in its shell. They were bound to the city now, to each other and to him, and surely that would be enough to hold back the sea demons.

He glanced sideways, to see Envar watching warily, and leaned his shoulder against the other man's. Envar put his arm around him, familiar and comfortable.

"Are you all right?" he asked.

Irichels nodded slowly. "I will be," he said, and for the first time believed it might be true.

Acknowledgments

As always, I'd like to thank Jo Graham and Amy Griswold for their willingness to read early drafts—this was a pandemic book, and their encouragement and willingness to travel with me was a bright spot in a bleak time. I'd also like to thank editor extraordinaire Athena Andreadis, who came back after the first read with a comment so simple and perfect that it should have been part of the book all along, and whose insight continued to improve every draft.

About the Author

Melissa Scott was born and raised in Little Rock, Arkansas, and studied history at Harvard College. She earned her PhD from Brandeis University in the comparative history program with a dissertation titled "The Victory of the Ancients: Tactics, Technology, and the Use of Classical Precedent." She also sold her first novel, *The Game Beyond*, and quickly became a part-time graduate student and an—almost—full-time writer.

Over the next forty years, she published more than thirty original novels and a handful of short stories, most with queer themes and characters, as well as authorized tie-in work for *Star Trek: DS9, Star Trek: Voyager, Stargate SG-1, Stargate Atlantis, Star Wars Rebels*, and the first season of Rooster Teeth's anime series *gen:LOCK*.

She won the John W. Campbell Award for Best New Writer in 1986, and won Lambda Literary Awards for *Trouble and Her Friends, Shadow Man, Point of Dreams*, (with long-time partner and collaborator, the late Lisa A. Barnett), and *Death By Silver*, written with Amy Griswold. She has also been shortlisted for the Otherwise (Tiptree) Award. She won Spectrum Awards for *Death By Silver, Fairs' Point, Shadow Man* and for the short story "The Rocky Side of the Sky."

Lately, she has collaborated with Jo Graham on the *Order of the Air*, a series of occult adventure novels set in the 1930s (*Lost Things, Steel Blues, Silver Bullet, Wind Raker, and Oath Bound*) and with Amy Griswold on a pair of gay Victorian fantasies with murder, *Death By Silver* and *A Death at the Dionysus Club.* She has also continued the acclaimed *Points* series, fantasy mysteries set in the imaginary city of Astreiant, most recently with *Point of Sighs.* Her latest short story, "Sirens," appeared in the anthology *Retellings of the Inland Seas,* and her text-based game for Choice of Games, *A Player's Heart,* came out in 2020. Her most recent solo novel, *Water Horse,* was published in June 2021, and *Fallen,* sequel to 2018's *Finders,* will be out at the end of 2023.